COMMUNITY
of
SCHOLARS

Mary A. Agria

A Novel

May 14, 2016

To John with deepest gratitude for sharing the journey
of a lifetime—for your selfless support as we follow the dream.
To Helice Agria, Kim Palermo-Bogardus,
Professor Jennifer J. Curry, Dr. Linda DeNoyer, Joyce Giguere,
Ellen and the Rev. Dr. William McGill, and Lydia Metzig
for their invaluable contributions to the manuscript.
To Sheila Kromas for her generous
design advice and Bruce Hembd of horndoggie.com
for his web design and technical support.
Without you, this work would be unthinkable.

visit Mary Agria online at www.maryagria.com

Copyright ©2009 by Mary A. Agria
ISBN: 978-0-578-01559-0
All rights reserved.

What readers and reviewers say about Mary Agria's novels . . .

TIME in a Garden,
"must-read for the contemplative gardener. . ."
Suffolk Times, 2006

VOX HUMANA: The Human Voice
A reflective portrayal of the ascent of goodness, reconciliation and love."
American Guild of Organists Magazine, 2007

IN TRANSIT
"Wisdom, the kind that only a lifetime of experience can wield,"
Dan's Hamptons, 2008.

COMMUNITY OF SCHOLARS
"A winner. . .captures the life of academia with amazing knowledge and sensitivity. Characters show beautiful development and personal growth." *Easton, MD, 2009*

"Richly drawn characters who continue to be haunted by ultimate questions of mortality and spirituality. . . pure wisdom." 5-Stars, Amazon.com

". . . one of my top ten best reads. The characters are beautiful. I loved this book. It garnered positive reviews from our book club." Barnes & Noble.com, 5-Star Review

"From the very first paragraph until the very last, I was hooked." 5-star ranking, Amazon.com

"A unique voice; excellent, intelligent, witty writing; simply wonderful . . . engaging, interesting, believable writing; pure magic." Gather.com

"One of the most thought-provoking, profound yet beautifully, simply written books I have ever read. It is so on target on life that it is scary. I intend to tell my daughter to read it now and then about every 10 years as it will change in meaning for her as she matures . . . begins to contemplate what is truly important in life." Naples, FL

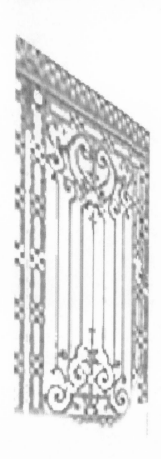

We are flawed and brittle glass,

yet in this glorious, transcendent place,

through grace we can be a window.

Speech by itself may vanish, a vain outpouring of sound.

But knowledge and life, colors and light,

when these in one combine and mingle,

they reveal in us awareness and awe.

Adapted from a 17th century poet,

George Herbert, *The Windows* [1633]

NY: D. Appleton & Co. 1857

Chapter **One**

A woman in jeans and a blazer, a scuffed green canvas book bag slung over one shoulder, had taken up vigil in the corridor outside A. J. Ferinelli's basement office in the Academic Center. It wasn't an everyday occurrence at seven o'clock on a Thursday morning in October. But it certainly was an improvement, A. J. decided, over the night janitor finishing his rounds.

Her back was turned, revealing dark hair in an intricate twist at the nape of her neck. She didn't hear him coming. They had installed new carpet over the patchy tile flooring of the building several months ago.

"Looking for someone—?"

She swung around in his direction. The reaction was a trifle too quick, anxious and he could sense the questions close to the surface in those intense blue eyes.

"Professor Ferinelli, we talked some time ago," she said, "at a faculty meeting. The schedule on the door says you come in early on

Thursdays."

A manila folder full of quizzes tucked under one arm made it hard to maneuver, but A. J. managed to shift his briefcase and keys so he could shake her hand. Her grasp matched her eye contact, straightforward. Still something about her body language, tense and guarded, told him whatever brought her here at the crack of dawn, it was not to discuss class scheduling.

"A. J.'s fine or just Ferinelli," he said. "That Professor business always sounds so fossilized, conjuring up images of ivy-covered halls and moss-covered faculty. Dinosaurs. Vaguely depressing."

A cautious hint of a smile played at the corner of her generous mouth. She nodded, "A. J. then."

At fifty-one, Ferinelli had the distinction of being the longest survivor among the younger faculty members at Bolland, a struggling four-year liberal arts college in mountainous rural Pennsylvania. Armed with a political science doctorate from the University of Chicago and eventually a night school law degree, he had begun teaching at an age when a lot of students were only starting their studies. They had given him tenure by thirty. Another record.

All that was not without costs. The most obvious was his once-curly mop of hair, a casualty of the stress dished out by a curmudgeon on his thesis committee. It never totally grew back, and what was left A. J. kept tightly cropped. Penetrating hazel eyes, the horn-rimmed glasses and lean, austere profile reinforced the look. All business.

"You're Pomerantz. Samantha isn't it?"

"Sam, third year instructor in developmental math. Once in a blue moon a course in college algebra if I'm lucky. Otherwise bonehead stuff."

"But doing something unusual with math anxiety, as I recall. Singing?"

"Jingles, rap, you name it," she hesitated, then launched into a restrained but catchy, "*Geometr-y-y-y is fun for me. Hey-heyyyy, yeh, woe-ah, woe.*"

"If you're thinking of giving American Idol a try," A. J. chuckled appreciatively, "you'd have my vote."

Sam flushed. "Corny maybe, but it works—reduces the stress, as long as your classroom is nowhere near mine. We laugh a lot."

6

"Fascinating, innovative teaching. I've got to believe even Pythagoras would sit up and take notice."

Apparently he should have as well. Although A. J. vaguely remembered he and Sam Pomerantz had talked before, he realized he hadn't been really listening. This woman cared about students, had a quick, creative intelligence, a sense of humor. Attractive, he concluded, in a unconventional way. It had something to do with her eyes—blue or green, it depended on the light.

"Thanks, but I really can't claim my approach is all that original," Sam said. "Of all people, Leibniz beat me to it, a little nugget from Intro to Philosophy 'back in the day'. The gist of it, music gives all the fun of counting, without actually counting. Students seem to *get* that intuitively, though when the light bulb finally goes on for them—well, as a teacher there isn't a bigger thrill in the world."

Visibly embarrassed, she dropped her gaze. "Sorry, I didn't intend to get into all that," she said. "I was just hoping . . . thought you just might have a minute . . . "

A frown settled in between his brows as he consulted his watch. "A seminar at eight, unfortunately. I'm giving a quiz. Constitutional Law. Barbaric scheduling a class before the caffeine kicks in, but it weeds out the faint of heart."

Sam's smile flickered, vanished. "Of course, I should have guessed . . . knew I was taking a chance coming here, but then I don't know many senior faculty," she said. "And when my . . . when the students need help, they say you can be trusted . . . "

That half question at the end spoke volumes. A. J. was willing to bet she hadn't talked to any of her other colleagues and his was the only name on her short list. Student scuttlebutt or not, he suspected the lack of options scared her, plenty. Not waiting for a response, she already had turned to go.

A. J. began fumbling with his keys. It wasn't exactly private out there in the hallway. "There's no guarantee I can help," he told her, "but if you can live with me having to dash out of here at some point—yes, this much I can promise. Everything said in this office stays in this office."

Muttering softly under his breath, he bent over the lock trying to get his office door to function, not easy since he accidentally had dropped the keys in the garbage disposal about a month ago. The door itself yielded to a gentle push, an anticlimax after all that effort. Sam followed him into the room, watching silently from just inside the doorway as he cleared away the debris on a battered leather sofa enough for her to sit if she chose.

"I was dead serious about the caffeine," he said apologetically. "If you give me a minute, I'll get the coffee going."

"Thanks," she nodded. "I'd like that."

Quietly she shut the door behind her. Not, he noticed, before a quick glance along the corridor in either direction. As he renegotiated the plugs in his overloaded electrical outlet, excused himself for a brisk jaunt down the hall for tap water and scouted around for unused coffee filters, he sensed her sizing up where she found herself, taking a measure of his turf before she tentatively settled in on the far end of the sofa.

It occurred to A. J., he probably should have turned his long-suffering housecleaner Margaret loose on this place long ago. A messy business, teaching. His floor-to-ceiling bookcases were crammed to overflowing with volumes, supplemented by stacks of papers and files on the floor. On the window ledge amid a collection of mismatched coffee mugs, half of which had a film of mold on top of the murky contents, stood an articulated plastic model of a skeleton, and totally out of character on the face of it, a marble bust of Athena. The latter was a lucky junk shop find, a copy of a copy of a copy—Roman from a Greek original, fourth century AD—hand-chiseled for the modern tourist trade before resin or pressed stone versions took over the market. The skeleton was sporting a crudely lettered stick-'em note that read, *Carpe diem.*

Time was not on their side. "So," he said, easing gingerly into his slightly off-kilter swivel chair, "what can I do for you? Whatever it is, I meant what I said. It stays behind these four walls."

Sam hesitated. "My career could be on the line here."

"Understood."

"It's the Dean—"

"Bremer."

"Yes."

A. J. felt a throbbing at his temples, suspected what was coming. Still, he waited for her to say it.

"It's out there in the rumor mill that the administration has the axes out, chopping programs," she said. "With enrollment tanking, they're looking for human sacrifices to balance the budget. I'm told my classes are on the hit list."

There was no point in mincing words about her situation. "Remedial courses were always on shaky ground around here," he said, "from Day One. When enrollments were on the skids a couple of years ago, alarmists forced through programs like the math equivalency exam to give students a way around the more flunk-happy faculty. It didn't mean the traditionalists among us liked it."

None of that would have been news to Sam or that hiring her was the Admissions Office's idea of a Plan B. When the competency exam proved to be so tough that few if any tested out, a developmental math course was put in place to help prep for the test.

"You would think it would be tough for anyone to complain, when the pass rate in math has been climbing steadily," she said.

There wasn't really a tactful way to explain. "Put yourself in the Old Guard's shoes," A. J. said. "A new guy on the block like you triples the math test-out numbers and students keep claiming you're doing it without giving away the store—"

"So there's gotta be a hitch. It's too simple to chalk up the change to solid teaching."

"You've got the general idea," he told her. "Rampant paranoia and hardball politics aren't so farfetched as bedfellows go—at Bolland or on just about any campus these days, I suspect. With few exceptions, across the board colleges are struggling with tight donor money and skyrocketing costs."

By now the coffee pot had begun to shudder, the sound of water just before it boils, on the edge. Appropriate, he concluded, given the expression on his colleague's face.

"Politics." Sam looked at him intently, drew in her breath, then let it out again slowly. "Well around here, we're talking cesspool levels. When I went to see Dean Bremer last week for a soul talk about the curriculum, I spent the better part of the hour—"

"Fighting him off."

Sam blinked. A deep flush spread across her pale features. "How did . . . you *already knew.*"

"Only that the Dean seems to be a serial womanizer," A. J. said quickly, softening his tone. "As an academic leader, the man came here with impeccable credentials, the champion of standards, truth, beauty and the liberal arts. Not exactly the embodiment of any

9

of those—certainly not what the faculty had in mind when the majority recommended hiring the man."

The coffee maker gave one last audible sigh, then silence. Grateful for the reprieve, A. J. ducked his head, intent on transferring the steaming brew into two of the cleaner mugs—though not without a swipe in each of them with a dish towel first. The results weren't exactly Starbucks, but better than nothing, potent.

Not the best of times to hand his colleague an open container of scalding liquid. "Cream or sugar?"

"Black's fine."

Sam just stared into the depths of the mug without a word, her expression unreadable. A. J. felt for her. Personally he had never been one of the Dean's fans. Still, this seemed like unusually brazen, even for Bremer.

Now in his mid-fifties, Dean Wilton Honore Bremer was an Oxford grad with a shock of prematurely white hair, two divorces behind him and an ingratiating charm he aimed at a fair number of single women faculty and staff over the past five years of his tenure at Bolland. But then, as far as A. J. could see, those attentions also seemed to end as quickly as they began.

"I don't mean to sound callous," he said, "or that I'm condoning any of this. A few students have complained from time to time. I'm sure you understand, for an individual professor it's tough to bring those concerns to the judicial committee when no one involved has been willing to go on record."

Sam winced. "Afraid of flunking out, I can empathize. He . . . I think it's an instinct with the man, sensing what he can get by with. But still, I have got to believe there are other colleagues who must suspect there's a problem—"

"I've not been privy to any of the speculation, if rumors are out there. Unfortunately, it's not unique to Bolland—an amazing number of good-old-boy-faculty have some borderline Neanderthal tendencies themselves when it comes to women," A. J. said. "Bremer also apparently knows how to hide behind the unspoken glass ceiling. No one ever said the man wasn't slick, that's the dangerous part. Someone needs to nail the guy—"

"If by someone you mean me," Sam said deliberately, all the while watching him intently, "you need to know, my first month here, Bremer and I . . . we had this unfortunate thing going."

10

It was coming back to him as she spoke. Crude faculty gossip had floated through the department some time back about this math teacher who ostensibly was getting it on with a Dean. Bolland was a small campus.

"Legally the situation is unambiguous," A. J. told her, not unkindly. "No means *no*—past history, irrelevant."

There was more, he read it in her eyes, something she wasn't ready to talk about. Odds on, his colleague was understating not just what had transpired in the Dean's office last week, but why. Evading his gaze, Sam eased forward on the sofa, took her time depositing her now half-empty coffee mug on a precariously stacked pile of books.

"Thanks for the coffee, for listening." She seemed suddenly self-conscious, as if afraid she had revealed too much. "But at this rate you won't . . . your seminar is going to be wondering if you—"

"They'll live. Don't give it a second thought."

She had begun gathering her belongings, her eye on the door. "Truth is, I'm really not sure what I'm doing here . . . what I thought you, what anyone could do."

"Ostensibly rank has some privileges, even at Bolland. For starters, I can keep an ear to the ground, try to sort out truth from fiction when it comes to possible cuts, try to figure out how much support Bremer really has out there."

"That would be helpful."

"In the meantime," he found himself saying, "if you're up for it, I suggest you let me buy you lunch in the faculty dining room."

Her head jerked up—Sam was no less surprised at the offer than he. It had been three years since his wife died. This would be the closest he had come to being seen alone on campus with a woman ever since.

"I'm not sure I understand," she said slowly. Her eyes never left his face.

"*Lunch.* It sounds like you could use a friend," he said evenly. "Plus the Dean hangs out in the dining room on a regular basis. At the very least, showing up over there with a senior faculty member, male no less, would confuse the heck out of the rumor mill. It's an in-your-face move as political gestures go, I'll admit."

"I've heard of worse," she said after a conspicuous pause. "It might just . . . yes, thank you. I would appreciate it. Very much."

"No problem. Noon?"

"I'll be there. Except we're going Dutch."

A. J. nodded. "You got it."

Hand on the doorknob, Sam turned and looked at him. Her smile was back, tentative but nice. "Wishful thinking, but you're right," she said, "I would love to see that sorry excuse for a human being on a fast track out of here. Trust me, he deserves it!"

A. J. just stood there staring at the empty doorway—not a guy's average office hour walk-in, that's for sure. Revving into high gear, he grabbed his briefcase, locked up and tore out the nearest exit in the direction of the main classroom building.

Sam Pomerantz was nowhere in sight, but her predictions were dead-on. Halfway across the quad, the carillon started playing the Bolland fight song, dashing any illusions he had about making it to his Con Law seminar on time. He burst into his second-floor classroom, red in the face and out of breath, to find the entire seminar watching for his arrival as if collectively expecting the ax to fall any minute.

The quiz. He had forgotten he was giving a quiz. His thoughts unprintable, A. J. rummaged in his briefcase for the questions and court cases he had run off the night before, unfortunately now MIA. In his haste, he must have left them on the desk. Sheepish at his out-of-character logistical faux pas, he told the students to fend for themselves, review their notes, while he sprinted back to get the missing folder.

Good God, they were young. A. J. stared out at the faces bent over the quiz sheets on the desk tops in front of them—vaguely making a pact with himself to start working out. Maybe even cut back on the blasted caffeine. His heart was still in hyperdrive after that humiliating relay across the quad. Whatever the cause of the abrupt time warp that followed, he found himself no longer a detached observer, monitoring what was going on in his silent classroom. Their struggles were becoming inseparable from his own.

All those questions, even the knowledge behind them, were never the motive, only the excuse—to push the limits of the known, the knowable. In the Testing itself, writ large, is where the journey began for him, where it always begins, the awe-filled, fearful pursuit of the inner sanctum, the holy of holies. The Life of the Mind.

Hunched over a gunmetal desk in the cramped steel cubicles of the library stacks at Chicago, he wrestled with the selfsame Great

Eternals, the accumulated wisdom of the ages. Towering walls of musty volumes became at once his sanctuary and his prison. Over the narrow aisles and drafty cells, bare bulbs hung from the ceiling, scant illumination at best. A. J. could have located the cardinal points of that cosmos in his sleep.

Library of Congress subclass HXHX1-970.7 Socialism. HX806-811 Utopias. The Ideal State. Library of Congress subclass JC—Political Theory. The State. Theories of the State.

Pushed to the limits, he would close his eyes, draw in the acrid-sweet smell of ink and paper, intent on internalizing the contents of the yellowing pages in his hands. *I will not let you go,* the Soul cries to the dawn, *until you bless me.* Heady stuff for a tousle-haired kid from Long Island.

Decades ago. And yet, for the man and scholar—the academic—he had become, even the simple act of stepping into the hushed confines of a bookstore, the smell of printer's ink, the sight of all those spines and titles turned outward could still evoke in him the same intense, inexplicable longing. Intoxicating. Unsatiable.

Those were different times in higher education. In the golden decades when he was earning his doctorate and the early years at Bolland, all it took was hanging out a sign, College or University, and the students came in record numbers. Dorms and building projects sprang up like cement block and brick-clad mushrooms on what often had been cow pastures. Grant money flowed freely, spent with equal abandon on essentials and amenities. Board membership promised the perks of a glorified country club, replete with a flowing bar. Civilized. Collegial. Whatever their issues with one another on campus, faculty socialized freely after hours, cultivated the mystique of a campus family.

Family. The images were like a knife twisting in his gut. All that was before he lost his wife, Anne, and their unborn son at the hands of a drunk driver. Three years of grief had been a relentless tutor. He learned to reach inward, grasp at the only constants left to him—his passion for teaching, his research. These alone had not failed him. These alone he could trust.

In his well-ordered universe, Sam Pomerantz standing in the hallway outside his office simply didn't compute. He had defined himself as a political scientist. The dynamics of human governance

13

were his stock in trade. But as he replayed Sam's story in his head, A. J. realized it had never occurred to him—not once—that while he had been withdrawing more and more from campus life, the community around him had not been standing still. The Bolland he thought he knew had been changing, evolving, mutating. *Not*, it seems, for the better.

He sensed the students were getting restless. The period would be ending soon and the bulk of the class had already packed it in. A few stragglers still hung in there, bent over their quiz sheets, confused and uncertain from the look of it. They weren't alone on that score. It was as if A. J. suddenly felt uncomfortable in his own skin—like a man abruptly and unexpectedly emerging from a long, in his case self-imposed, sleep.

"Tough stuff," one of the brighter juniors muttered, depositing his quiz on the stack piling up on his professor's desk. Tough stuff, indeed.

"We'll debrief," A. J. flashed what he hoped was a reassuring smile, "don't sweat it. There's still a good week before midterms. Consider this a trial run."

Three minutes to go. There wasn't much sense in prolonging their misery.

"You've given it your best shot," A. J. said. "Let's wind it up, call it good."

A guy could hope, anyway. Gathering up the remaining exams, A. J. headed back to his office, where a preliminary run at grading several random tests confirmed his worst nightmare. For all his prep time, there were still far too many blanks on the answer sheets to generate anything approaching a normal bell-curve. Several students had already guessed as much—dropped by to see him, anxious about the results. By noon he had a monster headache and was late for lunch.

At least if he had handpicked a time or cast of characters for orchestrating his impromptu show of support for Sam Pomerantz, he couldn't have done a better job of it. The faculty dining room was crowded, a microcosm of departmental and divisional politics in action. As usual Bremer was ensconced front and center with a couple of his cronies from Natural Sciences, and over in the far corner, A. J. saw an historian locked in animated debate with an adjunct in languages and a tenured member of the art department. Perfect.

Professor Enoch Slaughter, senior psychology guru, his tie askew, was balancing a tray in one hand and a battered leather briefcase in the other. He was mumbling to himself as he picked his way between the chrome and Formica tables to his usual spot, something about what had or had not transpired in his day.

It was the predictable list—campus gadfly, power broker, nervous newbies—one that hadn't changed much since A. J.'s last appearance in the faculty hangout. The dynamics at work in the campus lunch room were his intellectual life's blood, with one unsettling twist. He suddenly found himself seeing the assemblage through someone else's eyes, not just his own.

Like any community, Bolland had never been without its proverbial warts and moles, the stuff of indulgent humor and much head-wagging over the years. A. J. had always defended the cast of characters as vaguely eccentric, harmless. Sam Pomerantz had put a face on that lie. The campus of her experience had become a snake pit, with precious few resources apparently with which to extricate herself. *Except him,* at least as she saw it, a sobering thought.

At first glance she seemed to have given up on him, bailed, but then A. J. spotted her, standing off to his right just inside the door—alone, chewing on her lower lip. Sam looked up from consulting her watch, visibly relieved to see him. His heart went out at her determined attempt at a smile.

"Sorry . . . I tried to call but I got your voicemail," he said. "On the way out the door, I had a last minute, panicked walk-in."

"Amazing what a D on a pre-midterm quiz will do for a prof's popularity."

"You guessed it," A. J. chuckled softly, shook his head. "With midterms in two weeks, the guy was . . . does anyone still say *freaked?*"

Sam wasn't laughing. "Freaked. Right now, it makes perfect sense to me."

"I hear you," A. J. said in undertone as he reached out and helped her readjust her shoulder bag that was in danger of sliding to the floor. "It's too late for us to back out now. We're already an 'item'. . . *showtime.* And if this display of solidarity of ours is going to work, subtlety is *not* going to cut it."

Sam's eyebrow arched. "I'm not sure I follow—"

"*When they mess with you, they mess with me.* Crude, but

effective. I suggest you take a deep breath, brace yourself."

"Bring it on . . . I think . . . "

With a reassuring smile and his hand at her elbow, A. J. deliberately drew her close alongside him, then aimed them toward the snack bar counter. Sam had fair warning what was coming. Still, reflex took over. She stiffened at his touch, seemed about to pull away before a subtle tightening of his grip stopped her.

"Sorry," she breathed. "I wasn't—"

"No problem. We're good."

A. J. felt for her. This was going to be a heck of a lot tougher than she thought. Jaw tight, he didn't allow himself to back off an inch as he waited for Sam to order lunch, then did the same himself.

"If it helps, this macho stuff—invading someone's space—isn't my style either," he told her quietly after the lone snack bar worker was out of earshot. "But then you already know that. I think you also know, before you start fishing around for your wallet, it makes sense to let *me* pick up the tab."

Sam blinked, appeared about to protest. Instead, she forced a tight smile, let out her breath in an audible rush.

"Now, that wasn't so hard, was it," he said.

"You're kidding, right?"

Chuckling softly to himself, A. J. laid a single tray on the counter directly in front of them. The student working the snack bar didn't ask. He just loaded the tray with enough silverware, napkins and condiments for two before turning back to the grill to rescue several burgers—A. J.'s among them—from a potential conflagration.

A. J. and Sam made eye contact. "You okay?" he said.

"I could ask you the same thing. First a shellshocked student, now this. Some would say you're a glutton for punishment."

"Or something. That student is Pre-law, my advisee," A. J. winced, "and our little come-to-Jesus moment was way overdue. He *knows* nonstop memorization is par for the course. The review session was loaded with dire warnings to nail the basics of the cases we've been studying . . . names, majority and minority opinions. I even cut the class a break, heavily slanted the quiz toward multiple bluff or guess. Heaven knows what the guy was thinking. But then he wasn't the only one who had a meltdown—just by far the brightest."

"Cocky, lazy or all of the above?"

"Distracted," he amended. "Joel Van Susten. The guy is trying

16

to do it all—captain of the tennis team, student government, editor of the student weekly and a damn articulate leader when it comes to campus causes. Unfortunately, the downside tends to be a substantial gap between promise and performance in the classroom. I ought to have cracked down on him ages ago."

"Or maybe you're being a tad hard on yourself *and* him," Sam said. "Joel stuck it out in my course, twice, until he finally nailed the math competency exam. Aced it."

"Now why do I think it was *you* who had something to do with that?"

Their lunches were up. A. J. caught Sam's hint of a frown, but outside of that she didn't put up a fuss when he shoved a ragged assortment of coins and bills at the counter attendant. It was more than enough to cover her fruit yogurt, side salad and mineral water, plus his burger and cholesterol-laden plate of breaded jalapeño poppers with dipping sauce. The coffee—thick, black high-test—was his fifth cup of the morning.

"Combat pay," A. J. told the harried snack bar employee as he shoved the change into the tip jar sitting on the counter.

The guy grinned. "See ya in class, Ms. Pomerantz," he said.

Sam gave the young man a reassuring thumbs-up. "Good job on that worksheet," she said. "Go for it!"

Grace under fire, A. J. had to hand it to her, despite the rocky start. Awkwardly balancing their tray and with Sam in tow, he crossed the dining area and staked a claim on the last remaining table for two, somewhat removed from the thick of things.

"Perfect," he said. No sense pushing it.

He would have loved to force eye contact with Bremer, but the Dean was having none of it. It was impossible by now to miss the openly questioning looks some of their colleagues shot in their direction. Mercifully, Sam didn't appear to have noticed. With a puzzled expression she had been watching A. J. sort through and distribute the items on their lunch tray.

"Problems?"

"Just thinking," Sam hesitated, "you certainly have an interesting notion of food groups . . . "

His explosion of laughter was enough to turn heads at several of the neighboring tables. "Unlike certain past Commanders-in-Chief," he said, "broccoli is about the *only* green thing I enjoy. Not on

17

the menu. The rest are more or less tolerable, if well disguised. Breading, lots of sauce, creativity is good."

Sam's eyebrow arched. "Somehow . . . I guess I would have figured you for a fellow health nut. No red meat. Low everything."

"Certifiable, maybe. Health . . . doubtful," he shrugged. "Too many students, chronic insomnia. I could put together quite a list."

His eight o'clock Con Law class was no accident, he explained. When Contemporary Political Issues, his survey course, had the dubious distinction of winning excellence-in-teaching honors a half-dozen years running, all it accomplished was to send his enrollments through the roof. He wasn't about to flunk out the overflow and the administration was opposed to quotas. So, just let the schedule weed out the less motivated. Passive aggressive, but it works.

"Some quid pro quo, you also have to *teach* at that hour . . . !" Sam's laughter faded almost as soon as it began.

"Why, Ferinelli, you've deigned to join us!"

Startled, A. J. slowly laid down his fork. He knew that voice. The sensual undertone—Tennessee Williams meets way too many BBC costume dramas—was a dead-giveaway. New was the malice fueling it.

Tray in hand, self-styled "Brit lit" expert in the English department, Winona a.k.a. Winna Dougherty must have gone out of her way to stop alongside their table. For some time now, A. J. had the uncomfortable feeling the woman—a twice-divorced ash-blonde, late forties—had more on her mind than the Bronte sisters whenever their paths crossed on campus.

Winna didn't give him a chance to respond. *"And* with our own *Ms. Pomerantz,* I see."

Sam was tracking down the last bit of kiwi at the bottom of her yogurt container, which didn't totally explain the slow flush spreading across her cheekbones. A. J. had to admire her grit. When she looked up from the task at hand, her eyes were a steely gray in the face of Winna's blistering scrutiny.

"Hello, Winna," she said.

"So, are you folks meeting—or eating?"

A. J. wasn't about to let the woman join them. "Sorry," he said, "solving the problems of the college, Winna. Some other time."

The look Winna shot in Sam's direction could have frozen

solvent. "Have *fun*, you two!"

Instead, the woman headed for Dean Bremer's table. Audible even over the escalating conversation level in the room, she held forth on enrollment ratios and academic standards. Pointed, too pointed.

"Sorry, that was my fault," Sam said softly. "I didn't intend to drag you into this."

"Winna is in a class by herself," he said. "I'm not sure how much clout she has, if that's what you're worried about."

"She has enough. Tenured, plus she sits on the faculty Personnel Committee."

Something in Sam's voice stopped him, mid-bite. "And you think she has you on some personal hit-list," he said.

"Rumor has it, I had the honor of displacing her in Dean Bremer's address book. Only Winna actually *enjoyed* the status."

"Ouch."

Eyes averted, Sam was making an art form of accordion-folding an unused napkin left behind on the tray. "She chaired the search committee when Bolland hired me—knows how badly I wanted this job after teaching endless overfull sections of intro math at a community college in Ohio. Adjuncts like me were two notches below union scale from the custodians and grounds crew. So, when Winna called to set up an interview here, I thought I had it made."

"I can imagine. Winna would have given you an impressive dose of the usual Bolland wannabe-Ivy hype."

"Try the promise of a decent salary," she started to bristle, caught herself, "and yes, students with a touch of fire in the gut. As another woman on the faculty, I honestly thought Winna would be on my side. She certainly talked a good line, early on anyway."

There was no arguing with the pain in her voice. "Winna is out for Winna," he said gruffly. "You don't deserve this."

She just looked at him, then slowly straightened in her chair. "According to the college catalog, I understand you earned both a PhD and a law degree."

"Civil," he said, "passed the bar, but not practicing though."

"*Could* you . . . ," she breathed, "take a case, I mean?"

A. J. looked at her, hard. "If you're thinking of legal action, I would think twice," he said slowly. "Only a handful of harassment cases ever surfaced around here in my day, all unsuccessful. In the end, they always came down to He-said-She-said. And all of them

19

were internal campus grievances—nothing as risky, publicly combative or embarrassing to the institution as a lawsuit. When an in-house complaint fails, at least it's all in the family. Awkward, uncomfortable, but potentially survivable."

He could read the uncertainty in her eyes. "The thing is, I really need a lawyer who knows this place . . . hoped you might—"

"I *have* drafted grievances before," he said, "if it came to that. And one of my best friends is a labor lawyer, local—a darn good one. Problem is, what winds up on those documents is not the issue. The tough part, the nitty-gritty of the process, you would have to be prepared to level not just with me, but publicly and out loud with every single colleague on this campus. Brutal."

Sam didn't say a word, but he noticed how her gaze lingered momentarily in the direction of the table, now empty, where Bremer had been sitting. Somber, A. J. concluded, beginning to realize what she was up against.

Without their noticing, the lunch crowd had been thinning out. Classes changed at one and these were prime-time afternoon teaching slots. A. J. was acutely aware how their peers would have been processing this subdued one-on-one.

"In any case, this is no time or place to talk about it," he said. "If you don't have plans for Friday night, I suggest dinner. This isn't something you should be handling alone. An evening would give us some time, some privacy to discuss your options."

Friday. That was tomorrow. She hesitated, toying with the empty yogurt container on the table in front of her. "Five-thirty. My place is fine . . . since you won't let me buy lunch, I'll whip up something. It's the least I can do."

"Six," he smiled. "And dessert's on me."

Something in her face told him she was getting the wrong idea again. The taut set of her mouth and the way her dusting of freckles stood out against the porcelain of her skin were dead giveaways.

"Mousse," he said gently, "I'm talking about *mousse*, Sam—chocolate, straight out of a deli case, but edible. No strings, no agendas. And I promise you, whatever you choose to do in the end, you won't have reason to regret coming to me about this."

Those expressive eyes of hers couldn't hide much. When it came to harboring regrets, on some level, she already did.

20

Chapter Two

Not quite sure how it came about, A. J. found himself in chinos, button-down-collar dress shirt and a very uncomfortable rep-stripe tie at the wheel of his Toyota. On the passenger seat alongside him lay a bottle of Chilean red and a deli container of amaretto-laced chocolate mousse. It was a Friday night and he was headed to dinner at the home of a colleague—a woman—he barely knew.

Sam Pomerantz. If called upon to summarize on a narrow-ruled index card a profile of the woman he was meeting, his cramped and illegible jottings would have produced less of a biography than for any random student in one of his classes. *Instructor in Mathematics. Untenured and worried about her job. Bright, creative. Great teacher.* Tough or foolhardy enough to go *mano e mano* with the Dean.

Yet, here he was. And her sketchy vitae wasn't the only mystery in a riddle in a conundrum on the table. If pushed to articulate why he found himself in that position at all—trying to help the woman with what had to be a difficult legal situation at best—a single word sufficed. *Justice.* Justice in truth not just in theory or the abstract. That, and perhaps the simpler fact, Sam had asked.

On the way out the door yesterday in the faculty dining room, she had scrawled her street and house number in permanent marker on a flimsy cafeteria napkin for him, along with her phone number. Unlisted, she made a point of telling him. The address led him to a tiny Seventies-vintage modular, rented most likely considering her instructor's pay. To A. J.'s surprise, her house was a scant mile from his own. While the neighborhood seemed marginal, the house itself looked like someone was making a concerted effort to reverse the demographics. The gray of the siding might have been peeling, but the front door sported a fresh moss-green paint job. Out front at either side of the steps stood the drying, frost-ravaged remains of what obviously had been thriving beds of perennials. All of it Sam's doing, A. J. suspected.

She must have been watching for him. His hand had just shot out, aiming for the doorbell, when he heard her slide off a safety chain and begin fumbling with the deadbolt. She stood there in jeans and a simple but dressy teal vee-neck sweater, visibly uncomfortable at the prospect of letting him into her living room.

"Burglars?" he said.

"Bremer."

At something in A. J.'s face, she stepped aside far enough to let him into the tiny foyer. "Whatever my credentials in the classroom, I never pretended I could claim the same for my taste in men," she said. "I told you, for about six seconds when I first came to campus, I actually was deluded enough to think I had something in common with that low life. It made sense to change the locks."

He just looked at her, only now beginning to comprehend what she was telling him, what she had been facing. Apparently stalking, for starters. And he could do the math. It would seem Sam quietly had been coping with the Dean's intimidation for much of her stay on the Bolland campus.

"That was three years ago." It wasn't a question.

"Meaning, considering what I knew about the man," she said dully, "I had no business going to his office alone last week."

"I didn't say that."

Sam hesitated, shook her head. "No, you didn't. But if you thought it, you wouldn't be the only one. It's nothing I haven't asked myself—why on earth I thought it made sense to try to confront him."

"*Power concedes nothing without a demand . . .* Frederick Douglass. You suspected your job might be in jeopardy, Sam.

Understandable. You wanted a shot at a tenure track, believed the Dean was capable of holding that hostage—"

"I was *stupid* . . . gave Bremer the only excuse he needed and he took it. Tried to, anyway."

Sam didn't elaborate, beyond that, about what transpired. The way she retreated back inside herself, managed to avoid eye contact, spoke volumes.

"I know what I told you about the problems of pursuing a harassment case," A. J. said carefully, "all of it true. But I'm not sure exactly what you're implying here. Assault is an ugly word, but if that's what this was, all bets are off. I'd be the first to say, it belongs in criminal court—"

"And tell them *what?* You said so yourself, it's my word against his. And next thing you know, I'd be dodging some smarmy lawyer's suggestive posturing about what *is* or *is not* sexual or consensual or . . . ," she broke off and on an out-rush of breath, forced herself to meet his steady gaze. "Yesterday you urged me to think this through . . . well, I have. This is pointless. I'm sorry—I've wasted your time."

A. J.'s eyebrow arched. Her modest entry hall was beginning to feel uncomfortable, downright claustrophobic. Sam had the cornered look of someone casting about for the exits. Problem was, it was *he* who was the interloper here.

"Hardly a waste of time judging by the smells coming from your oven," he said evenly. "Let's try a do-over, shall we? I'm A. J. Ferinelli and I believe you're . . . "

He left it to her to fill in the blanks. Sam hesitated, her deep flush betraying her embarrassment.

"Not much of a hostess, apparently—I haven't even let you set foot in the living room. The salad isn't done, my oven timer should be going off any minute . . . I'll be right back!"

With that, she turned and took off like a shot toward the kitchen, leaving him to follow at a distance—troubled, replaying in his head what she had told him. From the doorway, he watched silently as she added Gorgonzola cheese, almonds and dried cherries to whatever else was already in the bottom of a striking antique spatterware bowl on the counter in front of her. Tension drained from her face as she worked, totally absorbed, oblivious to his presence.

In one hand he was still toting the recycled plastic grocery bag which housed the dessert, in the other was the bottle of passable table wine. "Refrigerator?" he ventured.

"The mousse. Of course . . . go ahead." Sam quickly relieved him of the wine and began rummaging in one of the kitchen drawers. "I've got a corkscrew around here someplace. They say it's best to let a red breathe, but the quiche is ready now. I turned the oven off."

"Subtle. Three food groups at least."

Sam stopped what she was doing and a quizzical frown tightened between her brows. "*Seven*," she said. "As for your fondness for broccoli—you'll find it in both quiche *and* salad."

Her gotcha-smile snuck up on him. If this was theater on her part, pulling herself together while her world was crumbling around her, she was damn good at it. Instinct told him this woman was no whiner. A survivor. Though he could see she was fighting a losing battle with the corkscrew.

"At the risk of sounding like a chauvinist or worse," he chuckled softly as he gently eased the bottle from her hand, "how about I handle the wine."

She didn't protest. A. J. uncorked the bottle and wandered out toward what had to be the dining room with it, the intention being to fill their glasses. One look at the delicate etched-crystal stemware, depression-glass candleholders and matching serving pieces positioned cheek-on-jowl on the compact table top, was enough to change his mind. She caught him standing there bottle in hand, looking down at the elegant place settings, the soft pastels of the handwoven placemats and linen napkins.

"Problems?" she said.

"Considering this is a red and those placemats aren't, I think it's safer if you do the honors," he winced. "At Thanksgiving, I was always one of the cousins who got stuck at the card table in the hall. Plastic tablecloths and disposable forks. You get the general idea."

With obvious pleasure, Sam took her time filling the fragile-looking long-stemmed wine and water glasses. "A fetish of mine," she said. "Crystal, like fine china, is meant to be enjoyed, if that's what's worrying you. I read somewhere glass and china become brittle, break or chip if they sit for long periods of time in the cupboard."

"Interesting. Use it or lose it, who knew?"

"I am not making this up," she frowned, trying not to laugh.

"Apparently there's something about handling porous materials like they're alive that strengthens the molecules or keeps them more resilient."

"I'll take your word for it."

Resilient. Pretty much what he would have come up with by way of a character reference, he decided. His hypothetical Pomerantz file card was becoming more crowded. Looking around Sam's space, it also had begun to occur to him, this wasn't at all what he would have imagined for a math instructor's taste. There wasn't anything trendy or overtly techy, not a bit of chrome or tempered glass anywhere in sight.

Everything about the place said, *traditional* in a minimalist sort of way. Classy. The colors were woodsy and earth-tones—from the cool sage of the walls to the homey, unbleached canvas drapes. She had furnished the cosy dining area and what he could see of the equally unpretentious living room beyond it with early 1900's American farmhouse antiques. Along with all the intimidating glassware, her weathered drop-leaf table had been set with period china and, in an age of stainless flatware, with what had to be genuine silver. On the ornate oak sideboard stood a stoneware crock filled with dried weeds and grasses.

Living alone didn't define who she was, he concluded. She was obviously comfortable projecting herself into her environment, showing she cared deeply about having beautiful things around her.

"You have some amazing antiques," he told her. "Hard to find these days. My wife used to prowl the local Penny Saver looking for yard sales, though there aren't many bargains out there any more. Folks tend to know what they have."

Her hands swathed in oven mitts, Sam had just re-emerged from the kitchen carrying a steaming ceramic dish that she eased onto a slate hot pad she had on the ready for it. "Most of these pieces were in the family," her smile didn't reach her eyes. "My folks were downsizing at the time and I couldn't bear to see them just wind up in some dealer's window."

Something told him he had touched on a sore point. When she made another run to the kitchen for the salad, he quietly changed the subject. It wasn't hard to make small talk about her cooking, everything was fabulous. As it happened, they had barely begun to tackle the feast when the doorbell rang. Insistent.

As she stood up to answer it, he instinctively started to get up as well. "Not necessary," she told him. "I'll be right back."

Even with company in the house, A. J. couldn't help notice, Sam made a point of cracking the door first with the chain on. It turned out to be a pint-sized kid, African-American, eleven or so, wearing jeans and a Bolland hoodie. He started through the doorway, hesitated when he caught sight of A. J. sitting there.

Visibly uneasy at A. J.'s presence, the kid thrust the envelope in her hand. "Mom sent me," he mumbled, "somethin' came this afternoon for you. She says to tell you she signed for it."

Sam had grabbed her book bag from the hall tree in the entryway and began fishing around in the contents. All the while the neighbor kid stood scuffing his toe on her door sill, shy but expectant. Obviously the two of them had some kind of a game going.

"Just a minute, Ja Ron, okay."

She came up with a handful of change, extended it in the boy's direction. The kid's grin lit up the room as his fists closed around the stash.

"If you hurry, I think the corner store is still open," Sam told him. "Last time I looked, they still had those rubbery sour fish things."

The look on the kid's face spoke volumes as he gave his benefactor an awkward hug, all elbows and pent-up energy. "Hey, sweet . . . thanks, Sam!"

"Just be sure to save me some of those goodies for later," she called out to his retreating back, then shut the door, fumbled to reattach the chain.

Sam winced. "Sorry about that. I can't imagine why anybody would be sending me certified mail," her back half-turned, she began to work open the envelope.

"No problem," A. J. teased, "though at this rate, I suspect it's probably a good idea to turn off the old cell phones before your quiche gets totally—"

He couldn't miss the audible intake of breath as she retrieved what had to be a letter, scanned the contents. Short, he gathered. Intuitively he was on his feet.

"Sam, are you—?"

He never got the rest out. Whatever this was, it was definitely not okay. She turned, that single crisp sheet of rag bond clutched in her fist, looking at him in mute appeal.

"The *bastard*," she breathed.

Bremer. Jaw tight, Sam didn't have to spell it out for him. *Payback time.*

"Don't panic," A. J. said, riveted by her eyes. "We'll handle it."

She shook her head. "Too late. I've been fired. Effective the end of the academic year."

The air in Sam's living room seemed unnaturally quiet, like the weird calm people tell about just before the earthquake strikes, when the knot of fear in a guy's gut reminds him the ground isn't really steady. She had to pass A. J. on the way back to the table, stumbled. The awkward, fleeting contact between them was enough to sense she was cold, trembling, half in shock.

From the quick perusal he gave the document she shoved his way, as dismissals went, this one was brutal. Three terse sentences spelled out the grounds—financial constraints, sorry, turn in your keys. Technically, it was a nonrenewal of contract. Topping it off was a familiar Hancock-esque flourish of a signature at the end. *Bremer.*

The timing was fiendish. If a guy was in the mood to be paranoid, on the face of it, this could be interpreted as a calculated slam, aimed at A. J.'s simple public show of support for his colleague at lunch yesterday. When it came to Sam, the Dean clearly was going for the jugular.

She had slid into her chair, their utensils and meal still spread out on the table where they had left them. Food was the last thing on A. J.'s mind right now. All he could think, as he stood there looking down at her, was how ashen white she was—that, and graphic flashes of her alone in Bremer's office with the man's hands all over her.

"I'm so sorry, " her voice was low, "should never have . . . you had no idea what you were getting into when you agreed to—"

He willed her to make eye contact. "After everything he . . . everything that man has done," A. J. choked on an expletive, "you still believe this is somehow your fault, some grim reflection on you. Sam, that morning in my office you wondered how I knew Bremer gets off playing things right up to the edge of the law. Latest case in point was an advisee of mine—a mother, Hispanic, with two kids—sweating through an accounting degree. Professor Slaughter accused her of cheating on one of his psych exams, reported the incident to the Dean. Bogus of course. When the woman retook the test, she aced it. But Bremer still threatened to put an incident report in her file. Technically, he was within his rights. But *ethically* . . . outright minority and nontrad bashing on the guy's part. Something like that on her record would have made it impossible for her to ever be certified—"

"And she blew the whistle. Is that what you're saying?" Sam said, chin set. "Of course not, or we wouldn't even be having this conversation. The student's smart, knows the drill and so do I. When in doubt, cruise along under the radar unless you're willing to risk ruining . . . "

Sam didn't have to finish. They both knew in all likelihood, her career was already in shambles.

As A. J. slid back on his chair, he evaded her gaze. "You're right," he said, "it took some major muscle flexing, my threat to file a lawsuit on the student's behalf, for the Dean to back down—sheer bluff. I got lucky."

"How many lives has the man destroyed," she said, "and when does it stop, *if ever?*"

In the silence that followed, the dawning awareness in her eyes was an answer of sorts. When it came to potential whistleblowers, with her pink slip lying there on the table between them, she was as likely a candidate as any.

A. J.'s mouth felt stiff. "I am not going to hit you with all kinds of cheap platitudes about not letting the man get away with it. But just know this, if you do decide to make a stand, you can count on me to be there, whatever it takes."

Too proud to break down, he thought. She was rigid with the effort it took, but didn't make a sound. With a shock, A. J. realized she had brutal practice at it, most recently in Dean Bremer's office.

"To be honest," she said dully, "I'm really not sure I'm even ready to talk about this, much less haul out the laptop and start putting together some sort of a sordid chronology of dates, innuendos . . . worse."

"I assume you've kept a journal, something to document all this, chapter and verse."

Sam winced. "Not at first and not everything, but yes. The last six months especially."

"Good. We could work with that. I took the precaution of

28

laying hands on a couple of sample successful grievances—brought them along. You might feel more comfortable . . . it might be less intimidating if you lay out a rough draft alone of what happened, before we try to tackle the legalese together. There's no deadline, but I recommend sooner, rather than later."

Sam drew in a long breath, let it out again slowly. "We're about to head into midterms, so I can't promise you . . ."

"*Meantime*," he said, cautiously raising the paper-thin wine glass in front of him in her direction by way of a toast, "your wonderful quiche is getting cold, Ms. Pomerantz, and I don't know about you, but to me right now working on the rest of the bottle of Chilean red seems relevant. Let's say we top it off with a goodly share of mousse before I head home to shovel a week's worth of mail off my dining room table, get a jump on grading those quizzes—let you sleep on this whole business."

Eyes wide, Sam let his reaction sink in, as if half-expecting judgment or censure, finding neither. "The students were right," she said finally, her voice low. "You're a decent man, Ferinelli."

A muscle twitched uncomfortably along the edge of his jaw. *Decent.* It wasn't exactly the adjective that came to mind. For three years this woman had been walking the same corridors, caught up in her own private hell, while he crossed the quad a half dozen times a day, detached from and desensitized to the ongoing rumors swirling around the Dean and his alleged conduct. No longer.

"I'm not so sure about your character reference," he said, "but I certainly feel confident recommending the salad. Incredible, and that coming from a guy who hates green stuff."

"Must be the broccoli," she told him.

"Does the trick every time."

With a wry twist of a smile, A. J. reached up and began to tug awkwardly at the knot of his tie, eventually felt it loosen a notch. The sense of relief was palpable.

It seems they had arrived at a tacit understanding of sorts, to get beyond the letter-folded sheet of rag bond lying on the table—the Dean, Sam's possible grievance and whatever came after. No agenda but the moment. And no small display of courage on her part, he decided, *considering*.

Granted, at times small talk could only do so much to bridge the silence that won out between them. In those moments, A. J.

quietly opted to take charge, regaling her with hilarious tales of student exams past and present. The high point, or low point depending on how one looked at it, was the tale of a history major who was asked to define *Grand Peur*, the reign of terror following the storming of the Bastille during the French Revolution.

"Literally 'Great Fear', right. Only the kid mistranslates it as 'Great Pear', identifies it as a nickname for the last French king."

"Pear," Sam frowned. "How on earth could somebody come up with that one?"

"Would you believe, the kid thought it was because old Louis was so incredibly fat."

"You're kidding," Sam gasped in between peals of laughter.

"Dead serious. Unfortunately."

Still laughing, she stood, began to clear their now all-but-empty plates. "Funnier than heck, though not a hint about the menu, I hope," she said. "I just worry after all this chick food, you're still hungry."

"You're kidding. Everything was terrific. Except you're dealing with a diehard choco-la-holic here, hence the mousse. If you tell me where the plates are, I'll take care of the logistics."

"Stay put," she told him. "I can manage."

A. J. didn't make an issue of it, listened instead to the sound of her loading the dishwasher, through the kitchen doorway watched her busying herself with dessert spoons and pressed glass parfait glasses. She was quietly humming to herself as she worked, something freeform as melodies went, obviously of her own creation. It was a habit, he expected, from when no one was listening,

All that while, a question kept surfacing in his head, a missing piece of the puzzle, one he hesitated to share out loud. He gave her time to dig into the lush amaretto-laced concoction before he risked it.

"You never volunteered and I can't help wondering," A. J. said, "how you chose to wind up in academe in the first place?"

"Bolland, you mean. The usual ads in the Chronicle," she shrugged.

"That, too. But I was thinking more 'the big picture' stuff. Math, college level teaching . . . judging by sheer demographics, not necessarily the easiest field for a woman to crack." The words were barely out of his mouth when he found himself regretting them. He could tell instantly he had struck a nerve, caught her off guard.

"That's important?" she said slowly.

"Only if it is to you. And I'm beginning to get the distinct impression it is, Sam."

Silent, she just stared at the table top in front of her. When they finally made eye contact, he caught the faint tightening around her mouth.

"Fair enough . . . only I'll warn you, I didn't take too well to those same questions around the dining room table while growing up either," she managed a weak attempt at a smile. "Multiply your most out-of-it campus geek by the umpteenth power and you pretty much have my childhood in Phrenel Springs, North Dakota."

"The rural Midwest. I would never have guessed," he told her.

Sam grimaced, as if she expected his reaction. "You wouldn't be the only one," she said, "but there it is. A child of the Heartland. My folks ran the last struggling hardware in fifty miles. Trust me, it didn't take long for them to suspect I had been dropped on the doorstep by passing aliens. The 'Sam' speaks for itself about their expectations—except the hoped-for son-and-heir wasn't to be. Backup plan was I marry some local ranch kid and keep the store afloat. That was unlikely after I came home with a tattoo and started messing around in a wannabe punk band with a couple of underachieving townies. Anything to avoid keeping the family books in perpetuity . . . "

They made eye contact. Sam's ragged intake of breath trumped anything he might have said in that moment.

"And then I got lucky," she said. "End of my junior year, a counselor gave me an ultimatum. Risk dropping out at the rate I was going or graduate early, *right then*, with more than enough academic credits. Her alma mater, Beatrix—this tiny blip of a women's college in Massachusetts I never heard of before—was offering me a full-ride half a continent away. I didn't even blink, just took their scholarship and ran."

"Eighteen and totally on your own. A lot to handle."

"Seventeen . . . and not as rough as you might think," she told him. "I had a lot of help and some great teachers. And in a weird sort of way, despite the medieval dress code, a nun for an advisor and three years required religion for a self-professed agnostic, I actually fit in. Childhood stereotypes that women don't do numbers can be pretty pervasive. It was considered moderately "cool" among my

31

classmates to excel at the very subject many of them struggled to master."

"You and a uniform," he chuckled, shook his head. "Something tells me, I would have loved to have witnessed that."

"Let's just say those heinous Beatrix College blazers certainly forced me to look beyond orange hair and a nose ring to assert my identity and independence. But once I stopped banging my head against the wall, I didn't have far to look. I always knew where I stood when it came to proofs and equations . . . "

"Structure," he guessed.

Sam looked pained. "Face it, I badly needed that. But, no. In retrospect, I think it was the desperate hunch—hope, maybe—there might be some cosmic truth in all those numbers, the Eternal Music of the Spheres, whatever you choose to call it."

Something in what Sam said was vaguely familiar. "I remember reading that some argue as we search for symbols to capture the spiritual," A. J. said, "'God' and 'math' are more or less interchangeable."

"Barrow," a smile tugged at the corner of her mouth, "John middle-initial-D., English physicist, mathematician and cosmologist. Somebody around here besides me has actually heard of him. I'm impressed."

"I was probably channel surfing and hit NOVA en route to C-Span."

"I'm still impressed."

It had to be asked. "Clearly your passion," he said, "and yet you ultimately chose applied math, not theoretical."

"Not much demand out there for a woman who sits around counting angels on the heads of pins," Sam told him. "And I know where my strengths are, can live with that. As is, I came the closest to slipping some order-of-the-universe stuff into the classroom when I was teaching at the community college. We adjuncts had a pretty free hand as long as we took attendance . . . and at least some of the kids occupying those seats were big-time into crystals, black holes and crop circles—willing to suspend disbelief. At Bolland, denominational or not, pulling that off has been a lot harder."

"I can imagine," A. J. told her, "with some of the purists in the hard sciences on campus breathing down your neck about objectivity. Meanwhile you're out there bringing pop culture, to say nothing of philosophy—God forbid, even something that might smack of the 'spiritual'—into your classroom. Risky stuff."

Sam shrugged it off. "Nothing so noble. Like my career itself, my teaching style more or less found me. It isn't much of a stretch from 'heavy metal' in some dork's garage to singalong formulas with Sam in front of 30 students. After tutoring so many of my dorm mates at Beatrix for four years, a graduate assistantship was more or less a foregone conclusion."

"I assume by then your family must have been—"

"Preoccupied," a shadow passed over her pale features. "About the time I headed off to grad school, the store finally went under. Mom and Dad forsook the amber waves of grain for a trailer park in Florida. They missed both graduations."

"You still see them . . . your folks?"

"Cancer and a heart attack, within a couple of years of making the great trek south."

"I'm sorry," he said.

Sam's expression had taken on a faraway look. "Stuff happens. It is what it is. In the end we finally had our moments, time to make our peace with the course things had taken. Not all of it, but enough. I'm grateful for that."

Suddenly so much made sense, A. J realized. The reaction must have shown itself in his face. Sam ducked her head as a flush of awareness spread across her cheekbones. She shifted in her chair and a wisp of dark hair worked its way loose from her austere up-do, began to trail along the curve of her cheekbone.

"Anyway, you know how the personal side of the equation turned out . . . not exactly like setting formulas to perky show tunes," she told him, still avoiding his thoughtful gaze. "I'm not so sure my profs at Beatrix would still consider me one of their success stories—despite all the magna, summa stuff at the time. But then I never thought through the downside of Beatrix either, how woefully overprotected I had been those first four years out on my own."

"Growing up rarely comes cheap. We can't always anticipate the price tags."

"True. Just maybe though, I'm finally listening to that outspoken nun-of-a-mentor of mine, declaring a moratorium on beating up my myself—excising not just guilt, but *regret* from my working vocabulary. Woulda-coulda-shoulda's may not be as

33

destructive, but pretty darn close."

"Even when it comes to Bolland"

She looked him square in the face. *"Especially* Bolland." What he read in her eyes was enough to rob any man of speech.

"Well, if it's any consolation," he told her after a while, "if life can ever come *too* easy, then mine certainly is a cautionary tale. I wasn't born grading multiple-guess exams, but close. Two uncles had their doctorates and Mom wound up as an elementary school principal on Long Island. My two sisters, both older, went into education. Meanwhile Dad was duking it out as a legal eagle in the corporate world, so hardscrabble politics was Sunday dinner table fare."

"No adolescent yearning to chuck it all and enlist, ship out on a tramp steamer, join an ashram?"

"It might have helped if I had," A. J. said. "In retrospect I was spoiled rotten, woefully unprepared for what came after. Like you, I finished my education, grad school anyway, so much earlier than my peers. I dated around, sure, but never seriously until Anne. And after she . . . after my wife's accident, I just caved—had nothing to hold on to but a failed altar boy's faith, this place, class schedules, going through the motions. We Ferinelli's had always been close, tons of cousins, grandkids, dogs and all the trappings of an extended Italian-American family. Suddenly it was too difficult even going there. Literally or figuratively . . . "

A. J. broke off, stopped—hadn't intended to, wasn't quite sure how he wound up revealing so much. Without giving it a second thought, he had just given this woman a glimpse into his head and heart he had never unpacked in quite that way before, not even to his closest friends on campus, colleagues of decades' standing.

If Sam sensed how uncomfortable he was, she didn't show it in the silence that settled in between them. It was she who chose to end it.

"A lot in common, when it comes down to it," she said quietly. "On the surface of things, who would have thought it, Professor Ferinelli."

A. J.'s smile didn't reach his eyes. She wasn't the only one who had begun to come to that conclusion.

"Unfortunately, it's getting late," he said, abruptly downing the last of the wine in his glass. Easing his chair away from the table, he got to his feet, stood looking down at her.

"Sorry . . . I really hate to leave you with cleanup detail," he told her, "but there's that stack of quizzes waiting for me to grade. It's time I get going."

Sam studied his face before responding. "I could say it's been fun, but under the circumstances, that seems a bit of a misnomer," she said evenly. "I'll call you, if and when I decide to go ahead with all this. Regardless, I seem to have some last-ditch job hunting to do."

The grievance, her pink slip. To his chagrin, A. J. realized he had forgotten momentarily what had brought him here in the first place. It didn't seem either the time or place to suggest she use him as a reference. After an awkward round of thanks on both sides, he snagged the keys from his pocket and headed out to the Toyota.

Sam followed him out into the yard, but at a conspicuous distance. Through the windshield he saw her standing there, hands clutched tight around her, while he navigated the cracked and buckling pavement of her driveway. A. J. managed to dodge her precariously positioned metal mailbox—tough with other distractions on his mind. Top of the list, he couldn't help speculating whether she had any intention of really following through with what they had discussed.

Something in the set of her shoulders as she turned, headed briskly across the lawn and up her porch steps told him that her decision to file the grievance or simply cut and run was no slam dunk. She never looked back.

Chapter Three

Changing night owl and weekend sleep-in habits comes hard. Still, by nine-thirty Saturday morning, dressed for the job in fraying jeans and a work shirt worn thin at the elbows, A. J. had run through two loads of laundry—including the borderline disgusting dish towel he had smuggled home from his office. He had cleaned out the corner of the basement in the immediate vicinity of the washer and dryer. Both projects were long overdue, a factor which in A. J.'s mind didn't totally explain the zeal with which he tackled them. The basement especially was a backbreaking business and led to a sizeable heap at the curb anticipating trash day.

By the calendar it was October. He could have sworn it felt more like mid-February, the restless time known on campus as the "tunnel" term—so-named because at the end of it, students and faculty alike begin to catch a glimmer of light. Semesters end, academic years lurch to a close bringing lazier summer days, a greatly reduced course schedule, a chance to regroup. The rhythm of the academic seasons was embedded in A. J.'s body clock. It was a silent alarm going off inside him, especially since his Anne was no longer there with her golden smile to remind him now and again there was more to life than class periods and syllabi.

For now, A. J. settled for mindless grunt work to help switch off all the introspection, ruminating and analyzing that were the life's blood of his existence. The potential for quick-and-dirty fixes around him, he quickly discovered, was endless.

His back porch door was falling off its hinges and only needed a little wood filler and some elbow grease to remount the thing. It was as good a place as any to start. Barely a third of the way through the first set of screws, a familiar voice stopped him, cultured and sonorous, used to an audience.

"Looks like good therapy, Ferinelli—the academician's perpetual instinct to ferret out the proverbial hawk from a handsaw."

George McDowell, division chair and chair of the original search committee that hired him, was not the kind of guy who just showed up in people's back yards on random Saturday mornings quoting out-of-context Hamlet. A. J. took his time wiping his hands on his frayed and faded shirttails before he reached out and responded to his colleague's greeting.

A good history professor and in A. J.'s eyes a mentor, George had steered his wet-behind-the-ears protégée through some pretty rocky shoals his first few years. He had pushed A. J.'s promotion through the ranks, sided with political science in a couple of nasty curricular battles. More recently he was there to help his colleague pick up the pieces in his personal life. A lot of memories.

"Scary times, George," A. J. said. "A little honest manual labor is good for the soul."

His colleague smiled. "I'm counting on it. Three more years for me. Sixty-seven seems as good a time as any to hang it up. After that—roses."

Cultivating his hybrids, like everything about the man, fit the stereotypical image of an Oxford don, from the tall, lean-boned frame and studied hint of professorial gray at the temples, to the steel-rim glasses and leather-elbowed wool blazer collection. A. J. had sat in McDowell's garden often enough, while he and Anne drank red wine with George and his wife, Bea—academic life at its most idyllic. Civilized. George tended those thorny acres with as much care as he expended on his meticulously crafted research on Civil War military strategy.

"I'll admit, I'll be glad when the semester's over," A. J. said. Out of sixty-four colleagues on the faculty, here was one with whom he had always been able to share his darker moments without fear of being misunderstood or used.

"Multiply your malaise by every one of those offices up and down the hall, Ferinelli, and you've got Bolland these days. Sometime I think admissions has one criteria and one only. Is the incoming student still breathing?!"

Deep in A. J.'s memory banks, an alarm was going off. As a teacher, George was always solid if not a trifle dull. And for all his scholarly cynicism, his mentor hadn't been one typically to carry the flag for elitism. "As teachers," George told him once early on, "our calling here is simple. We make the most out of whatever human material comes across our path."

A. J. had never forgotten it. The question was, had George. There was one way to find out.

"You heard, I assume," A. J. said, "about Sam Pomerantz."

Again A. J. saw George smile, but it was tighter now. A queasy sensation in his gut told him his instincts had been dead-on.

"If you're considering taking her side, charging into the lists," George said, shaking his head, "it's a mistake. There isn't a colleague in the division who would be with you on that one."

"She's a damn good teacher, George. She seems to be making a difference here, is getting a raw deal."

"Life's tough, I grant you. She's young, Ferinelli—new to the game. We've all made errors in judgment along the way. Sometimes they backfire. But let's just say, all those sterling teaching evaluations aren't always what they appear."

"Meaning?"

"You've read the debates at the highest levels in the academy these days—about the role of women in the sciences. All those gimmicks she uses might work . . . or they could be undermining the core curriculum, a way to get around the math requirement, forget how."

"I've seen the stats, George," A. J. said, choosing his words carefully. "The math department toughened the challenge exams after her first semester in the classroom, convinced she was giving away grades. Two years later, the students are still testing out once she has had a chance at them."

"And flunking out in Winna's intro to lit and in the beginning lab sciences."

The usual cast of characters. A. J.'s mouth felt stiff. "Makes

38

you wonder, doesn't it?"

"Reluctantly, I have come to believe some students just don't belong at Bolland," a scowl had begun to crease McDowell's elegantly composed features. "At a community college, maybe. After all, isn't that where she . . . where Pomerantz came from?"

It felt to A. J. as if a heavy band were tightening around his chest, making it hard to breathe. He couldn't imagine what in the hell Sam had done to get his colleagues so riled up. She obviously went the extra mile to teach her classes, tough but fair, tried to build student self-esteem helping retention in the process. It was no secret, if enrollments didn't stabilize, the school was in trouble.

"What you're telling me is—"

"You'll lose this one. And frankly, if half of what is going around on campus is to be believed about Ms. Pomerantz . . . let's just say, I'd think long and hard about going to the mat over this one. You're going to need a lot of support for your department to keep its second teaching slot."

The second departmental position was A. J.'s sanity factor—allowing him to hire an ex-CIA agent with a Master's degree who took over the global curriculum a couple of years ago. It saved A. J. a heck of a lot of prep time, made the course load more manageable. George wasn't through.

"You've served on every major campus committee, have published a half dozen articles," the older professor said, "won every damn teaching award this place has to offer, more than anyone on campus. If things stay on course, you're next in line for the Reuter Prize, a chance for the sabbatical year you've been angling for, to finish your monograph on utopian political models."

This man was A. J.'s oldest friend at this place. Until that moment, he still clung to a shred of hope he was misjudging this little visit—a senior colleague offering up a well-meant bit of advice, support never more appreciated than in the months after Anne's death. That was three years ago, three years in which the younger professor had taken himself out of the loop. And it had come to this.

"When I retire, Ferinelli," George was saying, "I always wanted you to . . . always thought you'd make a run at division chair. Something I would support, even now."

A. J. felt his hands clench and unclench, begin to shape themselves into fists. There was no doubt about it any longer. His mentor's ramblings were beginning to sound suspiciously like blackmail.

"George," he said quietly, "I cannot . . . won't stand by while a handful of our colleagues throw an effective and caring instructor to the—"

"I didn't come here to argue with you."

True enough. The Division Chair came to warn him. That much was evident.

"Is this . . . am I to take this as a threat, George?"

The senior faculty member flinched, as if abruptly realizing to whom he was talking. A. J. stared him down, message sent—received.

"I have nothing against Ms. Pomerantz personally," McDowell had the shuttered look of a man picking his way through a verbal minefield, "and she certainly is a most . . . attractive young woman. But I have become cynical enough to believe where there's smoke, there is often a whiff of truth wafting around somewhere in all those rumors. We're not just talking about the Dean, but the integrity and credibility of this institution. And there, my friend, it's time to draw a line in the sand. Your colleagues have always respected you enormously, Ferinelli. They can appreciate you've been isolated over the past few years, out of the mainstream of faculty life—understandable enough after everything you've been through. A day hardly goes by without my Bea remembering the wonderful times she and your wife used to . . . "

Everything he had been through. As his colleague saw it, Anne's accident was clouding his professional judgment and Sam Pomerantz was trading on his vulnerability to win support as she went after the Dean. If true, an indictment of both Sam *and* himself. Through a pounding in his ears, A. J.'s anger flared white hot.

If this wasn't personal, than what *was*, to hint at a more than collegial relationship with Sam and then dredge up the close friendship between George's wife and Anne, all in one breath. At least George had the common sense, if not the decency, to leave his friend's dead wife's name, literally, out of this.

When it came to trust and integrity, right now about the only thing A. J. had to go on were his instincts, telling him loud and clear Sam Pomerantz not only needed but deserved every single shred of help and support he could muster. Whatever was going on, whatever had prompted his colleague's visit, it wasn't just petty business-as-usual campus intrigue. Not when McDowell obviously was prepared to go to these kinds of lengths, even lay their very friendship on the line to stop him.

A. J.'s hand shot out, his face an expressionless mask. "Great seeing you again, George."

His colleague hesitated before he took it. "I'll see you at the faculty meeting," George McDowell nodded, turned on heel and never looked back.

The faculty meeting. The heavy hitters among the traditionalists had thrown down the gauntlet, the appointed date for their slug-fest no longer a mystery. Faculty meetings were set for the second Tuesday of the month, the next one just three days from now. With the big guns already rolling into place, A. J. knew he didn't have much time. Awkwardly retrieving his cell phone from his jeans pocket, he punched in a sequence of numbers. ASAP, he decided, he needed to update his speed dial list.

Sam picked up on the fifth ring. So did her answering machine.

"A. J., is it . . . hold it a second, okay." A warbly series of beeps, then her canned voice cut off. "That's better," she said. "My machine is older than the hills, so blasted annoying."

And essential. If all hell broke loose as A. J. suspected it was going to, flawed as her machine was, it at least it offered backup protection of sorts.

"I need to talk to you," he said.

Her silence spoke volumes. "Now isn't really a good time. I'm up to my elbows in—"

"George McDowell was just here." His tone told her the rest.

"Oh."

"I'll be there in ten minutes, Sam."

He broke the connection before she could protest. Grabbing his keys, he locked the house and headed for his fifteen-year-old Toyota. *Finally rusting out,* he hadn't noticed before, along the bottom of the doors. Even on a full professor's salary it made sense to drive the thing into the ground.

Sam was waiting out on the porch steps with her neighbor kid, Ja Ron, sitting at her feet. Her hair was down but loosely tied back with what looked like packaging twine. Judging by her paint-streaked jeans and rolled up shirt sleeves, A. J. guessed his phone call had interrupted major household adjustments on her end as well. There was a smudge of what had to be paint on one of her cheeks. When in doubt, shuffle the deck chairs on the Titanic.

At the moment, Ja Ron appeared to be showing her the inner workings of some kind of toy that transformed itself into a war machine with just a few deft twists. Would to heaven, A. J. found himself thinking, Sam herself proved as capable of reinventing herself.

She waved, flashed a tentative smile as he headed up the walk. The boy, on the other hand, didn't bother to conceal his disappointment at A. J.'s arrival. "What's *he* doin' here?" he mumbled.

"Sorry, kid," she said, "gotta go!"

"We were gonna play . . . you know, those warrior guys on your computer. . ."

"*Ci-vi-li-zaaaa-tion,* guy. Some other time, okay?"

A. J. stifled a smile at the notion of Sam into strategic video games. While he knew plenty of students who ate, slept and breathed hooking up on-line over stuff cryptically titled *Halo* and *Call of Duty,* he was utterly clueless with anything more complicated than a periodic mind-deadening computer solitaire marathon.

Ja Ron frowned. "You're gonna kick butt and I'm gonna miss it."

"Right now the Prof here and I have a different kind of kicking butt to do. Work stuff. Don't worry, I promise to save you some of the action."

Sam tousled the boy's tight-cropped Afro, then hand on his shoulder, nudged him gently in the direction of home. Leaving sneaker marks in the still greening late Fall grass, he shuffled his way back across the lawn to his own yard, protracting the exodus as long as possible.

"That was quick," she said as the boy moved out of earshot, scanning A. J.'s face.

"I was wrong. You haven't got a lot of time—"

"Time?"

"For some tactical maneuvering of your own," he said as he followed her into the house. "I'm not here to pressure you. But if you have any intention of filing your grievance with the Personnel

42

Committee, it would make sense to do it before the next general faculty meeting on Tuesday. McDowell paid me that visit to warn me the good old boys are among the moving forces behind your pink slip. How much do you want to bet you're on the agenda Tuesday?"

"This can't be happening," she breathed, sank down on the love seat just beyond the entryway.

Seating in her tiny living room was limited. A. J. settled into the antique Morris chair facing her, giving her time to let the shock value wear off. He remembered Sam's reaction from the faculty dining room yesterday, the way she caught her lip in her teeth like that when she was nervous, weighing her options.

"Of course, your pink slip won't come up formally," he told her finally, "if that's what you're imagining. Someone will bring up the issue of 'pending dismissals' from the floor, so it's tough to anticipate, tougher to respond. Of course the discussions will be so civilized and veiled, your name would never even be mentioned. There will be tap dancing around the cast of characters, but everyone would know—and so would you—every posturing word was aimed straight at you."

"I don't believe this."

"The faculty meeting doesn't change the game plan, just the timetable—that is, if you were leaning toward pursuing a grievance," he prompted gently, knowing it was unlikely she had given it much thought, considering what she apparently had been doing with a paintbrush since he saw her at dinner last night.

"Would I like to stop Bremer from ever doing this to anyone else," she said, "of course, who wouldn't? Especially now when I know I'm not the only one the man has been jerking around."

"But—?"

"I guess this is as relevant a time as any to tell you, I haven't been totally honest with you." She hesitated, then plunged ahead, evading eye contact in the process. "You've been very supportive and I thank you for that. I truly do. But you have to know before this goes any further, I am not really a sterling test case for anything."

"At issue here is the Dean's conduct, Sam, not—"

"You need to hear this," she insisted softly. "There was . . . it's years ago now, back in grad school. I had this problem with my Master's thesis committee. Things with one of my advisors got way too personal, *messy*. Somehow when I was trying to land the job at

Bolland, Bremer found out. At first he seemed so supportive, wonderful. But it didn't take long to figure out the man is bad news, sadistic—abusive. I broke things off."

"And Bremer let it stand?"

"Eventually, except for the random suggestive phone call, usually in the middle of the night. Or he would show up at my house on some pretext, garbage like that. When I threatened to blow the whistle, he resorted to blackmail. After the incident in graduate school, he said, no one would ever believe me. My career would be history, he said. Even in his office last week, he made it plain if I ever complained about his conduct, it would be all over campus in a heartbeat I make a career of sleeping around to . . . "

Fill in the blanks, A. J. thought as a grim string of possible scenarios flashed through his skull—to get her degree, hold on to her job, make sure she got tenure. Suddenly George McDowell's innuendos made sense and at least some of the leverage behind Dean Bremer's hold on Sam had become painfully clear. A. J. cleared his throat.

"So, I'll understand," she said, "if you might be . . . if you're thinking maybe it would be best to just let it go after all. I planned to spend tonight dusting off my resume—"

"Hell, no," he bristled, momentarily taken aback at how fragile she assumed his support for her might be. But then after everything she had experienced, could he truly blame her.

"What you've told me complicates things, Sam," he said, deliberately choosing his words, "but certainly doesn't change the bottom line. You came here in need of a supportive campus community. Wishful thinking perhaps, but not unreasonable as expectations go. Bremer sensed your vulnerability, used it—cynically, brutally, indefensibly—which makes all this his problem, not yours, any way you cut it."

"Tell that to my colleagues. Regardless of whether I go after the man or not, we both know I have to try to get out of here. And we know what a job search would mean right now with all this hanging over my head. Any reference check would be a dicey game of Russian roulette, from Bremer's office, on down."

"They have no grounds to attack your teaching. It's why Bremer and the boys have decided to go for the old tried and true, below-the-belt politics. George McDowell made it pretty clear Euclid himself could be teaching your courses and the standards-police would be in an uproar if what he was doing got kids through the math requirement," he told her. "Bizarre as it sounds, it's not politically correct these days actually to have to *teach* the students."

"So you're saying, this really isn't about how totally . . . naive I was in my personal life at all, or the fact I so woefully misread what kind of a man Bremer was. The real issue is *remedial math*?"

A. J. winced. "Academic standards, anyway. If you carry the keep-out-the-riffraff arguments to their logical conclusions, that's where you're bound to end up."

Sam looked ill. "They would actually trash my life just for thinking it's possible, wanting to help those poor, shellshocked—"

"Small consolation, but McDowell was right when he insisted, from his point of view, this isn't personal," he said, "all appearances to the contrary. The job description itself is the target. The fact *you're* in the particular faculty slot, incidental. But if you still have any illusions about how vicious this could get, Sam, you're right. Now is the time to bail. I won't hold it against or think the less of you if you do."

"McDowell's visit . . . it means they've already gotten to you, too," her voice broke, steadied again, "just for taking me to lunch."

A. J.'s jaw hardened. "Not an issue. If you go through with this, I'm with you, Sam. A thousand percent. George already heard as much from me this morning, loud and clear."

"And what is that going to cost you? I have a right to know."

A. J. shifted uncomfortably in his chair. "Do I need to buy a gun? *No.* But I'll admit, George McDowell came armed with an interesting list. If I was thinking about a sabbatical next year—forget it. Then there's the second faculty line in my department I've been trying to protect."

He left the business about the division chairmanship out of the mix. Even George was having trouble dragging that into the equation. As for questioning the motives for supporting Sam's case, A. J.'s blood still boiled at the very thought of what his mentor had been implying.

Sam sat in silence, factoring in what A. J. was telling her. "Any off-the-rack book on employer-employee relations would tell me to get smart. Just give it up," she said. "It was your gut reaction the first time we talked about this—not what I was in the mood to hear at the time, but I respect, appreciate the honesty. If anyone knows the politics of this place, it's you."

A. J. winced, *not exactly his take on things.* Sam didn't give him time to register a protest.

"But then a guy learns a lot, too, living out on the prairie," she said. "I must have been seven or eight the first time I watched a coyote on the prowl. I was sitting on a swing in this park down the street from where my folks lived. The coyote was far enough away, I never knew exactly what it was he was chasing. I just saw these clouds of dust rising above the clumps of grass and sage as the two of them circled, dodged and wove their way across the barren field. At first I thought, maybe they were just playing . . ."

A. J. knew he had heard that note in her voice before. It was whenever she talked about growing up, her family, anything that reminded her of those years in the Dakotas.

"The coyote would pursue and fall back, pursue and fall back," she said. "It had to have been an hour and still he and the nameless, faceless creature out there were locked in this desperate dance. It would be dark soon and the animal the coyote was chasing looked like it was getting tired—its circling and darting became tighter and tighter. By now it must have known it had become a toy in some terrible cosmic game. Finally it came to a full stop and just sat there. Funny thing was, so did the coyote. It was as if he expected any minute the game was going to continue. Or maybe he's bored, I thought. He'll give it up, let the other animal go."

"But he didn't," A. J. said evenly.

"No. And for years afterward, I kept having these vivid nightmares—remembering . . ."

"Powerful, those kinds of memories."

"In all fairness to the coyote, the guy was just thinking, *dinner,*" she shrugged. "I know that now. It's the whole problem with Aesop's fables, the fairy tales we concoct for ourselves to make some sense of why we human beings act the way we do. We feel obligated, somehow, to project our own penchants for violence and cruelty on the 'lesser creatures' But then, I suppose when you think about it, a coyote's not exactly in a position to complain."

With the fingers of one hand, she was tracing the delicate curve of the chair arm, as if reminding herself where she was. Reconnecting. This was her living room, her terrain, a half a lifetime

46

away from the brutal world of predator and prey she had been describing to him. In theory anyway.

"Bremer's dismissal letter," she said finally, "the whole timing of it, I've been thinking about it. And I believe it was meant for you, as well as me. I reread the Handbook. Procedurally dicey for the Dean, doing it the way he did—but even that didn't stop the man. There is no way that Bremer is going to let this . . . let me just go away quietly. He thinks he has the upper hand and he's going to play it. Firing me was only the beginning. That's true, whether I choose to grieve him for his conduct or not. Bottom line? Common sense tells me I can't turn and run, play the victim here. But that doesn't mean I have to drag you down with me."

A. J.'s answer was to get slowly to his feet, inviting her to join him. "My decision to make, Sam, and I've made it," a half-smile tugged at the corner of his mouth. "And unless I've badly misread what you're telling me, you've all but made yours as well. I assume you've got a laptop around here somewhere. If you really intend to file a grievance by Tuesday's faculty meeting, we've got a hell of a lot of homework to do."

By midnight the draft was done. With the two of them hunched over her computer, Sam had put together a compelling and carefully crafted account of the Dean's harassment, stalking, and intimidation. Even with the squalid details lying there in black and white, in A. J.'s mind there was no way her terse, dispassionate outline could catch even a fraction of the ruthlessness of what Bremer had done.

It was a classic tale of personal and professional exploitation, a brilliant yet vulnerable woman pitted against power and a kind of facile, unscrupulous charm wielded by a man who knew how to exploit both. With her contract renewal at stake, Bremer tried to coerce first unthinkable abuse, then Sam's silence. That done, he canned her—knowing in the current faculty climate all the positive teaching ratings and retention figures in the world wouldn't help her. Faculty these days were watching their own backs. The few support letters from colleagues would be tougher for Sam to get now.

When she haltingly described the ugly encounter with the man in his office and how he had hustled her out of there afterward as if absolutely nothing had transpired—with his secretary conveniently in

47

waiting right outside his office door—it took every bit of willpower A. J. had not to get in the Toyota, drive over to Bremer's elegant Federal Revival home and kick the shit out of him. The sick, arrogant bastard.

"I had to get out of his office and said as much. Bremer just looked at me with a cynical smile—chilling, depending on my silence," she told him. "So help me, I wasn't going to give him the satisfaction of falling apart. 'Did I ever tell you,' he said on the way out the door, 'you're absolutely *beautiful* when you cry?'"

Pale yet defiant through the whole brutal narrative, there was no question she was telling the truth. Whatever the woman's flaws, dishonesty wasn't one of them. He remembered what she told him about her childhood, involuntarily found himself picturing her as a girl—those incredible eyes and all the pain behind them, trying to make sense of the silent violence she had witnessed playing itself out among the sagebrush and prairie grass.

"Time to call in the cavalry," A. J. said.

Stifling his anger, he used his cell phone to call his buddy Jake Burroughs, got him out of bed. A tough country lawyer and graduate of Temple, for all his aw-shucks demeanor Jake hadn't lost a labor case in ten years. After another four hours subjected to the lawyer's meat ax, the grievance was ready, signed and lying on Sam's coffee table. Judging by the pale light filtering in through her living room windows, the sun would be up soon. Sunday morning—not exactly anybody's idea of an idyllic weekend.

"I owe you one, big time," A. J. told his friend, "combat pay, a good stiff drink, something."

"Later," Jake yawned, "that's for sure."

Even the caffeine wasn't working any longer. Sam was still on her feet, too, but barely. There were dark smudges under her eyes, not the first or the last night's sleep she would lose over this.

The quick hug she gave the attorney when they finished was understandable, gratitude, nothing more. Still, as she began to detach herself awkwardly from Jake's flannel shirt front, A. J. caught her uncertain look as it slowly dawned on her how her gesture could be interpreted. He felt for her, remembering how warm and spontaneous she had been with her neighbor kid—suddenly finding herself forced to second guess what clearly had to be the habit of a lifetime.

Her voice was low. "I don't know how . . . Jake, how can I

possibly thank you for all your—?"

"You just did."

Jake's growl of a disclaimer was meant to defuse and reassure. But A. J. was glad Sam couldn't see what he could—the raw, undisguised worry in his friend's eyes.

"Talk to you later, buddy!" Jake said.

Wrapping his massive grip around the handle of his beat-up briefcase, he let A. J. walk him to the car. He also made sure they were out of earshot before he ventured the truth.

"We've made her case as strong as possible," Jake said

A. J. could read the hesitation in his friend's tone. "There's a *but . . .* "

"Sam's one heck of an attractive woman, downright yowzah from what I've seen of that old boy's club of yours. She's a mathematician—suspect in itself for anyone of the feminine persuasion. Spontaneous, she wears what she's feeling on her sleeve, seems to be a terrible judge of character when it comes to men, present company excepted, of course. A hugger. I've seen employers hang a defense on less."

"Sam Pomerantz is no—"

"I know that. You know that," Jake shrugged. "Still, it's her life and conduct they're going to put on trial. It would help if we could establish a pattern of abuse on Bremer's part—as in, the guy gets his jollies shoving women around, professionally and otherwise. The minute Sam tried to stand up to him on his own turf, it became personal for the man. Left to his own devices, he'll try to bury her. And it appears he may have plenty of help. Hells bells, the woman has a heck of a lot at stake here and even if she wins, she'll lose! And she knows it. Long term, she won't be teaching here, that's a given, regardless of the outcome. And worst case scenario . . . not anywhere."

"Damage control?"

"She files her grievance and wins clean, nails the Dean and keeps her job," Jake's eyebrow arched. "I'd say with the good-old-boys like McDowell lined up against her, the odds are nil . . . even less. She gets the college to settle and moves on, especially if the press gets hold of it and there's a fund drive coming up? Better. Her best shot may be they seal the files and at least give her a snowball's chance of salvaging her career. A gag order could be negotiable.

Provided, of course, it becomes in Bolland's best interest to muzzle Bremer in all this. That could happen, on procedural grounds, if nothing else. In the end it wasn't the FBI but the IRS that did in Al Capone."

"Alternatives."

Jake shook his head. "It's not going to be pretty—taking them on. Tricky. You could be an enormous resource, behind the scenes, as she starts to pump out resumes. You have the clout to help cultivate and control her references, maybe even minimize random fishing expeditions by some eager HR-type out there."

A. J. kneaded at the hard knot forming at the base of his skull. Among other things, he had one killer headache, not the first since Sam showed up on his doorstep.

"I ought to warn you," A. J. said. "That business about McDowell makes me uneasy. I get the distinct feeling, going after Sam may be just be a smoke screen for some larger agenda. Unfortunately, I've been so totally out of the loop, it's risky to even hazard a guess what the real game plan might be."

A quizzical frown had begun to settle in between Jake's shaggy brows. "The same thought had occurred to me in passing," he said slowly. "But then it wasn't the *only* agenda I've been wondering about here, guy. Before we go too far with all this, it might be very helpful for me to know."

A. J. felt the color rise in his face, momentarily broke eye contact. *Leave it to Jake to call a spade a spade.* The thinly veiled question wasn't aimed at Bremer and company's motivations, but a heck of a lot closer to home. As a tenured professor, why would he put his own career on the line like this for a junior faculty member he barely knew. He already had heard George McDowell's take on the same subject.

No question, in Jake's case there wasn't a shred of ill will at work. But the very fact both men had raised the issue couldn't help but pull A. J. up short, big time, make him question what he had been playing at. He had assured Sam Pomerantz, from the outset, his only motive in supporting her was the principle of the thing. Anything else, after what she told him in confidence about her childhood, her sheltered college experience and obvious personal vulnerability, was unthinkable—borderline irresponsible.

What had George McDowell said about smoke and fire? High

time, A. J. decided, to shut down anything smoldering back there in his subconscious. For good.

"Strictly professional," A. J. said, jaw tight, as he looked his friend square in the face. "Sam asked for my help. If you insist on finding some cosmic significance in all this, then maybe I'm just a sucker for lost causes."

"Maybe," a half-smile twisted at the corner of Jake's mouth and his tone lost its probing edge. "Welcome back to the human race, old friend," he said softly. "It's been a long time coming. Too long."

Mercifully, whatever else his friend was thinking, he appeared to let it go. A. J. felt a tightening in his chest, found himself blinking away the image of his Anne, smiling out at him from the recesses of his memory.

"I realize it might appear I'm flirting with conflict of interest issues on multiple fronts here," A. J. said. "Fact: Sam is likely to need me as a witness. Fact: everything I've heard from students about Bremer is confidential. If it comes to building a case, I couldn't easily testify publicly to any of it. Also fact: coercing students to come forward on their own, under the circumstances, might not be in their best interest. There is simply no way to maintain anonymity in this place. Too small."

"Sam might have picked up rumors among other women faculty."

"Not likely," A. J. told him. "She came here under a political cloud and I gather has been fairly isolated since. Given the budget cutting going on, colleagues around here right now would be sitting on their hands. Or worse, gathering the firewood for the pyre."

"We're back where we started. A tough gig."

"So," A. J. persisted, "we help Sam regroup, track down women faculty who already bailed, are teaching elsewhere. Or recent grads. With degree in hand they would be less susceptible to whatever that low life Bremer has to dish out and probably couldn't care less about campus politics."

"What ever. You know the players, so when you come up with something, call me," Jake said. "No hurry, buddy. By the time we factor in the appeals process, this whole thing could easily drag out for years—"

Years. Instructor salaries were at a bare subsistence level. Fast as all this had been going, A. J. hadn't thought of the obvious. A few things his law degree taught him. Justice isn't a given. It certainly isn't fast. Long before Sam saw a deal or a dime, she would be broke and living out of a U-haul.

Chapter Four

When in doubt, teach. A. J. knew the drill. This time the relevant bullet points were all there, timely beyond his wildest imaginings on his course syllabus. *Restraining orders. Anti-stalking laws. Title IX.* He had just challenged the students, off the top of their heads, to cite evidence of recent court cases or news stories involving gender bias or sexual harassment. Through a cloud of chalk dust, he was jotting down their responses, discouragingly prosaic so far.

"Supreme Court decisions about employer see-no-evil management practices," Joel Van Susten threw out with a stifled yawn from the back row.

The rest of the class just looked blank, eye-balled their fellow-student as if he had grown a second head. A. J. suppressed a grin. Whatever issues he had with Van Susten's work habits, he had to admit, the kid was brighter than hell, didn't miss much.

"Point is," A. J. said. "We're seeing a growing body of laws, precedents, sentences to fit the circumstances, some designed to punish and others to protect. At times more aggressive than others. You'll catch a feel for those kinds of issues in the textbook's essays on domestic violence—for starters."

A dozen faces were trained on him, drinking it in. There was nothing like life intruding on those hallowed halls of learning to get the old adrenalin flowing.

It was Monday mid-morning, barely two hours after Sam filed her harassment grievance. By now it was all over the Bolland campus. Sam Pomerantz was going after the Dean for alleged unprofessional conduct. *Alleged.* Knowing what he knew, the word was starting to set A. J.'s teeth on edge.

"All right, *sexual harassment, gender bias, sexual discrimination,*" A. J. challenged the class. "Definitions! Where does it start—in the work place, the dorm, in the classroom or closer to home with how we're raised or the friends who help shape what is acceptable and what is not."

A. J. timed it so the class ended before anyone could respond. As a teacher, it was his job to drag the good, the bad, and the ugly out into the open. Make them think and keep them coming back for more. If the results just happened to help Sam Pomerantz in the process, so much the better.

On the way back to his office after class, A. J. made a detour to check out his mailbox. Sorting through the clutter, he found a letter—unsigned and obviously mass produced—that momentarily stopped him cold. Vicious and libelous, it accused Sam Pomerantz of indiscretions with students and colleagues alike, then laid out the crass scenario of a woman maneuvering to keep her job at all costs. It was a far cry from Sam's own understated, clinically dispassionate account of vulnerability and betrayal.

Disgusted, A. J. tossed the copy in a blank manila file folder in his office desk drawer, intending later to share it with Jake. No point in giving it credence by showing it to Sam. If, of course, she didn't already have it. The tone made it abundantly clear what the author of the letter was capable of—including the chutzpah to send *her* a copy.

It turns out, A. J. didn't have long to speculate. Sam showed up herself around eleven, just standing there in his office doorway, not saying a word. Her tweed skirt, crisp white blouse, sweater coat and brown leather boots were understated, had poise and professionalism written all over them.

Still, A. J. was glad he was sitting down at the time, pouring over his lecture notes for the rest of the week. The hard feel of the floor under his feet helped him weather the gut wrenching anguish he read in her eyes. A single, letter-fold sheet of photocopy paper was clutched in her hand. He already had seen the contents.

"It's starting," she said.

A. J. nodded, shifted uncomfortably in his chair. "I gather you've met our not-too-subtle campus hate-monger. Not new," he hastily added, "to you or the situation, by the way. Over the years, any time something happened on campus with major administration-embarrassing potential, vitriolic brew like that pops up around Bolland . . . or worse, winds up in the hands of the local press."

No one ever had proven where the things were coming from. Certainly A. J. had his suspicions. Most of them kept coming back to an embittered language teacher, Richard 'Tricky Dick' Craighton. To look at the guy, he was a vain and wrung out shell of a man who should have retired at least five years ago. Instead, he had begun to vent his spleen publicly at faculty meetings, a practice the various factions on campus had learned to use and play to their own advantage. He was capable of worse, most definitely. In A. J.'s book, if the school closed tomorrow, the guy would have considered it a victory.

Sam stepped into the room, eased the door shut behind her. Stashing her book bag alongside his battered sofa, she sat. From the neutral vantage point of his swivel chair, A. J. studied the set of her mouth, the faint flush along her cheekbones. A glint of steel flickered in her eyes as she returned his gaze, but there was a catch in her voice, betraying her uncertainty.

"I can't imagine what you must think of me," she said, simple fact, devoid of self-pity.

"What I can't imagine," he told her, "is the courage it took to walk across the quad or into your classroom this morning—to know that instead of rallying in your defense, there are colleagues out there who feel no qualms about savaging what's left of your life."

"Don't . . . please. Don't try to excuse this. I brought it on myself. Insecure and gullible, wanting Bolland so badly, needing to fit in that I—"

Lonely. Unbidden, the word popped into his head. With a shock, A. J. realized it was one he understood.

"Sam, I've said it before. What's happening here has nothing to do with you," he said carefully. "Twisted as the reasoning may seem, the cabal out there truly believes they are defending some intellectual high ground. McDowell made that abundantly clear on Saturday and ostensibly the man has been my friend for twenty years."

As it turned out, his one-time mentor's visit had the opposite effect from the one intended. Among other things, it had driven home a disturbing reality. None of their hands were clean when it came to Sam's situation, A. J. admitted, his own included.

It was time to recognize his isolationism for what it had become. He had chosen to lock himself up in his classroom with his grief and heartache and ignore what campus politics had been reduced to in the name of protecting standards or whatever the justification might be. It had been easy enough to do when he wasn't on the receiving end. Problem was, Sam had put a face on the realities behind the myths he had cultivated about his life's work. There was no going back.

"You see the consequences of stonewalling change," he said, as much to himself as her, "and of arrogance beyond comprehension. This is about teachers who have forgotten why they chose the profession in the first place. You are experiencing academic life at its very worst—have gotten in the way of someone's agenda, Sam, that's all. You're expendable and you'll pay for it."

"I wouldn't care so much," she said, "except for the students. I've seen firsthand what the system does to them. They deserve a heck of a lot better."

"Of course. But then so do you."

A. J. shoved back his chair, got up. "Screw 'em, we're going to lunch," he said, grabbing his leather jacket from the top of the file cabinet. "Faculty dining room."

Eyes wide, she started to respond, hesitated, began again. "I know you mean well, but we all have our limits," she said softly, "and this is mine. Forgive me if I give it a pass. I just *can't* . . . "

"Sam, I've been in this place twenty years," he told her. "If you don't stay in their faces out there, yell your head off at women's volleyball, take in the gosh-awful open mike night coming up next weekend—you name it, it'll only get worse. Whoever is behind this and for whatever twisted, despicable reasons, will be smelling blood. You're right not to delude yourself about how civilized this place is. They'll move in for the kill."

"And if you're seen with me, they'll—"

"I'm in their crosshairs already. And you know what, Sam . . . I don't give a flying—"

The f-bomb wasn't a staple in his arsenal, but he used it now, dwelling on the word with a ferocity that surprised even him. Sam's gasp of awareness told him he gotten her attention at last.

"I've spent half my life here," he told her, "always loved this place, warts and moles and all—still do, I tell myself, in spite of everything. But I cannot and will not let you hang out to dry on the line alone. Not and live with myself. McDowell & Co. already know that, loud and clear."

This time it was beyond her to stifle the tears. But just the way she stood there letting them fall, chin high, tore at his insides.

"I already owe you so very—"

"Nothing. You owe me absolutely nothing," he said. "You're a colleague and I'd like to think, becoming a friend. I'm doing this as much for me as you . . . and much against my increasingly cynical instincts of late, I'm doing it because I believe, simply put, it's the right thing to do."

His tone pretty much cut off discussion. Sam took a swipe at her cheekbone with the back of her hand.

"At least this time lunch *is* Dutch," she said, "or on me, take your pick."

He could picture her standing there in the faculty dining room, brow crinkled in concentration as she rummaged in her book bag, until she finally located what she was looking for. With all of their colleagues watching, she would thrust a crumpled ten-spot at the counter attendant, gesture inclusively at both their trays. *No one owns me*, her flash of movement said. *Forget that at your peril.*

"Gutsy, Pomerantz, I'll hand you that," A. J. said evenly. "Don't tell me . . . it's something in the water supply back there in the Dakotas."

He regretted the attempt to lighten the mood as soon as the words were out of his mouth. Sam didn't crack a smile. "I appreciate the atta-girl," she told him, "but I was always taught that courage presumes the luxury of a choice."

Monday afternoon. Four-eighteen. The campus was heating up despite a bone-chilling rain that had begun sending the first of the leaves down with it. Conditions in the dingy under-the-stairs office of the Bolland student newspaper, *The Campus Voice*, were tense, overpopulated. It wasn't every day the students got to take on a Dean.

Editor-in-Chief Joel Van Susten had taken charge, hunched over the draft of page one and a red pencil in hand. In his radical-message tee and shredded jeans, the shaggy-haired senior could have passed for a dropout from the Sixties—an impression subtly contradicted by his captain-of-the-tennis-squad tan that had 'preppie' written all over it. With an impatient gesture, he plunked the sheet of revisions down next to the closest computer keyboard.

"Did anybody run a damn spell check on this thing? Journalism 101. Definitely not smart for the lead story on Ms. Pomerantz to misspell harassment *and* grievance . . . *four times.* Ferinelli is bound to show up here any minute for a read-through."

Her face a fiery red, sophomore Liz Diamond skimmed the corrections. This was her work Joel was skewering.

"Don't get in a bunge," she muttered. "I told you I'd fix it. I'll fix it."

"We're running out of time here, people"

Fighting words under the circumstances. "*You* try rewriting the lead article umpteen times in less than an hour. I didn't see you volunteer."

Joel flashed a sheepish grin. "You type faster."

"True."

"And it's your byline. You earned it."

Liz blinked, took a deep breath. "Thanks . . . or something."

There was the little matter of the hate mail that was bound to follow. Still, fair was fair. She had been sweating over the lead article on Sam Pomerantz and the Dean nonstop since the anonymous letter trashing the Math Instructor began circulating on campus yesterday. Then barely an hour ago, a second letter—also unsigned—appeared under the newspaper's door, accusing the Dean of a pattern of unprofessional conduct. *A bombshell.* And anonymous or not, one that gave powerful credibility to Sam Pomerantz's claims.

"Time to stop tap dancing and start kicking butt," Joel had told his crew. Meanwhile, there he stood, checking his watch for the second time in as many minutes. Grumbling quietly to herself, Liz appeared to be fixated on the text scrolling on the computer screen in front of her.

"You can bet this letter also went out to the town's weekly," Joel said. "Thing is—we're set to run first. If we had tried for a scoop, we couldn't have planned it any better. Twenty minutes, kiddies . . . let's do it, get this rag ready to run. We make the deadline and our printer will have just enough time to run a thousand copies before close of business. Crackpots have fed us 'tips' before pushing one agenda or another, too hot to handle. But this is different, worth getting right."

He was losing his audience—the mass of humanity in the room had begun to scatter. Bolland's cafeteria had already begun serving dinner. When Liz pulled copies of her latest draft off the printer, Joel faxed the piece, along with the second anonymous letter, to Professor Ferinelli's office. The originals had barely cleared the innards of the cranky fax machine when A. J. himself showed up on the doorstep, tie askew and out of breath.

"Okay, Van Susten—source."

"No clue." Joel shared the original of the terse message. "Letter No. 2 was shoved under the door about an hour ago. I checked the hallway to see who delivered it. Nothing out there. I thought the last paragraph especially offered some juicy possibilities for an editorial."

A. J. scanned the contents, then passed the note back to his student—though not before committing the final paragraph to memory:

Before people crucify Professor Pomerantz, they ought to know she isn't the only one. At least a dozen other women on campus could give the Personnel Committee an earful about what Dean Bremer considers 'getting close to the students, faculty, staff'. Nobody should have to put up with this kind of crap to get an education. What has all this got to do with higher learning?

"Unsigned. Standard copy paper and the font seems to be Courier," A. J. speculated. "Campus computer labs and a lot of the offices use Courier as a default. The Dean has this weird fetish about

59

imitating typewriters. That second note could have come from just about anywhere."

Joel nodded. "Liz is reworking page one based on the second letter, beefing up the tone. I thought I would let the dust settle, wait until next week to do an editorial."

"Smart, under the circumstances."

By now the professor had moved on, was looking over Liz's shoulder himself at the computer screen. *Good stuff,* despite the occasional rough spots in the young woman's grammar. If Jake Burroughs thought it would help legally for Sam's case to go public and possibly dredge up other harassment cases in the process, Liz certainly did both with her article.

"I plan to stay down at the print shop until the edition actually comes off the press—work on memorizing those Con Law cases while I'm waiting," Joel was saying coyly. "Then crack of dawn a bunch of us are going to slide copies under every student and faculty door, personally. We'll stack whatever's left in all the usual campus pickup points. Dorms, student and faculty lounges, the cafeteria and faculty dining room, for starters. That way if the powers-that-be try to pull the mass copies, it will already be too late. The edition will be in circulation."

"Good thinking," A. J. fought a smile.

If only the student displayed half as much concentration and persistence in class, he thought—although at least, from the sound of it, Joel was trying to get his act together. As the newspaper's advisor, A. J. knew all too well how tough it was keeping even a slim six-page edition going every week—enough to distract anybody.

The other names on the masthead of *The Voice* read like one of his Con Law class lists and volunteerism from other quarters in the student body was not exactly overwhelming. The priorities of most Bolland undergrads were far crasser. Scoring brews or hot dates, racking up scores on the gridiron were 'biggies'. Those worried about the unemployment line down the road were dead-set on finagling internships that might give them a leg-up on the rest of their graduating class. A handful zeroed in on getting into a decent grad school. That was where Joel was coming from initially, until A. J. tried some arm-twisting and got the kid to sign on as editor-in-chief his senior year. There were no other candidates.

"You want relevance?" he had told Joel point blank when the

60

student had piped up in class last spring complaining about the general state of political life on campus. "There's plenty of gritty stuff, if you know where to look."

Leave it to Joel to remind him of the conversation now. "You were right about 'slime' when it comes to campus politics," Joel said. "Nasty, but then rumors about the Dean have been out there for years. I won't let this one get away from us, Prof—not when finally we can get the goods on our campus *Lecher*-in-chief Bremer."

A. J.'s eyebrow arched. "Sounds personal, Van Susten," he said carefully, "a dangerous way of doing business."

To his chagrin, he recognized the hypocrisy in the warning as soon as he gave it. In so many words, this was exactly what his friend, Jake, had been hinting. But then, whoever said it was mandatory for someone to take their own advice.

"Whatever my shortcomings, ingratitude isn't one of them," Joel muttered by way of defense. "Pomerantz chewed me out plenty and ran my butt ragged. But I gotta hand it to her, the woman got me through bonehead math. We were cautious when the first piece of hate mail showed up on campus. But after this second letter, the harassment allegations can't be a coincidence. Legally, we should be covered, right?"

A. J. chuckled. Not just the headline in *The Voice* but that homework assignment in Con Law on harassment was about to get a heck of a lot more interesting.

Right there, he made a seat-of-the-pants decision not to enlighten the students about his conversations with either Sam or Jake or the collaboration behind Sam's grievance. Except for protecting the students from libel, he wasn't about to put his own spin on the article in *The Voice* either—or try to use his influence with the paper's staff as a personal trump card in Sam's grievance strategy. With what he knew, it would have been easy enough.

"A direct quote from the second letter about Bremer," Joel frowned, "I mean, would using it be safe? We have backup. A couple of staffers have heard first-person about students with similar horror stories."

A. J. stifled a smile. The guy was learning. At least he asked.

"Credibility wise, the lack of a signature won't wash," A. J. said, "so Liz has done it right. Don't quote—summarize content and remember to use the word 'alleged'. If worse came to worse . . . let's just say, on deep background I could count as the second source, if you need to verify the accuracy of a pattern of harassment. And of course, you called Bremer?"

Joel nodded. "Got his voice mail. In the last paragraph Liz wrote he wasn't available for comment. So legally there we're—"

"Covered," A. J. said. "Just in case, I also faxed both notes and the draft of your article over to my friend's law office for a second opinion. If there was a problem he would have called by now."

Joel had the look of a sprinter tensing at the block. "Then we can—"

"Go for it." From force of habit, A. J. took one last look at the headline—the biggest type and the biggest odds of a mistake. "Liz, just one thing."

"Spell check, *Harassment*," she winced. "I know. I did. Twice."

"I assume . . . ," A. J. hesitated, "does Professor Pomerantz know about any of this?"

Joel shook his head. "No answer, office or home. So, I was planning to—"

"Don't," A. J. said quickly, "I'll take care of it."

The spell checker was running yet again, then the printer. "Done," Liz said.

Joel leaned over her shoulder and awkwardly hit the copy-file sequence, went on-line and pulled up the address of the printer. "It's outta here. So am I. I'm going to wait it out at the printer's until the issue is off the press."

Liz followed at her editor's heels, not about to be left behind. In two quick strides, A. J. managed to catch Joel with his hand still on the door knob.

"Van Susten, Liz . . . solid work," he said, clapping the two of them on the shoulder.

Joel grinned. "Thanks."

The walk back across campus was wet. A light drizzle was turning the leaf-covered walkway across the quad into a skating pond, just what A. J. needed to clear his head. It wasn't the only slippery slope he needed to navigate. For starters, despite his assurances to Joel, he had no intention of calling Sam about what had just transpired. Under the circumstances, the more deniability on both his and Sam's part, the better. For good measure, he made a point of turning off his cell phone and disconnecting the land line overnight, didn't reactivate either one until crack-of-dawn the next morning on the way to his two-hour class.

The precautions paid off. Sam's call caught A. J. in his office next morning. Even with all the steel and concrete around him, filtering out a good chunk of the signal, he caught the fear in her voice.

"The secretary in the Dean's office called, foaming at the mouth about some headline article in *The Voice*. I hadn't seen it until a couple of minutes ago, but Bremer sure wants to see me. *Now.*"

"Not without me," A. J. said. "And Jake, if I can get him. I'll meet you in five minutes, in your office. Wait for me!"

The phone tucked awkwardly against his shoulder, A. J. started scrawling a note in thick black marker on a yellow legal pad canceling his class. Not unheard of. But it was something, it occurred to him in passing, he hadn't done since his wife died, three years ago.

By now he knew Jake's number by heart. His friend picked up on the third ring.

"Sam just got a call from Bremer's office about that article in the student rag I faxed over to you yesterday," A. J. said. "Command performance."

"Has she seen it?"

"No."

"Good, keep it that way. I'll meet you there," Jake said. "She shouldn't go in there alone."

"Damn straight."

Already in the hallway, A. J. clicked his office door shut behind him, locked it. Great timing. Joel Van Susten was coming down the corridor in his direction. Groggy and yawning, with an impressive case of bedhead, the student had a stack of newspapers under his arm.

"Post this cancellation notice," A. J. barked, handing him the sheet he had ripped off the legal pad, "on my classroom door over in Richter hall."

"Wha-zup, Prof . . . is everything—?"

"The natives are restless. I'll fill you in later."

Taking the stairs two at a time, A. J. struck daylight, headed across the quad toward Sam's office. Her door was closed but he knew better. He knocked, identified himself.

"Thank heavens," she said, pulling open the door. "What's going on here? I found a copy of *The Voice* under my door, just started to read the front page article on—"

"Toss it in the pail or better yet . . . here, you don't even have a copy of it," A. J. reached out and took it from her.

"But the Dean thinks I—"

"Let him think whatever he wants. You're going to sit there in his office and listen. Say nothing. If the asshole is smart, he will do the same. . .which should make for one short meeting. As is, with any luck, the guy just might hang himself if you give him enough rope. You filed a grievance, within your rights. It's par for the course for Bremer to assume *you* sent the second letter to *The Voice* or engineered the student article. Though for the record, as their advisor, I was the one who okayed—"

"You . . . what . . .?"

Back up, A. J. told himself. Go slow. "The student paper got a tip just before deadline last night. When they couldn't reach you for a comment, I didn't encourage them to track you down either. If the Dean asks you, you can honestly say you know nothing about it," he told her. "Ditto, when it comes to any knowledge of the article in *The Voice*. Van Susten and Liz wrote it. I didn't touch it. Not a single word—except to make the guys spell harassment right. It's their paper, not mine. Or the administration's."

"Does Jake—?"

"I faxed him both letters and the article last night. After you called this morning, I got him out of bed. He's on the way over to the Dean's office as we speak. When is Bremer expecting you?"

Sam looked at her watch. Her mouth was stiff. "Three minutes."

"We'll start. Jake said he'd meet us there."

As they negotiated the outer doors to the administration building, they ran into a colleague from the business department. His smile and greeting had the half-asleep, noncommittal feel of someone who hadn't yet seen the latest.

Bremer's secretary, on the other hand, was cold, perfunctory and didn't wait to announce their presence. Standing there in a pencil skirted brick-red power suit, she just unceremoniously opened the Dean's door, let them into the inner sanctum. As A. J. made a point of shutting it again behind them, he and the secretary made eye contact. The look she shot in his direction bordered on thinly veiled contempt.

Whatever the Dean had expected, it was not A. J., or when he joined them about four minutes later, Jake either. The lawyer's breathing had the desperate edge of an out-of-shape marathon runner on the last five-mile stretch.

In spite of himself, A. J. smiled. Where on earth did Jake get those flannel shirts? The contrast couldn't have been greater. Even anticipating what boiled down to a back-alley rumble, Dean Bremer epitomized professional gray flannel decorum.

"I'm *disappointed*, Ms. Pomerantz," the Dean growled, "shocked . . . aggrieved at what's happening here. You saw the student paper." It wasn't a question.

"Just the headline this morning," she said. "*After* your call. I didn't have time to read the article."

"And the second anonymous letter—"

Sam didn't even flinch. "I assume you mean the anonymous hate mail that apparently popped up yesterday in everyone's box—including mine," she said, "personally and professionally ripping me to shreds. If there's another letter, I haven't seen it, have no idea who sent it or why."

"I submit you *do*, that you . . . "

"Bremer," A. J.'s hands were balled into fists at his side, "you're treading on damn thin—"

Eyebrow raised, Jake cut him off. "*Now, Dean Bremer . . .*"

A. J. knew that voice. It was all wounded innocence, enough to stop anybody, himself included, mid-charge. Jake was just getting started.

"I do believe," the lawyer said, "we seem to be heading off in a . . . shall we say, most inappropriate direction here. Is this a formal hearing of some sort? I guess I missed that. Oh, well . . . if that's the case, it would be advisable to tell that to my client."

The Dean's eyes were a dead giveaway. The man was edgy under all his moral indignation, outgunned and he knew it. If A. J. had to make book, the college President had already laid hands on the student paper as well as the trash-Sam letter preceding it, had given Bremer one heck of an earful.

Even more likely was the President's source. A. J. would have bet a month's salary it was Bremer's secretary at work here, playing both ends against the middle. Ever since the woman had resolved the discrepancy between roots and hair, from bleached blonde to a power-statement shade, the rumor mill had it she would not be adverse to moving over from the Dean's to the CEO's office if the opportunity arose.

Interesting how complex one's loyalties can get when a promotion is on the line. Then again, maybe the proverbial rats were beginning to look for the life boats.

Jake had taken the initiative. Bulldog fashion, he was not about to let it slip. "By the way, what *is* the personnel grievance and appeals process around here?" he said.

A. J. had to fight back a smile at that particular bit of theater. Jake already knew, had poured over a copy of the faculty handbook from cover to cover at Sam's house in the middle of the night on Saturday. The first step was a formal written grievance to the Faculty Personnel Committee, followed by a hearing culminating in a faculty recommendation to the Dean. With the Dean a party to the case, it probably would be kicked upstairs to the President, or if necessary, the Board of Trustees. The last resort, if it got that far, was civil court.

A. J. sensed Jake Burrough's game. Make Bremer go on record about due process, signal loud and clear that legal eagles would be watching him, every step or misstep of the way. Above all, Jake was clearing up any misconceptions the Dean might have that Sam was alone in this.

Bremer had the stone-faced look of someone outmaneuvered and resenting it. "It goes without saying," the Dean said, "as a party to the grievance, I would absent myself—except, of course, to present my case."

If anyone believed that, A. J. thought grimly, they would believe in the tooth fairy. The only way the Dean got by with his slimy shenanigans all these years was because he had accumulated enough ammunition to pull the right levers with uninvolved faculty and his victims alike.

Grudgingly, though, A. J. had to admit the Dean was smart enough not to hang out over the edge alone on something like this either. Someone on the faculty or board, in turn, had to be not just backing, but most likely using him. But who, and why? A. J. was convinced all of this was far too calculated and risky to originate with a few of the Old Guard with delusions of turning Bolland into the

"Fair enough," Jake said. "I guess, then, we're out of here. The day is still young and I'm sure, Dean Bremer, you have a lot of work to do."

His face stiff, expressionless, Bremer nodded. On the surface anyway, what began as an explosive situation was resolving itself with a whimper.

Once out on the quad again, the sun was trying to burn through. A. J. drew in the crisp October air, not so much trying to clear his head as to leave every hint of Bremer's office light years behind him. Silent, Sam walked alongside him, eyes fixed on the ground at her feet. With her jeans jacket and her book bag slung over her shoulder, she could have passed for a coed.

"What happened in there?" she said finally.

"Round one," Jake ground to a halt, tucked his battle-scarred briefcase under his arm. "Some territory marking, pissing on trees and phone poles . . . that's about it. I think Bremer got the message."

A. J. broke stride and the three of them stood there together watching the campus come alive around them. "Maybe," A. J. said, "probably wishful thinking, though. The man knows he will have to work underground now, which makes him potentially more dangerous. We'll be able to judge better after one o'clock. Though just in case, I suggest we all get out our bulletproof vests."

At Sam's puzzled look, he reminded her. "The faculty meeting."

"I guess I was suppressing it."

Jake grimaced. "You know, boys and girls, I can't . . . it's inappropriate for me to—"

"You can't be there, I know," Sam forced a smile. "No sweat, Jake. I'll leave my Uzzi at home, just in case I'm tempted to go postal at the moment of truth."

"Sounds like a plan!" Jake nodded, shot a veiled glance in his friend's direction. "And *you*, Ferinelli . . . ?"

A. J. didn't dignify that one with a response but the look he returned in his friend's direction pretty much said it all. Stifling a grin, Jake ducked his head, flipped quickly through his dog-eared pocket calendar. "So, any word on the personnel hearing?"

Sam shook her head. "Still too soon."

"The clock is ticking. Their response has to be filed within the month," A. J. said. "Unless they, or we, request an extension."

"I still need those witnesses," Jake reminded them. "Names, dates—"

"You'll get 'em."

Quick as he was to reassure his friend, A. J. was harboring no illusions about how difficult it could turn out to be. It was one thing to send anonymous letters to the student newspaper. Persuading women to come forward and testify in front of the Faculty Personnel Committee was something else entirely.

He was remembering the sophomore from Waupsonamie who had been caught smoking dope out behind the new track and field facilities. A. J. shuddered to think what it had cost her to get Bremer to lobby on her behalf, personally, at her suspension hearing. The coed had dropped out a semester later.

But then Sam had helped a lot of students in her three short years at Bolland, much to her own peril as it turned out. Maybe Joel Van Susten wasn't the only one who remembered or cared.

Chapter Five

After more than two decades of teaching, A. J. had good reason to be wary of student follow-through. The intentions might be good, but the proverbial flesh had plenty of distractions. As it turns out, the staff down at *The Voice* pleasantly surprised him. Fresh from posting A. J.'s note about the canceled class, Joel and Liz had polled a fair cross-section of their classmates, then took up watch outside their professor's office, armed with a proposal. Instead of generic case studies on harassment, they hoped A. J. would assign an official class project on Sam's case.

No was never easy given that level of enthusiasm. A. J. settled in at his desk, half an eye on the message light blinking on his phone.

"What you do outside of class, that's none of my business," he said carefully. "But Sam Pomerantz and I are colleagues . . . friends. It would be unprofessional for me to use the course deliberately on her behalf."

"Profs bring in stuff about campus politics all the time," Joel protested. "Academic freedom, right?"

"Not this prof," A. J. shook his head. "Despite what you may see going on out there, academic freedom was not designed to empower faculty to bite the hand that feeds them or circumvent campus governance. If I personally support legitimate campus protest or teach to the issues, that's one thing—totally ethical, I have no problem with that. But in my book that freedom doesn't extend to hiding behind the students or using them to stick it to the institution with impunity. Even the Bremers of this world have their right to due process."

"And if the institution is wrong?" Joel said. "From where I stand, Professor Pomerantz sure deserves support for—"

"Dangerous," A. J. said. "If 'support' looks like an orchestrated conspiracy, it could hurt her politically as much as help."

"Like she was putting us up to this?"

"Exactly."

"Bremer always creeped me out," Liz said, her distaste apparent. "Coming on like Mr. Charm in that obnoxious voice of his, *I'm so great I'm humble.* Give me a break! It's hard to imagine him getting it on with—"

"Beside the point, Liz. Harassment is like *rape,*" A. J. found the word sticking in his throat, an ugly reminder of everything Sam had told him. "Attraction has nothing to do with it. The real motivator is manipulation, control, power."

"On a smaller scale, think about how ethnic jokes work," Joel told her. "The principle is to set up a victim, create a sense of superiority."

A. J. fought a smile. Just when he was ready to give up on his star advisee, the guy came up with something like this. "You're right, the parallels are interesting," he said. "Bring it out in class next time."

Joel had the look of someone who knew they had been finessed. "Well, at least we may have come up with a candidate for Ms. Pomerantz's witness list. Last night when we talked with Andy Duncan, he—"

"Duncan?" A. J.'s mental antenna went up.

A senior Pre-law major from Omaha, Andy was headed for the FBI if he could manage to pass the physical. Intrigue and conspiracy theories seemed to be Duncan's middle name. Partly to keep the guy out of trouble on campus, A. J. had hooked him up with the athletic trainer, who currently was doing his darndest to bulk the guy up a little.

When it came to research and sniffing out legal precedent,

70

Andy didn't need any encouragement. The guy was obsessed with cloak-and-dagger politics. Even mention an issue and the student would show up with a stack of printouts gleaned on-line, at times after what had to be a significant amount of hacking. A handy thing—the Internet—with a limited library budget.

"We met Andy on the way back from the printer," Liz said, "and he talked us into going to see Charlotte Anui. You must know her—radical, connected, someone other women go to."

A. J. remembered without prompting, back row center in his Fundamentals of Politics course a couple of semesters ago. On paper, Charlotte was brutally outspoken about gender politics, economic and social justice. In class, she didn't say a word.

Apparently it took the better part of an hour for the trio, crammed into the front seat of Joel's turbocharged Cobalt, even to find the woman. Charlotte's apartment was downtown over an abandoned furniture store. Address numbers were in short supply.

"I tried to explain why we, why Professor Pomerantz needed her help," Liz said, "but Char's four-year-old kept wandering through in his cartoon-character PJ's to see what mom's 'stew-dents' were—"

"Bottom line, the conversation was going nowhere," Joel said with an impatient scowl. "The woman's body language was straight out of an Intro to Psych course, crossed arms and a look on her face that had *lost cause* written all over them. I laid it on the line. With just a semester left until graduation, why did Char feel she had to defer to Bremer, when a good professor's career was at stake? All we needed was names—women who may have had run-ins with the Dean. And then Char said it. *Okay, you're right, Pomerantz wasn't the only one. It's high time to cut the crap and—"*

Almost word-for-word the text of the second anonymous note," Liz beamed. "I ought to know, because I retyped the darn phrase at least a dozen times trying to paraphrase it for my article."

"That did it," Joel admitted. "We pressed harder and Char accidentally let slip a name—"

"*Grace.*"

At that, A. J. sat up and took notice, and not just of the withering glance Joel shot in his fellow-student's direction. "Grace Denison," the professor said slowly. It had to be.

The woman was a standout in his Political Philosophy course last Spring. Attractive—way too young-looking to be the mother of a high school student. Divorced and on her own, vulnerable. The Big Three, apparently, when it came to Dean Bremer's taste in women.

"You got it," Liz enthused, "by the time we left, Char agreed to give Grace your phone number. We've got a witness."

"Potential anyway," A. J. conceded, anything but encouraged by the machinating it took to come up with even that single possibility.

The three of them were no longer alone. A student was hovering in his office doorway, from the look of it her Con Law quiz in hand. In the changing of the guard, A. J. forgot all about the phone. It was nearly noon before he finally punched in the message retrieval code to find that Liz hadn't been exaggerating. The call was from Grace Denison, wanting to talk with him. She left her unlisted phone number.

Except by now, A. J. had one heck of a headache and it was a very long two-block sprint to make it to lunch with Sam. The local deli was a calculated exception to their campaign to be seen on campus—less stressful, considering they had barely an hour to get their heads together before the faculty meeting.

"They're good students," Sam said when A. J. told her about Joel and his buddies' dogged intrigue on her behalf. "Loyal."

For a while there, A. J. had been seriously considering deleting the word from his personal thesaurus. "I suggest holding the thought," he said, "because as far as the faculty goes, we're about to face the firing squad—"

"You, maybe. When it comes to firing, you recall I already have the Dean's pink slip stashed in my book bag!"

A. J. winced as he caught the pun. Sam already was disappearing in the direction of the restrooms. The debris left over from lunch occupied his hands, if not his thoughts as he cleared the table. He was checking his cell phone for messages when a flash of movement caught his attention.

Sam was back—threading her way through those crude wooden benches and tables as if all the tiredness and brutal stress of the last several days hadn't even touched her. It hadn't occurred to him earlier what she was wearing, but it sure as heck did now. To her austere flannel slacks, modestly cut tank top and jeans jacket, she'd added a gauzy scarf, vintage inlaid silver necklace and matching earrings. Both stones and the silk were like her eyes, pure turquoise.

A. J. didn't trust himself to speak.

"Survival 101," Sam apologized as she joined him, "it may take a bit of doing to pull it off, but never let them see you sweat."

"I think it's safe to say, you just redefined the concept."

She dropped her gaze, managed a self-conscious little laugh. "Sleight of hand, courtesy of the history channel," she said. "Clever folks, those embalmers back in ancient Egypt—amazing what some blush and mascara will do. Under the circumstances I figure, what the heck, give the chauvinists over there something to really gossip about."

Her reality check was unintentional, but effective. They both knew what, in all likelihood, lay ahead. Gathering their belongings in silence, an awkward distance between them, the two of them began to strike out along the apartment-lined street toward the Bolland campus.

Sometime in the past hour, the front had begun to move through and fitful gusts had begun to tug at the branches of the maples overhead. Dead ahead, ankle-deep now in falling leaves, stood the massive wrought iron gates to the campus. As if only now seeing it for the first time, A. J. sounded out the ornate lettering in his head:

Bolland College,
founded 1852,
to dignify man and glorify God.

Noble goals, considering where they found themselves.

Beyond the gilded arch, a broad walkway led to the central quad surrounded by the main classroom and faculty office buildings. Their path lay up and to the left, toward the massive Natural Sciences building sprawled across the shoulder of a terraced hillside. The hall was named for its donor, Owen Cornelius Acton. An alumnus although he technically never graduated, Acton was brutally self-made and never tired of proclaiming it. The story goes he allegedly amassed his fortune in an empire of offshore distilleries during Prohibition. That last bit of Bolland history wasn't a mainstay of campus recruitment brochures.

Still, for all the ambiguity about the man's ethics, his legacy fit. *After all, the guy was a chemist of sorts*, A. J. chuckled to himself as he made the connection. When he shared the story with Sam, he thought he saw the knot of tension between her brows finally begin to loosen a little.

"*All for God and country.* It's hard to take the rhetoric seriously, considering the source," she said. "I like that."

Their laughter more comfortable now, the two of them began to climb the ivy-banked stairwell leading upward toward the white columned brick facade of Acton Hall. None too soon, A. J. found himself thinking. Although it wasn't forecast, he could have sworn it felt like rain.

An odd time for the doggerel verse of the Alma Mater to go limping through his head—the artistic contribution, such as it was, of some alum back 'in the day':

> *O hallowed halls, our fairest Bolland, we,*
> *thy loyal children, lift the sacred flame*
> *and look to thee to harbor Knowledge true.*
> *We humbly here sweet Wisdom's light pursue.*

The Beacon on the hill. Not much truth or light in what was on the afternoon's agenda.

A. J. never fully appreciated the irony of Acton, either, as a setting for the monthly faculty governance ritual, meetings he had been sitting through for over twenty years. On the outside, the hall was a picture-postcard image of the austere simplicity and classical idealism of academic life. Inside the central lecture room with its steep-pitched rows of seats, the place had the aura of a gladiator-and-lions arena, pretty much anticipating what usually went on once the faculty showed up on the scene. The next hour-or-so wasn't likely to be an exception.

When he and Sam arrived, the room was still surprisingly empty, the headcount nowhere near a quorum. Sam followed his lead, settling in alongside him in the middle bank of seats, about half-way down one aisle. The location was strategic, offered a bit of a buffer from their colleagues who tended to prefer either congregating near the back, to the side out the line of fire or right up front and in-your-face for the benefit of whoever was chairing the meeting.

No surprise, their arrival provoked a lot of shuffling and

74

surface noise. "Holding in there?" A. J. whispered, as he leaned down to retrieve the copy of the agenda which had fluttered to rest at Sam's feet.

She managed what could pass for a smile. "The vultures are gathering."

True enough, but it was difficult reading the corporate body language to figure out from where the attacks were going to originate. In front of them, in a block, sat the rest of the math department, tenured and most definitely not on their side. Winna was off on the fringes near several members of the foreign language department. Psychology was dead-center down front. McDowell had not yet made an appearance.

The seats were hard and uncomfortable with the old-fashioned flip-up wooden writing tablets which forced a tense, unnatural airline posture. Complete with pre-flight jitters, A. J. thought grimly, his own included.

Up on the dais, President Dornbaum, flanked by a stony-faced Dean Bremer, was getting ready to chair the session. By now the faculty secretary had counted heads at least a half dozen times as stragglers came in. Dornbaum made an art-form of staring down latecomers.

Three minutes into the preliminaries, a hand shot up—Richard Craighton. A. J.'s prime suspect for campus mail assassin was about to make his presence felt. "Point of order, Mr. President," Craighton said in a sonorous, megaphone voice which sounded like it was coming from all four corners of the room simultaneously. "It appears to me a quorum is, in fact, not yet present."

Five minutes of pontificating later, the man had managed to slam his absent colleagues, the next half-dozen latecomers, and the general state of faculty morale which contributed to a thorough breakdown, as he saw it, in respect for the governance process. It was an impressive display.

Yet another count—after which, indeed, the quorum had materialized. It was going to be a long afternoon. The tactic was simple. When in doubt, stall. Huddle, set up for the play, then call a time out.

The psychology department chair Enoch Slaughter launched a similar attack on the process. "Am I correct," he said, agenda and contents clearly in hand, "we are not to hear the anticipated report from the Curriculum and Planning Committee?"

"The committee's not scheduled to meet until next week," President Dornbaum said stiffly. "The chair will report next month—"

"Point of order, Mr. President," Slaughter persisted. "As faculty we received a memo from the Admission office last week informing us, as we speak, they are strongly promoting programs which in point of fact may not be available next fall. Given the urgency of the situation and decisions already being made which would impact Planning's deliberations, it would appear . . . prudent to suspend the agenda and meet as a committee of the whole to—"

Motion made and seconded. There it was, buried under the rhetoric and Roberts Rules of Order—*The Game Plan.*

Slaughter and his co-conspirators were intending to bypass the normal process and ram through a resolution in a public forum which, if left to committee, would never pass. They would ax remedial programs, and most likely other vocationally-oriented curricula, as a way of balancing the budget. It would shut Sam and others like her out in the cold.

"*Point of order*, Mr. President!"

It wasn't the fate of the curriculum that had brought A. J. to his feet, demanding the Chair recognize him. Sam looked up at him, lips clamped tight. Everything in her upturned face nevertheless managed to signal, *No.*

"Mr. President," he said again, more quietly now. "What my colleagues are proposing here is at best grandstanding, and at worst, an unproductive use of our time. We have duly elected committees working on issues of institutional program priorities—"

"President Dornbaum . . . I object," when the chair did not respond, the male voice from the back of the room persisted. "While I respect the concerns expressed by my esteemed younger colleague, Professor Ferinelli, as a senior member of this faculty for thirty-plus years, *I must disagree!*"

A. J. slowly turned toward the sound, felt himself go cold but managed to keep his feet. Brutally rational and publicly assaulting his one-time protégée, George McDowell was about to lead the charge. Personally.

"For some time now," McDowell went on, "I've had grave doubts about the viability of this institution's committee system. They

76

meet rarely or in secret. In the main they do not represent a cross-section of the faculty."

True enough, A. J. found himself thinking. Much easier to snipe from the sidelines than risk losing your power base by serving on a committee and publicly supporting causes which could be construed as unpopular.

His long-time mentor and friend wasn't finished. "For nearly a century and a half, Bolland has espoused a mission dedicated to quality and excellence of education. It's no secret that early on I had my doubts about the new administration's budget and retention priorities—both of which seem to be potential threats to that mission. Repeatedly as a faculty we have called for the need to attract qualified students. We have demanded that Admissions adheres to strong, consistent standards in recruiting."

Jaw set, A. J. forced himself to keep his feet, hear George out without giving his one-time mentor the satisfaction of relinquishing the floor. President Dornbaum's face had taken on a dour, uncomfortable look. None of this was new.

"All that aside, we appreciate that the administration is facing difficult, wrenching decisions which may at times appear . . . harsh," McDowell said. "To act boldly is essential. Bolland needs to stay focused on the programs which traditionally have been its source of strength. That means to ignore pressures leading us in the direction of trends which lack substance . . . or which lower standards in the name of inclusivity. Especially given the unfortunate recent speculations about a possible *merger*."

Sam's pink slip. The recent move to discuss partnership opportunities with Emmaline-Wattrous, the former women's college down the road. The link between the two agendas was finally adding up.

A. J. silently aimed a couple of well-chosen expletives at himself for not figuring it out a long time ago. During the September start-of-the-year faculty meeting a month ago, President Dornbaum abruptly had appointed a committee to begin face-to-face meetings with a team from their sister institution. The intent, he claimed, was to explore the possibility of what he ambivalently called 'programmatic partnerships'. Fighting words, if 'partnerships' equated with 'merger'.

Everyone in the room, Dornbaum included, had caught McDowell's threat. If merger was coming or even officially on the table, some of the power-hitters on the faculty were prepared to drag out the artillery to stop it. The first warning shot had just been fired.

"These are troubled times," McDowell said. "On some fronts the Administration appears to be moving in, shall we say, *controversial* directions with a possible merger. But merger or no merger, if consolidation becomes a necessity, on one thing there is consensus. Better that *they*—the administration—make the tough choices than *we*. After all, we cannot be expected as a faculty to devour our own . . . *even in the case of programs of dubious quality.*"

Under all his civilized verbiage, George McDowell was delivering an ultimatum. The bottom line was to protect senior faculty at all costs. McDowell all but announced publicly, if the firing of junior faculty in general—Sam in particular—stuck for whatever reason, the senior faculty would support it. Neither he nor his colleagues would have been so enthusiastic about granting Dornbaum such blanket powers if they thought things might go Sam's way instead.

There was nothing in any of that about the students or where they fit into all this. Nothing about Bremer's deplorable lack of ethics.

Still on his feet, knuckles white against the seat back alongside him, A. J. sensed Sam shift forward subtly in her chair. It would be suicide for her to join him, but then this was her career, her programs and students McDowell was skewering openly now, impassioned and deadly. Taking no chances, A. J. slowly took his seat alongside her. Imperceptible to even the cluster of colleagues farther down the row from them, his hand came to rest tentatively on hers in the process. It was icy cold.

Out of the corner of his eye, A. J. saw Dean Bremer, who until this point had been sitting inconspicuously alongside his boss on the platform, straighten in his chair. The man's gaze appeared to linger in their general direction. A half-smile or what passed for one tugged at the corners of his mouth.

"Mr. President!" This time the voice calling out from off to one side behind them was both young and female.

A. J. half-turned in time to see Julie Schechter, Assistant Professor in Accounting, shoot out of her chair. Her hands were clenched on the edge of the seat in front of her and her voice had the crisp edge of a practiced debater.

"I'll save my distinguished colleague, Professor McDowell,

the trouble of pointing out my youth and relative inexperience at this college," she said. "But as a former controller at one of the fastest growing small companies in this town, I know numbers and I know bottom lines. Debt levels around here appear to be deadly. Unless as faculty we get our heads out of the sand and admit the possibility of change, those very winds of change are going to blow venerable institutions like this right off their foundations—"

"*Ms.* Schechter," McDowell's verbal slam was glacial, deliberate—as a fellow tenure-track faculty member, the customary form of address would have been Professor and everybody in the room knew it. "*Ms. Schechter,* I believe I have the floor."

Julie ignored him. "I remind you that as an *Assistant Professor* at this . . . august institution, I have a right and duty to make my priorities clear to the administration, as do you, *Mr.* McDowell. But there are processes for this. Circumventing governance is not one of them. I move that Curriculum and Planning be urged to make recommendations to this faculty no later than our next regularly scheduled meeting!"

"Second," a voice from the back called, male.

"Out of order . . . I protest," Enoch Slaughter whined from down front. "There's already a motion on the floor . . ."

True enough, but by then who was counting. The damage already had been done. Julie Schechter had publicly called McDowell out, figuratively waving the Faculty Handbook in his face in the process.

The undercurrent of side conversations in the room intensified. Had Julie's department—Business, or at least a faction within it—broken ranks, or was Julie acting on her own? A. J. felt Sam's death grip on the seat-divider lighten up a little.

"If, as our distinguished colleague implies," Julie insisted, "decisions are being made now which we as faculty ought to help shape, then I, for one, would urge that end runs such as the one he is proposing, *cease* immediately. Standards, I grant you, are important. So is procedural integrity."

President Dornbaum fumbled with the microphone on the podium, half-knocking it loose in the process. His efforts triggered a high-pitched, grating squeal that set A. J.'s teeth on edge.

"In my position as chair," Dornbaum said, finally getting the siren-like shriek under control, "I feel it is totally inappropriate to speak for or against the motion before us. But I do feel compelled to point out to you, as your president, with the press attention and rumors in the community over recent events on campus, this institution—already in a difficult financial situation—may find itself even more so."

Dornbaum didn't wait for the undercurrent to die away. "Anonymous letters, innuendos—what we have here could be construed as a . . . deliberate, *malicious* attempt to inflame public opinion, discredit the institution," he said. "We're talking about a general loss of confidence among students, alumni, friends of the college . . . to say nothing of potential major donors. We need to act with dispatch and discretion, realizing as we do so, this kind of negative publicity can be devastating to the life of an institution, especially for our upcoming annual major gifts drive . . . "

The guy's oratory stopped short of a bottom line. A. J. couldn't tell if the President was proposing to terminate Sam on the spot and hustle her off campus or to hang Bremer out to twist in the wind. Or both.

"*Bull . . . pure unadulterated . . . bull*," a voice in a stage whisper came drifting down from several rows behind them, "There the guy goes again with his donors—all but ready to drop a million each. If we had a nickel for every one of 'em in the past four years, we could all retire."

Hilarious, A. J. thought, if it weren't so damn tragic. At least he and Sam weren't the only ones in the room who weren't laughing. Amid the muffled scattering of groans and chuckles, the anonymous second to Julie Schechter's motion stood and identified himself. Dean of Students, Fred Urban, was an unlikely champion of red tape and protocol, but there he stood, flushed, angry and determined to be heard.

"Donors or no donors," he said, "I hope you are not intimating you are prepared to aid and abet ethical and intellectual hypocrisy, *Mr. President.*"

A. J. could count on the fingers of two hands the times the Dean of Students had spoken from the floor at a faculty meeting. And never like this. Julie and Sam couldn't have asked for a tougher ally or one with more credibility.

Fred was an alum, a Bolland Hall of Fame legend, lettering as both defensive center on the gridiron and point guard on the basketball court. In his three years as Dean of Students, he had made a point of what he openly called a conscious effort to 'swim above the cesspool'. A. J. made a mental note, before the week was out, to get the guy aside for an 'after five' conversation, something long overdue.

Dornbaum flushed. "Dean Urban, I fail to understand—"

"Neither do I, sir . . . I haven't the faintest clue what the *real* agenda might be here," Fred said coldly. "Well and good, all this lofty rhetoric about standards and traditional values. I have to *assume* it's in the context of equal concern for how we put those principles into practice, in our own professional as well as *personal* conduct. I'm speaking here of both faculty . . . and *administrators*."

Everyone in the room had read *The Voice*, knew just whose conduct the Student Dean was attacking. Bremer's smile had hardened into a grim mask. The relationship between the two Deans had been shaky at best, but then Fred wasn't through.

"I, for one," he said, "want no part in an institution which does not adhere to the same high moral and intellectual standards it holds up for its students, rather than attempting to sweep misconduct under the rug. Although I too deplore the impact of negative publicity, we have the appropriate committees to process such issues, Personnel and the Judicial Committee for starters. I feel safe in saying there are others in this room who will be anxiously waiting to hear the outcome of their upcoming deliberations."

Imperceptibly the tide had shifted. Fred had changed the playing field from battles over curriculum and seniority to Sam's accusations of sexual harassment, a political slam-dunk.

The Student Dean hadn't lost his gridiron physique. It was so still in the room, A. J. thought he heard the rivets on the guy's chair loosen in protest as he sat down. Dead silence prevailed, awkward, before mercifully the faculty began to vote with their feet—noisily gathering briefcases and heading for the exit, taking the quorum with them.

Fun or no fun, time flies. A. J. consulted his watch, a good forty minutes had passed. At least for this go-round, the threat to suspend the agenda, appeared to have come and gone. After another twenty minutes of sputtering, positioning and posturing, a disgruntled President entertained a motion for adjournment.

Sam shifted in the seat alongside him, caught A. J.'s eye. She was making a valiant effort to smile. "All sound and fury," she whispered.

"Signifying a hell of a lot, unfortunately," he said. "Once again the place is ungovernable."

"For a minute there, I half-thought Dornbaum was prepared publicly to fire either me, Bremer or both of us on the spot."

You and me both, A. J. exhaled sharply, trying his best to minimize how close to the brink they might have come. Making a show of gathering his briefcase, he stood. His free hand extended, he invited Sam to do the same.

"I wouldn't put anything past those guys right now," A. J. said as the two of them exited the room past the quizzical stares of their few remaining colleagues. "We're the only business in the world, except maybe the theater, where to talk is to act. At least on stage they make no bones about the sham and artifice of it all."

"Was all of that just . . . was Dornbaum bluffing?"

A. J. shrugged. "Moot. You saw the look on McDowell's face. This isn't over, not by a damn sight. If merger talks mean Bolland truly is looking at a fiscal Apocalypse, time most definitely is on the conspirators' side. The longer things drag on, the more likely they are to prevail . . . if and when merger becomes a necessity, they'll simply throw the junior faculty under the bus."

"I see," Sam said quietly.

What do you say after something like that? Their pace across the quad brought them alongside the female accounting professor who laid it on the line in the faculty meeting. Off duty like this, without her game face on, Julie Schechter was anything but the picture of kick-butt-take-names professionalism she had painted minutes earlier. With her flame-red hair, pert stride and petite features, she could easily have been on her way to cheer-leading practice.

"Julie, you were incredible," Sam said. "If you hadn't taken that pack on—"

"Someone else would have."

"First year here," A. J. shook his head, "it took guts."

Julie laughed. "The word is *Chutzpah*. I'm Jewish, an odd duck in itself on this campus. Besides, if I get sick of this, I can always go back to the private sector. A heck of lot more money and a heck of a lot more civilized, despite all this community of scholars stuff bantered around the halls of this place. Sometimes I think our venerable ivy is eating away at more than just the mortar!"

That thought had occurred to A. J. while listening to his colleagues vivisect one another. He'd forgotten during those three years he had pulled back from the political side of campus life, just how disgustingly self-serving the whole process could be.

"So," he said, "after this, are you going to wind up talking to yourself over there in the Business Department?"

Julie shook her head. "Doubtful. It helps that a lot of the 'reducing standards' stuff was aimed at us, too. Bolland appears to have never quite recovered from the shock of transforming the Economics curriculum into a genuine management program."

"And Bremer?"

"No love lost there. Most of the guys I work with came out of the corporate world. In general, they seem appalled at a number of the liberal arts faculty who still find it professionally acceptable to behave like cavemen around their women colleagues. If not actually pulling us 'girls' around by the hair, then darn close!"

"Anywhere else," A. J. said, "this kind of . . . garbage would trigger lawsuits that would make the administration's head spin. Face it, Bolland has been fairly isolated out here on our little hillock in the Alleghenies."

Julie winced. "And to think Henry Kissinger once said that politics in higher education can be so petty, precisely because the stakes are so miserably low."

True enough, if a guy forgot about the human costs and the whole business of integrity, A. J. thought. Pedestrian traffic was starting to pick up on the quad, with classes about to start. It was time to opt for circumspection. Badly as he wanted to test the waters about the merger issue, A. J. knew this was neither the time nor place.

"At least I hope you don't feel so alone, Sam," Julie said. "I'm only sorry we haven't gotten to know one another sooner. There are no guarantees what my colleagues in Business will do and I don't sit on the Personnel Committee. But for what it's worth? *Give 'em hell!* I've heard some stuff from my female students that would curl your hair and would be happy to say so. Just name the time. I'll be there."

As an ally, A. J. suspected, the woman wasn't quite as tough and devil-may-care as she projected herself to be. Still, whatever else came of the faculty meeting, the balance had begun tilting in a more positive direction. Sam was no longer alone.

Chapter Six

If A. J. had to define his mood, it was punchy. That faculty meeting easily could have turned into a public brawl. It hadn't. And at least now the agenda and some of the players were out there in the open. Harder or easier to confront, that was the question.

Strategies would keep. Right now, all he wanted was to postpone the inevitable—a night alone in his study with warmed-over leftovers and, most likely, way too much domestic red. Sam seemed at loose ends herself, in no hurry to go. At any rate without planning it, the two of them wound up in the corridor outside his basement office while he fiddled, yet again, with his cranky lock and key.

"Nothing wrong with this office of mine that a good bonfire out on the quad wouldn't fix," he sighed. "One of these days I have got to rent a dumpster and just start pitching stuff."

"Sorry about that—you've already wasted the better part of the day, thanks to me," Sam looked around her as if only now realizing just where she was. "Time to split, check my voice mail and head home so you can salvage something of—"

"At least save yourself a trip back to your office," he said, "the phone's all yours, Sam, if you need it."

She hesitated. "Right now I'm not much in the mood to encounter random colleagues over there, I will admit."

Leaning against the file cabinet, A. J. waited while she entered the ID code to retrieve her messages. "Wrong number," she announced. "One down and two to go."

Perched on the edge of his desk like that, she looked freer, happier than at any time in the past five days, since she first showed up in the hallway outside his office. "At that rate," he said evenly, "what say I talk you into taking what's left of the afternoon off, both of us. Get loaded, rob a bank, I'm open to suggestions."

Sam flashed a tentative smile. "Have you got a pen?" She wasn't waiting for an answer, had reached down and gingerly fished around in the overfull wastebasket for scrap paper. A. J. retrieved a ballpoint out of his shirt pocket, popped the plastic cap, and extended the pen in her direction.

"Student." Receiver tucked under her chin, she scrawled out a name and phone number. "A death in the family so she'll miss midterms. A really neat kid. Plays the oboe, runs cross-country. She's scared to death of Pythagoras."

She again keyed in Delete, then moved on to the next message. A frown settling in between her brows, she replayed it without comment. Twice.

"I think you ought to listen to this," she said.

She held out the receiver. The voice was disguised, an ugly rasp of a sound. A. J. couldn't tell whether the caller was male or female.

"Give it up," the voice said, throwing out the C—word along with a string of other choice obscenities. "Give it up while you still can."

"Archive it," A. J. told her. "We'll record the damn thing, try to figure out who—"

Sam shook her head. "Forget it."

"It *could* be important to document—"

She silenced him with a look, reached up and worked open the clasp holding back her hair. Then with a quick, impatient gesture, shook her head, sending the dark, silken waves cascading down around her shoulders.

"Right now, all I want," she said, "is to get off this campus."

"Done," he said quietly. "Name it."

"Drive somewhere, anywhere," Sam shrugged. "Find the wildest spot around here, then walk. No people, just trees and the last

85

of those tough mountain wild flowers hanging on among the rocks. I need to feel the raw wind in my face, remind myself there's life out there that's hard and brutal, but never," her voice broke, hardened, "never, ever willfully malevolent."

"My car's in the faculty lot."

She looked at him, her expression unreadable. "So is mine," she said. "I could leave it here, pick it up later, but we need to stop at my place first, anyway. I usually keep a pair of cross-trainers in my desk drawer. In all the commotion I forgot, wore them home last week."

A. J. followed her at a distance, sat with the Toyota on idle at the curb while she abandoned her aging Hyundai in the driveway and headed for the house to retrieve more sensible shoes. A smile tugged at the somber lines of his mouth as his gaze kept coming back to the car's raffish, two-tone paint job. Hard to miss. When he spotted the unfamiliar vehicle in the faculty lot earlier in the morning—black with a plum-colored driver-side door—he had no idea it was hers. It hadn't been around last weekend when they were working on her grievance.

The sound of his own car door startled him. Silent and her expression unreadable, Sam joined him in the front seat, cross-trainers in hand.

"Interesting paint job on your hatchback," he said, casting about for small talk while she struggled with her shoulder belt.

"Somebody sideswiped me downtown, didn't bother to leave a note," she winced. "I've been sliding in from the passenger side for weeks, but finally lucked out, found a replacement door. Hitch is, repainting would cost more than the thing's worth. My students have started this contest, suggesting I detail the door with refrigerator magnets—everything from 'Got Root' to Einstein's Formula of Musicality . . . "

"Musicality?"

"A little in-joke," she said. "E=F-flat."

All those years of trumpet lessons weren't entirely a waste after all, A. J. chuckled quietly to himself. He got the joke. "Go for it! After all, that model's an Accent, isn't it?" he said.

Something in Sam's laugh told him any chit-chat, at the moment, was a bad idea. Instead, he got them on the road. The lingering threat of rain had abated. Half-blinding in its intensity, the late-afternoon sun slanted through the windshield. A. J. shifted awkwardly in his seat trying to escape the glare, finally cracked the driver-side window to clear his head.

He had no idea where he was taking them, nor had Sam asked. The miles sped past. It was the sign for the Morgan Ford Sanctuary that decided it for him. Clicking on the turn signal, he guided the Toyota through the tight series of curves leading to the tiny state park. Fifteen miles of trails. On a weekday like this, they would have the place to themselves. Almost anyway. A solitary car had staked out a space in the dirt parking lot.

A. J. started to head the Toyota in that direction, spotted the student vehicle parking permit in the back window, smiled. Emmaline-Wattrous College. A hint of movement in the back seat, told the rest of the story. Someone else, it seems, had enough of higher learning and all that went with it.

"Give the kids a break," he said under his breath. After a split-second hesitation, he sought out a parking spot some distance from the maroon junker.

Sam caught where his attention had been straying and flashed a ragged hint of smile. "Sometimes I wonder if I was ever so young."

"No room on the cake for the candles. Somehow I don't believe that."

"Depending on the size of the cake," she said. "But if you must know, the Big 4-0, in a month."

Older than he thought. "I've got a good ten on you. So, if it's a power walk you're planning—"

"Not my thing. So, we can forget the oxygen tank." Sam had reached down, began substituting the well-worn cross-trainers for her black dress shoes. "Actually, I have a lot of fun keeping a yearly wildflower log, where I saw what and when. We math types are big on quantifying stuff."

"I'll keep that in mind. Unless I'm seeing double, the trail map over there seems to have lots of little numbers."

Their laughter felt good, a relief after the awkward silence building between them for most of the trip. While Sam finished tightening her laces, A. J. locked the driver's side door and wandered over to the official park signboard.

His thoughts were a jumble, like the tangled multi-colored routes of the trail system on the park signboard. Whatever her colleagues were thinking right now, this woman, Sam Pomerantz, was proving to be anything but the unidimensional, career-driven single professor he might have assumed. Enough of a techie to spend fun time on her laptop, she was at home in the kitchen, earthy-crunchy about gardening and the comings and goings of the local plant life. The more she opened up and let him into her world, the less A. J. presumed to have her figured out.

After a couple of easy stretches, her palms braced against the hood of the Toyota, she joined him at the weathered signboard, quickly scanned the maze of routes winding through the park site. "Swamp, Bog, Devil's Glen," she read. "Sounds suspiciously like what we were just doing over in Acton Hall at the faculty meeting. I thought the goal of this junket to get away from all that."

He laughed. "There's always Morgan's Meadows on the yellow trail, a half-mile this side of the glen. It doesn't say, but I would assume no crampons or climbing gear required."

"Don't tell me you're going to wuss out already! Actually, the Devil's Glen sounds interesting, probably out of the wind, too. We aren't exactly dressed for this."

In the end, she picked the route and set the pace. A. J. found himself content to settle back, watch the strong, easy rhythm of her stride and her dark hair catching the breeze behind her. The silence between them was different now. Broken by bird calls, the occasional sighing of the wind sent showers of leaves drifting down around them from the canopy overhead. *Comfortable,* he found himself defining his mood—like Sam's battered cross-trainers, their laces spliced in spots but serviceable.

"By the way, the parking sticker on the junker in the lot back there reminded me," she told him. "I'm thinking of driving over to Emmaline-Wattrous later this week—drop off my resume, do some networking. Ten miles isn't a major effort and with all the buzz about merger, well it just might make sense regardless of how this whole Bremer thing goes down."

Not just talk, A. J. was convinced of it now. "Covering your bets could be a smart move, Sam," he admitted reluctantly, surprised at how much he would miss her on campus if it came to that. "It never hurts to have a backup plan. Emmaline-Wattrous has quite a strong developmental program. They pride themselves on innovation."

"And as a former woman's college, they're big on tackling

gender-biased learning difficulties. Math and science, not surprising, heads the list. I led a faculty seminar over there last fall."

"You do that sort of thing a lot?"

"Some," she said. "A month ago I actually got a call from a publisher about my manuscript for a sing-along-with-math text for use at a college level. The editor got a tip from a colleague who had heard my pitch at a regional math educators' meeting. ROCK 'N MATH is the working title, but obviously I'm open to suggestions."

"I had no idea you were writing a book. Impressive." If Emmaline-Wattrous were smart, he decided, they would snap her up in a minute.

"There's nothing firm yet," she said, "but the reviews and editor comments so far seem promising. I walked the guy through the intro to numbers theory, 'Seven-come-eleven-it's-PRIME-prime-PRIME', to convince him the darn sing-a-long teaching approach really works, once people stop howling with laughter and try it. But I'm not counting my chickens until I see the omelet. The textbook publishing industry is a tough business these days."

No tougher than their own, A. J. winced. He found the terrain becoming increasingly familiar as the trail approached some kind of watershed. For some time now the path had been following a small stream and intuitively their pace adjusted itself to the hypnotic murmur of the water beside them. The valley was narrowing, the stream becoming more restive in its bed. From the look of it, the glen itself couldn't be more than a block or two away at this point, he thought.

Rounding a bend in the trail, Sam stopped and quietly signaled him to do the same. Directly ahead of them lay a small clearing, strangely lush for the time of year. At the edge of the meadow, three deer—from the look of it, a family—had been grazing until the sound of human presence disturbed them.

A. J. blinked, found it suddenly tough to catch his breath. Late afternoon sun glistened on the animals' russet bodies. Their heads lifted and eyes fixed wide on the trail, they waited, wary. Then deciding eventually it was safe, they began to move on.

Sam had done likewise, had begun to head out again along the trail, a fact that escaped him entirely. Oblivious, A. J. stood stone still on the spot where they had watched the deer, caught in what became a churning whirlpool of images welling up out of his subconscious. *He knew this place.* With the eyes of memory, past and present blurred until he lost all sense of time or direction.

It was late summer and milkweed clouds drifted on the breeze. Pale golden hair fanned out against the damp meadow grass, his wife Anne's, tousled by their love-making. A shower of sunlight obscured the contours of her face, the soft curve of her breasts. He half-shaped her name, it hurt just to look at her. She was so alive in that moment, A. J. could have reached out and touched her. His body taut with desire, he willed her to look at him, expecting the sensual honey-warmth of her eyes.

Instead he found himself face to face with a deep and unsettling blue, as turquoise and cobalt as the Aegean, bottomless enough for a man to drown in. *Sam.* These were Sam's eyes—riveting, questioning, achingly beautiful for all the dark secrets behind them. She was standing there quietly on the trail, disturbingly close, watching him.

"Something . . . what . . . ," he heard her say, felt her hand come to rest tentatively on his jacket sleeve. "A. J., are you okay?"

He read the confusion on her face, as stunned as he by what had just transpired. Apparently when she didn't hear the sound of his footfalls, Sam turned back and had quickly closed the distance between them. The genuine alarm in her voice got him moving, on autopilot but moving, nevertheless.

"I'm fine," he stiffened, mentally shook himself alert. "Sorry for holding you up."

She dropped her hand, but was smart enough not to give his brusque disclaimer any credence. In those seconds it took to catch up with her, he knew his face must have served as a trail map of his very soul.

"What is it?" she persisted gently.

A. J. felt a muscle jerk along his jaw-line. "We . . . my wife, Anne, and I, walked this trail the first summer we dated."

"You should have *told* me."

"Something . . . those deer triggered it," he said. "I had honestly forgotten."

"Do you want . . . we should go—"

"No," A. J. shook his head, scattering the last wisps of what it was he had been seeing. "I'm good. Let's go on." Not entirely true.

Sam started to say something, hesitated. "Your wife's accident

90

. . . it happened the spring when I came to interview at Bolland. At the time I remember thinking how devastating it would be to—"

"Three years," he told her. "It took almost half that time before I could even hear her name without feeling like I had died out there on the highway with her. In some ways, I guess I had."

"I can't tell you how sorry I am."

"Don't be," he said gruffly. "I loved her, we had more in our ten years together than most people *ever*. . . "

All that sounded far harsher than he intended. Sam flinched, subtle but he caught it, visibly stung by what he realized must have sounded like a thinly veiled indictment of her, what was happening in her own life.

"That was uncalled for," he said quickly, felt the color rising in his face. "Sam, I didn't mean . . . would never—"

"I understand," she said softly, "apology unnecessary. I can't even imagine what it must have felt like to love someone so much, to have a wonderful life together and then . . . "

As hugs went, the one that ensued took A. J. by surprise and just who initiated it was no less a mystery. Sam's dark hair brushed against his face, subtle as a caress, as her arms twined around his waist, drawing him close. Like a drowning man, he found himself breathing her in like the air and the sunlight, lost in a rush of emotions he couldn't even begin to comprehend.

"In my own obsession with all the heartbreak on campus," she whispered against his shoulder, "it can be so easy to forget, to lose sight of what really counts."

Yes, it was. And risky as it was, at the very least this woman finally deserved the truth. They both did.

His throat tight, A. J. reached behind him and caught her two hands in his, gently disentangled himself. Even at arms length, her hands clasped in his, there was still no simple way to tell her. What had begun as 'principle' on his part, then a case of one hurting human being reaching out to another, had inexplicably evolved—for him anyway—into something else entirely.

"It's only fair . . . I need to be as honest as I can about my meltdown back there," he said carefully. "Yes, true, Anne was part of it, but not entirely. I've let, even forced myself to forget so many things—including what it feels like to truly need anything or anyone, to want more in my life than class schedules and division meetings.

God knows how, but none of those defense mechanisms have been working for me lately. And after this, I have to believe you have a very good idea why."

His vulnerability was there for her to read in his face, naked and undisguised, all of it aimed in her direction. A. J. sensed the catch in her breath, the subtle awareness before she started to pull away.

"Flattering," she said dully. "But you really have no idea what you're letting yourself in for."

"I think I do, Sam."

She dropped her gaze, her arms crossed tight in front of her. With the sun sinking behind the high cloud bank on the horizon, the day was beginning to cool off quickly.

"Sam, what is it you're so reluctant to tell me?" A. J. said, gently raising her chin with thumb and forefinger so he could see her eyes.

What he saw told him a lot, not just her tears welling up, but the hint of long buried memories behind them. She managed to step out of reach, then just stood there, her back to him.

"We'll be running out of light soon if we don't keep moving," she said, her voice barely audible. Squaring her shoulders, she struck out along the trail toward the glen more aggressively than ever.

There was little left for A. J. to do but follow, silent and troubled, memorizing the stiff set of her shoulders. Occasionally her step faltered on the uneven ground and it took every bit of willpower he had not to reach out and steady her.

Every nerve ending alert, he found himself replaying their fleeting moment of intimacy, such as it was. He could have sworn the way Sam clung to him, whatever she had been feeling back there, it was more than just a question of shared pain, real and close to the surface as that was. And then something had intruded, spooked her, sent her fleeing back inside herself—leaving him utterly at a loss to comprehend what it might have been.

"You . . . we don't have to do this," he said. "We're both exhausted. It's been a god-awful week."

"I'm game, if you are."

They had reached a small creek with no choice but to go back or cross it, pick up the trail again on the other side where it wound along the twisting course of the stream. The water was swift after several days of late-autumn rain but well below flood-stage—treacherous, nevertheless. Sam slowly searched out safe passage over the slippery rocks, A. J. close at her heels.

Just beyond the water's edge she stopped, so abruptly his hands shot out to keep himself from plowing into her, steadying them both on the precarious slope. Her voice echoed back from the hard walls of the glen in front of her, a barely audible whisper of sound.

"You're right," she said, "I have got to tell you this now, A. J. Because if I can't, or don't, I'm not sure if I'll ever get up the courage again . . . "

Her voice had a tight, artificial cadence, almost as if she was calling up the words, the memories, from some invisible tele-prompter on the rock face in front of her. "Ten years ago my life pretty much fell apart," she told him. "Academically my undergrad years at Beatrix landed me a scholarship for grad work at one of the tonier state universities down the road. By the time I was finishing my Master's course work, the department considered me to be some kind of *wunderkind* and the doctorate was a foregone conclusion. The department assigned this statistics guru to Chair my thesis committee—one of those Mediterranean-god types all the women ogle on the quad. It was common knowledge, the guy's marriage was troubled. I sensed an attraction, worried we were spending way too much time together, but at first didn't know how to deal with it. One thing led to another . . . "

Something rustled in the bushes, too small for a wood grouse or pheasant. Startled, Sam's voice broke off, then steadied again.

"I'm not proud of what happened . . . a single night was enough to regret it. I quickly broke it off or tried to. He wasn't used to women just walking away. It was uncomfortable, difficult, but I stuck to my guns. Too late, it seems . . . I was pregnant . . . "

Subtly, A. J.'s hands shifted on her shoulders. Wherever this was going, she needed to know he was there for the duration.

"You chose to tell him," he said, "about the baby."

At first a quiet out-rush of breath was her only response. "I felt I had to," she said finally, "a colossal mistake. All hell broke lose. His wife found out and went ballistic. She wanted me out of his life, he said, out of the department and out of the profession if she had anything to say about it. And she expected him to make it happen, whatever it took."

"Surely the guy couldn't have . . . Sam, tell me he didn't *buy*

93

that."

She finally turned so that she could look at him. In the process, A. J. felt his hands lose contact, slip helplessly to his sides.

"You could call it that," her harsh whisper of a laugh died as soon as it began. "He wanted the good life and his wife held the purse strings—old money, a great deal of it and every penny of it hers. The department came within a hair's breadth of believing I had plagiarized one of his unpublished manuscripts. It was his word against mine until the Dean intervened—a scholar and a gentleman, thank heaven. He heard us both out, demanded the guy resign from my committee, made sure the department reevaluate my work. Then just when I thought my life had hit rock bottom . . . "

The sound of the rushing water was thundering in his skull. *Her baby.* The possibilities were beyond words, all of them devastating.

Sam just stared at the ground at his feet, her face deathly pale. "They . . . his wife couldn't have a child and I kept getting these threatening calls, insisting the baby was *theirs*. Time was running out. I was desperate, panicked, had no money for a lawyer—couldn't bring myself to risk some crazy judge would give them custody, just couldn't. For better or worse, I found a clinic prepared to . . . intervene . . . "

A. J. felt as if the ground had suddenly opened under his feet. "Dear God, Sam . . . you . . . do you have any idea what those people could have—"

"Of course. Legally they could have buried me. They were vindictive enough and would have done it in a heartbeat if they had known," she said. "And so I lied, let it be known I had *lost* . . . "

From the anguish in her voice, it was more the truth than she knew. Her voice broke off on a half-sob of recognition. They were so close, A. J. could feel her breath on his skin. By simply raising a hand he could have reached out and touched her, but her body language defied him to move an inch.

Arms crossed tight against her chest, clutching her shoulders where his hands had been, Sam stood ramrod stiff on the trail in front of him, eyes closed, breathing ragged. Her face was like the rock around them, impervious, unreadable.

"I had finished my course work and had a viable thesis design," she said finally, visibly willing herself to make eye contact.

94

"But when an adjunct's position opened up in Ohio, I grabbed it and never looked back. Unless you count living like a nun and ten years of therapy—five of it just to feel safe enough to sleep through the night. Eventually, I started to turn what should have been my thesis into the draft of a textbook. When Bolland advertised a job opening, I applied."

Where Bremer violated her trust all over again. A. J. felt his gut twist but jaw clamped tight, he waited for her to finish.

"None of what I told you showed up in my graduate records, of course," she said. "When asked, I chalked up the unfinished doctorate to a change in priorities—true enough. But somehow Bremer picked up on something when he ran an off-the-list reference check. No one ever said the man isn't smart. He knew all the right buttons to push. Not only had he backed my candidacy at Bolland, but he promised to make sure the past never surfaced again."

Sam's voice trailed off, steadied again. "I was so relieved, grateful beyond belief. He was charming, persuasive. I hadn't dated in a very long time. That, of course, was before I found out what the man was really like."

"And you seriously thought," A. J. began, his mouth stiff, "any of this would make a difference in what or how I—"

"Oh, but it does," a shadow of a smile played momentarily at the corner of her mouth, "don't you see? If not for you, then me. What's the term of choice these days . . . walking wounded, damaged goods . . . emotional road kill? Those students, my classes were the only things keeping me on more or less an even keel for over a decade. And since Bremer, I haven't let anyone close, *no one*. Simply *couldn't.*"

It wasn't quite the truth. "But you showed up on my doorstep."

"Yes."

A. J. forced a breath, let it out again slowly. "For the record, I don't regret you did, not for a second," he said quietly. "But life changes when you've seen the far side of hell and survival demands a whole new set of rules—trust and honesty take on a different kind of urgency. In that you aren't alone, Sam . . . trust me."

Anne and the baby. He saw her blink, remembering how this all began for him.

"Bottom line, I will not . . . cannot lie to you or myself any longer, even if the truth scares us both witless," A. J. told her. "I've never been one of those lightning-bolt kind of guys, tend to think everything to death. Which is why I would be the first to admit I don't fully understand what I'm feeling here—except I don't believe it's just the survivor instinct finally rousing itself with a vengeance. Bluntly put, for me this has ceased to be professional. Even Jake sensed the attraction, and from the get-go, called me on it. I dismissed it, because I had made you a promise. No strings, period. It was a promise I fully intended to keep. But then you and I both know life is nowhere near that simple."

The emotions washing over her face were powerful, conflicting as she met his steady gaze. A. J. suspected she had seen the same agonized awareness in his own eyes a quarter mile back on the trail. Life had done its best to break them both and yet, here they stood. For a terrible moment he thought she would just force her way past him and start power-walking back toward the trail head. Instead, her face unreadable, she crouched down and began to search for something amid the rocky boulders at their feet.

Cautiously A. J. eased himself down alongside her, no easy business on the uneven terrain. As he watched, she carefully lifted a clump of moldering leaves that had fallen among one of the wider clefts in the rocks.

He found himself holding his breath. "I don't . . . Sam, are you—"

"Am I okay? No. But I intended on sharing something with you back at the trail head," she managed a wan smile, "my own little reality check. I thought maybe it wasn't too late in the season. Sometimes even in winter, there can be a whole world down there."

Tucked in the dark crevasse, he hadn't seen, but did now. Nestled down there among the crevices were spongy mounds, rolling hillocks of brilliant yellow-green with a forest of fragile-looking crimson shoots and stalks rising above them.

"Beautiful," he said. "Like a Grant Woods landscape, only in miniature."

"A tiny microcosm, life—all kinds of it," gently her fingers untangled some of the feathery tendrils until they began to strain toward the sun. "Tenacious, all these little guys, doing their thing under the most unimaginable conditions, waiting for us to find them—sometimes when we least expect it."

"I suppose you know what all this green stuff is called."

"Some of it anyway," her forehead wrinkled in a frown as she thought about it. "Common mosses, *Sphagnopsida, sphagnidea*. I won't bore you with all the jargon. Those red spikes are called *sphorophytes* . . . "

"And the larger shiny leaves?"

"Bunchberry shoots, odd because they usually grow in colonies and not quite in this precarious a soil. *Cornis canadensis*, I love that name, a member of the dogwood family."

A. J. chuckled, shook his head. "Sorry, Latin was never my forte. I'm not sure I have the makings of much a botanist."

"Pure bluff on my part anyway," Sam flashed a rueful smile. "I gave up on memorizing the genus and species names a long time ago. And for all my pretensions about ticking off those lists in my wildflower books, whatever I'm looking for isn't always about the thrill of the chase either. Sometimes I just need to remind myself there is so much beauty still out here, in spite of everything, hanging on for dear life, when the sturdier prairie plants like the ones we passed in the meadow gave it up with the first signs of a frost."

On a sigh, she took one last look at the improbable Eden at their feet, then gently replaced the leaf cover as she had found it. "Anyway, I wanted to show you. A life lesson in there somewhere, I keep telling myself."

She made eye contact, her face flushed, disarmingly close. As A. J.'s hand closed around hers, he found it icy cold from handling those wet leaves and exposure to the near-freezing water.

"You need to know, where this goes from here is in your hands, your choice to make," he said evenly. "*Yours,* Sam. And whatever I feel, I have no option but to leave it to you to decide exactly what all this means—to set the limits. Friendship or more than that. I'll take what ever it is you'll let me be in your life . . . "

She drew in an audible breath. "It should be pretty obvious navigating interpersonal minefields isn't exactly my strong suit."

"I'll risk it."

The question was, would she? That part went unasked and unanswered. Instead, evading his scrutiny, Sam slowly extricated her hand and began to clamber to her feet. Hunkered precariously where she had left him alongside the rushing water, A. J. tried to straighten his aching back in order to join her.

Sam stood watching him in silence. "Need help down there?"

"Truth . . . I may never get up again," he grunted. "If you decide to bail, some park ranger is going to find me here next spring, frozen to death in fetal position. Face it, my knees are a lot older than yours."

A hint of a smile tugged at the corner of her mouth. "A decade, right? Not much of an excuse in the great scheme of things, *Professor* Ferinelli."

"Tell that to my fifty-one-year-old knees."

Their laughter echoed in the narrow glen, a fragile bond between them, as with a lot of good-natured jostling Sam supplied the leverage he needed to master his footing on the uneven ground. A. J. seized the moment and the proximity, coaxed her gently into his arms.

"I don't know about you," he managed, still trying to catch his breath, his forehead resting against the silk of her hair, "but this old geezer is running on empty."

Against all odds, for once she didn't flinch and actually let him hold her, even when she felt his lips brush against the bare skin along her temple. A. J. knew it couldn't last. Still, his heart beating its way out of his chest, he embraced the closeness for what he knew it to be—a tenuous glimmer of healing for both of them.

Whatever he had assumed when Sam Pomerantz had turned up outside his office, in her heart and gut, this woman was no fragile victim, desperately in search of a colleague who would go to the mat to save her career. Flawed, yes, but then he had plenty of demons of his own to worry about. Her decision to reach out, her very presence in his life was nothing short of a miracle.

Sam already was finessing a safer distance between them. "Persistent," she said, "I'll give you that."

Chuckling softly to himself, he watched her begin to rummage in her backpack, judging by her puzzled frown to no avail. "And from where I stand," his voice was low, "you're one of the most amazing women I've ever met. Funny, bright as heck—"

"*About to be blind as a bat,*" Sam shrugged impatiently, "despite all the emergency gear I schlepp around in this darn backpack of mine. Power bars, got 'em. Umbrella and band-aids, don't leave home without 'em, and check—we're all set for snake bite. Classic OCD, a textbook case."

A. J.'s eyebrow arched. "You've seen my office. I'm hardly

one to start casting stones when it comes to compulsions. The clutter has been accumulating for two decades."

"Which still leaves us out here in the middle of nowhere sans flashlights. And in fifteen minutes give or take, it'll be so dark we won't see our hands in front of our faces." Sam managed a sheepish smile. "Though compared to the morass we've been wandering in at Bolland, I suppose, no sweat."

Bolland With a start A. J. realized, he had honestly lost sight of the disaster of a day that had landed them here in the first place.

"No time like the present," he said.

When he extended his hand, Sam took it. Laughing at the precariousness of their situation, the two of them began to pick their way along the slick, dew-drenched path of mud and wood chips toward the trail head. At least the terrain was vaguely familiar, A. J. consoled himself, as he narrowly managed to dodge a half-exposed tree root.

They were passing the clearing in the meadow where everything had changed so abruptly for him, *empty now*. Blindsided, he found himself naming his gut reaction for what it was—subtle, but a very real sense of loss. Unsettling on multiple fronts, but then this was neither the time nor place to deal with any of it.

Sam had been dead on. By the time his boots finally struck the dirt expanse of the parking lot, it was truly dark. The maroon junker with the Emmaline-Wattrous sticker was nowhere in sight. Even out on the highway again, other vehicles were few and far between. The countryside seemed all but deserted. As the harsh glare from the Toyota's headlights swept the landscape, trails of mist rose over the creeks and ditches, a gossamer white. Beautiful.

Alone, the two of them. A. J. turned the notion over in his head, as if inexplicably they had become the only people left on the planet. He was accustomed to silence, less so the unanswered questions rushing in to fill it. A. J. felt acutely consciousness of time passing, aware of and begrudging every mile taking them home and away from each other.

He weighed and just as quickly discarded the possibility of dinner at his place, decided to drive Sam straight home instead. When he tested those intentions out loud, Sam didn't object. Apparently he wasn't the only one who needed the space to process what was happening between them.

99

But then, as his Toyota sat on idle in her driveway, neither of them made a move to go. Stalling for time, anything to prolong the moment, he told her about the ongoing fiasco with his Con Law quiz. He worried out loud that he needed to make darn sure the students had every chance to raise their scores. Sam just sat there watching him in the dim light from the dash panel, her hand poised on the door latch.

"So, consider this a raincheck," he told her. "Pasta primavera. My one culinary claim to fame. I make the sauce from scratch, my grandfather's recipe. Unfortunately tonight it's strictly leftovers and a midterm to write."

"Lesson plans on this end," she hesitated, "but thanks—yes, I'll take you up on the offer. Or we could eat out somewhere, maybe take in a flick."

Both public settings, safer—not surprising under the circumstances. A. J. smiled, nodded. "Good. Tomorrow?"

"The weekend."

"A deal," he said.

Silence. Then her free hand shot out and came to rest gently along the somber planes of his face. "You've been incredible," she told him, "really . . . I mean it. Not just today, but about everything."

With that she was gone, shutting the door behind her. He waited in the driveway until he was sure she was okay. The porch light flickered once after she was inside, then after a playful strobe-like tattoo, stayed on. Thrusting the car into gear, A. J. pointed the Toyota toward his own place.

The day-old casserole in the refrigerator was soggy. A. J. had been right about how hard it would be cranking out the midterm. He found himself discarding several drafts before settling on questions he hoped wouldn't flunk out the whole bunch of them. A rare occurrence, he found himself in bed by ten o'clock and slept through the night in spite of confused and unsettling dreams whose content by morning eluded him. He chalked it up to stress—the faculty meeting and then all the fresh air on the trail.

At first light he threw on his jeans, dress shirt, sport coat and tie, topped them off with a lightweight parka against the chill. He hadn't walked to work in so long he couldn't remember, but he pushed himself to cover the two miles in time for office hours. The campus was strangely quiet after all the commotion surrounding yesterday's faculty meeting. Not surprising, the student body was oblivious, sleeping in, waiting for the last minute to tear into class.

Once at his desk, he slugged down the last of the cold coffee left over from the day before and used the downtime before class to review his lecture notes. A last-minute phone call almost made him late, yet again. Dean of Students Fred Urban's voice on the line was guarded, a terse proposal to meet. Tonight. Whatever Fred had in mind, he wasn't letting any grass grow under his feet.

A. J. took the precaution of scrawling the agreed upon time in his day planner. This was one meeting he had no intention of missing.

Noon came and when A. J. still hadn't seen or heard from Sam, he called her cell, found himself forced to leave a message on her voice mail. "Just called to say, Hi," he said. "Let you know I was thinking about you." More, in fact, than he would have thought possible.

Chapter Seven

It had been a long time since A. J. was a party to an 'after-five' conversation over a beer in the back room of Smithy's. The notorious working class bar dominated a rural crossroads only a scant six miles from Bolland, just over the ridge of the mountain but lightyears removed from campus in clientele. Dark and crudely furnished, the pub drew the local family crowd early on, replaced after nine by the red-neck faction and half-wasted, unemployed mine workers pouring out their anger by the pitcher.

If anything, the place was even dingier and more depressing than A. J. remembered. He left his suit jacket in the Toyota, but his dress shirt stood out like a sore thumb, even with sleeves rolled up and open at the neck. It would have seemed inconceivable barely a week ago to find himself on a Wednesday night, nursing a Rolling Rock on tap while Dean of Students Fred Urban laid out a take on campus politics that hit unnervingly close to the one A. J. had begun to foment in his own imagination.

Fred showed up, punctual to the minute, in jeans and a Pittsburgh Steelers jersey that had seen better days. First impressions left no doubt whatsoever, here was a guy who was aware of the way the game's played and who could hold his own, on the gridiron and off. Perfect, considering both the clientele around them and the unwritten agenda on the scarred wood tabletop between them.

"I can't prove it," Fred said, "but I'd be willing to bet a year's wages that McDowell, Slaughter and a handful of tenured faculty are hell bent on scuttling any kind of consolidation talks with Emmaline, even if it means taking Bolland itself down in the process."

A. J. must have let his gut reaction—caution—show in his face. Fred leaned forward, deftly avoiding the bar-ware and crock of shelled peanuts cluttering the space between them.

"I know it sounds crazy, Ferinelli, but I'm not paranoid and I am *not* wrong on this one either. Add up the bizarre cast of characters who spoke up yesterday, apart from you, me and that accounting professor. Throw in the predictable elitists, disciplinary purists and standard bearers for the Liberal Arts, plus a few burnouts trying to hang on until retirement, maybe one or two folks who just like a good fight . . . I'm sure I've forgotten someone—"

"When you put it that way, a rather odd coalition."

Fred chuckled, leaned back against the booth. "I'm sorry if that offends you, they're your colleagues and all. But I'm a guy used to sizing up the jerseys before I take off down field. Safer that way. And there they all were, huddling up behind McDowell—not my nominee for quarterback—getting set to run interference for a terminally flawed Academic Dean. All of 'em armed with platitudes about standards, seniority and the Bolland Way. The whole scene strikes me as just a wee tad too . . . coached."

"If not McDowell, then who's calling the game plan?"

"My money is on someone else among the faculty from the late Seventies, the bunch who tried to unionize but got their hands slapped by the Board. Yesterday's Young Turks wind up today's Old Guard. All of 'em are lot older now and very much tenured, well aware of what an actual merger could do to their seniority. You noticed how they never said, *consolidation talks*. It was always worst case scenario. *Merger*, nail the damn doors shut and dispose of the key."

"To my knowledge there hasn't been any talk of a union in decades."

"Officially, maybe," Fred's shrugged, "but I've been told, the same ringleaders have roused themselves occasionally to push select agendas. Sometimes they were out to chop or push programs, more often to do in people. For a while before I got to campus, Student Life was going through a Dean every six months. You can guess the soft spots in the line these days. It's where they'll hit you every time."

"What the senior faculty wanted wasn't *all* negative," A. J. said carefully, "at one time anyway."

He found himself reconstructing in his head the coalition that had backed an innovative honors program with a heavy-duty student research component some fifteen years ago. *Good stuff.* A. J. had been involved in that maneuvering himself, saw a Dean go under in the process. Idealistic and relatively new to campus politics at the time himself, A. J. hadn't thought too deeply about where the support was coming from or how.

It was toughest to write off McDowell as a pawn in yesterday's faculty meeting. Despite the historian's recent backyard visit, A. J. still clung to now distant images of his one-time mentor as an academic of the old school, basically above the fray, holding forth under a tree—at his feet the disciples prepared to toss gratuities into the hood of the scholar's doctoral gown. It was a story straight out of the Middle Ages, apocryphal perhaps. Every profession has its mystique. Early on when McDowell had talked about the tradition to A. J., it was with a wistfulness bordering on envy.

No more. Someone clearly had persuaded McDowell to take sides. And the driving force behind that sea-change, A. J. realized, had to be someone much, much tougher.

"What do you know about Ray Ellison?" Fred said.

Damn, but the guy was good, A. J. winced. He took his time, along with a deep draught of his Rolling Rock, before responding.

"Comes from a third-generation-unemployed railroad family," he said. "The story goes Ellison worked himself through Ontowona State the hard way, shoveling coal by day and running a Saturday night poker game—at which the man never lost. Supposedly a damaged cartilage in his knee, souvenir of a bar fight, kept him out of Vietnam. He helped ramrod a teaching assistants' union at Ontowona . . . affiliated with the Teamsters."

Ellison always bragged they modeled their labor organizing tactics on the late-Sixties grad student revolt at UW-Madison. A. J. saw the Student Dean's eyes narrow.

"Certainly explains the guy's instinct for the jugular," Fred said evenly. "One that professorial veneer of his can't totally mask."

A. J. didn't allow himself to react one way or the other. An edge to Fred's voice told him, loud and clear, that nothing A. J. had shared was entirely new. Or unexpected.

"Okay, just suppose you're right. Suppose the impetus is coming from Ellison," A. J.'s mouth felt stiff. "Then why let Sam Pomerantz take the first hit? Much as he may like a scrap, Ellison never seemed the type to bother with demolishing the little guy in the great scheme of things."

Fred looked uncomfortable. "Sam's a friend of yours, right? I assume you've told her she can't take this personally. The cabal would see her as collateral damage—a target of opportunity trying to protect Bremer. And make no mistake, protecting the Dean is essential, if the goal is to bring down the Big Man himself."

"Dornbaum," A. J.'s eyebrow arched. "That guy is about as much of a threat as a Chia pet."

Fred chuckled softly. "Don't underestimate *El Jefe*. I'm beginning to think Dornbaum's very cluelessness is why the Board has backed him, almost without fail, these past seven years. He lets them spend endowment like it's funny money in a Monopoly game. He makes governance fun. Which makes the other potential victim in the coming coup even stranger . . . "

When A. J. didn't venture a guess, the Student Dean enlightened him. "I'm talking about the newly-elected power behind the throne," he said, "the guy who single-handedly appears to be dragging Dornbaum toward some semblance of fiscal accountability—"

"The new Chair of the Board."

Fred grinned. "You got it. From what I saw of the closed-door meeting when he was elected—before they kicked us peons out, of course—it was clear the younger faction on the Board finally had their fill of the old regime's shenanigans. Which didn't necessarily mean Dornbaum's cronies were out for the count."

"Board Chair, Doc Radisson." An eyebrow-raiser, for sure.

"You know the man."

"Some. Socially on and off after I started using him as a resource in some of my classes. He seems like a good guy."

"Bucking the tide though," Fred shrugged. "And think about it . . . what better way to give the kumbayah faction on both campuses cold feet than to flatten both our cheerleaders for merger after they've barely taken the field."

Bolland and Emmaline weren't unique in raising the issue of partnerships to improve a college's economy of scale. As a market, Pennsylvania was notorious for more private colleges per square inch than almost any other state in the union. Nasty, as competition went. In this case, the two campuses were within a stone's throw of each other in neighboring towns along the same Amtrak line. Historically there were strong connections among Board members and graduates of both places.

"Unlikely, isn't it," A. J. said, still playing the Devil's Advocate, "to merge with a former woman's college, when here at Bolland we always have been coed?"

"Math, Ferinelli. With Bolland's focus on traditional athletics, we're struggling with a higher than normal male-to-female ratio. You add up Emmaline's 500 students, mostly women, and our 650, three-quarters men, it would just about balance out."

"There are the two schools' church relationships. Tricky."

"Different denominations, but compatible," Fred said. "The real bottom line—no football rivalries to muddy the waters!"

"Priorities," A. J. shook his head. "Go figure."

He still wasn't convinced it was totally safe to let his guard down with Fred. Not in dispute, the Student Dean obviously had been giving the whole mess considerable thought.

"True, Emmaline-Wattrous has the lion's share of the cash," Fred said, "mainly from their weekend and evening program for older students. But they're landlocked up against the side of the mountain. Bolland's got the acres and dorms . . . unfortunately also declining head counts and debt. From a bottom line point of view—a marriage made in heaven. Set up a shuttle between the two campuses. Voila. Bolland even beefs up its Title IX team sports."

"Okay, if some kind of a partnership makes dollars-and-cents long-term, then the faculty opposition must center on tenure," A. J. insisted.

"Right . . . you heard those guys, yesterday. Bolland has 64 faculty, high for the total enrollment. An actual merger with Emmaline-Wattrous would be a perfect chance for the Board to trim that ratio down to size."

"Cut the dead wood," A. J. nodded, "without wandering into an impossible legal thicket. And the movers and shakers on the faculty must know that."

106

"Big time."

Fred uncoiled like a finely tuned jungle animal. Shoulders square against the high wood of the booth, he just leaned back and let A. J. spin out the possibilities, all the while listening intently.

"So, let's assume the faculty at Bolland drives the place into the ground," A. J. said, "makes what's left not worth the pickings. The Emmaline-Wattrous Board goes away mad, permanently. With the merger off the table, the solutions have to come from within. Dole out the pink slips on a last in, first out basis . . . which slashes all those suspect vocational programs our more conservative liberal arts advocates keep complaining about. Bolland limps along as always, stripped of nontenured faculty, on life support maybe, but still viable enough that most of the tenured crew stays on the payroll."

Fred was grinning now. "Interesting, isn't it."

"Like using dynamite to fix a splinter. I can't believe anyone can be that—"

"Naive? Self-absorbed? Gullible? I *can*—believe it, at least of the guys on the fringes, used to lots of come-the-revolution talk and not a great deal of action. Trust me, the Ellison's of this world damn well think they know exactly what they're doing. Poker is the man's game and he apparently plays it like a bloodsport."

"How widely is all this discussed out there?" A. J. said.

"No idea," Fred shrugged. "The administrative cabinet is busy treading water most of the time. I'm not on the Board Chair's speed dial. And if the President suspects what these guys are up to—let's just say, nobody's talkin'! Neither was I, until now."

Thoughts racing ahead, A. J. ran his hand over what had once been his crop of thick, dark hair. The possibilities were mind boggling. "And Bremer, where does he stand in all this?"

"A survivor. This buddy of mine is on the staff at Washtenaw. Bremer served there, if you can call it that, before coming here. Washtenaw privately quotes the same chapter and verse—harassment on an epic scale, much like the pattern Sam Pomerantz is describing. How Bremer managed to stonewall his proclivities when he interviewed here, I'll never know. The guy's a former historian, a student at Oxford with—"

"George McDowell." A. J. said.

Fred looked surprised he knew, but covered nicely. "Give the man a cigar," he said.

Odd bedfellows, McDowell and Bremer, but after George's bitter elitist ramblings in A. J.'s back yard and the man's willingness to lead the charge publicly against Sam in the faculty meeting, the common denominator was apparent. McDowell was prepared to back the Dean for one reason and one only. Bremer could be a powerful ally in stopping a merger and protecting senior faculty.

Suddenly, A. J. regretted not having gotten to know Fred Urban sooner. But even as the thought occurred to him, A. J. knew he was being unfair to himself. His wife, Anne, had worked in the Student Life sector when he first met her and up until her first miscarriage. Since her death, he found the whole aura surrounding those familiar offices hard to handle.

"What you did yesterday was gutsy," A. J. told Fred gruffly, "but it's going to take more than scoring points at a faculty meeting to derail this one."

Fred nodded. "What is happening to Sam is the tip of the iceberg. There isn't a junior faculty member on this campus whose position is safe—starting with that accounting professor who threw herself in front of the cannon yesterday. They'll be gunning for her now. Staff, ditto, always among the first to go. The more effective a job you do, the harder they will have to go after you, and one way or another, the spoilers control the evaluation process. So much for the Handbook and due process!"

"Meaning, all the ranting at the faculty meeting about quality is nothing but a smokescreen."

Fred laughed. "Who can oppose defending something like standards—they're like motherhood and apple pie. Except in this case, the rhetoric is just aimed at confusing the real agenda, to scuttle the merger at all costs, even risk gutting the place, if that's what it takes to do it."

"If you're right, you could have laid your job on the line yesterday," A. J. said slowly.

Fred shrugged. "Fact is, I'm good at what I do. I could have bailed six months ago if I wanted to. But then, I still have a pin in my shoulder from the gridiron out back and alumni tend to remember stuff like that. Besides, I like this isolated corner of academe, despite all the sewage percolating up around this place at the moment. Great students."

True enough, A. J. thought—if Fred Urban were any measure

of what Bolland had been turning out over the years. And great faculty, too, if one looked hard enough. Fred was right about Julie Schechter charging to Sam's defense at the faculty meeting, perhaps not quite as vulnerable as Sam herself, but close.

For the first time since he walked into that bar, A. J. managed what could be considered a genuine smile. "For what it's worth, Fred," he said, "none of this comes as a surprise."

"I can understand you might distrust my motives. For whatever reason, your own colleagues have chosen to leave you out of the loop."

It never occurred to A. J. that Fred might have doubts of his own about agendas, including how willing he would be to get his hands dirty if things got messy. The Dean of Students was certainly within his rights to know just where A. J.'s loyalties lay.

"I left myself out of it after Anne died," A. J. said evenly. "Way too long, apparently."

Fred looked uncomfortable, as if only just now remembering. "Your wife . . . I'm sorry. I'm told she was the heart of our department. Even after she left, every time I met her on campus she was so gracious and vibrant—"

Alive. The silence was awkward.

"She really cared about this place," A. J. said finally. "So do I, though at the moment, exactly *why* escapes me. Bottom line, if you're wondering, my allegiance is to Bolland, not just my peers out there. One heck of a lot of my life is tied up in this place."

A. J. told him in detail about McDowell's visit, proof positive he wasn't about to leave Fred twisting alone in the wind. "McDowell already knows we part company on this one," he said. "When it comes to definitions of what it means to save this place, Fred, you and I are of one mind—you can count on it. The *how*, I'll admit, gets a great deal trickier."

The Student Dean extended his hand and A. J. shook it. Their eye contact was sure and steady.

"Suggestions?" Fred said.

"Let me sleep on it."

Which didn't change the fact, they had to do something and soon. For starters, when the waitress brought their bar tab, A. J. quietly paid it.

The house was dark when A. J. arrived home, felt especially empty. A flashing light on the phone's answering machine pleasantly changed all that.

"The week is getting away from me," he heard Sam's voice say, chatty to the point of breathless. "Sorry, I'm going to have to bail on our little trysts in the faculty dining room for the rest of the week. Julie Schechter invited me to lunch tomorrow. A first. Of course, if you're still on for hanging out on the weekend, I'm game . . . provided I dig in on a set of quizzes in the meantime. But by now you probably have another stack of your own, right?"

Just before the machine cut off, she added a quiet, "Oh . . . and I've been thinking about you, too."

It was too late to call her. A. J. gave in to the irrational need to hear her voice, did the next best thing and replayed her brief message before he erased it. Time to douse the living room lights and limp off to bed himself. All the unaccustomed exercise, first the glen at Morgan Ford and then the walk to campus, was catching up with him. Exhilarating as the one-on-one with Fred had been, it was also damn stressful. A. J. stared at the ceiling in the darkness a long time before he finally drifted off to a dark and dreamless sleep.

With Sam out of the picture, A. J. spent Thursday lunch alone at his desk with take-out junk food from the cafeteria vending machine and over-brewed coffee left over from his office hours. His chance encounter with her on the quad mid-afternoon was way too brief. They hugged, set a time to get together on the weekend before Sam hustled off to the library to do some photocopying. For a split-second, as he watched her crossing the quad in her cut-to-the-chase stride, he found himself feeling oddly bereft.

The plan was to meet Friday at three in the faculty parking lot, then drive fifty miles over the mountain for dinner and a movie in Ontowona. At the appointed hour, Sam showed up in jeans, belted ivory knit tunic and her boot-length sweater coat with its oversize collar framing her dark hair. She was smiling, more relaxed and visibly at ease than A. J. had ever seen her.

"You're looking amazing," he said, suddenly feeling very

self-conscious in his jacket and tie, a conspicuous departure from what had been his decade-long on-campus uniform of open-at-the-neck dress shirt and jeans.

"You're not looking so bad yourself—ready to get out of Dodge," she teased. "Do your research, Prof?"

A. J. laughed. She pretty much had him pegged, right there. In fact, he had come armed with on-line printouts of everything playing in a five-mile radius of their destination, including not just the multi-screen theater, but the university art cinema, the screening room in the community art center and a couple of outlying small cinemas specializing in budget ticket re-runs.

"Overkill, but yeah," he said.

She was already studying the encyclopedic stack of community calendars he had thrust in her direction. "I'll admit my brain is fried after two sections of algebra back-to-back," she said "Anything jump out at you in all this?"

"A blockbuster costume epic plus a new sci-fi thriller have been getting good reviews, then there's a cop chase, an off-the-wall comedy or an apparently so-so chick-flick . . . take your pick," he told her as he eased the Toyota into gear. "I left out a disaster remake of dubious quality—after watching the decks tilt all week at Bolland, I'm not sure I'm up to watching any more boats in trouble."

"The sci-fi sounds good, I heard that, too. Right now, late night talk shows are obsessing about it. I'll admit I'm into futuristic stuff, not everybody's cup of tea."

A. J. laughed. "Would you believe you're riding with a Trekkie, albeit the original, not the later reincarnations. And for the record while we're on the subject of final frontiers, I wrote my thesis on American utopian communities, am trying to recast it as a monograph."

"Idyllic. Okay, with that in mind, how about that costume epic? Several reviews waxed eloquent about BBC-types having hot, steamy sex surrounded by opulent Edwardian architecture."

Fraught, A. J. chuckled softly to himself, especially given the latest rumors making the rounds on campus—namely, that he and Sam were "doing it" with some regularity, among other places, in the back seat of his Toyota out behind the sports complex. An embarrassed Fred Urban had given A. J. what had to be a heavily censored head's up yesterday at close of business over the phone. The

111

wealth of detail had "Winna Dougherty" stamped all over it. Forget the fact, you couldn't get a parking spot in back of the stadium even when a game wasn't scheduled.

A half-smile lingered as A. J. turned the image over in his head. Sam caught him at it. "A private joke," she said, "or can I tag along?"

"Just shaking my head at the incredible imagination living in a small town seems to breed into the gene pool," he said.

"Oh."

It had started to rain. Hard.

"Lovely!" A. J. grumbled, flicking on the windshield wipers.

They were passing the outskirts of the town of Bradenton where Emmaline-Wattrous was located. *Chicks man,* someone had scrawled in spray paint on the official sign, along with a makeshift arrow pointing toward the site of the College, a half mile off the highway.

"By the way, I drove over here Wednesday," Sam told him. "An interesting afternoon."

A. J. kept his eyes straight ahead on the ribbon of asphalt ahead. "Math department?"

"The Academic Dean. I had called in the morning, just on a whim, to see if she would be around."

"Stasia Smith," he said. "I met her once. Tough. Outspoken."

"Five feet tall and just as wide, but quick to spot trends and act on them. Much to my amazement, she canceled an appointment, agreed to see me. Her secretary called me back after she'd arranged it. Told me to bring a resume."

A. J. picked up on the laughter bubbling to the surface. "They offered you a job."

"Not exactly," Sam chuckled, "I should be so lucky. I think it's a consultancy. Apparently someone proposed packaging their developmental programs on the web, found a donor to fund it. Heaven knows what the whole operation is going to cost."

"And they're thinking about you to develop and run it."

Sam had turned and was staring at him. "How did you know?" she said finally.

"Just a guess."

"It's tempting," she said, "I'm as big a computer junkie as the next guy, but there's also a more traditional opening in

112

administration—"

"Their director of Developmental Studies has turned in her resignation," he said, "effective end of the summer term."

"Spoilsport. You knew."

Something in her voice warned him he had gone too far. She had wanted to surprise him, tell him herself in her own way.

"Just rumors," he told her quickly, "speculation they might be losing some staff. Really though, that's fantastic news, Sam."

"My only worry is, with all the talk of merger, I could just be wandering into another shooting gallery."

"Possible," A. J. admitted. "If the merger should materialize, there may be layoffs on both sides, not just Bolland's. In which case, both sets of faculty might consider their junior colleagues expendable."

"So," Sam sighed, "nothing changes but the color of the jerseys."

She may be relatively new to four-year campus politics, but she was learning fast. At the risk of adding yet more rain to her parade, he had to tell her.

"Fred Urban and I polished off a pitcher out at Smithy's Wednesday night," he said. "Let's just say, if you and I are getting paranoid about all this, we aren't the only ones. He is absolutely convinced there is a faction at Bolland trying to sabotage the merger and they aren't the least bit fastidious about how they do it"

"In a merger, where would you stand in the pecking order?" Her voice sounded too casual, as if she had been thinking about it.

He shrugged. "Depends. If I'm remembering correctly, Emmaline-Wattrous is down a slot in Poli Sci and uses adjuncts to supplement the one tenured line. With my seniority at Bolland, I should be all right. It's more than I can say for a lot of the Old Guard around here."

"At Emmaline-Wattrous, rumors are circulating about organized resistance."

His antenna went up. "From their side?"

"No, just Bolland's. Right now at Emmaline the prevailing mood is to suspend judgment."

"Fred Urban said as much. He thinks Ellison, McDowell, Slaughter, and the rest of them may try to rock the boat just enough to make Bolland less of an asset. One way of scuttling the merger.

With their jobs on the line, the Bolland faculty may feel they've nothing to lose."

"Only it's other people's lives and jobs they're risking, too," she said. "And the life of a hundred-fifty-year-old institution." It was sadness and disbelief, as much as anger in her voice.

"Fred chalks up all the intrigue as an occupational hazard, to arrested development on their part. He equates it to those post-adolescent dorm jocks he rides herd on every night, flirting with booze and disaster on these god-awful mountain roads. Tenure, I suppose, can do it to you. It makes you think you're invincible."

"With absolute job security," she shifted impatiently in her seat, "I'd say they are."

A. J.'s hands flexed on the wheel as he thought about it. "A buddy of mine in the advertising game once said, Where things really get crazy is when you start *believing* your own P.R. The market in higher ed is too tight, too unforgiving, and the donor money too scarce these days for that kind of posturing and gamesmanship. More and more schools are resorting to adjuncts across the board—even my Alma Mater Chicago now uses 'temps' to teach their undergrad classes, something top tier schools would never have done in the good old days. Anyway, tenure was never meant to condone any of this. If the situation gets bad enough in academe nationwide, who knows what the courts might do, to tenure and everything else. It's dangerous stuff, toying around with witch hunts and programmatic book burnings. At Bolland the keepers-of-the-flame appear to have gotten the matches out."

"Sounds like you and Fred are getting ready to rumble."

"If Fred had his way," he admitted, "I suspect he'd have us join forces with the new voices speaking out for solvency on the Board. Politically, it would help them to have someone inside the faculty *and tenured*, standing out front with a spear and horned helmet."

He hadn't intended to let an edge of sarcasm creep into his voice. Sam picked up on it immediately.

"And you're not sure you're up to it."

"Something like that."

"Your decision to stay out of it," she persisted, "does it have anything to do with me and my grievance?"

To his chagrin, he realized she had come to the truth quicker than he had.   In A. J.'s mind, the evening with Fred cast serious doubts on his own ability to read the mood on campus. Worse, he suspected he may have misled Sam about how to approach the Bremer problem, as well.

"I should have seen this coming," he told her. "With a negotiating team for a potential merger already in place, guys like Ellison are running out of time. Your grievance plays right into their hands. They couldn't care less about you, or Bremer, or whether justice is served. They'll drag you through the sewer if they think it creates the negative publicity they need to stonewall and stall. No one can ask you to take that kind of abuse."

Jaw tight, he studied the rivulet of water trying to make an end run around the wiper blades. It was high time he got the blasted things replaced.

"In your shoes," he said, "I'd think hard about shaking the dust off my feet, take what Emmaline has to offer and run with it."

"Just like that."

A. J. mulled over a response as he tried to second-guess the driver up ahead who appeared to be having trouble holding the appropriate lane. "You're eminently marketable," he said finally, "so are people like Fred and Julie. Me. . . dicier, but I stayed out of the jungle for nearly three years now, taught my classes. As long as I stuck to my scholarly treatises on political governance models, they left me alone. They would do it again—"

"Provided you kept your mouth shut about me or the merger."

"Tough, I know, for a professor," he managed a grim smile, "when words are our stock in trade."

"Except something happened in the glen at Morgan Ford," she said. "We've both had a brush with avoidance and denial in our day—can testify how well they work."

A. J. felt as someone had just punched him, hard, in the solar plexus. "Sam, if Emmaline-Wattrous thinks you're litigious, they could change their minds about you and their job opening."

"I already laid it out there for Dean Smith, all the gory details. You forget, Emmaline used to be a woman's college. None of this impacts Dean Smith's offer. They want me. They respect the decision to fight, wouldn't expect me to do otherwise."

"Are you *really* sure you know—?"

"What I'm doing. Does anyone ever? That said, yes, I believe

I do. I could ask the same of you, you know."

He sensed her watching him. "Putting my own career on the line is one thing, trying to restore some sanity at this place," he said. "But standing by, a voyeur, while you throw yourself in front of the cannon is quite another. I'm not at all sure I can stand by and watch."

"Without your help last week, I don't know what I would have done," she said quietly. "But I'm a big girl and this isn't only about my career any longer, about working out my anger or getting my pound of flesh—not even whether I'm willing to stand on principle, for the sake of every woman Bremer ever hurt. It's time to stare down my own demons and move on. Long past time. I can't ever let what happened with my graduate advisor and then with Bremer happen to me again. In some bizarre way, I think filing the grievance, for me, was my personal line in the sand. I've drawn it."

He had pushed her enough. The choice was hers to make, not his.

"I just hate the thought of what those guys could do to you, especially if Fred and I join forces and start to push back," he told her. "You know what Bremer did when you confronted him. A part of me says, lower the stakes a little. Don't corner the man—"

"Trouble is, you can't do that."

"No," he admitted, surprised how easy it was suddenly to say it. "I can't."

Fred had left him the space to think about it. Well, he had. Most important, it seems, he had talked it over with Sam.

"You're right," he said, "about knowing when enough is enough. Sam, I have no intention of going back to what I was since Anne died. You saw to that, the minute you showed up in the hallway outside my office. And if I didn't care so damn much that we do this thing right, the *us* part of all this—take our time and get to know each other—I would turn this car around right now and . . . "

Her knowing hint of smile supplied the rest. For starters, he would make love with her until neither one of them knew what time or day it was. And after that, the two of them would just have to figure things out.

Chapter Eight

Both Sam and her attorney Jake Burroughs were closer to the recorder. Still, it was A. J. who got there first, slammed off the power switch. "That incredible . . . ," the rest was largely unprintable.

His living room got ominously quiet as his colleagues processed the content of the recording—though A. J.'s reaction pretty much said it all. The deposition Jake was replaying from Dean Bremer's secretary was disturbing enough, distorting almost beyond recognition Sam's version of what had gone on behind the massive hardwood door of the Dean's office the week before she was pink-slipped. Hardest to handle was the palpable venom behind the woman's account.

Snugged alongside A. J. on his floral print living room sofa throughout the entire wince-inducing replay, Sam didn't say a word. She didn't have to. If this was the tack Bremer was going to take at the hearing next week, A. J. had been right. She was in for a rough ride.

"Nasty, as fiction goes," Jake said evenly, "but easy to refute. If the woman heard half of what she claims to have, her auditory prowess belongs in the record books. Bremer's damn office door, if I recall, is close to three inches thick."

"Isn't there . . . I assume there is some way we can suppress this kind of garbage," A. J. said.

Jake shook his head "I was pretty damn blunt all through the deposition about what defamation of character can lead to. You see the results. It is what it is. Still, I've got to believe the woman will tone things down some when I'm eyeballing her in front of a room full of witness. I hinted we could produce a half dozen students who can and will testify to Bremer's bizarre notion of professional ethics over the years."

Joel, Liz and Andy had been busy. Two more former students had been persuaded to testify. Another two had come forward on their own, all variations on the same unpleasant theme. Several other women on the faculty had been subjected to suggestive calls and innuendos, but none had agreed to go on record except Julie Schechter.

"Then there's the committee itself," Jake said. "How do faculty members on Personnel fit into the sandbox politics around here?"

"Obstacle number one, Winna Dougherty." A. J. said. "Supposedly she had serious designs on Bremer at one time. Unfortunately, Winna also tends to support her male colleagues rather than other women on the faculty. It seems to have been a pattern over the years."

Jake looked up from his dog-eared legal pad. A. J. was mentally trying to run the rest of the list, but was drawing a blank. Amazing how quickly a guy could suppress all the players and maneuvering that surrounded faculty elections.

"Sam, help me out here—"

"Mike Alonski, from history and Flo Battersy from education," Sam obviously had done her homework. "We've always gotten along well and they're fair-minded, I think. Mike is up for tenure so that could be a vulnerable point for him. As for Flo, some on Personnel may fault her for supporting my approach to learning styles."

Jake looked puzzled. "Explain."

"Most professors teach using logic and oral techniques," Sam told him. "Partly it's the way they were taught themselves, partly we inherit those kind of preferences. So, when a prof gets to the podium he or she tends to—"

"Drone on and on," A. J. winced. "Don't remind me. My own teaching ratings went up enormously when a custodian accidentally pitched out my lecture notes and I had to start winging it. In desperation, I even dragged Jake into class to lead us in some case simulations. Hate to admit it, but the students love it."

For the first time that evening, Sam managed a smile. "Shucks," she teased. "I had hoped it was the faculty workshop Flo and I taught that was making a difference. Not just the whims of the custodial staff!"

Jake's eyebrow shot up. "You two may be having fun with all this edu-speak, but you lost me."

"In traditional lectures," Sam said, "a lot of students just zone out. They learn far better either by getting their hands dirty or through a fast-paced mix of oral, visual, and written techniques."

"The Sesame Street generation, thirty-second sound bytes. I never thought of that," Jake chuckled. "When A. J. started sending all those hordes of fresh young interns down to the courthouse every semester, I just thought he was looking for a break!"

"Good stuff, internships. Your buddy here saw the light!"

A. J. shot an uncomfortable look in her direction. "Unfortunately, some of our colleagues still tend to dismiss multi-level teaching as psychobabble. Or protest they're expected to pander to a Gen-X-Y-Z character flaw."

"Technically, if you're talking about our current crop of learning miscreants, it's *Millennials*—"

"What . . . *ever* . . . the point here is good teaching, right? I'll admit some of my colleagues go so far as to actually withhold knowledge rather than teach it—make issues as complicated and obscure as possible to prove how intelligent they are. And many of the worst offenders I know probably squeaked through grad school themselves."

"Math is notorious for it," Sam nodded.

Her lawyer looked incredulous. "You're telling me either the faculty rationalize their own unimaginative teaching or massage their own bruised egos at the expense of the captive audience in their classrooms. The ultimate kick—humiliating yet another generation of students."

"Most faculty who behave that way aren't consciously sadistic, I'd like to think," Sam said. "But the end results are pretty

119

much the same. They had trouble with the process themselves, which validates perpetuating it in a strange sort of way."

"The good news, Ellison and the real power hitters aren't on Personnel," A. J. said, as together he and Sam finished ticking off the remaining two committee members. "Why go on record in a committee vote, when it's much more fun to sit back and let the newbies stick their necks out."

The last two names on the Personnel Committee list had plenty of personal reasons not to back the status quo. Marcus Cowley's promotion to associate professor had languished for three years thanks to Ellison and McDowell. The excuse was that Crowley's work with a local juvenile detention center was considered 'lightweight' compared to scholarly publishing in his field. For her part, Eleana Turic from languages had complained for years about Bremer for giving her a hard time over upgrading equipment in her department.

"In other words, four of the five 'jury of your peers' on Personnel might be prepared to suspend judgment long enough for us to make the case," Jake said.

A. J. never had a chance to weigh in on the subject. He grabbed for the phone, got to it before the answering machine kicked on. Voice mail had been programmed to pick up almost immediately, ever since the initial flurry of hate calls when Sam filed her grievance.

"Professor Pomerantz," the woman's voice was stiff, halting, "I don't want to do this, but I won't be testifying before Personnel next week. A couple of months ago Security caught my daughter smoking pot behind the stadium with a couple of her high school friends. Up until now the Dean has agreed not to pursue it. I've decided I can't, won't risk jeopardizing—"

A. J. knew the voice, quickly set the call on speaker phone so his colleagues could listen in. "Grace," he said. "Grace Denison. It's Ferinelli here. Sam's lawyer is with me. So is Sam. Did the Dean threaten—?"

"Not in so many words, no."

"Grace, please," he said, "listen to me."

"Professor Ferinelli, I . . . tell Ms. Pomerantz, I'm sorry."

"You tell her your—"

Dial tone. A. J. frowned, sat down, still cradling the inert hunk of plastic in his outstretched palm. *If you would like to make a call,* the computerized voice began. A classic Anglo-Saxon expletive summed up A. J.'s response to that suggestion.

"Unfortunate," Jake said, "but not unusual at the last minute in cases like this. There still are three—"

Sam forced a smile. "And what would you like to bet Bremer's gotten to them all. One way or another."

She wasn't far off the mark. A. J. prepared to drop the other shoe.

"Eleana Turic cornered me yesterday in the library," he told them. "Apparently if she doesn't vote to censure Sam, or at least abstain, Winna personally threatens to hold up the woman's budget requests into the next millennium."

"Blackmail," Sam breathed.

The lawyer shook his head. "Technically, maybe—but this is a professional hearing, not a court of law. Normal laws of evidence don't necessarily apply."

"Sam can't just sit there and let Bremer and company savage her in front of her peers," A. J. said.

"I thought I was just imagining it, but now . . . suddenly it all makes sense," Sam's voice shook, steadied again. "I swear someone was in my office last week, in the files. I didn't tell you because a quick check didn't turn up anything missing. But there are four cabinets of stuff in there. I wouldn't necessarily notice."

Jake's scowl was back. "Anything I should know about, Sam?"

"Some of my old journals . . . potentially damaging, I suppose, if taken out of context. But I checked. Nothing seems to be missing."

"The photocopy machine is ten feet down the hall," A. J. reminded her. "We all have access."

Jake was on his feet, stuffing tape, recorder, and miscellaneous documents on A. J.'s coffee table into his briefcase. His exertions still left behind an amazing array of clutter.

"Damage control, kiddies! I'll make the rounds of the potential student witnesses personally tomorrow. At least we'd find out how far the defection seems to be going."

"Julie Schechter over in Business might agree to talk to Eleana," A. J. offered, "or any other members of the Faculty Personnel Committee who may feel pressured. It can't hurt to know there are colleagues out there who want to see an even-handed

121

hearing of this case."

"What would it take," Sam speculated, "to find some crack in what seems like a united front going after remedial studies?"

"Good question," A. J. said. "Maybe it's time the Dean of Students and I have another one of our heart-to-hearts."

Sam's tweaking him about his diet must be having an impact, A. J. decided. Even from his perspective across the table at Smithy's, he found himself mesmerized, incredulous, as Fred Urban finished up his second plate of frog legs. The things were saturated with enough grease to give the average customer a heart attack within an hour of consumption. As a precaution before he dug into the second breaded mound, Fred had taken a break long enough to stash his latest go-everywhere tie in the pocket of his jeans shirt.

"Insurance," he shrugged. "Can't afford any more close encounters with my entrees. After this rugby model is history, I'm down to one with a cartoon character on it. The student interns chipped in and bought it for me last Christmas."

"Don't tell me," A. J. chuckled, "the Flintstones."

Fred looked pained. "One thing's for sure. This sure as hell ain't Bedrock. I stopped laughing at the whole circus on campus a long time ago."

Well into his second beer, A. J. had just spent the better part of a half-hour laying out his cautious take on Sam's divide-and-conquer strategy. "So how about we encourage some dissension in the ranks?"

Sounds like fun to me." Fred had the look of man already mentally rolling up his sleeves.

"Game plan?"

"Three choices, as I see it, maybe four, Ferinelli. Classic gridiron strategy. Power or finesse our way through their line, try for an end run . . . last ditch, a hail Mary or punt."

"Right now, they've got numbers on their side," A. J. reminded him. "On a campus like Bolland, even a half dozen irate faculty can count as a critical mass. Whatever they're planning, they also have a head start on us."

"Okay, then. We don't try to outrun 'em either. In my play book, that leaves a pass."

"Up and around," A. J. speculated, "as in, over their heads. What's your take on the administrative cabinet?"

"As things stand, I wouldn't trust a single one of Dornbaum's crew to stick their necks out about the color of paint in the restrooms. Tackle a gang of faculty on the warpath? Forget it!"

"Which leaves the Board of Directors or Divine Intervention. Some of those new Board members besides Doc *must* have bought into the possibility of a merger—or guaranteed, we wouldn't even be talking about this!"

Fred scowled. "Funny you should mention it," he said. "I had a visit from Board Member Harry Lentz yesterday . . . not on our side, that's for sure."

A. J. set down his glass of Rolling Rock. It was no secret on campus the retired power company executive—paunchy and balding, with the florid look that promised a heart attack down the road—had found a second calling in life poking into campus politics, usually with unfortunate results.

"A guy's gotta get the real dirt on what's going on around here," Harry once was overheard to say, when asked about his all-too-frequent unannounced campus visits. "Get behind all the official administrative whitewashing. I can't believe a thing in those damn reports."

Problem was, any faculty member with an ax to grind knew he or she had a ready-made conduit to the Board. Harry also subscribed to the tabloid conspiracy theory of history that says *good* news is *no* news. The wilder the story, the better, as far as Harry was concerned. All that fit Ellison and company's agenda perfectly.

"The guy's a loose cannon, Fred. If old Harry gets his hands on this—"

The Student Dean groaned. "And they wonder why the place historically went through administrators like grass through the proverbial goose! Our illustrious Prexy, Dornbaum, may not be so dumb after all—stay sloshed most of the time, let the inmates run the asylum. As for rabble like me, try 'dean-ing' when anybody and everybody knows that end runs are not only condoned, but encouraged. Thanks to Harry, the lunatic in the chemistry department almost had the Board investigate my sector for violating athletic policy because I had the counseling center begin hand-holding all the poor souls he was flunking last semester. No one in their right mind would have steered those kids into chem in a Fall semester anyway, not enough hours in the day for scrimmages and all those hours of lab work—"

"Unless their advisor happened to be one of the Chemistry professor's cronies," A. J. chuckled sympathetically, "trying to help pad the guy's enrollments. So what was Harry sniffing out this time?"

"Harry has it on good authority," Fred said, doing a credible imitation of Lentz at his most pontifical and self-righteous, "there are *elements* on this faculty who are giving away grades and demonstrating poor judgment when it comes to faculty-student relationships. They even use the student newspaper to push their own agendas."

"Well, that pretty much takes care of both Sam and me."

"Join the club," Fred said. "He *demanded*—note the word—as one 'in charge' of the life of students on this campus, I look into it immediately. Even on my best days I would never pretend to be in control of 'the life of students' and neither are the students themselves, most of the time."

A. J. laughed. "And failing that?"

"Lentz thought President Dornbaum could be persuaded to find ways for me to make it happen."

"Ouch."

"It gets worse. Harry, it seems, suspects the same 'subversive' elements on campus are pushing for a merger with Emmaline-Wattrous—a marginal institution academically, as he sees it. Goal of the Emmaline Board is 'to tarnish Bolland's strong national reputation'. Which according to Harry, is on a par with the best any Ivy League institution has to offer."

"You're kidding," A. J. said. "The guy actually believes this?"

"Absolutely. Forget minor details like our endowment is among the lowest in the state for schools our size, our labs hopelessly outmoded and our student body shrinking like low tide in the Bay of Fundy. And by the way, in his rush to 'stem the tide of mediocrity' around here, Harry is proposing Admissions reject all but the upper twenty percent of high school applicants starting a year from fall."

A. J. topped off his beer from the pitcher, then downed a hefty share of it. He could just imagine what Harry would make of Sam's run-in with Bremer. Remedial math was bound to be on the guy's hit list.

"Our Board Chair, Doc Radisson lives up in Ontowona. His son graduated from Bolland and went on to law school," A. J. said. "Before I got the kid as an advisee during his second semester, he was well on his way to flunking out—a combination of rotten advising and a too-heavy class schedule for any sane person to handle. Doc and I have had soul talks over the years about the state of the state at Bolland The guy has strong contacts on Emmaline's Board."

"Could you do a bit of judicious politicking?"

"At least I know he could give us the lay of the land," A. J. said. "I was planning on driving up there on the weekend, anyway. There's one way to find out, I'll ask the man."

"Great timing. Just before the first go-round of Faculty Grievance hearings. At the rate Harry is going, if the Personnel Committee doesn't skewer Sam, then Lentz—personally—will organize the lynching party."

A. J. stared glumly at the oak of the table top, scarred with what had to be generations of initials. "The students are scared to death of that bottom feeder Bremer," he said. "We've had a few change their minds about testifying."

"If worse comes to worse," Fred said, "you and I can fill the gap. Lord knows, I've had my hands full with a Bremer-generated student caseload over the years."

"All well and good, but we sure better have a backup plan. Right now I wouldn't put anything past the Dean if he thought it would get him out of this."

Ed Radisson, known universally as Doc, was out in his garage doing some body work on the hull of his vintage fiberglass trimaran when A. J. showed up in Ontowona on Saturday with Sam Pomerantz in tow. It took some fancy tap dancing on his part to get her to agree to come, but she was there.

"I feel like a piece of horseflesh on the block," she had told him in the car on the way over. "I've never even met the man. He's bound to suspect day-old fish after everything that's been going on."

"It's awkward, I know," A. J. said, "but at least give Doc a chance to put a face on a name. From the character assassination Bremer is engineering, the Board is likely to think you're running around campus with whips and leather, howling at the moon. Behind the scenes, Doc could make a dent in that perception."

Sam sighed. "You did warn me this was going to be tough. I guess I thought, hoped maybe, you were exaggerating."

"Second thoughts?"

"No. Just tired, sick of it and it's barely been a week—the hearings haven't even started yet. I can't imagine what I'll feel like by the time the issue reaches the Board of Trustees, if it ever does."

A. J. tried to coax a smile. "Try me . . . I can be as self-righteous about doling out pep talks as the best of 'em," he offered. "Adversity builds character. Look both ways when crossing. Remember the Alamo."

Sam laughed. "Right now I'd say I can identify more with Men in Black," she said. "Never leave home without a loaded gun!"

At least, she hadn't lost her sense of humor. Much as he loved teaching, if truth be told, there were days A. J. himself found it difficult to keep his own growing feelings of cynicism about the political climate on campus from impacting the classroom. If this was a community of scholars, he had seen precious little evidence of it lately.

Doc Radisson's garage looked a lot like what A. J. remembered of the man's office—genial clutter, but functional. In one corner a gas heater was putting out BTUs, a given for anybody intending to mess with fiberglass in November in Pennsylvania. More fit in his late-sixties than A. J. had ever been in his life, Doc had the weatherbeaten look of a man who should have been skippering an America Cup crew or riding off into the sunset in a commercial for a Land Rover. Doc wiped his hands on a hunk of ragged toweling before shaking first A. J.'s hand, then Sam's.

"What brings you up to this neck of the woods?" he said. "I hope you're finally deciding to take me up on sailing this thing in June."

Over the years Doc had tried his best to wean A. J. from his books long enough to fill his lungs with something besides recycled classroom air. At least there were seven months of winter weather ahead this time to get A. J. off the hook. Just looking at those outriggers on Doc's trimaran was enough to sense this baby would take off like a bat out of hell.

"You know how I feel about boats," A. J. told him. "If the tilt sends a six-pack sliding, it's time to head for the slip."

Doc laughed. "Now you know how I feel about your 'invite' every semester, Ferinelli, to talk about medical ethics to your Contemporary Political Issues class. Gives new meaning to 'hanging over the board'."

Doc flashed a conspiratorial wink in Sam's direction. Truth was, the man was a natural in the classroom. And for all his protestations about being just a plain old country doctor, A .J. would have trusted the guy with his life. Doc had an uncanny way of sniffing out the essence of problems, and when he did, running them to ground.

Right now, A. J. noticed, the Chair of the Board was not having much luck concealing his appreciation for Sam's jeans-clad presence. Set off by the subtle-patterned green silk top she was wearing under a black leather bomber jacket, her eyes took on the color of a tropical sea, a hard combination for any man to ignore.

"Pomerantz." Doc turned the name over thoughtfully. "You're . . . developmental math, the instructor who—"

"Is trying to nail the Dean," Sam winced. "Not surprising my notoriety precedes me."

Doc smiled, shook his head. "Bremer is slippery. It's a gutty move, taking him on."

"Or stupidity. Take your pick."

"From what the grapevine tells me, smarts are not remotely an issue here. My own son could have stood a hefty dose of your math-angst therapy. Testing-out took the poor sod a record three tries. Frankly, from what I've seen of those exams, if a comparable level of math would have been a prerequisite when I went to the university, I would have never made it through Pre-med."

"Moot," A. J. said. "Saving student hides is not considered politically correct in some quarters these days.

"A strange business . . . academe," his friend muttered, as something that could have passed for anger flickered in those steel-gray eyes. "Especially nowadays. How folks make a virtue of kicking

127

out customers, then turning right around and competing like nuts for more warm bodies with the next school down the road is beyond me! Forget mundane issues like who's going to come up with the payroll if there's no student body."

"It's gotten to be a game," A. J. said. "A sick one."

"Potentially fatal." Doc ran a hand over the still uneven surface of the trimaran hull. "There are 30 colleges out there in a ninety-square-mile area. If I had to make book, we'll lose a bunch of 'em in the next two decades."

"So, you believe the merger with Emmaline-Wattrous—"

"Is just common damn sense," Doc said.

A. J. toyed with just how far to push it. "Not to everybody."

When Doc didn't react, A. J. sketched out his own interpretation of what some of the faculty might be plotting. He wasn't quite as frank as he had been with Sam or Fred, but wasn't holding back much either.

"Bottom line," A. J. finished, "if they scuttle the merger, and if the budget goes south, they play the trump card—offer up the younger faculty and support staff. It's as wild a scheme as any for protecting senior faculty lines."

Doc didn't seem either put off or surprised. "Let me get this straight," he said. "You're telling me long after Bolland's a cow pasture again, those with tenure will have their pensions and can rest easy knowing they saved the world from mediocrity."

"Maybe a bit blunter than I'd put it. But yeah, you're close enough."

"Ironic, isn't it?" Doc told them. "The senior faculty can't lose by supporting Bremer. If the Dean wins, they get rid of a junior faculty member—a woman, no less. Emmaline-Wattrous was a woman's college, so their Board might well have second thoughts about hitching itself to the kind of governance that condones harassment. Scratch one merger. Even if Sam wins, the grievance process creates enough of a stink, enough bad publicity, that Bolland's enrollment and finances are bound to tank—at least temporarily. Another minus with Emmaline."

"Precisely," A. J. said.

"So, you two," Doc said thoughtfully, "apparently someone on campus is hell-bent on getting a head start on thinning the ranks of the junior faculty. What can I do to help? Call it a Hegelian

128

nightmare—history repeating itself—or a classic case of where there's way too much smoke, it's time to call 911, but that guy Bremer is way beyond due. Good for you, Ms. Pomerantz, for wanting to take the guy down!"

"Thanks for the vote of confidence . . . I think," Sam said, forcing a smile. "Call me realistic or paranoid, but it seems prudent to have a backup plan. I'll leave a couple of copies of my resume . . . just in case you know of any job openings. For the record, I worked my way through undergrad school helping a medical practice with its books."

Doc laughed. "I'm impressed. A tough job."

"Amateur hour compared to campus politics," A. J. told him. "On that score, I was going to suggest you might explore ways, Doc, of diffusing a couple of reactionary Board types who have been messing around the edges of Sam's grievance—"

"I assume you mean that old rabble-rouser Harry Lentz."

A smile bordering on sheepish tugged at the corner of A. J.'s mouth. Doc knew a heck of a lot more than he had been letting on.

"Obviously, you're way ahead of me," A. J. shrugged.

"Trouble with those I-ran-my-business-with-an-iron-fist Board types like Harry, is they have unlimited phone calling plans and unfortunately see Bolland as their personal sandbox. Great, as long as they can crow about the place around the pool at the club. It gets a lot nastier when they start trying to run the place on a day-to-day basis."

A. J. laughed. "Whatever Dornbaum or Bremer's merits or lack of them, I don't envy them a minute dealing with those wannabe micro-managers on the Board. I've heard at least once a week Harry shows up in an office, demanding that someone just 'get in there and fire those faculty sons-of-bitches' whenever the mood suits him!"

"Too bad you never chose to put some of your political horse sense to the test," Doc said, suddenly serious. "The place certainly could use a decent dean . . . "

"You're kidding—manage that zoo? No way!"

Doc just smiled, took a casual swipe at a lingering rough spot in the fiberglass only he could see. "Ya never know. I suspect, if you're patient long enough—maybe not as long as any of us think—there just might be an opening."

The drive back to Bolland was tricky, stressful. Fog was rolling up over the mountain as it often did on late fall evenings, reducing visibility out in front of A. J.'s beat-up Toyota to barely a foot or two from the center line and the edge of the asphalt. Window down, Sam was straining to spot deer or other potential dangers cloaked in the dense white shroud.

It didn't make for easy conversation. But then Doc Radisson had given them plenty to think about. By the Eugenia town limits, the fog had lifted enough to see the clusters of light marking the first isolated neighborhoods. As A. J. nosed the Toyota toward home, the muted wail of sirens—emergency vehicles—trailed off along the garish orange-neon-lit avenue of lights heading in the direction of Bolland

"Sounds like the natives are restless," A. J. said. "Another kegger and some joker pulled the fire alarm."

Still, pure reflex, he had tensed at the sound. *Anne.* And then it occurred to him. The recent meltdown at Devil's Glen aside, he couldn't remember when he had last thought about those awful hours after the accident, her death and their baby she was carrying, the wreckage his life had become in the space of a heartbeat on a rural highway. His wife's photograph was still tucked safely in his wallet, but the contours of her image were beginning to blur—like those first ghostly trails of mist on the mountain.

A. J. shifted in his seat. In the process, he caught a quick glimpse of Sam, silent and tense, in the darkness beside him. It was late. The conversation with Doc and the looming struggles over Bremer and the merger were still so front-and-center on both their minds.

"I make a mean margarita," he offered casually, only half expecting her to take him up on it.

"Sounds promising."

So did a hint of something in her voice. A. J. bypassed Sam's street and steered a course in the direction of his own place, wondering if he had volunteered more than his cluttered refrigerator and depleted liquor cabinet could deliver.

Fumbling with the house key, he felt her watching him. Once inside, her closeness eroded whatever remaining restraint he was prepared to muster. A. J. drew her against him, searching for her mouth—only to find it already upturned toward his. Warm, their fleeting contact told him, inviting more. With some difficulty, he eased the door shut behind them.

Her laugh was nervous. "Hello . . . !"

His own voice caught, steadied. "Hello, yourself."

In the dim light coming through the transom from the carriage light outside, A. J. could read her half smile, the anticipation behind it. Aching with his need of her, he slowly lost himself in the taste of her mouth on his. Her hair flowed like quicksilver against his skin. On a sigh, she settled closer into his arms.

"Sam," he whispered slowly. "Are you sure this is what . . . "

The rest went lost with the strident ringing of the phone. Best ignore it. Though it finally stopped, it quickly began again. By the sixth ring it dawned on him, his answering machine wasn't going kick in and stop this—a turn-off to put it mildly.

"Hold that thought," A. J. breathed.

He gave up fumbling for the receiver in the half-darkness, connected with the switch instead. Light flooded the room. This better be good.

"Ferinelli," he growled.

"She's dead."

A choked intake of breath from the other end of the phone line followed that pronouncement. The voice sounded young, male, most likely a student. A. J. couldn't place it.

"She left a note. That bastard Bremer . . . "

A note—suicide. "Slow down," A. J. said carefully, trying to fit a name to the raw panic in the disembodied voice. "I need to know who this—"

"Joel. It's Joel Van Susten. We planned . . . she and I were going to meet at her office, drive up to Ontowona. But when I got there she wasn't . . . she was . . . "

Suddenly the emergency vehicles A. J. had spotted near campus made sense. He couldn't imagine what the hell Van Susten was mixed up in to get him that upset.

"Who," A. J. demanded, "meet who?"

"Julie."

A. J. repeated the name, drew a blank, then turned it over again quickly in his head. There was only one Julie on campus filed away in his memory banks. "You're talking about Julie—"

"Schechter. I showed up early and her office door wasn't locked," the student said. "I dialed 911, knew right away . . . tried CPR until the EMT's got there. It was too late."

Joel found the young instructor dead on campus. That much was becoming brutally clear. Piecing together the ugly details were coming harder.

"Joel, you've got to tell me what—"

"Bremer. Somehow he found out Julie and I were dating." Joel choked on an expletive, his voice wracked with anguish. "The EMT's said even a half hour earlier and I could have . . ."

Joel was seeing a faculty member after hours. A. J. tightened his grip on the receiver. He always vaguely wondered why, despite Joel's disingenuous charm and tennis player good looks, the young man had seemed immune to the parade of coeds throwing themselves in his path. Eventually A. J. concluded, perhaps his advisee was gay.

Wrong, again. Still, straight-arrow Julie Schechter was the last person in the world A. J. would have suspected of taking that kind of chance. Student-faculty relationships were officially censured, although they weren't out of the realm of the probable or possible on campus—Dean Bremer's liaisons among the more notorious.

Knowing Julie, there had to be something more at work here to risk that kind of relationship and the whiff of scandal that potentially could have followed. But then Joel wasn't a typical Bolland senior either, older for starters, had taken time off for a stint in AmeriCorps after his freshman year, which narrowed the age gap.

Those veiled references the student made to Bremer sent cold chills down A. J.'s spine. Joel wasn't telling the whole story and the phone certainly was no way to find out.

"Van Susten, where are you?"

Silence. "A pay phone. The Seven-Eleven. My cell quit on me."

A half-mile away. "Get the hell over here," A. J. said, "now."

The phone went dead in his hands.

Chapter Nine

Sam took the terse news about their colleague in silence, alone on the sofa and her hands clutched tight in her lap. A. J. saw her visibly pulling back inside herself—anything but how their evening had begun. From her reaction, it didn't seem to come as a total shock to her that Julie and Joel could have been a couple.

"It happens," she said quietly. "There's nothing wildly out of the ordinary for a guy like Joel to hit on a young female faculty member—or for her to be tempted to reciprocate. Look around. For a highly educated woman professor or instructor, the local bar scene and its gun-totin' culture aren't exactly match-dot.com."

They didn't have long to speculate. A. J. still had the phone in hand when a wild-eyed and shaken Joel showed up on the doorstep. The student clearly needed to talk, grieving the unthinkable.

"Joel, you have got to tell us," Sam coaxed gently. "This is not something you or anyone can handle alone."

The student shuddered, his voice almost inaudible. "You could say, I fooled around a lot my freshman year, finally got caught at it. The Big H—lucky, I suppose, it wasn't AIDS. Typical undergrad solution, when in doubt, drop out. It seemed easier to get my head on

133

square out in the middle of the desert on the Reservation cleaning the trash out of irrigation ditches than to explain why I was dodging invites to frat parties because I wound up with herpes and assumed my love life is permanently in the crapper."

"But you came back," A. J. said. "Not the easiest thing to do."

Joel's laugh was terrible. "Just what a guy wants on the old transcript. Twenty years old, back on campus as a sophomore—living like a monk," the student grimaced. "But then Ontowona has a support group for just about anything, including singles living with STD's. I turned up at my first meeting and there was Julie. She began teaching at Bolland *after* we started hanging out."

The student didn't wait for the questions bound to follow. Instead, he drifted off into a disjointed account of what he knew of Julie's sheltered Long Island childhood, her mother's Jewish-princess aspirations for her, the decision to enroll their only daughter at a tough and pricey undergraduate school a good day's drive from home. None of that would have prepared Julie for her freshman-in-college crush on the captain of the cross-country team or what came of it.

"The guy had been dumped by this rah-rah cheerleader type," he said, "was down on dating. Julie took his attentions at face value. When she started having problems, she walked in at the campus clinic, got the bad news. Face it, those aren't subjects a good Jewish girl discusses with her mother. She did the right thing, went to the guy intending to warn him—only to find out he already knew."

"You mean he slept with her," Sam said softly, "without telling her she was at risk?"

"Worse. Not nearly that random. Apparently the creep planned it in some kind of bad-ass way, so she wouldn't ditch him—made it tougher for her to go out with anyone else. When she tried to break things off anyway, the guy got drunk, took off and drove his car under an eighteen-wheeler. They called it an accident, Driving Under the Influence. For her it was the ultimate guilt trip. Believe me, it took months after we met before she even let me take her out for a cappuccino."

It was dead silent in the room, except for Sam's stifled gasp of awareness. For all her bravado at the recent faculty meeting, Julie had been carrying around a mountain of hurt and except for Joel, had let no one close enough even to guess how alone, how vulnerable she was. Joel couldn't have had the foggiest notion how close to home his

134

brutal narrative had hit.

"We were colleagues, for what," Sam said, "a year? And I never knew, never suspected, not a clue."

A. J. cleared his throat. Sam only was putting into words what he had felt so acutely himself ever since he had gotten to know her—a deep regret at how insular the academy had become, how much heartache, even inhumanity, reared its terrible head beneath the ostensibly civilized veneer of campus life.

"On the phone, Joel," he probed gently, "you hinted Bremer was somehow involved."

The student's face worked. "I don't remember much about her note—mainly rambling, incoherent apologies to her family. The upshot was the Dean knew Julie planned to support Ms. Pomerantz at the Personnel hearing. But he had found out Julie and I were seeing each other, must have threatened to raise issues of unprofessional conduct if . . . "

"Blackmail," Sam finished for him, her voice devoid of any emotion. "If Julie didn't back off, Bremer would 'out' the two of you, take her down with him."

The look on Joel's face spoke volumes, the dawning awareness of his role in all this. With the best of motives the student had done his own share of pressuring witnesses over the past weeks, never suspecting what he was unleashing every time he and Julie must have talked about the whole Bremer affair.

"I should have sensed something was wrong," Joel said dully. "She was having trouble sleeping the last couple of days—apparently had these prescriptions. On the desk in her office, where she knew I wouldn't miss them, were all my letters. So before the cops showed up I shoved the letters in my backpack, knew it was what she . . . why she . . . "

The student laid the thick stack of carefully bundled notes on the coffee table in front of him. If protecting Joel was Julie's intent, the brutal truth was she had died for nothing. Even if his name was never mentioned, his 911-call would have made the link public quickly enough.

"We were making plans," a hard edge had begun to creep into Joel's voice, "to keep things going while I slogged away in law school somewhere. And then Dad got in the picture, leaning on me to take over his damn car business. Julie took my side, kept telling me to go my passion . . . "

The student's voice broke. "Yeah—well, tomorrow, I'm going all right, turning in my withdrawal. *Shit*, maybe I'll just throw my junk in the back seat and split. This place sucks."

Her face tear-streaked and paler than A. J. had ever seen it, Sam had been listening without comment through the rest of Joel's rambling confessional. In the silence that followed, she eased forward on the edge of the battered couch. The movement, however subtle, drew the student's eye contact.

"This isn't your fault, Joel," she said softly. "Or Julie's. Blame Bremer, even me if you want, but don't do this. I understand how much you're hurting. But Julie was right, you've come too far to abandon all your hard work, just walk away . . . "

A. J. sensed the wistful edge in her voice for what it was. This was the closest Sam had ever come to admitting any regrets about not finishing her own doctorate.

"Gotta have the paper-cred," the student chuckled, a bitter rasp of a sound. "For what, after this? I never thought . . . but stuff makes sense now. Julie was trying to find a way to say goodbye. She set up that time to meet at her office on purpose, though she never met me on campus before. She knew I would find her . . . "

Joel had slumped forward, head in his hands. His whole body was shaking, and the strangled sound of his breathing was painful to witness.

"For what it's worth," Sam told him slowly, "Julie hinted at something when we went to lunch last week. I never fully grasped how important it was then. We were talking about how difficult it is as a single woman to cope with some of the stuff that goes on around here. She made it pretty clear there was someone she really cared about—"

Joel's head jerked up, his eyes cracking with anger and self-loathing. "Not enough to live for. Not damn near enough."

The student was on his feet, half turned toward the door. A. J. was quicker, blocking his way.

"You're staying here tonight, Van Susten," he said. "Then tomorrow we're going to sit down and figure out some way to—"

"What ever it is, count me out. I'm done here, *finished.*"

Sam's voice stopped them both, cold. She was on her feet and reaching for the sweater she had slung casually over the sofa arm.

"This is over," Sam's tone was fierce, brooking no argument. "I started this grievance business and I'm ending it. Right here. The semester is all but over. Bremer will have my resignation in the morning—only a gesture since the man already canned me—but at least these are *my* terms, *my* timetable. By January with any luck I'll be on staff at Emmaline-Wattrous. No hearings. No more strong-arming students or anyone else to come forward. I only wish, Joel, for your sake I had come to my senses before it was too . . . "

Her voice broke, trailed off. One look at Sam's face was enough to tell A. J. it was futile to intervene.

"Joel, I'll make sure you have a copy of my resignation letter, for *The Voice"* she said. "I trust you'll know what to do with it." Her hand already was on the front door knob.

"It's late," A. J. said, "no time to go wandering around out there alone. Joel will understand if I drive you home."

Sam waved him off. "Thanks, but no," she said. "I'll be fine, always carry Mace. The walk will do me good."

She gave Joel a lingering hug, managed to evade A. J. entirely. He had no choice but to let her go. Joel was standing there numb and silent, like a man on the edge.

"I'm sorry," Sam said, "sorrier than you can imagine."

Then she was gone.

Joel was true to his word. So was Sam Pomerantz.

Despite A. J.'s impassioned protests, Joel hung around on campus only long enough to pass along Sam's resignation letter to the staffers on *The Voice*, wrote one last editorial passing the torch to Liz and left town. A. J. was able to finesse at least one thing. He set in motion the process by which Joel could still graduate without finishing the spring semester's course work. It wasn't hard, under the circumstances, to write a compelling case for translating life experience into equivalents that met the student's few missing departmental requirements.

Meanwhile, Sam wasn't returning A. J.'s calls. At Julie's memorial service she sat alone, pale and withdrawn on a folding chair on a side aisle. The Bolland chapel was packed, so it was easy enough for her to slip away immediately after the service ended. For several days afterward, A. J. finessed a detour past her house after work, hoping to spot her car, then gave up. It wasn't going to do either of them any good for her to peg him as a stalker.

The students put out one last edition of the student newspaper before final exams, with Julie's obituary and the text of Sam's letter of resignation plastered across page one. Liz, the new editor, asked A. J. to write an editorial informally on behalf of the faculty that would run parallel to Joel's. He didn't trust himself to do it. Even with an overrun, all the copies were snatched up in minutes.

Given Julie's suicide note, police interviews regarding the young professor's death were perfunctory. The campus gossip mill was strangely hushed as the details filtered their way through the institution's grieving corridors. One thing Julie Schechter had accomplished in death that had eluded her in life. For the first time a few brave souls were publicly calling for Dean Bremer's resignation.

Which left one very large question mark. Was President Dornbaum finally cornered enough to act? A. J. had to believe the man was not a total fool. With hints of the scandal surrounding Julie Schechter's death making headlines in the local press, the Dean was becoming a liability the President couldn't easily ignore. Then again, judging by memos and pronouncements over the years, Dornbaum appeared to be more glitz than substance. Both the Dean of Students and Doc Radisson had attributed the president's survival in office to throwing a good party and to being enough of a raconteur to keep board members like Harry Lentz amused, rather than by virtue of any particular administrative skill.

A. J. doubted if the President even knew most of the faculty by name, himself included. Which made it all the more baffling when he found himself summoned formally to a "conference" in the executive suite in Founders' Hall. He arrived to find an agitated and somewhat befuddled Dornbaum waiting for him—alone, at the far end of an enormous, mahogany board table.

The man always reminded him of an overdressed water bug, darting erratically over the surface of a situation, all flashing eye contact and gestures, with no discernible forward motion. None of which, A. J. had to admit, made him any less dangerous. The President's smile could mutate from smug to mean-spirited in a heartbeat.

After a full ten minutes of pontificating, while A. J. sat in silence gritting his teeth, Dornbaum got to the bottom line. "In recent weeks some Board members have proposed making you a Special Assistant to the President for Campus Affairs, with the understanding you would get to the bottom of certain . . . rumors that seem to have been circulating widely on campus and in the community in recent months—"

"Rumors?"

"That unfortunate affair with the young accounting professor, of course. But of late some Board members also have suggested *fiscally* we may not be as solid as we would like to be."

Fiscal sleaze compounding the political. If there was a bottom to the morass, A. J. saw no sign of it. "Why me?" he said.

The President's momentary hesitation confirmed what A. J. had begun to suspect. This was not Dornbaum's doing. Someone was forcing this.

"It's my understanding in recent years you were . . . you have been, shall we say, politically *neutral*—?"

Not exactly a plus, A. J. winced, to be considered out of the loop, clueless, unlikely to know where the bodies might be buried. "Rather tough, staying neutral. Given the circumstances."

Something of his skepticism must have communicated itself in his face. The President looked pained.

"Then, if you prefer . . . shall we say, *beyond reproach*."

A. J. would have disputed whether the two things followed. He was finding it hard to live with his own culpability in the intrigues leading up to Julie Schechter's death. As a political scientist he also knew enough about the Nazis and a whole pack of other –isms to spot survivor guilt when it reared its head. In this case, it was his own.

And when they came for me, wisdom had it, there was no one left to stand up and be counted. "This assistant," A. J. said, "would report directly to the president?"

"To the Board."

At that admission, if possible, Dornbaum looked even more uneasy. *An assistant to the President with direct access to the Board.* No wonder why Dornbaum was so skittish, why all the posturing about ethics. Title aside, a direct reporting relationship to the Board meant Dornbaum himself was a potential target of suspicion.

The question here, A. J. concluded, wasn't whether he was being used. That was a given. The bottom line was by whom, and why.

"I need to think about it," A. J. said.

Dornbaum's flicker of a smile didn't reach his eyes. "Fair enough. But I'll need an answer by Friday."

Three days from now. Enough time, A. J. thought, to force Sam to see him, to talk things out with the Dean of Students and Doc Radisson. The prospects were beyond intimidating, a no-win, he suspected, whatever came of it.

In the end, it took camping out on Sam's doorstep to get past her defenses. She arrived home after work to see A. J. hunkering on her front step, under the watchful eye of her neighbor's son, Ja Ron.

For a while as she sat there in her hatchback in the driveway with the motor running, he thought she might actually slam the vehicle in reverse and just keep going. Even after she cut the engine she took her time, head down, rummaging on the floor for her purse and briefcase. Just when he was about to give it up as a lost cause, she finally locked up the vehicle, started slowly up the walk in his direction.

When it came to bargaining chips, his hands were empty. "I know you don't want to see me," he said, "but we need to talk."

Sam was walking circles around him. She hadn't said a word, not even a simple hello while she fussed with collecting her mail and unlocking the door. Mercifully, as the house door swung open, she stood aside enough to let him pass.

A. J. had to blink several times to try to get his bearings, before he recognized what should have been familiar surroundings. Stacks of cardboard boxes were piled everywhere in the front hall and the tiny living and dining rooms. All of them appeared carefully labeled and numbered in bold permanent marker in Sam's distinctive block printing.

Logic and statistics, he read silently. *Basic Geometry, Algebra, Course notes,* and *Kitchen stuff.* Sam was spelling out the parameters of her life on those cartons. Wherever their destination, the move was taking her away from him. The very thought made him sick at heart.

It finally dawned on him, he would have to volunteer what she was not about to ask—what had brought him here. There was no point in beating around the bush.

"Someone has pushed the President to offer me an administrative post," he told her, "as a trouble shooter, fiscal and otherwise, reporting directly to the Board. Supposedly to clean up the mess over there."

Her eyebrow shot up. "And you said you would take it."

"I don't know. Maybe. I said I would consider it."

"Congratulations."

Her tone said otherwise. Sam had taken several manila folders out of her briefcase. Evading his gaze, she suddenly appeared intent on integrating them into carefully arranged stacks on her cluttered dining room tabletop. On the face of it, she was no longer listening.

"Sam, I know what you think—"

"Do you."

"That they've bought me. Or McDowell, Bremer—or heaven only knows who—might be using me to cover their tracks, preserve the status quo. Nothing, by that way, that hasn't occurred to me."

"Obviously, you don't need my opinion, one way or the other."

A. J. hesitated, picking his targets. "Let's just say, I'm not ready to give up on the place . . . or us for that matter, to head off to the monastery or bag it all and open my own law practice. Not yet anyway."

"Poli Sci meets life, real-politik versus cut and run," Sam chuckled softly. She left their personal status out of the mix entirely. "Good for you—keep your options open. Smart in this business, I've discovered."

Her edgy sarcasm surprised him, on multiple levels. Had the offer from Emmaline fallen through? A. J. had just assumed from the boxes she was headed there. It had never occurred to him she might be at loose ends herself. Since Sam dropped the harassment suit, the Bolland gossip mills had been unusually quiet.

"The deal with Emmaline-Wattrous . . . you've heard something."

Sam returned to her paper shuffling. "I signed the contract

141

yesterday. Three years as Director of Developmental Studies and an option to renew."

A. J. hadn't realized he was holding his breath. The offer was better than either one of them had hoped, built in a parachute of sorts. Emmaline must have wanted her badly. So she was safe. As safe, he corrected himself, as anything ever got in this business.

"I'm glad," he said, only half meaning it. Any way he cut it, they were bound to see a lot less of one another. It made sense for her to give up her rental and move closer to the Emmaline campus to cut some of the commute time.

"Well, *you're* certainly right on track," Sam said finally. "Doc said you would wind up in administration."

A. J. winced. "Not a done deal. I have until Friday to decide. Dornbaum wasn't exactly enthusiastic about the prospect, I'll admit. He hinted at some pretty serious fiscal problems, Fred Urban's worst nightmare."

"And you'll be standing there conveniently with a bull's eye painted on your back."

"Not necessarily a career breaker what ever comes of it," A. J. shrugged. "It's a part-time job so I would retain tenure and could always go back to the classroom full-time. Other faculty have done the same thing from time to time."

But never like this, he found himself thinking. Not potentially with the very future of the college at stake.

"You realize for every bit of garbage you dredge up over there, the faculty—all of them—will hold you personally accountable," she said. "And if and when the Board gets sick of the mess . . .well, you know what they do to messengers."

A. J. caught the unspoken. She still cared enough to want to protect him. That was something, anyway.

"But then, who am I to tell you what to do with your life, right."

"Sam, *don't*," he said quietly. "Don't do this. You have no idea how much I've missed you."

"We're in the wrong business for relationships," she was evading his gaze. "For all our good intentions, A. J., sooner or later like everybody else, you would find yourself forced to *use* it."

A. J. recoiled, fought to compose himself, not entirely succeeding. "Is that what you truly believe?"

Sam just looked at him, her expression unreadable. "Or we wind up using each other," she shrugged. "Either way, I'm not prepared to let that happen, not any more. Not after Joel and Julie Schechter."

The way things were going he figured he had nothing to lose. "The only thing I'm not sure of," he told her, "is whether I'm prepared to risk bucking Dornbaum alone, without you to keep me grounded. Whatever happens, Sam, I can't promise you it will be easy or I wouldn't let you or myself down in the process. I can only promise, I would never knowingly make you *regret* that you—"

"Dangerous," she said, "making promises you can't possibly know you can keep." Her smile was indescribably sad.

"So," A. J.'s hand closed in on the dull ache building at the base of his skull. "I guess that's it, then. Will I . . . when will I see you again?"

Sam hesitated. "I'll call . . . after the holidays sometime, when I'm more settled over there at Emmaline. Meantime, you have a lot on your plate, I'm sure. The time between semesters is always crazy. We could both use a break."

"I assume you've rented a truck," he said. "You'll be needing help with the—"

"Thanks, but the Athletic Director loaned me half the woman's basketball team for the move. I'll be fine."

It had become abundantly clear, whether he took the job or turned it down, as far as Sam was concerned, he was on his own. Her hug on his way out the door was guarded, perfunctory, and felt suspiciously to A. J. like a goodbye. At least she didn't add insult to injury by throwing in, *Merry Christmas*. Until she mentioned the holidays in passing, A. J. had honestly forgotten.

The reaction from Doc Radisson and Fred Urban was not quite as pessimistic, but food for thought, nevertheless. A. J. broke the news of Dornbaum's offer with the two men over far too much Rolling Rock in a back booth at Smithy's.

"I'm not sure whether I should be offering congratulations or condolences," Doc said, "though it's certainly high time somebody at

Bolland got some sense and started turning over rocks."

"It occurred to me you could have been the one who engineered all this," A. J. wondered out loud.

The Board Chair didn't seem put off by the question, though his face was expressionless, revealing nothing. "It's no secret a subset of the Board is concerned with the way things are headed," he shrugged. "You know how I feel on the subject."

"Whatever the official agenda," A. J. said, "Dornbaum and crew might try to co-opt the whole process."

"Possible. The guy certainly left quite a trail of heel marks when the committee-of-the-whole dragged him kicking and screaming to give you a call," Doc said. "I don't have to tell you that guys like Dornbaum and Bremer play rough. Hence the little fail-safe about the Assistant reporting directly to the Board."

A. J. grimaced. "All well and good, but you could look on Dornbaum's caving in as life insurance. I'm also damn sure Harry Lentz will be putting in his oar—yet again. Legitimately, for once."

"When you put it that way, Ferinelli," Fred said, "the job has all the appeal of walking on bare razor blades or swallowing glass. But it just may be Bolland's last chance and I hope to heaven you take it. If anyone can ferret out how deep the cesspool is, it's you."

The Dean of Students hesitated, stared intently at the wisps of foam clinging to the bottom of his mug. "For what it's worth, you also ought to know I was always a scramble and scrap kind of player, especially if I knew I could trust the quarterback to do the right thing at the moment of truth. I'll watch your back, run interference as much as possible, you can depend on it."

Trust the players, trust the process, trust the outcome. A. J. wasn't sure any of the variables were realistic. Doc called the situation at Bolland just another sordid case of history repeating itself. If true, then Sam might have every reason in the world to fear not just for Bolland's future, but for his own. Everything certainly pointed to a larger systemic failure that went well beyond one man's power to cope. For proof, he only had to consider the unsettling rise and fall of colleagues like George McDowell for whom A. J. once had held the greatest respect.

At least Sam was out of the line of fire. If Doc knew she had withdrawn her grievance and had taken a job at Emmaline, the man was tactful enough not to say a word. Two sleepless nights later, in which Sam's wistful smile continued to haunt him, A. J. realized for better or worse, he had his answer.

He got up, showered and shaved, then self-consciously donned his one and only business suit before heading for campus. From the look of it, he wasn't the only one taken aback by his appearance, gray flannel or otherwise. The President's eyebrows lifted as he saw the professor standing, briefcase in hand, in the doorway to the executive offices.

"Ferinelli. I gather I can count on you, then."

A. J. wasn't about to tackle that one. "I've decided to take the job," he said.

Day One in the administrative suite was not auspicious. The president ushered him, unceremoniously, into a closet-sized sitting room off the main reception room. "Feel free to get settled in your new office," Dornbaum suggested, whatever that might entail. Before he could ask to what end, the man already was moving on.

"Lunch," the President said, "I've scheduled lunch so we can hit the ground running, talk about the possibilities."

A. J. spent the morning shuffling between his faculty office and the administrative suite organizing a second work place. The logistics were as superfluous as the new job itself appeared to be, all form and no substance. Lunch didn't alter his assessment. On the way over to the Student Union, Dornbaum was more concerned about dealing with the state of the paint job on the railings outside the gym and on the soffits of several of the buildings than the conduct of the Academic Dean or the bottom line in the finance office.

Forget details like the fact paint won't even dry below 50 degrees, A. J. thought grimly. As they walked, the first tentative snowflakes had begun to drift down on them from the sullen gray sky overhead. During their supposed working lunch, the president's priorities kept straying back to the need for new china and crystal for the presidential dining room, though how the man intended to pay for any or all of that, never came up.

It got worse. As the two made their way back to the presidential suite of offices, A. J. could have sworn he saw Sam coming toward them on the quad. She was dressed in a turquoise and gray ski jacket, head bare to the rising northerly wind. As the distance closed between them, he saw it was just the bookkeeper from the campus business office. The woman's name escaped him. Patricia sounded familiar or some variation on a theme, something ending in a vowel.

"Looks like Channel 9 was right for once," he called out to her in passing, "we could be in for quite a storm."

The woman broke stride, visibly uncomfortable when A. J. stopped as well. "It certainly looks like it," she said, "though I'm not sure I totally trust weather forecasters who refer to themselves as members of a Storm Team."

Her tone, the arched eyebrow that went with it, told him she wasn't just talking about the weather. A. J. winced, "As in don't look for trouble, you might just find it?"

"Something like that."

With the look of someone desperately searching for the exits, the bookkeeper turned and headed back in the same direction from which she had just come. Oblivious to the awkward exchange, the president had begun to gesture for A. J.'s benefit at what he termed the 'substandard' end-of-the-season trim job on a cluster of evergreens that looked perfectly acceptable as it was.

What was it Leon Botstein once said, A. J. fought back a grim twist of a smile—*that the job of a college president was right up there on the career ladder between running a tanking Fortune 500 company and a down-at-the-heels B&B.*

President Dornbaum had stopped mid-sentence, was looking at him with a quizzical expression on his face. "Indeed fortunate you're joining us, Ferinelli. Sound decision and high time we get some new blood in here. Help us shape up the place."

An unfortunate choice of pronouns, A. J. decided. *Us,* whoever the rest of that shadowy *us* might prove to be.

"It would help logistically, sir," A. J. speculated out loud, "to have some sense of how *you* envision the priorities, where and how I would best begin." Right now, half the battle seemed to be to keep the president on task rather than obsessing about campus aesthetics, real or imagined.

"Talk to the various department and staff divisional heads, I would suppose. Several of the board members might want to offer their perspectives—"

The man already had lost interest in their chat, leaving his new assistant with very little to go on as mandates went. Still, something clicked in A. J.'s head as he watched the president wander off again

146

into his own clubhouse of an office.

Priscilla. It finally came to him. The woman on the quad was named Priscilla.

Make a point, A. J. told himself, to call the bookkeeper before close of business. Whatever was making her so uneasy, it couldn't hurt to try a follow-up. When he did, things didn't quite turn out as he imagined.

Mistake number one was to meet Priscilla Fowler in the same executive dining room in the student commons where he had met with the President. At Dornbaum's insistence, the place had been renovated some months ago to create a more up-scale ambiance. It hadn't been easy, since the walls of the tiny dining room were cement block. For starters, maintenance had painted everything an overpowering ash gray with a wide green, burgundy and navy wallpaper border set tight against the ceiling. Furnishings consisted of a few imposing Queen Anne style reproductions—Colonial chic masking institutional drab, hardly the environment to put anyone at ease. From the get-go, the campus bookkeeper was poised on the edge of her seat, as if half-expecting to find a hidden microphone buried in the fake silk flower arrangement on the table between them.

"You . . . you're the one who was helping Sam, weren't you," Priscilla said, by way of introduction. It wasn't a question. "The women on the staff really respected her for her teaching, felt she was getting a raw deal. Believe it or not, the staff learn a lot from students about which way the wind is blowing. But then you also learn quick around here, you're better off if you just . . . "

"Keep your mouth shut?" A. J. finished for her.

Priscilla flushed. Evading his gaze, she had begun to trace the beads of sweat forming along the fragile stem of her water glass.

"You've been here now . . . what," he said, "about three years or so."

His implication was clear enough—long enough to know what, if anything, was going on. Priscilla didn't answer immediately. Sharp, he thought, cautious. The woman knew darn well he had access to that kind of information in her personnel file, including the in's and out's of her job description and time at Bolland He also certainly would have briefed himself before he took this meeting.

"Five," she said. "I've been here five years. Two in payroll and since then on General Ledger."

"Receipts. Donor gifts."

"And disbursements," she said.

Again A. J. could sense the shutters slamming in place. This conversation was going nowhere. As he walked her back to her office after lunch, it finally occurred to him what the problem was.

"All this high finance is way too complicated for an hour over lunch," he said. "Could I interest you in dinner, Saturday. Off campus, if you would prefer."

Priscilla looked at him strangely. "I'm not so sure that is—"

"Face it," he said quickly, "the President's dining room is not exactly conducive to soul talks about budgets and fiscal projections. You pick the time and place. At least I can spring for a decent meal off campus for your trouble."

A. J. felt a subtle stirring in his memory banks. Something Sam had said—an invitation that led him to a different place entirely. *A Friday night after work. Her dining room—with him wondering what he was doing with all that damn crystal of hers on the table between them, as breakable as it was beautiful, catching the light.* He shaped her name again, willing himself to feel the crushing ache that began to build inside of him every time he thought of her.

Sam. Through the grapevine, he heard she was hitting the ground running with a whole package of new academic support services at Emmaline-Wattrous. Regional press was glowing and plentiful. If that continued, the Emmaline recruiters would be cutting into Bolland's market in no time flat. Suddenly irrelevant, utter damn nonsense—all of it. All of it, except her. And the fact he loved her.

A muscle jerked along the edge of A. J.'s jaw, reminding him where he was. Across the table, Priscilla, sat silent, watching him intently.

"If you'd prefer, Ms. Fowler, we can meet in my office—"

"No," the woman said, "it's all right. The Grist Mill, Saturday, around seven."

"Good," he nodded. "See you then."

He couldn't bring himself to say he was looking forward to it. The Grist Mill was an unpretentious restaurant-slash-tavern in a historic complex of buildings along a narrow country road five miles outside of town. The drive itself seemed far longer—too many trucks. As the miles ticked past, A. J. felt a growing sense of uneasiness at what he was potentially unleashing. At least the bookkeeper's choice would minimize the chances of prying eyes and the speculation bound to go with it.

Priscilla got there on her own, apparently had arrived early. From her expression when they first made eye contact, she too was beginning to have second thoughts about the whole thing. The bar was packed, from the look of it with revelers fortifying themselves for an office Christmas party going on in the private banquet room. The holiday was less than a week away and all the lights and holiday cheer struck him as vaguely depressing.

"Is it true," Priscilla said, her chin out and steel in her voice, "your job is to look for irregularities with the books?"

"Dirt under the fake Persians in general, not just fiscal," A. J. corrected her. "Ostensibly it's the plan. Although I'm not sure anyone really thinks the problems will conveniently present themselves. Dornbaum has been unwilling even to admit there could be issues."

Priscilla was staring down into the depths of her gin and tonic, doggedly intent on retrieving the solitary slice of lime hidden amid the ice cubes. "There's dirt, all right," she said, "and plenty of it."

A. J. paused, his frosted glass of Rolling Rock in hand, unsure how or if to respond. He didn't want to push her.

"Bremer," he said finally.

"I'm talking about the books."

And we both know it. That part went unsaid.

"I've heard locals in town have been gossiping for some time now about Bolland's practice of deferring payment of bills six months to a year or more," A. J. said, watching for her reaction. "If the budget were balanced as the Board treasurer maintains, none of that should be necessary."

A frown was settling in between his dinner companion's brows. When she didn't respond, A. J. persisted.

"I gather there's more," he said.

"Yes."

"As in—?"

"Raiding endowment in the name of investing in physical plant upgrades. Diverting targeted donor gifts to the operating budget instead to keep up with expenses. Booking gifts at more than their market value to reconcile the bottom line, spending bequests before somebody actually dies . . . "

A. J. straightened in his seat. He didn't know a heck of a lot about IRS regulations, but he could smell major trouble and this fit. "So, what you're saying is—?"

"We're running about a million in the red annually and nobody even knows where the money is going. So many expenditures are off the books it could take months or years, if ever, to figure out what the budget really ought to be. In the meantime, we're hemorrhaging funds we haven't got."

"How long are we talking here," A. J. said. "Years, decades—?"

"How long has all this been *going on* . . . or how long until we hit rock bottom? If I had to guess the former, ten years, certainly before my time. The deadline to Armageddon, now that might be harder to predict. We're maxed out on debt. If enrollments don't improve, try half as long as it took to get in this shape. Worst case," Priscilla just shrugged, "a lot could happen between now and May."

A. J. straightened abruptly in his chair, "Sonofa . . . "

He caught himself. The woman was looking at him like a deer transfixed in the headlights, terrified she had said too much.

"I have to insist, if it's your intention," she said, "to use me as a some kind of a source for any of this, I . . . "

A. J. forced himself to maintain eye contact. He had made it plain enough before either one of them said a word, anything she told him was off the record.

"I told you, meant it, this goes nowhere," he said evenly.

She averted her eyes. "Sam trusted you."

His face felt hot, like his hands against the frosted sides of his pilsner glass. He didn't consider Sam Pomerantz a success story by any standards. What was it Sam had said last time he saw her—*don't make promises you can't keep?*

"You realize," he said slowly, "this could cost you your job, the minute whatever I uncover becomes public. And it will become public, Priscilla. No matter what I do."

People in her situation made terrific scapegoats. If they knew and said nothing, they were in a bind. Even if they came forward as she had done, they were still likely to get the ax.

"I am not going to jail for them," she said.

Them. That was one area she had skirted entirely.

"Who," he said, "who's involved in this?"

150

When she didn't respond, he took a chance. The VP for finance was a given.

"The President," he said. It wasn't a question.

The color was deepening along the ridge of her cheekbones. But still she said nothing.

"The President, Dean Bremer? The Board . . . ?"

"Some of the Board. Not all."

Her silence told him Dornbaum and the Dean were assumed. He should have known.

"Harry Lentz," he said.

With an agitated gesture, the woman slid sideways on the seat of the booth so he couldn't see her face except in profile. Forget the fact they hadn't ordered or eaten.

"I think I better go," she said.

Much as she was wary of her immediate bosses, it was Board the woman feared the most, or at least a part of it. That made sense. The power base of Board members was in the private sector, Priscilla's logical escape route.

"I'm sorry," he said, "that was uncalled for. Putting you on the spot like—"

"This could destroy my career," she said, calmer now. "I need to protect myself, consider my options."

A. J. recognized the rhetoric. He had heard it once before. This was Sam talking and Priscilla made it pretty plain up-front the two women had discussed this, recently from the sound of it. Reading between the lines, Priscilla too could be on the verge of bailing out.

"A reference—is that it," he said. "If you're . . . if you need one, I would be happy to help."

The woman slowly nodded. "I have an interview next week with a major accounting firm in Harrisburg."

Spooked enough, A. J. winced, to be putting substantial miles and some intimidating mountain roads between her and the problems at Bolland "Done," he said, "just let me know where to send the letter. Or better, I'll phone ahead before you show up over there. You just tell me what's most helpful."

The relief in her eyes was embarrassing, given how little she was asking of him or how at risk she was. Hardest to swallow was the fact he really knew almost nothing of the people who were prepared to lay their careers on the line to help fight the status quo. He was

151

thinking partly of those staffers—and now Priscilla—who were willing to come forward to help nail the Dean and restore some measure of integrity to their workplace. Courageous and principled, with everything to lose.

"Your resume," he said. "Make sure you get me the latest version."

Made clumsy by her haste, Priscilla was already pulling on her coat. The two of them had never even gotten around to ordering. When she left, A. J. half thought about just paying their bar tab and heading out as well. Instead he settled in, ordered a steak—rare—and picked away at it for the better part of an hour, very much alone with his thoughts.

On multiple fronts his Christmas holidays were turning out to be grim, the worst A. J. had experienced since Anne's death. Legitimately this time, he justified turning down his family's invitations to come East with tales of out-of-control workloads. Priscilla, the bookkeeper, hadn't exaggerated one bit what lay ahead of him—or Bolland. Although most of the campus was officially on break, the staff in the business office had begun taking their usual mid-fiscal-year pulse of campus finances, with one major difference. This time, A. J. insisted on a copy of the budget and photocopies of the ledgers. He saw to the photocopying himself.

Bottom line, if anyone still was maneuvering behind the scenes to influence the outcome of the quickie internal audit, they were going to have to be damned circumspect about it. At the moment, print size was the only visible enemy. Armed with a strong light and a large-number calculator, A. J. stacked the welter of documents in manageable piles on his living room floor and started spot-checking numbers.

When President Dornbaum had gotten wind of what was going on, he had protested. In the end he backed off. A. J. already could sense the guy was positioning himself to assume the role of the knight on white horse, in search of likely guys to take the fall.

Priscilla, at least, was out of reach. A powerful letter of reference from A. J., laced with words like honesty and integrity, did its job and landed her the Harrisburg job. The night before she left, she turned up on A. J.'s front porch, a U-haul hitched to the back bumper of her fading red Chevy. Visibly flustered, she handed A. J. a poinsettia. Its pot was swathed in green foil and the festive ribbon holding it in place had suffered a great deal in transit.

"Happy Holidays," she said. "I realize it isn't much. I owe you a lot."

"There's some doubt who owes what to whom." The plant felt heavy in his hands, unwieldy. "But thanks. I'll do my best not to kill this thing . . . "

"Or Bolland"

A. J. forced a smile. "Given what's in those books, it's something I can't so readily promise."

The woman wasn't smiling. "In any case, I'm outta here," she said. "You've gotta live with these guys, I don't. My sainted grandmother had this expression—"

"Keep your nose clean?"

"Watch your backside."

A. J. laughed. "In six months I just might be asking you for a reference."

"Call," she said, "any time."

Chapter Ten

It wasn't Priscilla's voice A. J. intercepted on his answering machine the Friday after New Year. His week had been particularly contentious, frustrating, and even a rare Friday night at home offered no promise of sanctuary. The house was dark and uninviting, with a teeth-gritting chill that comes just before a winter storm. He had just started to cobble together some kindling in the fireplace when the phone rang. It was six o'clock—the witching hour.

For the past month he had taken to screening his messages, ever since he started getting a random mix of anonymous calls tied to his snooping around in the books. Sometimes the callers passed along tips, credible and otherwise. Just as often, he met with bursts of profanity or outright threats.

It took him a while to find the phone. *Caller unknown.* As usual, the caller ID on his phone wasn't helpful in identifying the source. So when the leave-a-message instructions kicked on, playing his own voice back at him, A. J. was not predisposed to intervene.

"For what it's worth," he heard a familiar voice say, "I misjudged you. Priscilla called and I just wanted to tell you how very much I appre—"

"Sam . . . *wait* . . . !"

As he cut into the line, the cordless phone began to emit a persistent chirping sound. *Low battery.*

"Damn . . . this blasted phone," he said. "Hold on. I'll be back in a second—"

A. J. made a beeline for the hard-wired extension on the night stand next to the bed. He hoped to heaven she hadn't hung up on him. "Still there?"

A husky undercurrent of laughter reassured him. Cursing silently to himself, A. J. tried to unsnarl the phone cord enough to sit on the edges of the coverlet. Cabbage roses. Anne had picked out that quilt the Christmas before she died. Especially since Sam's exodus, the lush and sensual pattern had become out of sync with what was becoming a monastic existence. Still, A. J. couldn't bring himself to replace it.

"You sound beat."

A. J. chuckled. "Out of breath. Hope you know CPR," he said.

"Tough. Long distance like this."

He decided to chance it. "We could remedy that easily enough."

"Suggestions."

"Dinner. You name the place."

He ticked off the seconds, waiting, got as far as a-thousand-eight. An eternity.

"I'll meet you," she said. "The Mill."

Twice in a matter of weeks, A. J. felt his stomach tighten at the thought. Neutral territory. Mathematically the place had to be equidistant, to within a tenth of a mile, from their two campuses. But then at least Sam was willing to see him.

"About six-thirty," he said, already fishing in his pockets for the Toyota keys.

"Make it seven."

Time for a quick shower after all his sweating over ledger sheets. "I'll be there."

She was waiting for him in the bar with a glass of red wine and a paperback for company. Down at the other end of the gleaming strip of cherry wood, a couple of good old boys had their heads together. Arguing, A. J. was willing to bet, about how best to hit on that babe in the jeans and the black molded-to-fit sweater. The look they shot in his direction as he joined her was vintage Stone Age.

155

"Sorry," he said as he eased onto the stool next to hers. "Got caught behind a truck."

"No problem. I was late myself."

Sam stashed the book in the denim bag lying between them on the bar, but made no other move to greet him. Moot, since their stools were close enough to guarantee intimacy, just by breathing. He caught the subtle scent of her hair, blindsided by the chain reaction it triggered and the slow ache building inside him.

Get a grip, man. Through clenched teeth, A. J. called to the bartender and got his attention long enough to stake claim to a Yuengling on tap. What the heck, he thought, as he passed on his usual Rolling Rock. *Live a little.* Things were looking up.

"Salud." Sam tipped her glass toward his.

He noticed she hadn't opted for Happy New Year. At least she was here, an improvement over the way the last one ended.

"You've been busy," he said.

"Oh . . . the papers. You've seen, I guess."

"Hard to miss. Especially the photo spread with a shot of you down in the Emmaline game room, kicking butt in some Guitar Hero battle of the bands," A. J. chuckled, shook his head. "All sorts of hidden talents. Who knew . . . ?"

Sam flushed. "Why they pay me the big bucks, huh? You remember, I used to play in this gosh awful punk band in high school—pathetic, the whole bunch of us, but then you know what they say about math and music. Only goes to show you never know when stuff is going to come in handy."

"Certainly great buzz for jump-starting your programs."

"Though not totally fair," she said. "Most of the programs were already in the works for six months before I got here and all that plays better in theory in the media than in practice. But yeah, thanks. If all else fails, it'll look good on the old Re-zum."

The waitress was eager to seat them, not a bad idea. A little distance right now struck him as prudent, the way things were going. He couldn't seem to get the photo of Sam out of his mind, apparently caught mid-game, surrounded by students, a wicked hint of a grin on her face. The guys in the shot looked about the way he felt at the moment, half wondering what had hit them.

The Mill's menu was depressingly familiar, slim pickings for all its length. Although he had all but memorized the offerings once

156

before, A. J. poured through the list of entrees, twice, before settling on the same unimaginative choice he made the night of his soul talk with Bolland's bookkeeper. All the while he sensed Sam watching him, her own menu still unopened on the table.

"Priscilla says you've been busy yourself," she said, "turning over some pretty scary rocks."

"Imagine your worst nightmare. It wouldn't come close."

"Bet the upholders of truth, beauty and traditional academe are relishing every gory misplaced decimal point."

"Not exactly their mood, judging by my answering machine," A. J. said.

The catch in her breathing spoke volumes. "Sounds also like you've already ventured pretty far out on the proverbial limb from what Priscilla told me," she said finally. "A lonely, thankless business."

"You could say that."

It fit—the part about being alone. At least she hadn't said, I told you so. Sam was contemplating the dwindling Chilean red at the bottom of her glass.

"If it helps, none of this seems to have scared off the Emmaline-Wattrous Board when it comes to a merger," she said. "Nobody is talking much around me, though. I'm still too new, a defector and not exactly one of *them* yet, hence automatically suspect."

Swapping war stories about work had an uncomfortable edge, with their two employers actively in negotiations. "The whole drill is enough to keep a guy up nights, more or less permanently," he shrugged.

"That explains it. You're looking worn out."

An understatement. One thing was obvious, A. J. decided. The move sure had agreed with her.

"You're looking great," he said. "Terrific, in fact."

Sam flushed. "Nothing like a change of scenery to get a guy thinking, figuring out some things. Coed or not, Emmaline is still trying to cultivate some of the same atmosphere I experienced back in my old undergrad women's college days. Knock on wood, I just may be finding my niche."

"Sounds very Zen. Anything earthshaking come of it?"

"Just your everyday meaning of life stuff," she shrugged, "like exactly what teaching means in my life, the whole academic scene, why I keep letting the Bremers of this world work me over. By the way, I also ran into that friend of yours Doc Radisson yesterday on campus at Emmaline—over there for some meeting or other."

If Sam's goal was to change the subject, she certainly was doing a great job of it. "So, what did Doc think of your change of venue?" he said, trying to sound more casual about her answer than he felt.

"Okay with it, I guess—he said he could relate to my soul crisis over what happened with Joel and Julie, hoped the goings on at Bolland didn't get worse before it got better."

"Amen to that."

"I unpacked a bit, was pretty frank about my struggles to adjust to life without a driving ambition to exact my pound of flesh or take on the social injustices of the planet. Doc made all the right noises. As he saw it, closure can be a tricky business, not always what it's cracked up to be. Maybe, he said, sometimes we just need to let somebody buy us lunch instead. So I did—let him, that is."

A. J.'s mouth felt stiff. "Doc's a wise man."

"And in a funny mood. He talked a lot about you, actually. The man obviously respects you a great deal."

At something she read in his face, Sam plunged ahead. "Anyway, armed with his little pep talk, I decided it was time to get a life or try to anyway. So, I laced on my boots, took the rest of the day off, drove up to the glen and checked out the cross country trails. It's sure cold enough for frostbite, but we're starting to get a snow pack along the path we took out there. Granted, I didn't get far without skis."

The path we took. That simple *we* of hers gave him hope. "It just so happens, I've got a couple of pairs of skis in my garage," he said.

Something told him the color rising in her face was not all traceable to the lingering effects of windburn. Sam finally gave the menu a quick scan, closed it again.

"We really didn't have a chance, did we," she said quietly.

"Bremer. The grievance—"

"*Us.*"

The single syllable covered a lot of territory. Sam hadn't chosen to define it.

A. J. managed a smile. "I honestly was surprised you agreed to see me."

"Ditto, considering the way I reacted when you came to me about taking that job Dornbaum was offering you."

"For the record," he said, "if there were a way to press the reset button and start over—with us, I mean—I would do it in a minute."

A. J. had seen the gesture before, the way she nibbled at the inside of her lower lip when she felt unsure of herself. "Have you . . . I suppose you didn't hear from Joel," she said.

"He's home apparently, degree in hand, working for his dad. I have it secondhand from a couple of his classmates who stopped by my office last week. They're planning to drive over to see him before the new semester starts."

"I had heard pretty much the same thing. I assume that early-degree business was your doing?"

A. J.'s face felt hot. A burst of laughter from the bar startled them both. Sam straightened in her chair.

"I guess what I'm really trying to say," she said softly, "is, I owe you an apology."

Increasingly uncomfortable with the tack their conversation was taking, A. J. wanted to cut her off, instead said nothing. Awkward as it was, if Sam needed to vent, he needed to let her.

"Guilt is a dangerous thing," she said. "I took Julie's death so personally. Blamed myself . . . and you, indirectly, for letting things get so out of hand. Then too, I underestimated you. Badly. Maybe I was trying to protect myself, but when Dornbaum offered you the administrative job, I just assumed . . . presumed that you'd wind up like Bremer and the rest of them."

"Reasonable enough an assumption, under the circumstances."

"But totally unfair. You never gave me any reason to doubt you. Ever. I should have trusted my experience . . . trusted you. I'm sorry."

"Apology accepted."

Sam seemed to take his gruff disclaimer at face value. At least some of the tension in her eyes was gone, the silence between them more palatable. The waitress was bringing their orders, a California salad for her and the usual slab of steak for him—rare, with a double order of fries. A. J. caught Sam's twinge of a frown.

"Don't say it," he grumbled, "I know. My carnivore tastes have hit an all-time low."

"A gun would be quicker."

"There *is* a solution."

Sam cocked an eyebrow. "A heart transplant?"

Not out of the question. His cardiovascular system appeared to be working double time. "Actually," he said, "I was thinking more along the lines of someone taking charge, shaming me into some degree of self-restraint."

"A personal food trainer. Interesting concept."

"Not exactly," he said. "I was hoping more for a vegetarian on call, charged with major lifestyle revisions. The exact job description is certainly up for negotiation."

The noise level in the bar seemed to escalate six notches. For her part, Sam was silent. "You're suggesting exactly *what*."

Go slow, he told himself, every nerve-ending alert. "For starters, you spend the weekend hanging out with an unrepentant junk food addict. I'll hide the chips and even serve whole-grain sawdust for breakfast, whatever it takes."

Sam was caught up in shaping a fork full of uninspired and largely unshredded greenery into a manageable chunk. Finally she gave up entirely. "Aren't we pushing our luck," she said. "If you would have asked me two hours ago what I would be doing tonight—"

"Can't be worse than what was on my calendar. Wading through spread sheets or sacked out in front of the TV, feeling incredibly sorry for myself," he told her. "Missing you . . . wondering what the hell I've been doing with my life. As it is, it's taken me far too many years to get my priorities straight. If there's one thing the last few years taught me, it's that time is precious"

"True."

"Besides," he said, "being a hermit isn't all it's cracked up to be."

A. J. decided he loved the way the smile lines crinkled at the corners of her eyes. They were so subtle sometimes, if a guy weren't watching for it, he might have missed them.

"I can't imagine you as a monk," she said.

"Yeah, well . . . "

It was A. J.'s turn to look uncomfortable. In fact, for the past year, he occasionally found himself spending time with a divorced single-mom he had bumped into in Ontowona in the DMV line. She had just escaped a long-term abusive marriage and turned out to be one of the emergency room nurses on call the terrible night after Anne's accident. Sheer coincidence—yet purposeful, he sometimes felt, as if they had been there somehow for one another when things were at their worst.

From the outset they both made it plain their relationship was a no-strings arrangement, a cautious and rather clinical antidote to their mutual loss. But then, all of that was before Sam Pomerantz showed up at his office door. Although the woman had called once since, when A. J. begged off she sounded almost relieved.

Sam was watching his face. "So," she said quietly, "your place or—"

"Mine. I can just see one of your students spotting my Toyota in your driveway."

"And turning me in to the vice squad," Sam looked amused. "It's the new millennium and Emmaline-Wattrous went coed, remember? But I do appreciate the thought."

Easing forward on the bench seat, A. J. tried to signal their harried waitress to produce the tab. When she didn't materialize, he resorted to dropping a stack of bills on the table, throwing in a patently undeserved tip for good measure and calling it even. After a brief search of the contents of her book bag, Sam came up with a set of keys.

"One minor problem of logistics," she said.

A. J.'s eyebrow arched.

"The weather," Sam said. "We've got two cars. That last two-mile downgrade can be treacherous on a good day and with what's brewing out there . . . "

"I'll follow you—we'll just take it slow." He kept telling himself the same thing.

It had started to snow and both of them had left their jackets in their cars. Shielding them as best he could from the dense swirl of white stuff greeting them beyond the reach of the rustic eatery's corrugated metal awning, A. J. guided their progress across the parking lot. The icy gravel made for treacherous going. Forecasters had been predicting a blizzard for nearly a week.

It occurred to him after she was safely inside her whimsical two-tone Hyundai, how dicey this was, on so many fronts. When he tapped on the driver-side glass, Sam cracked the window in response, a puzzled frown settling in between her brows. "Second thoughts?"

"The curve," he said, "four miles back. Even an hour ago it was getting really slick—"

Sam's laugh was taut, anxious, as she turned her face up to meet his. "Thanks . . . I'll watch it," she said.

Glistening droplets clung to her lashes and damp tendrils curled at either temple. God, the woman was beautiful. No wonder when he showed up at the Mill, the local red neck contingent had been ready to go for the gun racks in their pickups.

A. J. swore softly as a gust of wind drove sheets of sleet pellets across the windshield. It was tough to watch the road when what he wanted was her—dark hair spilled across the cool linen of the pillow, her delicate breasts rising to his touch. As it was, the pinpoint gleam from her vehicle's tail lights proved distraction enough.

The trip seemed interminable. All he knew was one minute Sam was easing her vehicle into his driveway, while he maneuvered the Toyota in behind it. The next, she was in his arms, the wind lashing through their light clothing.

"No parkas, either one of us," Sam shivered. "Real smart. Frostbite is a d-distinct possibility here . . . "

By way of a response, A. J. began tasting the wet snowflakes glistening on her upturned mouth. The heady scent of wet wool and silken feel of exposed flesh were proving impossible to resist. After a half-hearted attempt to move from lawn to porch, he found himself caught up instead in teasing little kisses along the column of her throat helped considerably by the deep vee of her sweater.

"So . . . beautiful," he whispered against her skin.

Her sharp intake of breath was involuntary, a subtle invitation. Through the taut fabric of her jeans, he felt her tremble as he fitted her body to his. At this rate, freezing or not, if he had his druthers in another minute he would be making love with her right there in the shadows.

"Sam," he groaned, "this is . . . insanity. Do you have any idea how long it's been . . . since . . . "

She could guess. At least she eased away enough to grasp at his hands. Laughing, she half followed and half led him across the deepening white crust of sleet and snow on the lawn toward his

162

darkened bungalow.

The front hall light was minus all but one of its three bulbs, enough for the two of them to dodge the major obstacles en route to the bedroom. A. J. was not in the mood to start throwing light switches and call attention to the omnipresent fiscal debris, empty junk-food wrappers and take-out cartons decorating every surface in the house.

But then, who was noticing. Made tentative by haste, their hands dealt with buttons and fasteners, anything that stood in the way of the intimacy their bodies were seeking. Sam slipped from his grasp long enough to find safe haven on the bed, the invitation in her smile impossible to misread even in the half-darkness from the room's nightlight. A. J. caught his breath—dumbstruck at the lush splendor of her naked flesh now stretched out before him on the coverlet.

"Dear God . . . Sam . . . "

His gaze traversed the curves of her breasts, then downward over the shadowed rib cage, lingered yet again. A soft wisp of laughter conveyed her pleasure as she watched him. Hunger and awe were in a war for control A. J. had the uneasy feeling he could lose.

As he slid alongside her on the bed, Sam's eyes never once left his face. He started to tell her, but she stopped him with a look. Instead, hands shaking, she drew him to her.

Still, he needed to say it. "I've fallen in love with you, Sam," he said.

On a sigh, her eyes half-closed. Everywhere he touched, her skin was on fire. Sam began to utter wordless sounds conveying her pleasure, urging him on. Dangerous, when it was restraint he was savoring, holding back the agonizing promise of surrender just beyond their reach. Her body lost in a trembling compunction of its own, she cried out his name. At that, A. J. came to her, pulled under into the same swirling torrent. Then silence. Time became measured in the gradual steadying of his pulse. With some difficulty A. J. finessed enough distance to see her face. Heavy-eyed, Sam smiled up at him. The first wild flood-tide was ebbing.

It was then he began to love her again, slowly this time, deliberately imprinting her body with his. All the experience, the joy and sorrow, of his fifty-one years went into the way he held her, defining and redefining love as he knew it in his imagination, satiating himself on her willing flesh until in the end there was

163

nothing left but the scent and touch and taste of her. Until they were both at peace.

The snow and sleet pelting against the windows had stopped a long time ago. Twined spoon-fashion under the rose-patterned coverlet shielding them from the chill morning air, they slept.

A. J.'s watch read ten o'clock. Just as panic was about to set in—what the hell was he doing sleeping in on a weekday—the faint smell of coffee brewing reminded him. It was a Saturday morning, and miracle of miracles, Sam was in his kitchen. All good, worth waking up for.

A quick pass through the bathroom ensured basic civility. Mirrored back at him, A. J. saw a man he barely recognized. A rakish shadow of stubble outlined his jaw. His hazel eyes looked younger, less jaded. Happy. Pulling on a pair of jeans draped over the hamper, bare chested and not bothering with shoes, he headed toward the faint sounds of utensils making contact.

"Smells good," he called ahead of him, not wanting to startle her.

He didn't let the frying pan he found her tending, spatula in hand, stop him. Sam was drowning in one of his dress shirts, only partially buttoned and braless he quickly discovered as he drew her back against him. With a groan of awareness, he buried his face in the gentle curve where her neck met her shoulder. She half pulled away, knew all too well what was on his mind.

"Omelets," she told him. "I am not going to let you distract me."

"I'm impressed—"

"Well, if you can control yourself, there's more. Homemade biscuits. They'll be done in ten minutes. Tricky. Apparently your oven bakes hot."

"I never knew that."

By now he had shifted his weight so his hands were flat against the curve of her belly, easing downward toward the gathered edging of her briefs. She was doing her best to ignore him.

"Well, it does—something is very wrong with that thermostat. Fortunately the m-marmalade I found in the fridge can cover a multitude of sins."

Fortuitous timing, her turning in his arms like that. She was quick enough to evade his hands, but not his mouth or what came after as A. J. set about exploring what lay within reach under her makeshift robe.

"Nice," he said. "A much better idea than breakfast."

Sam was having none of it. "Something . . . is something burning—?"

"I was thinking the same thing," A. J. chuckled.

"I'm serious, d-dammit. The biscuits . . . "

"So am I," he said. "But if you insist, there's a fire extinguisher next to the refrigerator."

Blue, acrid trails had begun to emanate from the vents on the stove. Still chuckling softly to himself, A. J. let her go. Apparently the temperature wasn't the oven's only problem. As Sam grabbed a dish towel and pulled the smoking pan out of the oven, they saw the back two rows of the fluffy creations had taken on the texture and general appearance of over-sized charcoal briquettes.

"See, the ones in front are edible," he said, "if we just surgically remove the lower crusts . . . "

"Darn it. I wanted this to be special."

"You have no idea," he told her.

Sam was not amused, told him so with a look of eyebrow-raised censure. Muttering in mock contrition, A. J. poured himself a cup of Sam's coffee, then clicked on the radio, hoping for a weather forecast, as good a distraction as any. Even the programming was against him. An NPR junkie, he had blundered into a program on sensuality and the music of Ravel.

"Then again," he said softly, "we could forget breakfast entirely and—"

"No deal. When we've cleaned up after ourselves—a novel idea, I see, from the pile of dishes in the sink—it's time to try out those cross country skis in the garage. I was on a hunt for your recycling bin and saw a pair and a spare. Five miles straight uphill ought to burn some of the gunk out of your arteries!"

His protests were going nowhere. Feeling at loose ends, A. J. wandered down to the bedroom and pulled on a turtleneck, well-worn ski sweater and a pair of waffle-soled cross-country boots that had languished in the back of his closet for years. It was only then he saw the second pair, smaller, standing alongside them. Anne's. Apparently when Bea McDowell helped gather her things to take to the hospital thrift shop, they had missed the boots.

Lost in thought, he took his time heading back to the kitchen. Sam was already dressed herself, in jeans and the dynamite sweater from the night before. Standing at the sink, she didn't see him coming.

A. J. watched in silence as she shut the now loaded dishwasher. "Found these in the closet," he told her finally. "While you lace on the boots, I'll check out the skis. The bindings probably could stand some tweaking after all this time."

At something in his voice, she straightened, quickly turned and looked at him, then down at the pair of boots clutched awkwardly in his hand. Her forehead crinkled in a frown.

"Anne's. I didn't realize I still had these," he told her.

"I never thought about . . . they should fit, or close enough anyway," she broke eye contact as she reached out for the boots. "Thanks."

On an out-rush of breath, he forced a smile. "So, how about I tie down the skis and poles, scare up a knapsack while I'm at it. In the cupboard to your left, there should be some energy bars, trail mix, something. Lord knows, I for one am probably going to need every calorie we can scare up at the rate we're going."

"Sounds like a plan."

A. J. headed out the front door, with some difficulty closed it behind him, all the while the wind threatened to tear it out of his hands. At his almost immediate return, Sam looked up from cobbling together their emergency trail pack.

"Don't tell me," she said. "The battery's dead."

A. J. didn't trust himself to speak. Fumbling through the yellow pages, he punched a set of numbers into his cell phone, waited.

"Chuck," he barked, "Ferinelli here. Got a tow truck free? There's this car in my driveway. Four flats."

At what he read in Sam's face, he averted his eyes. The twisting in his gut intensified. "Ten minutes . . . fine, we're not going anywhere," he said into his cell, snapped the case shut again.

166

The silence in the kitchen was unbearable. "Whose?"

"Yours," he told her.

"Oh."

This was no random act of vandalism. Whoever did this must have recognized her quirky two-tone car, knew she was here—wanted to let them know it. The damage was neat and calculated. The gouges in each sidewall, malicious as hell, all were designed to be beyond repair. His own car sat there, untouched.

"Hope the guy takes credit cards," she worried, "I don't have towing insurance."

"Forget it. Chuck's a friend."

A former student, actually, he explained. A. J. had cut the ribbon when the towing business opened ten years ago. It wasn't a typical career path for a dual history and political science major, but the small shop was going great guns, enough so it was getting tougher for Chuck to take off a week every fall to drive out to Hyde Park and spend a week digging through the archives of his idol, FDR. So much for a liberal arts education.

"Okay . . . so, why this," Sam said, "why now? Some irrate student upset over their semester grades . . . *who* . . . ? I'm not even in the picture at Bolland any more."

"Some psycho must have been watching this house," A. J. said quietly. "Decided to take a cheap shot at one or the other of us. Who knows in that . . . hell-hole. The two-tone paint job on your car-door is hard to miss. Believe me, when I find out who did this—"

"Tires are fixable."

"Not these."

"All right, replaceable. Some things are priceless. You said that, remember, it's how you got me here." Sam drew in her breath. "I won't let you risk yourself doing something on my account we'll both regret—or waste one moment on that pond scum. My coat's still out there in the car. *We're going skiing!*"

In a blast of frigid air and hanging on to the door for dear life, Sam ventured out onto the front stoop, with A. J. close behind. Good timing. A stolid brute of a truck had swung into view around the corner two blocks away, the rumble of its powerful diesel breaking the morning stillness.

The driver was a graying, shaggy tree-trunk of man, one of Chuck's most recent hires apparently. With gruff efficiency, albeit

167

cursing the sheer hellish cold, the guy winched Sam's car onto the bed of his tow truck. Double checking the tie downs, the man began to wipe his hands on one of his flannel shirttails.

"Chuck says he'll call you," the burly tow-truck operator said. "We're swamped right now with dead batteries."

A. J.'s handshake was lost in the man's massive grip. "Thanks. Appreciate it!"

"It may be tomorrow. Chuck may not have four of these in stock."

"No problem."

But it was a problem. That fact had nothing whatsoever to do with availability of four all-weathers. *Something dark and menacing suddenly had sprung up between them*, A. J. brooded as he nursed his Toyota through the fresh snowfall. He couldn't put a name on it.

The best cross-country trails were west of town at the Grenville Ledges. Sam had been there, offered to ride shotgun, intent on finding the route most likely to have been plowed. On the roof, the skis were vibrating in the wind, a high-pitched wailing tremor of a sound drifting back along the deserted roadway.

As he drove, A. J. found himself reliving a churning nightmare brew of memories, starting with the visit from the state police the day Anne died, then the terrible look on Sam's face when she got her pink slip. Joel was part of it, wild-eyed and broken, as he shared the story of Julie Schechter's suicide. Of a piece was the burly tow truck operator's faintly raised eyebrows when he first took in the damage to Sam's car.

"Radar," Sam said quietly.

Easing off on the gas, A. J. glanced down at the speedometer, glad he hadn't made matters worse by triggering the brake lights. The roads were relatively clear and he had been pushing forty-five in a thirty-five mile-an-hour zone. If Sam hadn't called his attention to it, he wouldn't have even noticed the squad car parked alongside an abandoned gas station.

"Hope the guy is just on lunch break."

Sam forced a smile. "Could turn out to be one costly weekend."

It already was, in more ways than one. Evil once again had reared its ugly head among them, shattering any remaining illusions they might have had the situation at Bolland was getting any better.

A. J. flexed his hands on the wheel and shifted upright in the seat, tried to focus. At least the cop hadn't chosen to pull him over.

"I'm sorry," he said. "You're right, don't need to tell me. I've got to let go of this."

"Easy to say. Hard to do. I've been there—"

"Done that. I know."

They both had. A semi passed them headed east, shook the car with its wake.

Simple, he thought, a world where you made things, bought and sold and transacted, trading cold hard cash for commodities people could taste and feel and touch. Not like higher ed where your product was words and ideas that could uplift and nurture, or wound and kill in such highly civilized fashion, capable of such meanness of spirit.

"When I was an undergraduate," he told her, "my favorite prof—the guy taught 'art in the dark', bonehead art history, of all things—got canned because he hadn't finished his doctorate. They'd given him an ultimatum, said they would let him go if he didn't. The chair of his doctoral committee had died and the replacement was this ambitious S.O.B. trying to make a name for himself, stonewalling the guy's research after he already had been working on the thesis for five years."

"Sounds familiar."

"Yeah . . . well, we students started a drive to persuade the university to keep him. Hell, the guy won every damn teaching prize the school had to offer. More than a thousand students and alums signed the petition. It took three huge binders to hold the support letters—"

"And they canned him anyway."

"You got it," a muscle jerked along the edge of his jaw-line as he remembered. "Leading the charge was this asshole department chair who later wound up skimming off departmental funds to put an addition on his summer home. The young prof lost his job. For his ethical lapse the Chair got a sabbatical, paid of course, provided he rehabilitate himself, whatever that may have—"

Out of the corner of the eye he caught Sam staring out the window at a stunning board-and-batten barn and the pristine Mennonite farmstead around it. Behind the immaculate white farmhouse and blizzard-white stretch of lawn, a queue of black, lilac

169

and blue work clothes were strung to dry along a clothes line. Stiffened by the sub-zero chill, their movements in the wind were almost human.

"It looks almost like a family, doesn't it?" she said softly. "A little parallel universe out there, dancing across the horizon."

A. J.'s hands tightened on the wheel. "Reminds me a lot of my doctoral research. 'Tis a gift to be simple. We academics prize ourselves so on enlightenment, the life of the mind. Still, I suspect these so-called 'plain' folks could teach us a thing or two about what it means to live in community."

"My old department chair said something once when I was going through that garbage with my own thesis committee," Sam told him. "I've never forgotten it. *Where is it written, that emotional and intellectual maturity go together?*"

A. J. smiled in spite of himself. "So what you're telling me is, nobody ever said this was going to be easy."

Sam turned in her seat so she could see his face. Gently she laid a hand on his, still locked in that death grip on the steering wheel.

"What I'm telling you," she corrected him quietly, "is be darn careful. If we didn't know it before, we know it now. Those guys you're playing with are dangerous!"

Chapter Eleven

While the enormity of the job at Bolland hadn't changed as second semester began, A. J.'s mind set certainly had. At least now he was no longer facing it alone. The weekend with Sam in his house and bed quickly turned into a week, then a month. It was subtle, this business of accommodating one another. At first some of Sam's clothes and books, then gradually more intimate signs of her presence appeared. Sharing an inch of shelf room here and a drawer there—those things were tangible. Of late, he was finding it hard to separate where her life ended and his began.

Outside their four walls, the winter was turning out to be protracted and rough. It wasn't just the road conditions that were bothering A. J. about Sam's daily commute to Emmaline-Wattrous. Since the tire-slashing incident, he couldn't delude himself any more that the conflict at Bolland ended with the campus gates. He weathered a couple of nightmare-plagued weeks, then broke down and ordered a security system for the house, bolstered by a motion sensitive yard light. When Sam came home from Emmaline late one night, she found both a fait accompli.

"Paranoid, are we?" she scowled. "The neighbors are going to have a hissy fit at those flood lights every time a rabbit moves out there in the bushes."

He shared her laughter. But the look that went with it was anything but amused. They were careful on other fronts as well. *Julie Schechter, Joel, Dean Bremer.* An unspoken consensus kept certain topics out of bounds in their personal life.

Still, for all the potential land mines, the two of them slipped into a kind of spontaneous domesticity, taking turns with the cooking and all the other necessities of life with an ease and humor A. J. would not have anticipated, given their very different notions of what did, or did not, constitute creature comforts. While his own housekeeping defied description, as with her equations and proofs, Sam was a neat freak. Yet, for all her need for order and structure in her routine, there was a lot about Sam Pomerantz that A. J. wouldn't have anticipated.

An intriguing mix of introspection and a go-for-it energy permeated everything she did. Hectic as their schedules were, he found her dragging him back into life with an elan that both surprised and fascinated him. She even coaxed him into trying his hand at computer games, teased him unmercifully as he laboriously picked out the bass line on classic rock tunes that took him back to his younger college days. He would tuck the sight of her belting out "What's Love Got to Do with It" at a student karaoke night in the Emmaline rec center as one of those once-in-a-lifetime memories that leave a guy saying, "And *that* woman actually has settled on *you*, lucky devil that you are." Though at times she was almost shy, even reserved, in the bedroom all bets were off. Most inconceivable was the thought of ever coming back to that house again without her.

It was past eleven one night. All languid curves, still glowing from their lovemaking, Sam's body was stretched out full alongside his. She shivered at the rasp of the wind clawing against the window panes.

"If you're cold," he said, reached down and snagged the quilt, pulled it over the both of them, "I could jack the thermostat up a notch or two. It sounds like it's getting wicked out there."

"No . . . I'm fine, really. Just thinking . . . "

At something in her voice, A. J. shifted so he could see her face. "Want to talk about it?"

"It's nothing really," she said. "Just wondering. Anne obviously put a lot of herself into this house, the reproduction

172

wallpaper, the fabrics," Sam said. "It's lovely."

Her eyes were half in shadow, an intense bottle-glass blue, watching him. The questions he read there had nothing to do with interior decorating. For the first time in recent memory, A. J. conjured up the familiar images. *Sun and green grass, the sound of laughter in the distance, and Anne's face golden-tan in the late afternoon sun.* The Anne of his memory was as open and uncomplicated as Sam was introspective, complex.

"The answer is, yes," he said evenly, "Anne chose the quilt, actually with a lot of help from Bea McDowell, the drapes, all of it. She really loved roses. And do I ever think about that life, about Anne . . . sometimes, yes. And even then, thanks to you, I can finally think of her and our years together without first remembering all the pain that came after."

It was the truth. His life was changing, and he with it. In every way that mattered, it was Sam's presence he felt in what was becoming their space to him, *her* he missed when he returned home to an empty house. But then Sam herself would have no frame of reference, except what had to be the constant evidence of Anne's decorating touches within these four walls—little things, but telling.

"It's just that sometimes I feel like she's still here," Sam said softly, "whether you intend it or not. From the pillows on the sofa to the watercolors hanging in the living room."

"I don't need to keep this place as some kind of shrine to her memory, Sam, if that's what you're wondering," he persisted. "The sofa can replace the wreck of mine at the office. You can pick out a new one. I'll head out to the hardware after work and pick up gallons of latex . . . just say the word."

Sam shook her head. "I don't expect you to wipe out what she meant to you and I'm not talking about color swatches," she said. "You never volunteered before, and it never seemed right to ask, but I know nothing at all about what she or what your marriage was like. Only that you lost her and it almost destroyed you. I think I deserve to know."

There was no easy way to start, but she was right. "Where else . . . we met on campus," he told her, "in the Dean of Students office. She was the secretary and the students loved her. At ball games, she'd holler louder than anybody, sit in the bleachers at a football game in a foot of snow. Lord help the other team if one of our guys got hurt.

She would be down on those sidelines, breathing fire. At the school dances, she knew all the latest moves—"

"So you asked her out."

"Not exactly. I wasn't a jock, had two left feet and the line was way too long—all these young, single faculty types hanging out in her office on the way to lunch. Of course all are gone now, victim of one institutional blood-letting or another."

"Some things never change."

True enough. Except among those missing faces was Anne herself.

A. J. forced himself to continue. "I can't say it was love at first sight, on her side anyway. One day on my way out of the faculty-staff lot, I accidentally backed over her lightweight titanium bike, a major splurge on her salary and brand new—totally trashed the rear wheel. Grand gestures to make up for it were out of the question. I had just bought this house, was still juggling grad school debt and finishing my law degree at night, so I proposed we work out a repayment plan over dinner. Six months later—"

"She said she'd marry you."

"Turned me down," he shook his head. "Twice. Anne had this 'Rule' about dating the hired help, professors anyway. She hadn't finished college herself, was worried I would get bored with trekking through the woods on foot or skis and nights camped out in a sleeping bag together in front of the fireplace."

"Romantic."

"Too broke to turn up the thermostat."

"But you convinced her."

"Wore her down is more like it. We scared up a Justice of the Peace on a Friday and were both back at work on Monday morning. Ten years. We had ten years. We wanted a family, but after two miscarriages, had begun talking about adopting. When we found out she was pregnant, she quit her job . . . talked about spending time with our baby, sewing nursery curtains and hand-knitting booties, the whole nine yards. She was well into the second tri-mester and had a doctor's appointment in Ontowona. We always went together. Except at the last minute, George McDowell called an emergency divisional meeting. Anne decided to drive over the mountain herself, alone—"

A. J. broke off, this was a hell of a lot harder than he thought. "When the troopers showed up on campus, the meeting in Acton was

174

showing no signs of breaking up. I followed the two guys out into the hall and they just hit me with it—she was gone. She never made it to the hospital. Apparently the oncoming driver was drunk, speeding and lost control The road was glare ice, they said, Anne and the baby never had a chance. We were driving a junker at the time, a big old boat of a van. No air bags."

He didn't have to add how devastated, how guilty he had felt. His thoughts a downward spiral, A. J. caught himself mentally steadying himself as he traced the faint play of light along the curve of Sam's rib cage. At the thinly veiled hunger in his eyes, she shifted alongside him and the delicate porcelain of her flesh tightened in response. She was reading him like a book.

"And so this scares you—I scare you," her voice was trembling, "because by now it's pretty obvious I'm not the type to make a career of baking sugar cookies and doing needlepoint, never will be. And if you admit to having *loved* all that, then—"

Then he would need to come to grips with the 'Why?' of their intimacy. Why choose a woman like Sam, so different from the Anne he had so deeply loved, who had fixed herself so powerfully in his imagination.

His intake of breath was involuntary. "Sometimes," he said, "I get the feeling you know me better than I know myself."

Propped on one elbow, A. J. leaned over and kissed the soft down of her lashes, then trailed along the lids where they were at their fullest, arcing downward. A soft whispering sob rose in her throat, Sam's eyes had clouded from turquoise to a troubled gray.

"I'm not about to start casting stones at women who get off on being soccer moms. I don't pretend to understand any more than you do what it takes to survive or to heal," she said. "My baby—boy or girl, I never knew—would be ten by now, the same as the neighbor kid of mine, Ja Ron's age. Not a day goes by without some reminder, something that makes me wonder if I can ever feel comfortable about the prospect of a swing-set in the backyard, joining the PTA. Then too, my biological clock is a decider, with a mind of it own . . . "

She didn't have to spell it out for him. These were questions A. J. knew he could not honestly answer himself, including whether he truly had it in him ever to want a family, especially a child, again. Even Sam's child. On a sigh, he gently buried his face against the subtle curve of her belly—his heart aching for them both as he felt its steady rise and fall. A delicate film of moisture glistened against her skin. The taste was warm and bittersweet against his lips.

"That man must have been a fool," he told her, "having this— *you*, the life he could have had with you and just throwing it all away."

By way of answer she clung silently to him in the darkness. He lay there, listening to the sound of her breathing gradually steady, until she drifted off to sleep. Alone with his thoughts, it was nearly dawn before he finally slept himself.

Time, he kept telling himself, we both need time. A. J. found himself repeating the mantra whenever he saw those insidious doubts began to surface in Sam's eyes, flickering in her smile. Unfortunately by now, time was one thing Bolland College had in short supply.

By late-February merger negotiations with Emmaline-Wattrous had stalled. The deeper into the fiscal crisis A. J. dug, the more damage surfaced from overspending, administrative irresponsibility and the related coverup on the Bolland campus. His first cautious estimates were, if the administration and board were willing tomorrow to bite the bullet and set things right, the college had slid at least ten million dollars into debt over a seven-year period. The wolf was at the door.

Donor windfalls President Dornbaum kept predicting had not materialized, nor were they likely to do so. From after-hours conversations with friends of the school like Doc Radisson, it was clear wealthy alumni and area business folk were reluctant to expend significant dollars on bailout drives, at least as long as reckless spending continued unchecked and with the leadership itself suspect. Even if the Board were to mandate tight controls, wiping out the deficit would be tough.

"Donors want their names on buildings and on scholarships," A. J. explained to Sam, as he mentally worked through the options. "Not at the bottom of a red-ink drenched ledger sheet. To gouge so much money out of operating expenses and restore the gutted endowment, set things straight, is almost impossible."

"Meanwhile, students seem to be expecting more creature

comforts and high tech support facilities than ever."

"Understandable," he said, "when their own tuition costs are soaring. The competition sure is gearing up to meet those demands."

He couldn't avoid the bottom line any longer. Ten tautly written pages, drafted over a tense and troubled week, summarized both the problems and conceivable solutions, such as they were. Another week of sleepless nights behind him, A. J. finished his report and formally submitted a copy to President Dornbaum, as well as the chairs of the Board and the Finance Committee.

The reaction came within twenty-four hours. Dornbaum called a special Board meeting. The agenda consisted of a single item. His report.

Ten minutes into the meeting, A. J. realized how right Sam had been. At least a handful of vocal Board members had begun aiming their guns in his direction. Apparently he was the only one who hadn't known in advance that Board Chair Doc Radisson was out of town, just a little too convenient to be a coincidence. At the head of the Board table the Vice-Chair Harry Lentz sat thumbing through the document. Not truly reading it.

"Dr. Ferinelli, your report certainly represents a great deal of effort," he said. "Clearly your recommendations require even more staff commitment. At the outset, I want to make a motion we upgrade Dr. Ferinelli's administrative duties to full-time."

Warning bells were going off in A. J.'s head. Lentz wasn't zeroing in on the report or its contents, he was going after its author. Transforming his job into a permanent administrative slot could jeopardize tenure. It was a possibility A. J. had fought from the very beginning. As an at-will employee, the change could open him up to dismissal if the political winds started gusting in directions other than toward reform. Gauging by how fast Lentz's motion was seconded and by whom, A. J. knew his suspicions were dead-on-target.

The second came from Chip Bollenger, a retired corporate hitman for a local construction firm. Bollenger was notorious for his penchant for booze, available women and nasty political intrigue. His gorgeous trophy-wife hosted every major charity event in town at one time or another. But rumor had it for every dime of the millions he ostensibly donated to the college over the years, the guy managed to wrangle at least that much in kickbacks—including cost overruns two years ago on a library roof already beginning to leak like a sieve, sending water down into the top two levels of stacks.

A. J. kept his tone more steady than he felt. A public board meeting, with his champion Doc Radisson out of the picture, was not the time or place to start a verbal brawl.

"I want to thank Board member Lentz for the vote of confidence. But for the time being, I feel retaining faculty status gives my position greater credibility."

Lentz quickly backed down, withdrew his motion, although the look the man shot in A. J.'s direction bordered on smug. It was an odd reaction, one that left A. J. feeling anything but vindicated. Whatever the Board member had on his mind, it wasn't over yet. Although the report was ostensibly confidential, A. J. would have bet a month's salary the grim prognosis would be out there in the faculty rumor mill within an hour. At least, he had to hope, the approaching midterm grading frenzy might slow down even the most rabid of campus conspirators.

A. J. had problems enough of his own on that score. For the second night in a row, he was camped out in his faculty office. He had just begun to shove the last stack of completed student blue books into his briefcase—why on earth anyone would name the damn exam booklets after the color of the covers, he couldn't fathom—when Custodian Henry Putnam's voice startled him.

"Workin' late, Doc?"

The unexpected bit of humanity in the night should have been reassuring. It wasn't, given A. J.'s mood.

Putnam always had an unshaved, unwashed aura about him, had collected a gallery of gothic tattoos. More to the point, in the past month or so, there had been a subtle change in the frequency of the custodian's midnight visits, enough to make A. J. cautious about what he left around the office after hours.

"Ready to give the place a going-over, Henry?"

"You guessed it!"

Putnam's ragged grin stopped short of his eyes. His glance darted from desktop to file cabinet, only then lingering on A. J.'s face. The work surfaces were bare, a conspicuous departure from the usual amiable clutter in his work space.

"Gotcha cookin' the books again, Doc?"

"Oh, the ledgers you mean," A. J. forced a smile. "Not lately. It's midterms."

"Hard-ass stuff, figurin' out who stays and who goes," Putnam's voice had dropped to conspiratorial growl. "If half the trash-talk goin' on around the place is true, ain't none of us safe."

A. J. could have sworn by now the man was on some kind of fishing expedition. "Not much fun wading through red ink," he said carefully. "Though you realize that it is way too early to speculate about possible cuts."

Certainly Putnam would be among the more vulnerable personnel on the support staff, low in the seniority pecking order. The guy also had a drinking problem. Several times in the past year or so faculty had circulated petitions formally protesting the slipshod custodial work on the night shift. A. J. vaguely recalled Putnam had been placed on notice, even suspended for a brief period.

Muttering under his breath, the janitor had moved on. After what seemed like far too long a time given the number of offices along the corridor in need of tending, A. J. heard the fire door down at the far end of the hall slam. To his relief, shortly after that incident, the guy stopped showing up for work at all. Problem solved. A. J. didn't take the time to check with Personnel to confirm whether the absence was voluntary or forced.

The weeks were running into each other, the stress level escalating with every passing day. It was a Wednesday night the first week in March, past midnight, and the light from A. J.'s basement office window was the only tangible sign of life on campus. Students would return to campus from spring break during the weekend. Classes would resume Monday.

A. J. moved quickly from the thought of suntanned undergraduates trying to settle down after having hit the Ft. Lauderdale beaches or wherever they went these days on break, to an image of Sam, bikini clad, stretched languorously on an oversize towel near the water's edge. Her familiar smile invited him to join her. Exotic greenery dotted the white sand, with nary a student in sight.

Nice, but fiction. The new man on the night custodial staff, an amiable and no-nonsense young Hispanic, had finished his rounds of the social sciences corridor an hour ago. A. J. still had course notes to review.

Much as he loved his teaching, it would be so tempting, he thought wistfully, to take the Board up on their offer of a full-time administrative post. Given the motives behind the deal, he had no choice but to reject the notion. Instead he had all but taken up residence in his basement cell of a faculty office, racking up eye strain and caffeine hangovers.

Sam was remarkably patient about the whole business. At least tonight, as so many other nights of late, Sam had an after-hours meeting of her own, which meant A. J. had wound up scrounging dinner in the cafeteria kitchen. He didn't relish heading back to an empty house.

"I'll be fantasizing about a bottle of California red and a major backrub." It was the last thing Sam had told him on the way out the door that morning.

A. J. half-smiled, remembering. "Great," he had told her. "You realize, of course, what I'll be thinking about for the rest of the day . . ."

Sam had laughed. "I was counting on it."

So was he. Which made the insistent ring of his office phone now all the more jarring.

A. J. made a grab for the receiver, identified himself. In the process the office clock caught his eye. He couldn't imagine who would be calling his office at this hour. The voice was muffled, like chalk on a blackboard, grating. Unfamiliar.

"Clairbourne's on fire."

The line went silent. Dumbfounded, A. J. just stared at the receiver in his hands. Clairbourne was the college's oldest and largest dormitory. It had been mothballed over mid-semester break with its heat turned down to save money, take some strain off the already astronomic fuel budget. The two hundred students in the residence hall would still be home on break.

A. J. swore softly, a sick and nameless dread building in his gut. With shaking hands he punched in 911.

Chapter Twelve

Even before the dispatcher could identify herself, A. J. started to bark out directions to the dormitory. The voice on the other end of the line cut him off. Someone, the woman told him, had already phoned in the fire call.

What the hell ? A. J. hung up the phone.

Forget locking the office. He tore up the basement stairwell, pushed open the safety bar to the nearest exit, setting off the security alarm in the process. Perhaps the anonymous call about the fire was nothing more than a false alarm, a prank.

Two steps out into the night were enough to lay that bit of wishful thinking to rest. With no moon, the sky should have been a black, overcast smudge. Instead an eerie Aurora Borealis of oranges and yellows danced overhead, spreading unearthly shadows across the quad.   Rounding the corner of the faculty office building, A. J. stopped dead still, stunned at the obscenity of what he was seeing.

Ugly tongues of flame were shooting high above the roof of Clairbourne Hall. The entire east wing was ablaze. A thickening vortex of smoke swirled upward, driven by strong gusts. Punctuating the angry roar, a deadly hail of shards suddenly began exploding shotgun fashion from the darkened windows of the west wing, raining down on the sidewalk below.

"Dear God," A. J. breathed. By any other words, it was a prayer. If anybody was in there, they wouldn't have stood a chance.

The words died on the wind. He was running again, hard, in the direction of the inferno. Heroics were out of the question. The blistering heat stopped him a good hundred yards short of the door nearest to the street.

Like a human voice in pain, the wail of sirens was getting closer. But slowly, judging by the protracted rumble and audible shifting of gears, too slow. Maintenance had been arguing about fixing the damn potholes on the access road as long as A. J. could remember.

A powerful headlight froze A. J. in its beam, half blinding him. Several dark forms were already springing from the first of the enormous vehicles, hoses snaking behind them toward the closest hydrant. A helmet-clad face thrust itself toward his, demanding to know if the dorm was occupied.

"Spring break," A. J. shouted, knowing it begged the question. He scrambled out of the way. Through the billowing cloud of sparks and ash, a thin pencil of light was coming in his direction. It was the new custodian, Rodriguez, on the run with flashlight in hand. His bronzed face was streaked with sweat.

"You called in the alarm?" A. J. barked, guessing the answer before it came.

"Yeah. But they already knew."

"Is anybody . . . the dorm would have to be empty, right?"

A scowl greeted that pronouncement. Something like fear glittered in the young man's eyes.

"On rounds over break," Rodriguez said cautiously, "sometimes things would be out of place . . . different. But I never saw anyone."

"Security?"

"I called about it, but they thought I was just imagining it."

Good man. Rodriguez had the sense to report it.

Let's hope they're right and the dorm was vacant, A. J. thought. And if it wasn't, maybe the custodian's double-checking had scared off the interlopers. Night security had been short-handed over break to deal with the budget shortfall. It wasn't his choice for economizing, but then Personnel had to start somewhere.

Around them now, a small army of yellow slicker-clad firemen was mustering a frantic defense. Too little, far too late, A. J. realized with a shock. Flames had begun making their way with breakneck speed from room to room along the second and third floors of the west wing. Barking orders into a walkie-talkie, a stone-faced fire captain was ordering the crews back and out of the building. From a discreet distance, hose crews continued to aim streams of water toward the inferno. And still the blaze raged on.

Near dawn the air became even colder, freezing or close to it. Despite the heat of the fire, a treacherous veneer of ice began to build up on the quagmire of melting snow wherever the spray from the hoses touched. The bluish glare of the emergency lights floodlit the branches overhead, a ghostly canopy of icicles dancing in the wind.

Even a down jacket was no match for the brutal cold. Hands thrust in his pockets, A. J. took shelter next to a fire-singed cluster of yews. It was there a grim-faced Dean of Students Fred Urban caught up with him. Together, the two of them kept vigil—alone for the most part—until just before first light, when Sam joined them.

"Thank heaven you're safe," she gasped as she slipped into his arms. The cold made it hard to breathe much less speak. "I only now heard about it on the radio. You hadn't come home and I had fallen asleep w-waiting for you to . . . "

She was shaking in the bone-chilling cold. A. J. tried to warm her body with his, awkward given their bulky parkas.

"You shouldn't have come," his voice was rough with concern. "This is madness. It's damn cold out here."

"I thought . . . I kept hearing sirens, was so terribly worried—"

"The campus is on break, remember. The dorm was empty, so at least no one was hurt. We'll get through this somehow."

Sam knew better. He had always told her in the great scheme of things, dormitory capacity was one of Bolland's few unquestioned assets. Until now.

Mercifully, she didn't call him on it. Together the three of them stared at the flames—Sam, A. J. and Fred Urban—a silent despair the only visible bond between them. At something, a deep cracking groan audible above the roar of the flames, A. J. tensed and started forward, stopped. As they watched, mesmerized, the roof on

183

the east wing caved in sending a shower of sparks heavenward.

Shoulders hunched against the cold, Fred Urban managed one last bleak look in the direction of Clairbourne. His face was terrible. Then turning abruptly, he began picking his way across the sheet of glare ice toward the central campus.

"It's frickin' over, man," he said, choking back an oath. "May as well pack it in." Fred never even looked back.

"Oh, A. J., sweetheart," Sam's voice was a raw whisper of sound, "I'm so very, very sorry."

Until that moment he had still believed in the existence of miracles. On a single choked outcry, he drew her to him, burying his grief against the silk of her hair. Arms twined around his waist, she held him like a child grieving some nameless woe for which there is no remedy. In the chill rain from the fire hoses, it became impossible to separate where her tears left off and his began.

By morning Clairbourne was a smoking, burned out hulk and the unthinkable, fact. Still checking for hot spots, a small squad of tired fire fighters were poking through the ruins.

It was only after Sam had gone home at A. J.'s insistence, and all but two of the emergency vehicles had left the scene, that he began to recognize what had been troubling him ever since he arrived so many hours earlier—the incongruity of it all. From the very beginning the fire seemed to be everywhere on all three floors. With fire doors everywhere, why had the flames spread so fast to the west wing?

Fire Chief Dunkerly, his badge and identity finally decipherable in the graying morning light, had begun to cordon off the site with a web of garish yellow and black lettered tape. His craggy face lined with fatigue, the Chief's somber mien only confirmed what to A. J. was becoming brutally apparent. *Arson.* It was as if even somehow thinking the word had made it fact.

"Ferinelli," A. J. identified himself. "We met last night. I'm the Assistant to President Dornbaum."

"Dornbaum. I assume the President knows?"

A. J. hesitated, choosing his words carefully. Security had standing instructions to call the President immediately in such circumstances. But if Dornbaum knew, he had not made an appearance.

"Am I justified in assuming we have a problem here?" A. J. said.

"From the speed of the fire, the burn pattern," the Chief said quietly, "it would not be unreasonable to suspect an accelerant."

"Arson."

The Chief's eyes narrowed. "If you had to guess at a motive?"

Try several dozen, A. J. thought, for starters. But he didn't say it, reluctant to contribute anything that might feed the already hyperactive rumor mill out there.

"Like any college, Bolland has its problems, " A. J. shrugged, "but what kind of sick-o would do something like that? A disgruntled former employee or student, maybe. Or every unpaid vendor with a grudge. I wouldn't even know where to start."

"Ferinelli, you said your name is. We need to talk."

A. J. nodded, knew the choices. He could stonewall and wait for the campus attorneys, try to control the spin, the prudent way of handling things. Or he could let it all hang out and try to help catch the sociopath who did this.

"Not on campus," A. J. said. "But off the record, yes."

They found the bodies around noon. Three of them—all charred beyond recognition—were huddled together among the twisted metal bed frames from a third floor dorm suite. Watching the grim procession of black bags being carried from the wreckage of Clairbourne Hall, A. J. knew whatever hopes he had harbored for salvaging this place were becoming remoter by the second.

It was not the first time foreign students or some kid escaping the parental nest had defied the dorm-closure policy over a break. The custodian Rodriguez's paranoia was, as it turns out, dead on. This was homicide. Chief Dunkerly's job just got one hell of a lot tougher.

First things first. They needed to identify the victims.

"Classes start again Monday," A. J. explained to Dunkerly. "Until then it'll be impossible to speculate who's missing."

"We'll need a base camp, an office somewhere on campus," the Chief told him. "It would help to narrow the possibilities before

185

we start looking for dental records."

In fact, the news services did their job for them. Within the hour, Bolland's switchboard was breaking down under the call load from frantic parents worrying it was their kid in one of those body bags.

By late afternoon, a flurry of faxes from Malaysia with medical records put names and faces on the tragedy. Three young business majors had been in the wrong place at the wrong time. They had made the fatal mistake of using the empty residence hall and a fellow dorm mate's computer to work on their senior theses. In a foreign land, even the room in which they had died, wasn't their own.

By now Dornbaum was on the scene and in his element, making all the unctuously reassuring disclaimers. A. J. couldn't bring himself to stay and listen. Red-eyed from lack of sleep, he did the only sensible thing under the circumstances. He went home.

Sam met him at the door, ready with the coffee. She didn't need to coax him to talk, just listen. Through the entire agonizing recital, her eyes never once left his face.

"By the time they've cleared away the rubble," he told her, "anything left of Bolland won't be worth fighting over."

"For what it's worth," she told A. J., "I love you."

Words failed him. Sam had never told him flat-out like that what their relationship meant to her and he had no doubt what the admission cost her. Right now, knowing what she felt was worth one hell of a lot.

The Bolland Board met in extraordinary session to weigh the alternatives. There weren't many. For once privy to those discussions, A. J. ground his teeth, silent, while Dornbaum, Bremer and company tried to gloss over the train wreck.

In the awkward pause that followed the official pronouncements, Doc Radisson caught his eye. "Professor Ferinelli," he said, his voice guarded, thoughtful, "we would be grateful if you would give us your take on the mood on campus as well."

A. J. hesitated, tried to mask his discomfort at being put on the spot. So help him, he wasn't going to lie, not after standing there and watching those students die.

"Terrified," he said, "though at least in the case of the student body, most of them aren't here to witness the worst of it. Quite apart from the fact there's an arsonist running around on campus, in two

186

days classes are beginning and a large chunk of the student body is without a place to live. The media is having a field day with the story. Rumors are circulating wildly about student safety, or lack of it, and parents are livid. Not much good news in any of that."

Dornbaum appeared to be checking out the finish on the board table. Bremer's face was impossible to read but his eyes darted from A. J. to the president and back again, unsettling in itself. For once even Board member Harry Lentz didn't react at all, appeared unusually subdued. In some strange sense, A. J. found himself feeling sorry for the man. Whatever line the faculty cabal had been feeding Lentz about their tactics to save tenure by scuttling the merger, for Harry it never could have included pulling the institution down in the process. Especially not arson and murder.

A. J. had to believe, despite his dislike for Lentz and the handful of Board members who sided with him, they were acting out of what they saw as concern for the place. At least one thing had come of the fire. The seemingly unshakable alliance McDowell and his faculty colleagues had forged with the rump-parliament of conspirators on the Board probably lay buried somewhere in the charred wreckage of Clairbourne Hall.

Once President Dornbaum got his second wind, he became strangely manic and upbeat throughout the rest of the meeting. A. J. chalked it up to desperation. When in doubt, the President turned back every question about liability and insurance with vague, optimistic platitudes—including the possibility of coming out of this tragedy with even enhanced facilities.

A. J. had his doubts. Make a note, he told himself, to check out—exactly—the status of Bolland's insurance. In the morass of statistics and line items he had been wading through over the past few months, those particular expenditures had not attracted his notice.

Right now, other priorities commanded his attention. Students were arriving back on campus from break to a climate of uncertainty and fear. A. J., other staff and administrators had dug in the weekend after the fire, working the phones to rehouse students in motels and private homes. When those options were exhausted, they resorted to setting up a mass shelter in the college gym.

A hastily organized memorial service on Tuesday for the dead Malaysian business majors did little to calm the waters. In a packed and eerily silent chapel, a wan and distracted President Dornbaum spoke about pulling together as a community. It was the second such communal time of mourning in less than six months. Only this time A. J. was sitting on the flower-draped dais full of dignitaries. And this time the faces of what he always considered his campus family looked estranged beyond hope of repair.

George McDowell stared off into some distant landscape only he could see. Ellison, Slaughter—they were all there but scattered through the hall instead of in the politically safe clusters that had become their trademark at faculty meetings. Seated halfway back on an aisle, a visibly distraught Joel Van Susten had an arm around the coed next to him. A. J. saw it was the reporter from *The Voice*, Liz Diamond, who never had learned to spell harassment.

A. J. sat there stony-faced, mentally concocting a formidable list of not just unspell-able, but unprintable words that might be relevant additions to the young woman's vocabulary. Sam chose not to attend the event at all, arguing A. J. had enough to handle as it was, without ducking veiled comments about her presence—some traitor in the ranks from Emmaline-Wattrous. Instead, the night before the memorial service, she simply cuddled alongside him, battling sleep to let him talk himself out.

Eyes closed and head throbbing, A. J. took in the scent of her, a delicate hint of vanilla. She had been baking again. Little had he imagined that morning six months ago when she stood outside his office, asking for his help, he would so desperately need hers instead.

"Sam, intentional or not, someone killed those kids. If it's the last thing I do—"

"You'll find them," she said.

Would God she were right. For his part, A. J. had ceased to be sure any more. About anything.

Chapter Thirteen

The knock on A. J.'s office door was tentative, barely audible. At first he thought he imagined it. No one would have been expecting him there, with the dignitaries milling around on campus and the Fire Chief still out there, trailing an entourage of his own.

"Come . . . !"

Silence. The knock didn't repeat itself.

Suddenly alert, wary, A. J. shoved back his desk chair and crossed the room in a half dozen quick strides. Standing in the corridor, half-turned to leave was a young woman, a coed by the look of it, in jeans and dark wool sweater, carrying a ski jacket with multiple day-pass tags hanging from the zipper hasp.

A. J. couldn't see her face until she swung toward him, wide-eyed. Frightened. It took a double-take for him to recognize her as Liz Diamond, Joel Van Susten's erstwhile protégé on the student newspaper staff. A. J. had just seen the two of them sitting together at the memorial service for the Malaysian students.

"Liz. Come in."

Sensing her hesitation, A. J. positioned himself so she couldn't change her mind and take off down the corridor. "It's been a while," he said.

She came into the office, but just barely. A. J. made a habit of leaving the door open whenever students were present, though not this time. Even safely insulated from public scrutiny, Liz sat poised on the very edge of his battered sofa, ready for flight.

"Joel and I were at the memorial service."

A. J. nodded. "I was surprised to see him."

"He hasn't been back here since . . . "

Not since Professor Julie Schechter's suicide, A. J. made the connection. The toll was mounting. He hadn't noticed before, but it was hard to miss. The physical resemblance between the two women was subtle, there nonetheless. He wondered if Liz—or Joel himself—had caught it.

"How is . . . Joel's doing okay, then?"

Liz shrugged. "Still working for his dad in the car dealership. It's not exactly what you think you're going to wind up doing."

"No. I suppose not."

Whatever was bothering her, she wasn't going to share it without some coaxing. The ridge of her knuckles stood out white against the dark faux leather of the couch arm.

"Liz, I think you came here for a reason," he said quietly.

"Joel doesn't know I'm here."

"Understood." A. J. nodded. Waiting.

"He says . . . Joel says the fire—"

"What about the fire?"

Liz broke eye contact. A. J. could barely hear what followed.

"When the fire happened," she said, "Joel said he wasn't surprised."

"Joel *knew*—"

"Not in so many words," she said quickly. "Maybe he . . . Joel could just be imagining this. I mean . . . you know h-he's been through a lot."

The young woman was on the verge of tears and if A. J. had to hazard a guess, felt a heck of a lot more for Joel Van Susten than the young man suspected. Her intake of breath was audible, even over the low hissing of the radiator.

"L-last semester . . . before Joel left," she said, "some students had been talking about how ticked off some of the faculty were about

190

the administration. The merger, all that stuff. Supposedly, in one lecture, the topic came up about campus violence."

"Violence."

"Like in the sixties," she nodded. "Campus protests, civil disobedience—even illegal stuff like wire-tapping, Watergate break-ins."

Arson may be extreme, but it certainly fit the bill. A. J. leaned back in his chair, trying to diffuse the tension in the room. You could taste it.

"Maybe it was nothing," she said. "But Joel heard one prof tell his class the biggest mistake you can make is play by the rules when the other guy has thrown out the rule book. He went on about these political theories, something about ends and means—"

"*Who could blame someone trying to save the state, if they use any means to get there.*"

"Do it, what ever it takes, Joel said. That was it!"

"Machiavelli," A. J. told her. "From *The Prince*."

The work was a staple of his Poli Sci 214, Political Thought. By now A. J. had taught the course often enough to spit out on command at least a passable paraphrase of that classic bit of cynical early Renaissance real-politik.

"Only the prof wasn't talking about government, Joel said. He meant Bolland."

"It's pretty standard intro fare, Liz," he told her, not unkindly. He had played Devil's Advocate himself with Machiavelli. It was a good way to get at the basic concepts of political ethics.

"The thing is . . . Joel said it wasn't so much what the prof said. It was *how* he said it."

"Justifying violence—"

Liz cut him off. "*No*. Not just . . . hypothetical," she insisted. "Joel described it more like a warning, almost like the guy knew something awful was going to happen."

A. J. swore softly under his breath. Even in his worst-case scenarios, he hadn't allowed his suspicions to run so far afield.

"And Joel believes," he said slowly, "this prof may have been hinting at the Clairbourne fire."

Liz nodded. "I tried to tell him to be really careful. That he shouldn't go over there and—"

"Let me get this straight, Joel is actually going to take this on, *confront* someone on the faculty about this."

Her silence was a dead give-away. "He already did," Liz said quietly. "This morning, after the memorial service."

Joel had a great deal of time to brood about Bolland since Julie Schechter's suicide. Enough, A. J. had to believe, for the young grad to build up a powerful rage, if that was what was driving this.

Not that A. J. blamed him. "Where is he?"

"Home. Joel was heading out right after he saw the prof."

"Liz, this is no time to hold back. I think you're telling me you saw Joel afterward, you know what he said . . . even who he—"

"Joel wouldn't say, wouldn't tell me exactly what happened. I only know he looked terrible, worse even than at Julie Schechter's funeral. The minute he . . . when his car was out of the campus lot, I came running straight over here. There wasn't anybody else I could think to tell."

"Liz, you did the right thing."

"If something happens," she blurted out, "I'd never forgive myself!"

Agitated, the young woman was on her feet and A. J. joined her, knew what she was thinking. Joel could be at risk, big time. But then Liz had left out a piece of the equation, important.

"And the professor," A. J. said evenly. "Did Joel say . . . I think you know who he was going to see. You have to tell me, Liz."

Her voice was shaking, almost inaudible. "Sociology. Professor Ellison."

Dead silence greeted Liz's revelation. Ray Ellison. When crossed, the man could be ruthless. Joel had no idea what he was unleashing when he went over to Ellison's office, no idea at all.

"You have to listen to me," A. J. said. "I want you to forget you ever heard any of this—forget you shared it with anyone. Stay clear of me in public. Above all, don't go anywhere near Ellison. Go to class. Don't speculate with anyone down at *The Voice* about what's happening on campus."

Liz nodded. A line of moisture had begun to well up along her lashes. Lip caught in her teeth, she bit back the tears that were threatening to overpower her.

"The students are scared as it is."

"I know," he said. "But don't worry about Joel. I will deal with this."

192

"P-Please . . . don't tell him who—"

A. J. flashed a ragged hint of a smile. "Of course not."

Weeping openly now, Liz was looking at the floor, unable to meet his gaze. He wanted to tell her it was going to be all right. The truth was, as things stood, if Joel was right about faculty involvement in the Clairbourne fire, nothing and no one would be safe until someone got to the bottom of this. What had Liz Diamond said about the examples Ray Ellison had used—phone monitoring, mail tampering? Sam's tires had been small potatoes if Joel's theory were to be believed.

By the time A. J. grabbed his parka, locked his desk and file drawers, then the office, Liz had disappeared. It would be at least a two-hour drive to suburban Pittsburgh, Joel's home base. Pray God, the heart-to-heart he had in mind with his former student wasn't already too late.

A light snow was falling, like dusty white clouds sifting down out of a gray sky. Traffic was light, the road slick. It would be dark soon. A. J. used his cell phone to check in with Sam while he gassed up about ten miles out of town, but caught his home answering machine. Thursday. Sam, he only now remembered, had some kind of a staff training session. She wouldn't be home until nine or later.

A. J. kept the message short, told her he had to go out of town. Careful as he was not to reveal the purpose or location, he was even more careful his tone didn't alarm her.

"Roads are probably too bad to make it back tonight," he said, "and it's going to be late before I'm done, so I'll phone you in the morning on the way home." He added one more thing before he clicked on the End button of his cell phone. "Sam, be careful."

Back on the highway, A. J. found himself struggling to take his own advice. Road conditions toward the west were deteriorating fast. His thoughts were churning like the eddies of snow swirling across the treacherous asphalt. *Ellison.* A. J. couldn't shake the images of those cold, inscrutable eyes staring back at him from the doorway of the chapel during the memorial service. Isolated, detached from it all. Still try as A. J. might, he couldn't bring himself to see his colleague, gas can in hand, meticulously dousing the threadbare carpeting of Clairbourne, corridor by deserted corridor. No, if Ellison or any of his colleagues were involved, it had to be far more circumspect than that. Instigating, goading maybe, but from a safe distance. The man was too damn smart, too manipulative, to actually light the match himself.

It was unlikely, A. J. had to hope, a disgruntled student would be that pliable, that open to suggestion. There were plenty of staffers who had reasons of their own to hate the place. Whenever the going got tough fiscally, those were the ranks which took the first hits. One thing was certain. In confronting Ellison, Joel accidentally had taken a powerful whack at the hornet's nest. If anything, the last six months had taught A. J. how tough it was to stay clear of—much less to divert—the vicious swarm that was bound to follow.

The exit ramp A. J. wanted was marked clearly enough. A quick bit of research at a convenience store confirmed the route from there. Straining to pick out the street signs through the wet windshield, A. J. slowed down. Two rights, then a left before he steered the Toyota to a stop outside a meticulously landscaped split-level. With a sinking feeling A. J. saw Joel's silver ice Cobalt was nowhere in sight.

The doorbell triggered results on the third try. It was hard to put a face on the silhouette—male, stocky build, above average height—standing in the flood of light from the entryway. Judging by the body language, the person was none too receptive to visitors.

"I'm looking for Joel. I understand he lives here," A. J. said.

"And you would be—?"

"One of his professors from Bolland It's important . . . I really need to talk to him."

The man shrugged. "Joel moved out several weeks ago."

"Apartment?"

"No idea. He didn't leave a forwarding address."

Transparent as lies went, A. J. thought, suppressing a smile. Joel Van Susten was utterly incapable of deceit and his father obviously was cut from the same cloth. This was a self-made man, owner of one of the state's largest car dealerships, but this wasn't business, it was personal with a heck of a lot more potentially at stake. If the senior Van Susten was trying to protect his son, it was time to take another tack.

"The name's Ferinelli," A. J. said. "You may remember me, from Parents' Weekend. Joel was one of my advisees."

"He talked about you from freshman orientation nonstop all the way to your course in Pre-law—says you single-handedly helped him graduate early. Yes, Joel respected you a great deal."

With that the senior Van Susten abruptly stepped aside and ushered his guest into the tastefully furnished hallway. It was only then A. J. realized he had been standing out in the bitter windchill without a parka. His hiking boots were leaving murky puddles on the pristine white carpet.

"I understand it's late," A. J. told him. "But it is absolutely imperative I find your son."

The senior Van Susten's face was a study in contradictions—concern and skepticism, for starters. "Joel drove over to campus this morning," he said, "called later to say he wasn't coming home."

It was as if a tight band were constricting his rib cage, making it tough for A. J. to breathe. "Did he tell you where—?"

"No, and he was damn evasive about why he decided not to come home. That's not like my son. Doc, I expect you to tell me what the hell is going on out there. The dorm fire, those dead students, now all the talk about arson . . . the story made headlines in all the Pittsburgh papers. If you think my son has anything to do with any of it, I can assure you—"

"No," A. J. said emphatically. "It never once crossed my mind. Joel is one of the most decent young men I've ever taught. He's principled, courageous. Maybe at times a little too much so."

The senior Van Susten's eyes narrowed. "I never went to college, but I'm smart enough to know when something is bothering my son. He's changed, ever since he went to that godforsaken place, especially since the young professor died."

His was the desperate fury of a father doing battle for his son over things beyond his experience, things he couldn't understand, much less explain or put in any kind of a context. The time for diplomacy had come and gone.

"Your son is one of the brightest students I ever taught," A. J. said. "I think . . . would be willing to bet, Mr. Van Susten, that Joel has stumbled on something, or thinks he did, about the dormitory fire at Bolland. If you know where he is—"

"My son has been through enough already. It damn near ruined him."

A. J. winced. "You have a right to be concerned. These people play rough. I have reason to believe Joel went to Bolland to confront one of them. He could have accidentally gotten in—"

"You're telling me he could be in danger."

"Yes."

A. J. sensed he was only confirming what Joel's father already suspected. Though tanned and ruggedly handsome, everything about the man suddenly seemed ten years older. His shoulders slumped and his face had taken on a faraway look.

"Joel didn't tell me any of this," his voice had taken on a strained, brittle edge. "But now his phone call makes sense. Truth is, I don't know where my son is. But it occurred to me as we've been talking . . . there *is* this friend of his, a classmate he hangs out with a lot. The kid didn't graduate with Joel, apparently sat out a semester to work for some security firm."

The senior Van Susten threw out of the name of a small town about an hour east, a good two-thirds of the way between Pittsburgh and the Bolland campus. It would mean an exhausting drive back in the direction from which he had just come. Still, A. J. felt as if a tremendous weight had just been lifted from his shoulders.

"Did he ever mention . . . could it be Duncan, Andy Duncan?"

Joel's father shook his head. "If he told me, I've forgotten. I just remember something about the guy studying for civil service exams and a lot of . . . weird bullshit about the CIA. I met him once a long time ago in this strange little blip on the map up in the foothills about a half-hour from campus."

The profile fit, it had to be Duncan. A. J. let out his breath in an audible sigh of relief and his hand shot out in the man's direction. "You've been a big help," he said. "I had better be on my way."

Joel's father hesitated, then gripped the hand extended his way as if some sort of understanding had just been reached between them. The two men made eye contact, reinforcing the bond.

"I just wanted to say," A. J. began, "you won't—"

"Regret this," Joel's father said, his voice hardening. "Damnit man, I already do, but what choice have I got. I promise you this, if anything happens to my son . . . "

He didn't have to spell it out. The senior Van Susten was not one to let life run roughshod over him or one of his own.

A. J.'s leather-soled shoes skittered on the icy sidewalk as he beat a path back to the Toyota. He had lost an entire hour, two if he counted the round-trip, driving to Pittsburgh. At least the man had

196

given him a shot at finding the needle in the haystack, ferreting out the place where Joel could be hiding. Technically a borough, the crossroads community of Wheelandale was popular with students on limited budgets who wanted to live off campus. Low rents made it worth the commute. But the real bottom line was it gave older students a place to hang out beyond the reach of campus security.

It was going on ten-thirty by the time A. J. hit the Wheelandale Borough Limits sign. He had no idea where he was going, had to hope the place didn't totally roll up the sidewalks after dark. The main drag consisted of boarded-up stores and decaying clapboard duplexes, fronted tight against the highway. A. J. kept a weather eye out for Joel's flashy Cobalt, to no avail. He had just passed the last cluster of ramshackle sheds and outbuildings when he finally spotted a seedy-looking bar up ahead, its official parking lot a virtual traffic jam of pickups and rusted-out junkers crammed in together. The place was still open, that much was obvious. Even with all the Toyota's windows frozen shut, the deep growling bass of the jukebox was beginning to set his teeth on edge.

Time to reconnoiter. Abandoning the car on the side of the road, A. J. stumbled a quarter-mile through a cratered minefield of frozen potholes on the shoulder in virtual darkness, muttering under his breath the entire time. Inside the bar the lighting was nonexistent, the smoke thick enough to slice and shrink wrap. The decibel level made speech impossible. It could take half the night just to get anybody's attention.

"I'm looking for a guy . . . name of Duncan," A. J. shouted as the bartender gave him the once-over. The less said of Joel's whereabouts, the better.

"Never heard of 'um."

"Wire glasses, average height," A. J. told him. "Works as a night guard somewhere around here—security."

"Scrawny guy. Used to be a student over the mountain at Bolland?"

A. J. nodded, his expression unreadable, helped along by what passed for ambiance in that black hole of a room. "Sounds right," he said.

"Check out the old Morrison place. Center of town at the blinker, take a right—about a mile down the road on the left there's this falling down barn. Fieldstone foundation, ya can't miss it. The

197

farmhouse you want is up the hill a couple hundred yards."

The bartender's attention was already turning elsewhere. At the far end of the bar, two locals were squaring off drunkenly over a video game.

"Thanks," A. J. nodded. His exit elicited about as much notice as a pebble tossed into a murky pond.

Safely outside, he filled his lungs with the chill air to clear his head. The bartender had to be talking about the intersection a scant half-mile back. Hanging a U-ie on the deserted highway, A. J. backtracked toward the flashing yellow caution signal before turning out into the countryside. Once off the highway, civilization ceased. The road was a maze of frozen ruts, shoulder-less, with trees spaced at odd intervals along the ditches. Deserted.

A quarter-mile ticked past, then a half. Out of nowhere a surreal blur of movement in the field off to his left caught A. J.'s eye—billowing clouds of ectoplasm—enough to cause the hairs on the back of his neck to bristle. Abruptly, the Toyota careened into what had to be major sinkhole, bottomed out.

"What the . . . ?"

With some difficulty, he managed to bring the vehicle to a shuddering halt. As he sat staring intently into the blackness, the ghostly specters finally began to take on a recognizable shape.

Cows, he muttered to himself, his hands still shaking on the wheel. *Spooked by a damn herd of dairy cows.*

The islands of black in their hides had been invisible against the darker patches of wind-swept ground—making the ragged animals appear like strange free-form shapes, ethereal clouds that levitated over the pasture. If he needed proof positive the whole business of the fire was seriously getting to him, the throaty rumble from the Toyota's damaged muffler was more than enough to do the trick.

At least he still had the presence of mind to clock the miles. As advertised, at point-nine he spotted the outline of broken timbers thrusting upward at odd angles. The bartender said he would see a barn, but this one had lost those bragging rights a long time ago. Clicking on the turn signal, A. J. veered off onto a grassy lane that turned out to be more of a two-track than a driveway.

Straining for traction in the frozen clay, the Toyota crested a slight knoll then wound through a copse of trees before A. J. caught

198

sight of his destination. Still farther up the hill, lights blazed from one end of a weathering wood-sided farmhouse. A. J. cut the engine, sat for a minute looking out at the sky—clearing now in spots and dotted with stars.

Damn dark, he thought, *once he turned those headlights off.*

Somewhere in the direction of the house a dog was barking, a harsh growl of a sound that sent a shudder of awareness through him. The Toyota was a goodly distance from the road, no turnaround in sight in the middle of the open field. Whoever was in the farmhouse would have long since concluded someone was out there.

No sense waiting. Snagging his down parka from the backseat, his hands thrust in the pockets, A. J. started to pick his way cautiously up the barren hillside.

Chapter Fourteen

"Who's out there . . . ?"

The sound of a door flung open and a sudden blaze of halogen from the yard light, preceded that demand. A. J. stood riveted on the spot, silhouetted and vulnerable in a wide-open expanse of snow-caked grass. The only thing between him and the farmhouse was what appeared to be an abandoned wellhead, too far away to offer any cover.

A. J. decided to take a chance. "Duncan. Andy Duncan!"

Going on instinct, he made sure his hands were visible, palms up and empty out in front of him. Jaw tight, he mentally braced himself for what ever came next.

"Who wants him?"

The voice was conceding nothing. In the dead silence that followed A. J. could have sensed a pin drop. What he heard instead was the contact of metal on metal—cold, ominous. He had never heard a shotgun being readied to fire. Some things one just knew.

"Ferinelli here," he called out over the wild pounding in his chest.

Silence was followed by a cautious, "Prof . . . ?"

A. J. counted to ten and started to advance. At least if he were wrong about who was on the business end of that gun, maybe it would be tougher to hit a moving target.

"How the hell did you find me?"

"It wasn't easy, believe me." A. J.'s laughter died as quickly as it began.

By now he was close enough he could begin to put a face to the shape that had moved into the open door frame, outfitted in combat boots and summer issue military camouflage. From the sound of it, Andy Duncan was preoccupied with engaging the safety mechanism on one of the most intimidating pieces of artillery A. J. had ever seen, close-up anyway.

"Glad you decided not to use that."

Andy forced a sheepish grin. "Me, too."

A. J. followed his former pupil into what turned out to be a low, drop-ceilinged living room. As his eyes adjusted to the minimalist light, he could make out a ragged scattering of overstuffed furniture, a sawed-off barn door passing itself off as a coffee table littered with mugs, books, a pair of binoculars, and a half empty box of shotgun shells. Against the far wall, a fireplace was producing an inordinate amount of smoke for the size of the blaze.

"Downdraft problems," A. J. speculated.

"Guilty. Know anything about flues?"

Someone else was in the room. The voice was coming from the sofa in front of the gaping fieldstone hearth. As A. J. watched, a very much alive and well Joel Van Susten stood and turned to face him, hand extended casually in greeting.

A. J. blinked, took in his former student's *There-Is-No-Planet-B* tee-shirt and the stubble along his jaw, topped off with the sheepish grin of a little boy caught in the cookie jar grin. Forget power handshakes. Uncoiling like a spring under tension, A. J. strode over and pulled his former student into a bear hug that needed no explanation.

"Damnit, Van Susten, you scared me witless!" The reality was a lot cruder. "What in the hell's going on here?"

"You're lucky," Joel said, "ten steps farther without identifying yourself and Wyatt Earp here was talking about letting you have both barrels."

A. J.'s smile faded. "So it went that well, huh."

Joel winced. "You heard."

"Ellison. Get real, man—do you have any idea what you're playing around with?"

"Funny," Joel said, "that's exactly what Ellison told me. Almost word for word."

A. J. swore softly under his breath. At the anger in his former professor's voice, Joel at least had the good grace to look contrite.

"Van Susten, what in the Sam Hill did you tell the man?"

First things first. Andy produced a couple of beers from the kitchen and the three men settled down on a huge and very uncomfortable braided rug in front of the unruly blaze. The beer tasted like ambrosia after his hellish drive.

A. J. couldn't help notice, before Andy joined them, he also made sure both shells and shotgun were conspicuously within arm's reach on the sofa. *Kids*, he thought, *playing cops and robbers. Out of their depth.*

"I wasn't sure what I was going to say to Ellison, or even that I *was* going to see him," Joel admitted. "Driving over from Pittsburgh for the memorial service for the Asian students at Bolland, something kept boiling away in my head, not anything I could pinpoint. Then I saw the guy standing in the chapel, smugger than usual, so damn above it all. There was no way I was going to let it pass."

After the memorial service, nobody was much in the mood for small talk, just in getting the hell out of there, Joel said. The campus buildings were all but deserted. He met up with Ellison in his office—alone, sitting at his desk. Even when he was enrolled in the man's class, the relationship between professor and student had been strained, vaguely comfortable.

Eyebrows raised, Ellison just stared at the former student leader standing in his doorway. "Wrong floor. Ferinelli's office is downstairs, Van Susten," he said.

Joel ignored the jab. "Civil disobedience. Last semester you spent a lot of time on it. Just curious, but would you say the Clairbourne fire fit the mold? The administration wants change—so burn the place down."

Ellison just laughed. But he put down the book.

"Sociology . . . I recommend it highly. Politics aren't for the faint of heart, Van Susten."

202

Damn, the man was enjoying every minute of this, toying with him. Joel didn't trust himself to speak.

"I recommend reading Machiaveli," Ellison said, casually hefting the burgundy-bound volume on the desk in front of him, "highly. Though I would have thought your *guru* Ferinelli would have thrown out the name a time or two, at least. Freshman elective, right—political thought."

"Cut the crap," Joel bristled. "And leave Ferinelli out of this, we're not talking theory here. Those students are *toast* and somebody out there lit the match."

Ellison's smile froze, Cheshire-fashion, then vanished. Much as he thrived on provocateur tactics in his seminars, this was escalating way beyond academic thrust and parry.

The professor's eyes narrowed. "I'm not sure, Van Susten, I like where this conversation is going . . ."

"Correct me if I'm wrong, Prof. But last semester you were pretty damn *sure* about the moral imperative of lighting fuses."

"That's what this is about—you came here to accuse me of something, Van Susten. In that case, up front, I ought to warn you—"

"Libel, I know," Joel told him. "Ferinelli had a whole unit on it and all the bullshit about free speech and academic freedom. Slander's pretty mild given what's on the plate around here."

"As in . . . exactly what."

"Try arson. Murder. Then of course, there's always the old stand-by conspiracy to commit."

Ellison's face was dark. It seemed hawk-like terrible. "I want you out of this office. Now."

"Or what . . . you'll call Security? Or maybe you'll just settle for dialing 911 once you're sure the match is lit."

Conversation ceased. Ellison just looked at him.

"Kid," he said, "you don't know what . . . or with whom you're fooling."

Joel had a hand on the doorknob. "I'm beginning to get a damn good idea," he said.

All through Joel's terse narrative, A. J. listened without comment. Privately, his head was reeling at the sheer audacity of what the student had attempted. Hands shaking, Joel managed to fish a joint from the depths of his backpack, lit up—inhaled and then while his face slowly composed itself, he let his breath go in a lung-cleansing rush. The bittersweet taste of cannabis filled A. J.'s nostrils.

For a split-second, the professor was young again as the lingering scent began to stir in the dark recesses of his memory banks, a vicarious throwback to his own rebellious years as an undergrad, conjuring up all manner of principle-fueled danger. A decade too young for the marches and protests some of his colleagues had experienced, he too had known his share of midnight plotting—righteous, angry. All of it, he winced, a young man's game, blissfully oblivious to the costs.

"Not the brightest thing you've ever done," the professor said finally, "but gutsy."

He wasn't talking about the pot. At least Joel had the sense to look sheepish. "I figured that much out quick enough," he said. "Ellison meant it, man. All I wanted was to get out of his office without coming to blows. I couldn't think of a safer place to lay low than out here."

"Maybe not *that* safe!"

For some time now, Andy had been standing at the front window, nursing his beer. He adjusted the slat blinds, finally shut them altogether.

"I hate to rain on your parade, Van Susten," he said, "but a set of headlights out there seems to be lost . . . or looking for something. That's the third time it crisscrossed past our driveway in the last five minutes."

A. J. arched an eyebrow in Joel's direction. His former student shrugged.

"Paranoia," Joel said. "With Andy it's an occupational hazard. You'll get used to it."

"What ever. Their left headlight is a dead giveaway," Andy shrugged, "it tracks high."

A. J. crossed to the window, convinced enough to check for himself. The slat blinds were cheap and not quite level. Even with them half-closed, he caught the two red pinpoints—tail lights—moving off along the road. It wasn't exactly a major arterial.

"Heading out of town," he speculated. "Probably just the bar closing. The guy's probably so drunk, he can't find his own driveway."

Andy scowled. "Come daylight, maybe we should start

tracking license plates."

A. J. nixed that one. Shifting gears, he began pondering excuses to strong-arm the two of them, keep them holed up here long enough for him to have a frank talk with the county sheriff. He had met the man once at a campus function. Right now an extra patrol or two out this way wouldn't hurt, either.

"For future reference, I would keep an eye on the rear view mirror anyway, Van Susten," Andy grumbled. "Just to be on the safe side."

"Yeah, right. Man, after my run-in with Ellison I had trouble just keepin' the damn car on the road. Ten minutes in the thug's office is enough to do it to anybody."

Without thinking, Joel had extended the half-smoked joint in his former professor's direction. A. J. chuckled, shook his head.

"Pass," he said. "One go-round as an undergrad was quite enough. I would think the last few hours were enough to sober anybody up."

"Funny . . . it's had the opposite effect on me."

"So, let me get this straight," A. J. said slowly. "Ray Ellison thinks you suspect he had something to do with the Clairbourne arson."

"The guy never admitted or denied it."

"Would *you* have, in his shoes?"

"Okay, so maybe I was over-reacting, goading him," Joel admitted. "I got pissed off at the guy's colossal ego. It was like he was jerking my chain, caught up in some I-am-the-font-of-superior-knowledge act. I hadn't intended to go after him quite so hard."

A. J. fought back a smile, knew where the young graduate was coming from. He'd been on the receiving end of Ellison's hubris-driven spleen a time or two himself.

"And you really came away from your pissing match believing—"

"Ellison is mixed up in the fire. I'd stake my life on it. Maybe I was out of line to turn up the heat, but it smoked out the truth."

An unfortunate choice of images. The butt of the joint cradled between Joel's fingers was getting uncomfortable. With an impatient gesture he flicked the glowing stub in a long arc into the grate.

"And the business about the 911 call?"

The former student looked pained. "All bluff, I just threw it out there. The Pittsburgh papers said somebody had called just after the fire was set. It could have been Ellison."

"Or some drunk taking a shortcut across the campus . . . it could have been anybody. I assume Ellison didn't react to that either," the professor wondered out loud, "one way or the other."

"In so many words, no. But man, you should have seen the guy's face. If he would have been packing a gun—"

A. J. had played poker with Ellison once. The guy rarely lost and never his cool. He must have been pretty upset if he let the mask slip, even a crack.

"If you're right," A. J. said slowly, "and it was Ellison . . . "

"Yeah."

It was A. J.'s turn to stare intently into the fire grate. By now the contents were more ash than substance.

"Sorry, Van Susten," he said finally, "everything you've told me plays great in the tabloids but none of that is going to convince a grand jury that Ellison set the fire."

"Great. So, bottom line, I'm screwed. The guy's going to sue my ass from here to Chicago."

"Not necessarily."

Joel and Andy just stared at him. A. J. explained.

"Academics talk for a living. They don't pour solvent on dorm carpeting," he said. "What if—and note I'm only saying, *if* Ellison were capable of talking someone else into lighting a match, then *who*."

"You want a list."

"A name," A. J. said. "At most we've got to be talking one, maybe two or three people involved. More and it would have been all over campus by now."

"A student," Joel speculated. "Some Sixties wannabees—freshmen mainly—seem to get off on all of Ellison's come-the-revolution stuff. It gets old, fast."

"Doubtful. For one thing Bolland was on break. The dorms were closed."

Joel scowled. "Okay then . . . maybe one of Ellison's faculty cronies. Like Slaughter."

"Whatever crazy tactics my colleagues on the faculty may have used in the past to shift the tide in their direction, murder isn't one of 'em," A. J. told them. "Revolution can sound good over a

206

couple of beers in Enoch Slaughter's basement, but on some freezing night on the quad, I don't think so."

With some half-hearted assistance from Andy Duncan, Joel ticked off a short list of staff who had gotten their share of dirt in recent years. In the end none of the candidates that came easily to mind seemed likely arsonists. It was one thing to spout off or vent to any and all comers, quite another to burn down dormitories.

Which left not much, A. J. concluded. Either that or they were looking in the wrong place entirely.

"Impulse," he said aloud. "All this is far too rational."

Through most of this Andy Duncan had been poking occasionally at the coals with the fireplace tool Joel had abandoned. A log was handy so he settled it on the grate. As it caught, the heat on the threadbare rug where all three of them were sitting began to escalate considerably.

"Drugs . . . booze . . . sex," Andy said. "The Big Three motivators, right. I mean, if the guy who did this isn't nuts, something had to trigger—"

A. J. sat up so fast that both younger men looked up. Startled.

"What did you say?" A. J. said.

Andy started to repeat it. Something clicked in A. J.'s brain.

"Booze and a grudge against the college," he added it up. "A hell of a temper—"

"The custodian. Nights."

"Henry," A. J. said, fishing for the rest of it.

"Putnam," Andy filled in the blanks. "He was so slow, the guys on my floor called him Putt-Putt. It drove the guy wild. He used to go around shuffling and muttering about setting a match to the place—frying us all in our beds."

Henry. Henry Putnam.

You've got a working phone here?" A. J. said.

Andy nodded brusquely in the direction of the sofa. Half-buried, muffled under the latest issue of the *Utney Reader* was a beat-up receiver, off the hook and trailing about a mile of incredibly tangled phone cord.

A. J. got a dial tone, punched in a sequence of numbers. "I'd like the phone number for Putnam," he said. "Henry. Anywhere in this area code."

Fishing in his pocket for a pen, he scratched out a sequence of

207

digits on the cover of the *Reader*, flashed a thumbs-up sign. Bingo. Except a quick test-dial drew nothing more than a recorded disconnect notice. After a second try, A. J. shoved the receiver back under the stack of newsprint where he had found it.

"Too easy," he said. "Phone's not in service."

Andy shrugged. "So tomorrow we make a run over to—"

"No way!" A. J. was on his feet. He riveted both young men with a look that would have stopped a charging bull.

"You're already in deep enough, both of you. Sniffing around on campus is my job and believe me, I'll do it. It's time for the police—"

Joel started to protest. A. J. wasn't in the mood.

"Van Susten, I just spent a hell of a lot of time cooped up in my Toyota tracking you down. Your old man made it plain my hide is on the line if anything happens to you. Not that I needed any reminder."

"You drove all the way to—?"

"Pittsburgh . . . and back. Damn straight. Now get this—if I catch either one of you on campus, I'll nail both of your shoes to the floor. Or have you jailed for trespassing. Whatever it takes!"

A. J. had never considered his an imposing face, much less handsome, although Sam told him once that outraged or determined, his features took on the edge of a man not to be messed with. For a second the two students just looked at him.

"Scar-r-ry." Joel ended on a low whistle under his breath.

"I meant it to be."

"You ever watched the *Sopranos*, Prof?"

Fighting a smile, A. J. stared him down. "Don't tempt me!"

Chapter Fifteen

It was three in the morning before any of them—Andy Duncan, Joel or a totally exhausted A. J.—packed it in for the night. At Andy's insistence, the two young men spent a good half-hour running an informal "security check" on the farmhouse. In A. J.'s book they needn't have bothered. To put it mildly, Andy had the bases covered. The FBI or CIA, A. J. decided, was missing a hell of a bet if they underestimated the guy's potential as a recruit.

Unlike A. J.'s Toyota sitting out on the knoll, a fixed target if there ever was one, the guy had stashed Joel's Cobalt under cover in a shed at the back of the property. The barking A. J. had heard was a German shepherd, also Andy's, chained to the back porch of the farmhouse. The array of computer gear strewn around the house was more sophisticated than the stuff in the campus administrative building. For good measure, alongside the base to Andy's phone was an array of off-the-back-of-a-truck electronics that could have stocked a small retailer, among them a basic phone-tap detector and a creditable anti-bugging device.

"Expecting company," A. J. laughed. "I'm impressed."

Andy flushed. "Okay, I'll admit it. As a kid I was a James Bond junkie."

"Figures."

A. J. sacked out on the sagging hulk of a sofa, anticipating a restless night. But when half-dozing, he finally checked his watch again, it was already 6 AM. It took a good minute to figure out where the heck he was. Through the groggy haze, he remembered. *Sam would be worried sick.*

Still dressed in the clothes he wore the night before, he got back on the road easily enough. Not, though, without a major caffeine fix. Joel and Andy hadn't stirred, so he got a pot of coffee going and left a note. Ten minutes from Bolland, A. J. broke out the cell phone.

He must have caught Sam in the shower. The answering machine kicked in before she picked up.

"Good morning, sleepyhead," he said.

"A. J., where in the world—?"

"Almost home," he could read the worry in her voice. "I was hoping maybe you didn't have to go into work until—"

"I'll be here," she said.

"Sam . . . thanks."

She broke the connection. After a glance at the speedometer, A. J. reluctantly opted for discretion. He was already pushing the limit, not too smart on only three hours of sleep.

Sam's car was in the driveway, the porch light still on from the night before. She must have been watching at the window. Half-way up the walk, he saw the house door open and then she was outside—in his arms, still clad in her black satin, spaghetti-strap nightgown with one of his fleece jackets thrown over it hastily against the cold.

"Hey, no worries," he teased as he took in her uncertain frown, "though if I'd have known what a little absence would do—"

Sam was trying to look stern. She wasn't succeeding.

"Not my idea of romance," she said, "keeping me up half the night worrying."

"You weren't the only one."

It hadn't occurred to him before spending last night on Andy's couch, it might be tough getting to sleep without her curled alongside him. Funny, he thought, what you miss.

Sam shivered. It was damn cold out there. Solicitous, arm around her shoulder, A. J. drew her with him into the house.

"Now," she said, "out with it. Did you fall off the face of the

210

planet? I half-thought of trying the morgue."

"Pittsburgh."

A conversation stopper. Sam just looked at him quizzically, waiting for the other shoe to drop.

"I was looking for Joel Van Susten, finally caught up with him at Andy Duncan's place in some crossroads burg a half-hour west of here, the one where all the upperclassmen hang out."

"Duncan. I don't remember the name."

"Joel's friend," A. J. said. "Andy's a senior, but sitting out this semester, definitely not the remedial math type. I know you've seen him on campus—he's one of those techno-geeks who likes wearing camouflage and goes around talking in computer-ese most of the time. Either he's headed for a career as a spook or doing jail time, take your pick."

Sam's frown deepened. "And you needed to go the see the guy, *why*?"

"Joel has gotten himself in hot water," he said.

What followed was an understated recap of what had transpired the day before, starting with Liz's visit and up to but not including A. J.'s concerns about Ellison. Sam had never been one of the guy's fans. The last thing A. J. wanted was to worry her any more than he already had, but then confidentiality and need-to-know ethics had never been an issue between them. She understood, it was part of the drill. While A. J. showered and changed, she busied herself in the kitchen putting the finishing touches on breakfast, a heck of a lot healthier than his caffeine and cholesterol-laced habits before Sam turned up in his life.

"That's my job . . . breakfast detail," he said. "You're spoiling me. Royally."

"After all your midnight marauding, I can't imagine how you're going to put in a full day over there."

A. J. shrugged. "I've thought about cloning."

"Vitamins, the seven food groups, a good night's sleep are a heck of a lot cheaper."

"I have a better suggestion," his voice was low. "How about I call in sick, we just hang out for a couple of hours. Just what the doctor ordered."

Aching and in need of her, A. J. drew her onto his lap and rested his forehead against the warm curve of her cheek, closed his eyes. "I love you, Sam," he said.

On a sigh, she finally eased out of his embrace, busied herself with the dishwasher, cleaning up the counter—anything, he got the uneasy feeling, that eliminated the need for conversation or eye contact. A. J. was polishing off his breakfast, had almost finished a second cup of coffee when she finally settled in again at the table across from him.

"I know you probably think I'm a whack job," she said slowly, "but there are times I still have a lot of trouble imagining myself—either one of us—doing this."

His eyebrow arched. "This?"

"The whole Ozzie and Harriet thing. Here you are, an unrepentant workaholic . . . and me, lugging around enough issues to confound old Sigmund himself."

A. J.'s throat felt tight. "Dealing with Bolland, I'm discovering, is enough to give anyone 'issues'. Believe me, if I had known what was lurking out there, I would never encouraged you to put yourself at risk with that grievance."

"But then, we might not be sitting here together, either. Win or lose, that wretched grievance taught me I had choices—my life didn't have to be some endless treadmill. In exile that first month at Emmaline, when I finally figured out you weren't a clone of every man who had ever turned on me or tried to trash my life, I knew it was up to me to pick up the phone . . . and I still had your number. A *sign*, I told myself."

"You aren't the only one on a learning curve here," he said quietly. "Work may not be considered a character flaw, but in my case—you're right, it comes damn close. I know I haven't exactly been there for you lately . . . can't even imagine what I would do if you would—"

"For the record, I have no intention of going *anywhere* any time soon. All I ask is, next time you're contemplating one of these midnight junkets, just bear in mind maybe we *both* need to get out of town! And if you want company when you finally decide to reconnect with your long-lost family out on Long Island, the answer is, *Yes.* "

A. J. was on his feet, coaxing her into his arms. A smile had begun to tug at the somber lines of his mouth. "How about Thanksgiving," he said.

"Thanksgiving it is . . . provided you survive 'til then. From

212

the sound of it, your last 24 hours were enough to wreak havoc with anybody's longevity."

"A lot of miles on the old chassis, I'll grant you."

On a sigh, she laid a hand against his shirtfront, levering some distance between them. "You know me by now, I'm not one for ultimatums. But so help me, Ferinelli, if tonight you aren't home by—"

"Six . . . on the dot," A. J. chuckled, "I promise."

His optimistic prognosis hadn't taken into account his Day Planner. He had given up walking to work over a month ago and the drive to the Bolland campus was too short to figure out how to juggle teaching a course and dispatching a growing stack of must-do memos, all before eleven o'clock, followed by a luncheon chat with a couple of irate faculty. As it turned out, his brutally over-scheduled morning turned out nothing at all like expected.

Half-way through his eight o'clock Intro to Politics class, A. J. looked up from a quick consult of his lecture notes to see a disheveled, ashen-faced Andy Duncan standing in the classroom doorway. Decked out in his usual army field gear, the guy looked all the world like a terrorist training-camp reject who had tried, unsuccessfully, to run a live ammo course.

"Prof—sorry . . . it's Joel," he gasped, "they've picked him up."

"They."

"The cops."

That got A. J. off his customary perch on the desktop. "When?"

"An hour ago."

Thirty pairs of eyes—instantly alert—were taking in the drama playing itself out in front of them. *Thank heavens for those review sheets.* A. J. had stashed the folder full of them in his briefcase. While Andy braced himself against the door sill, doubled over clutching his side and still fighting for breath, A. J. fished out the stack of the prep notes and tossed it on an empty desk in the front row.

"Your lucky day," he told the class. "Here's a twenty-minute head start on your cram sessions. We'll pick up again Monday."

Then he was out the door, dragging a hapless Andy with him. The public corridor of one of the main classroom buildings was no place for details. Knots of students already were starting to gather, waiting for classes to change. Once outside on the quad, a quick glance at the administrative lot narrowed their options.

"Your car," A. J. said. His own was parked-in by the campus maintenance truck.

"Loading zone. Behind the library."

"Keys."

Andy obliged. They were still clutched in his fist.

"Prof, I just knew . . . turns out the car we saw last night was the cops."

"Who tipped them off?"

Joel's friend shook his head. "No idea. We were still asleep. But they knew Joel was there. That's all I know."

"Arrested."

"Questioning . . . it's what they said anyway."

"Lawyer?"

"No. He told me to find you."

Andy's ancient VW started on the third try—sputtered, hung on. Before easing it into traffic, A. J. retrieved the cell phone from his suit jacket pocket, held it out in Andy's general direction. A fender-bender was not what they needed right now.

"Dial," he said, barking out a quick set of numbers.

Andy scrambled to comply. "Now what—?"

"Give . . . speaker phone."

With the phone balanced precariously on the dashboard, A. J. muscled his way through his friend Jake Burrough's staff until he hit paydirt. "Jake . . . it's Ferinelli here. I'll meet you at the county lockup. A student, Joel Van Susten—you met him during Sam's harassment fracas—has been hauled in for questioning. It's about the dorm fire."

"Van Susten," Jake sounded puzzled. "Vitals . . . remind me."

"Student body president, newspaper editor. He may have accidentally fingered one of the do-ees in the Clairbourne fire."

"Another student?"

"This don't-mess-with-me sociologist by the name of Ellison. Joel all but accused the guy of lighting the match."

"And now it's payback time," Jake said, "having the kid picked up by the cops."

214

"It occurred to me. How quick can you get to the station house?"

"On the way—I'll beat you there." Jake broke the connection.

By the time A. J. nosed the car into a vacant spot a half-block from the county detention center, whatever fatigue he was feeling from the all-nighter out at the farmhouse had metabolized into a surge of raw adrenalin. No sense trying to park closer. Jake Burroughs, he noticed, already had squeaked half-in and half-out of the last spot in the attorney lot, not quite ticket material but close. It would be hard to miss a vintage oxidized red 1977 Datsun 280Z with a spoiler and evidence of keying along the doors on the driver side from some sore loser of a client back in the day. The gouges were rusting.

At the intake counter, Jake was gesticulating wildly at a desk sergeant. The word Miranda, from the look of it, was beginning to make an impact.

It was hard to stand by and do nothing. But it's what A. J. found himself cautioning a shellshocked Andy to do while Jake vanished into the bowels of the department for the better part of a half hour. Short, A. J. concluded, given the possibilities. Judging by Joel's face when lawyer and client surfaced, even that interval of time had been more than enough.

"We're out of here," Jake told them gruffly, aiming his young client toward the double doors.

Not arrested. So far so good.

Once on the sidewalk, Joel made a beeline for the curb where he promptly retched his guts out. Watching the young man's agonizing struggle as he propped himself up against a fire hydrant wearing the same save-the-planet message tee from the night before, A. J. felt a white hot anger building inside him that had no outlet. It always kept coming back to the same bottom line.

What kind of professor—what kind of human being would do this to anyone? And it had to be Ellison behind this. No other explanation made sense.

Joel finally seemed to have weathered the worst. Still hunkered alongside the curb, his complexion had stabilized from puke green to putty gray.

"My office," the attorney told them. "Now."

Jake steered his client in the direction of his dubiously parked Datsun. A. J. followed with Andy in the VW. After two flights of stairs, with Andy trailing conspicuously behind, the ragged procession navigated the maze of corridors leading to Jake Burrough's tiny excuse for a law office. The conference room was unpretentious by any standards, stuffed to the gunwales with an oversized table and a circle of mismatched chairs, wall-to-wall credenzas with law books, all with the patina of rejects from a secondhand store.

"Facts. Let's have 'em," Jake insisted.

Ensconced morosely at the far end of the table, Joel looked incapable of rational thought, much less speech. A. J. took pity on him, quickly sketched his own visit to the farmhouse last night.

"This morning, when I left," he finished, "the two of you were still sacked out, Duncan. What the hell happened?"

"Eight-thirty two—I remember checking my watch, if that's important—we start hearing noises," Andy said. "By the time I crawled out to check who was ripping off my front door, some dude was kicking it in. Backing him up were three WWE thug-types, packing hardware on their hips you wouldn't believe."

A. J. could. And did. It must have given the two young men the scare of their lives.

"Joel wasn't even anywhere in sight—was in the can, in fact." Andy remembered. "But when they called out his name, demanded to see him . . . I mean, it was pretty clear they'd been watching the house, knew he was there."

So the car Andy saw with the malfunctioning headlight wasn't a coincidence. A. J. was half surprised that he himself hadn't as yet been paid a visit since his own Toyota was parked out on the open knoll close to the farmhouse all night—its license plate visible, hence traceable enough.

Andy wasn't finished. "There was enough of a posse out in the yard to start a coup in some Third World republic, ditto the hand-on-the-guns stuff. First thing you know there are about a dozen guys tearing apart the place. Right off they see the shotgun shells and start hassling me about a permit—no problem, though. And it wasn't loaded. So then they grabbed Joel and started grilling him."

"As in . . . ?"

"Had we heard about the dorm fire. Where had we been that night," Andy said. "It was my week to work nights. They sounded like they knew that already. When Joel said he couldn't remember at

216

first—they got tough and started pushing for him to come downtown. They didn't have an arrest warrant, still he didn't have a hell of a lot of choice."

Through all this Joel had been staring, pale and silent, into a mug of steaming tea one of Jake's minions had set in front of him. When he finally spoke, it had the effect of a bomb going off under the cramped conference table.

"Ellison," he said. "Ellison told them I had showed up in his office, threatened him. He said I claimed to know things about the fire . . . that I was acting suspicious—"

Some half-truths are worse than outright lies and Ray Ellison's qualified as rock-bottom. A. J. was on his feet so fast his mug and the last of its contents careened sideways, leaving a dark, murky trail behind it on the already battle-worn desktop.

Whatever he intended to say, the shock of upturned faces stopped him, cold. That, and his friend's quiet drawl.

"Vengeance is a dish best served cold, pal," he said.

A. J. blinked, hesitated, sat down. *Murderous rage.* As a scholar he had cultivated an image of what it meant—pure semantics, a dispassionate, clinical head-game. Violence had been as remote to him as Norse warriors marauding along the coasts of western England. He had caught a shadow of what it meant only twice before, once when that drunk behind the wheel killed his family and then the day he found out what Bremer had done to Sam.

So much had happened since. There was Julie's death and the fire in Clairborne. It was before A. J. fully understood how evil could root-and-branch permeate an institution he so deeply loved, to which he had dedicated his life. This was his student that Ray Ellison was trying to destroy, gutting the integrity of the professor-student covenant in the process.

A. J. believed in this pact with all his heart. Students came into class and suspended disbelief. Professors shared both truths and untruths and everything in between, their job to get at the heart of the difference. It was a mutual learning process which left both sides the richer for it. To violate the bond was nothing less than a violation of human spirit.

Hands shaking, A. J. righted the mug, containing the spill as best he could with a utilitarian stack of napkins Jake's receptionist had left behind. He caught the awareness, the concern, in Jake's eyes.

"So Ellison actually told the police he thought you did it, set the fire?" A. J. said.

"Not exactly. The cops didn't say that in so many words, but they inferred they were putting two and ten together. And when I didn't have an alibi at first . . . "

Smart, A. J. had to admit. For the sociologist to lie outright and try to pin the blame on Joel would likely have boomeranged and cast suspicion down the road on Ellison himself. As it was, the sociologist could wrap himself in platitudes about seeing-something-saying-something and pass himself off as a concerned citizen just doing his job.

"Where *were* you the night of the fire, Van Susten?" Jake persisted.

Joel winced, mumbled something unintelligible. A. J. knew survivor guilt when he saw it, but then Jake wasn't letting his client off the hook.

"Spit it out, man!"

"Here in town. At Liz Diamond's . . . you met her, the student reporter, now editor of *The Voice*. I spent the night at her place."

A. J. fought a smile. Jake wasn't through.

"The cops believed you."

"Maybe." Joel shrugged. "I don't know. They said they'd be checking out my story."

The attorney nodded. "Once more, I need to hear it from you this time. Not your professor or Andy's version. What *exactly* did you tell Ellison?"

Joel repeated to Jake what he had shared with A. J. the night before. Almost word-for-word, A. J. noticed, though clearly not rehearsed. This was the act of someone desperately trying to make sense of an experience larger than the emotions can comprehend. Which only left the business about the 911 call reporting the fire. Joel said the police pointedly reminded him he was already on record as the one who had phoned in Julie Schechter's suicide.

Jake didn't miss a trick, was bound to ask. "And did you? *Was* it you who made the call—about Clairbourne?"

"No. Hell, no. Liz and I were . . . it was the middle of the night, her apartment's a good mile from campus. I heard about the fire on the news like everybody else!"

"Except the guy who set it," A. J. reminded him.

218

"Or knew it had been set," Jake said. "Take your pick."

True enough. If Putnam had set the fire and Ellison had egged him on, then it was credible enough that Putnam had made a call to the sociologist to spill his guts about having done the deed. It wasn't out of the question either that Ellison had enough qualms to report the fire.

As for Joel, it was also likely the authorities would consider Liz Diamond a credible witness and put the Bolland grad far from the scene. Which meant for all their tough talk trying to shake the student's story, the cops didn't seem to have a clue who the actual arsonist might be.

"Ferinelli, I assume you were planning on taking your part in all this to the cops, including your little excursion out to the farmhouse?" Jake said.

A. J. nodded. "They just beat me to it."

"Time to 'fess up," Jake told him. "But not alone. And not without another run-through."

"Fair enough." In fact, A. J. no longer trusted himself to be objective, about the fire, Ellison—any of it.

"Just one thing, for the record," A. J. said, his full attention riveted on Joel and Andy. "What Ellison did . . . that is *not* what academe is about."

"If Ellison was caught up in this, how in the . . . ," Joel bit back whatever choice expletive was boiling up inside him, "how can the man live with himself, twist things to make it seem that I . . . ?"

The utter devastation in Joel Van Susten's voice tore at A. J.'s insides. A young man's loss of faith was not a pretty thing to watch.

"Spin doctors," A. J. told him. "We faculty are the ultimate masters of the black art. Ellison's bullshit about Machiavelli aside, it is possible he truly believes he is somehow on the moral high-ground here. The verbal pyrotechnics are just part of the game. You make him mad, call his bluff and he retaliates, pulls out his weapon of choice—rhetoric."

"But people get hurt," Joel said. "And that's for real."

"Yes."

"What if Ellison really did talk some poor jerk into it—into setting the fire?" Andy demanded.

"Same principle," A. J. shrugged, "only now he's covering his ass." A muscle jerked along the ridge of the professor's jaw, but he managed to leave the intellectual what-iffing at that.

Andy shook his head. "Some profession."

"Doesn't have to be that way. Any more than all cops—or lawyers—have to wind up crooks." A. J. shot a quick glance in Jake Burrough's direction. "Present company excepted, of course."

Jake scowled. "You passed the bar. I still don't see you tacking an Esquire behind your name, buddy. It can't be any nastier than what you've gotten yourself into."

The two of them had been feuding for years over whether A. J. was ever intending to practice law—despite the professor's passing the bar exams first try. It had taken Jake a second go-round.

"Incorrigible," Jake shook his head in disbelief, "you all should hear yourselves. The cops are thinking about locking one or more of you away for twenty to life and you're still debating the state of the universe. Van Susten, do me a huge favor—get your butt in grad school and let us moral relativists run things. It'll be a damn site safer with you and Ferinelli on the other side of the—"

"Admit it," A. J. said, "not half as interesting!"

For the first time that morning, Joel managed what could have been construed as a smile. As an ex-officio career counselor, Jake had pretty much hit the nail on the head.

By the time Jake Burroughs had laid out an iron-clad set of do's and don'ts for Joel and Andy, and had nailed A. J.'s hide to the wall about what he was or was not to reveal, imply or state on his visit to the authorities, it was after one o'clock. Andy and Joel took off for the farmhouse. Grabbing a stand-up lunch, the two older men headed back to the police station.

Under Jake's watchful eye, A. J. methodically laid out his version of Liz Diamond's initial visit, the trip to Pittsburgh and night with Andy and Joel in the farmhouse. He also made a point of putting Joel's confrontation with Ellison after the memorial service for the Malaysian students in the context of Professor Julie Schechter's death some months earlier.

"Van Susten was vulnerable and Ellison can be tough to take," A. J. told the detectives. "As a professor the guy's style has always been combative—he likes to challenge students to hit back intellectually. If he was actually goading Van Susten, it could explain everything that followed. Who knows what you or I or anyone might have said under the circumstances."

Any other suspicions about his faculty colleague, A. J. kept pretty much to himself, except to suggest campus politics were approaching a flash point well before the Clairbourne fire. A lot of talk was going around, in general, of an inflammatory nature.

When asked point-blank about prime candidates for the arson, A. J. singled out Henry Putnam, albeit with a few cautious provisos. "The guy had a drinking problem . . . plus one enormous chip on his shoulder," he said. "The students rode him pretty hard. Before the guy was fired from Bolland, supposedly he wandered around fantasizing out loud about burning the place down. Probably just idle talk, though booze maybe helped his resolve along."

"Could someone have talked him into it?" one of the detectives said. "Pushed the button and aimed the man."

A. J. shrugged. "Possible. Yes."

The detectives moved on. Despite their poking around the subject, they didn't appear to buy a conspiracy theory. Apparently the assumption was the arson was an inside job, someone who knew the campus and its buildings well. At least the name Putnam seemed to come as no surprise.

In passing, one of the detectives let slip to Jake the nature of the chemicals used to start the fire. Spirit master fluid—life blood of any college in the old pre-computer days. Trouble was, the stuff could have been found stored anywhere on campus. No longer used, tough to get rid of. The cans were a disaster waiting to happen.

It was beyond tough for A. J. to unload his version of things, without agenda or embellishment. Still, that was essential if his former student was going to cease to be a viable suspect. By the time he and Jake left the police station, he sensed at least he accomplished that much.

A. J. thought about hoofing it back to campus, but when his friend offered him a lift, he was glad for the company. Truth was, his still-smoldering anger over Ellison's treatment of Joel was bothering him more than he cared to admit. For all his reasoned, reassuring platitudes to Joel and Andy about professional ethics, for a split-second there in Jake Burrough's office, he had been operating on the basis of deep loathing for what his profession had become. Most sobering was to admit how readily he himself—under the right circumstances—might have been tempted to violate his own code of ethics in order to help his student.

221

"A crisis of faith, buddy," Jake said. "Classic."

A. J. winced, shook his head. While he recognized the diagnosis in Joel, he had never thought of himself in those terms.

"You give me too much credit," he told his friend.

"Why the hell do you think we've stayed friends all these years?" Jake growled. "It's who you are, Ferinelli—a cockamamie Pollyanna, a perfect foil for a wily old curmudgeon like me. It's been true as long as I've known you. And from the look of it, that Van Susten of yours is a chip off the old block."

A. J.'s laughter had an uncomfortable edge. "An occupational hazard . . . and why it was so hilarious comedian Shelley Berman chose us University of Chicago types to skewer back in the day. If a guy thinks too much, he can wind up schizoid over whether the proverbial glass is half full or half empty. While pondering the eternal truths, a guy winds up dying of thirst. Look at my track record. When Rousseau and the innate goodness of humankind stuff was starting to wear thin, what did I do? Switched disciplines and gave Dad's law and order a try. Not much principle in that kind of career path."

Jake wasn't laughing. "Van Susten is young . . . on as righteous a tear as he is right now, he'll pick himself up, try again. The Duncan kid's too cynical, way too juiced on conspiracy theories to let much of anything get under his skin."

Turning into the faculty parking lot, Jake kept the motor running. "Any way you cut it, it's you, my friend," he said quietly, "you're the one, Ferinelli, I'm worried about."

Chapter Sixteen

By the time Jake dropped A. J. off at the campus, it was four o'clock—a ten-hour day if you counted the drive back from Joel and Andy's place and the legal debacle that followed. The desk in his faculty office was a disaster area and he had promised Sam he would make it home by six, come hell or high water. Meanwhile, the message counter on his voice mail had maxed out at thirty-five. Grabbing a pen and handy sticky pad, he started to wade through the accumulated messages.

Students wanted notes from classes they had missed or a crack at a makeup exam. One tearful coed needed an appointment to talk about a term paper that had spontaneously combusted on her hard drive. Sam called to say, Hi. Someone—a woman's voice he didn't recognize and who didn't identify herself—left a message to check his email.

The worst of the bunch came near the end, a testy command-performance message to show up in the President's office immediately. It was followed by a cryptic request from Doc Radisson to phone him after close of business. Odd, the two messages coming together like that. A. J. replayed them quickly, looking for nuances. That the President was behaving out of sorts was nothing new. What Doc Radisson wanted, A. J. couldn't even begin to speculate. The guy wasn't one for idle chitchat unless it came to sailboats, and late March was way too early for that.

First things first. Dornbaum did not take kindly to unreturned messages. Almost as an afterthought, A. J. fired up the computer just long enough to check his email. Buried among the spam and complaints was an address he didn't recognize. Curious now, he called the document up on the screen.

Stunned, he had to read the brief text twice before he could connect sender and message:

Check the insurance. The business office routinely let bills like insurance 'ripen'—Bremer and Dornbaum's notion of economizing. Watch your back. P.

The initial leaped out at him. Only one name made sense. Priscilla, Bolland's former bookkeeper.

Even in his worst nightmares, A. J. hadn't contemplated her scenario. To be fair, working through the budget and ledgers wouldn't necessarily have revealed that kind of problem. Judging by past practice, checks often had been cut in a timely fashion and then tucked away in a drawer for lack of funds.

If Priscilla's email was right, the bottom line was devastating. The lost student housing would be irreplaceable. Potential lawsuits arising from the fire, both reimbursement for student property loss or damage and claims from parents of those three foreign students, would be staggering—enough to send Bolland into Chapter 11. Permanently. The President's office was clear across the quad. Armed with a printout of Priscilla's terse on-line revelation about the insurance, A. J. clocked the distance in less than two minutes. When Dornbaum's secretary saw him coming, she punched a button on the intercom without so much as a simple, Hello.

"He's here," she said. Unceremoniously, she aimed him at the inner sanctum.

What struck A. J. immediately was that Dornbaum was not alone. The President was ensconced in his usual spot on the massive black leather sofa. Dwarfed in a matching leather wing chair off to one side was the Bolland attorney, briefcase at the ready on his lap.

"Professor Ferinelli," the President said. "You're joining us."

Leave it to the guy to restate the obvious. The President gestured toward a second wing chair, uncomfortable under the best of circumstances.

"I thought it best to have Attorney Moran sit in on this. No objections, I assume."

A. J. nodded cautious assent. Whatever was going on, this was not your run-of-the-mill power play. "I just caught your message. You wanted to see me."

"I'll get straight to the point," Dornbaum said. "Under the circumstances your resignation would be preferable to . . . let's just say, the Board would appreciate your handling this in a civilized fashion."

A. J. felt a sharp wrenching in his gut. "You've lost me," he said, considerably calmer than he felt.

The President smiled, shook his head. "I'm talking," he said, "about your resignation from this institution, effective immediately."

The silence in the room stretched out well beyond an awkward conversational pause. "I remind you, President Dornbaum, regardless of the status of my administrative post, I am still a tenured member of the Bolland faculty."

"Moot," Dornbaum corrected him.

"Legally it was absolutely clear when I refused full-time administrative status, I would not in any way be compromising my tenure as full professor."

Bolland's attorney was a vicious little man with a predilection for pinstripe suits, the bravado of a snake-oil salesman and an ego to match. "I refer you to the fine print in the handbook, Professor. You'll find an interesting caveat under *I* for *Incompetence,* although malfeasance will also do nicely. Either clause makes no distinction between a professor's teaching or administrative responsibilities."

With a shock A. J. realized where this was headed. Sam's warnings were dead-on about the top dogs using him, letting him take the fall for their own ongoing fiscal mismanagement.

"And the grounds?" A. J. said, already aware of what their answer would be.

"It has come to my attention you either failed to detect or chose to ignore the fact the insurance on Bolland's physical plant had inadvertently lapsed before the tragic fire at Clairbourne."

Priscilla's email was too little, too late. "You found your scapegoat," A. J.'s mouth felt stiff, "intended this all along."

"In light of your distinguished past service, the Personnel Committee of the Board, despite their insistence on termination, is prepared to offer you a severance package, close the files."

A. J. had to hand it to the man, Dornbaum was a survivor. At least the man had the decency not to gloat, said nothing. By forcing the President to take an administrative assistant to clean up the mess, the Board merely had handed the man a way to weasel out from under. And from the sound of it, Lentz and his buddies on Personnel had prevailed. Even Doc Radisson, as Board Chair, had been unable to stop them.

With A. J. gone, both Dean and President could claim ignorance. No one would be around to contradict them. All the full Board would see is that A. J. had missed a fiscal problem so heinous it led to catastrophe. The attorney shoved both a sheaf of documents and a pen across the steel and glass coffee table between them.

"Note the last clause, Professor," he said. "We are prepared to pay you out until the end of the year. Your signature is required at the two X's and then again on the following page."

"And if I refuse."

"We'll fire you outright," Dornbaum said. "Here and now. In any case, clean out your desk by five o'clock. Security will stand by to—"

"When hell freezes over!" for a split-second the steely rage in A. J.'s voice stopped conversation cold. "The whole Board doesn't know about any of this, couldn't. Believe me . . . *sir,* they are going to find out."

"And risk a parachute. I think not, Professor."

"Try me!"

Dornbaum shrugged. "I hope you have deep pockets. Attorneys don't come cheap."

The punch line was still to come. "For the record, I do want to correct you on one point," Bolland's attorney said. "The Board went through channels. Our Board Chair was tied up in surgery, but Board member Lentz personally chaired the emergency session of the Personnel Committee that made the decision, then carried it on to the full board in closed session."

A. J. was on his feet. The resignation agreement was still lying where the attorney had left it, untouched much less signed.

"You'll be hearing from my lawyer," A. J.'s mouth felt stiff.

Dornbaum's eyes were hard. "If you aren't off campus by five, I'll have you arrested for criminal trespass."

At least the President was insecure—or cowardly—enough

not to demand the keys right there and then. Without a backward glance, A. J. left the office, then the building, all the while a growing checklist began to form itself in his head.

No sense worrying Sam, she would find out soon enough. Call Jake's office. Doc Radisson would keep. Dornbaum made it plain if there was butt-covering to be done, it might already be too late. At least the spreadsheets were at home for the most part. A. J. had taken to keeping them there under lock and key months ago, out of concern for what the former night custodian Putnam was or was not doing.

He had already unlocked the Toyota's driver-side door, hesitated only long enough to whip out his cell phone and start to key in Jake's number, when it hit him. The printouts for the past few months, the period immediately before the fire, were still in his office—fortunately not the closet of a space President Dornbaum had carved out begrudgingly in the administrative suite, but downstairs in the basement faculty retreat A. J. still used while working on his courses.

Shifting direction, he sprinted across the quad toward the social sciences office building. A quick glance down the basement corridor only confirmed how well orchestrated this all had been. Waiting for A. J. outside his office door—a pained expression on his face—was the day-shift security guard, Al Stinson.

A. J. had his keys in hand, was closing the distance between them. One look at the guy's face was enough to tell A. J. where things really stood. None of this was the security guard's idea. The two men had a long-standing thing going about their respective loyalties to the Eagles and the Steelers, the source of a lot of good-natured banter and ribbing between them. By now A. J. had come within ten feet of the door.

The guard showed no intention of backing off. "Sorry, Sir, I can't let you do this," he said stiffly.

A. J. forced a smile. "Lecture notes, Al. I assume it's not out of line to pick up my own lecture notes," he told him. "I still have a class to teach tonight."

A forgivable lie under the circumstances. The guard hesitated, slowly stepped aside.

It was all the invitation A. J. needed. Before Al could protest, he reached his desk, began rifling through file drawers at breakneck speed, pulling out folders and stuffing them into the half-empty briefcase he had left open on his desk. He breathed a silent sigh of relief for the foresight to hard-copy the email from Priscilla and slip it into his pocket before he showed up for President Dornbaum's little pow-wow. He suspected the plan was to freeze his access to the campus computer system as well.

All the while he worked, Al was fidgeting in the doorway, anxiously eye-balling the whole proceedings. "I suppose I really ought to check all your . . . those files you . . . "

A. J. was no more prepared to let that happen than the man was prepared to do it. "Done," the briefcase snapped shut as his thumb moved casually across the combination tumblers, locking the mechanism.

"Professor Ferinelli, I'm . . . ya gotta know, I was just following—"

"Orders. Believe me, I understand," A. J. said evenly. "Thanks very much for waiting."

"No problem."

A. J. left it to the guard to lock up behind him. By the time he drove downtown and hit Jake Burroughs' law practice, it was after hours. His friend was alone at his dimly-lit desk, surrounded by mountains of court documents. *Kafka-esque*, A. J. chuckled grimly, a scene straight out of *The Trial*. Still, the moment was no more or less surreal than what had just transpired over on campus.

Something, a sound, must have broken Jake's concentration. He looked up, froze when he saw A. J.'s face.

"What the . . . hell? Ferinelli."

A. J. managed a strangled laugh. "Client, to you. Business is picking up," he said. "Between professor and student, your billable hours just got considerably larger. In one day, no less."

"Surely, the cops don't think *you*—?"

"Dornbaum. I've been fired."

His friend hadn't moved so much as a muscle. "You're kidding."

"No."

"You're tenured."

"Tell them that!"

Jake was on his feet, hands splayed out against the desk top. "Those stupid sons of bitches . . . when—?"

"A half hour ago. Less maybe. I wasn't checking my watch."

"How the hell did they—?"

A. J. told him, starting with Priscilla's email and winding up with the run-in with Campus Security. "If you're contemplating an I-told-you-so," he said as he recited the list of documents he had managed to squirrel away off-site, "you're allowed."

Jake grimaced. "Not my style."

"So . . . what next."

"I suggest you get to the Board somehow if you can."

The Board. "The college attorney claims they knew, even sanctioned the decision," A. J. said. "Which could fit. Right after Dornbaum phoned, Doc Radisson also called my office, left a message on the machine. He wants to talk, though he didn't say, why."

A slow smile began to tug at the corner of his friend's mouth. "He didn't have to, Ferinelli."

A. J.'s confusion must have shown in his face. "Those dumb so-and-so's were bluffing," Jake said quietly. "Mercifully for you, Lentz and his crew must have gone around the full Board in staging their little coup. If I had to make a guess they acted without Board authorization or the Chair's knowledge."

"Which means—"

"Sue the bloody pants off 'em," Jake's voice grated like chalk on a blackboard. "Do you have any idea what due-process personnel cases like this are fetching these days? A couple of million—easy. Add in defamation of character, damages . . . I'll be visiting you in your villa on the Cote D'Azur."

"But winnable?"

Jake shrugged. "What have you got to lose? Besides, juries love juicy cases like this one, a chance to zing the bad guys, win one for the common man."

"You're telling me, Doc Radisson probably knows what's going down and that's why he made that call."

Jake laughed. "Buddy, chalk it up to far too many years in this slimy legal business, but I'd lay you twenty to one odds, there's already a counter-coup going on out there. You could just wake up tomorrow morning and find yourself running this freak show."

Chapter Seventeen

A quick phone call to Doc was enough for A. J. to confirm that Jake hadn't called the game plan to the play and down. But he was close enough.

"Be grateful you've got one hell of a loyal fan club, Ferinelli," Doc told him. "It turns out Bolland's ex-bookkeeper also fired off a copy of her email about the insurance, blind-copy, to six Board members. I was one of them. Bottom line, the Board is meeting in extraordinary session in the morning—and whatever comes of it, business as usual around here is no longer an option."

"Hopefully, collective wisdom will prevail," A. J.'s mouth felt stiff. "Right now, I've been put on notice to clean out my office."

Doc chuckled softly. "In your shoes I would think about postponing the move for 24 hours, Ferinelli. It just might save an awful lot of unnecessary shuffling of boxes."

There were others who needed to be kept in the loop. Dean of Students, Fred Urban, was one of them. By the time A. J. got home from a talk-it-out with Jake and Fred at Smithy's, well past midnight yet again, an exhausted Sam had fallen asleep on the sofa, still in her jeans and the teal sweater she liked to wear after-hours that looked so great with her eyes. A. J. stood there looking down at her while he tugged at the knot on his tie, finally succeeded in loosening it. He was on an adrenalin high that could have kept him going the rest of the week.

"Sweetheart," he said softly.

Groggy with the first flush of sleep, Sam stirred, frowned up at him as it began to register what time it was. His promised six o'clock had long since come and gone.

"This is not a habit I'm crazy about," she yawned. "Post-midnight cabals, mea culpa phone calls. No sex . . ."

In response, A. J. eased alongside her on the edge of the sofa, cradled her upturned face between his hands, kissed her gently on the mouth. Forget how beautiful she was, he had to tell her and tell her now.

"I would say, you told me so," he said quietly, "but first I had better find out how you feel about being the primary breadwinner, Sam."

"W-what . . . let's start this all over again, shall we? From the beginning."

"They fired me."

Sam just looked at him. "Not the kind of thing to . . . you're kidding, right. You're tenured. They *can't*—"

"They did. Whether or not they can make it stick," he shrugged, "time will tell. Theoretically, if I show up on campus tomorrow they're prepared to nail me for trespassing."

Sam's face paled, then flushed. She started to respond, but no sound came, only an audible gasp of sound before her jaw clamped tight. She was trembling.

"It turns out you were right," he said, struggling to keep his own voice even, "about everything. But I am *not* going to take this lying down. Jake is on it as we speak. And if Doc Radisson and his friends on the Board get their way, they are *not* going to let this stick either."

"Bremer, Dornbaum. Where are they in all of this?"

"They could be gone, both of them, by the end of the week. Or at least that's what Doc was implying. Jake suspects the opposition on the Board intends to propose me as interim to replace Bremer or maybe some kind of a combined position, until—"

"If this is some kind of sick joke," Sam swallowed hard, "I'm warning you . . ."

231

He shook his head. "I wish it were, for Bolland's sake."

"I don't understand."

"The fire. There wasn't any insurance."

Sam sat dead still as the reality of the situation hit home. "None of those losses were covered. And they're trying to blame the mess on you," her voice was barely a whisper.

"They can try, certainly did a creative job of orchestrating the whole thing. They're claiming the lapse in the policy was accidental and I should have caught it," he winced. "Though I've got to believe Doc can persuade the full Board to see the charade for what it is."

Sam was a mathematician, used to adding up the givens, factoring in the unknowns. What he just told her, the enormity of the crisis, was well beyond logical calculation.

"What you're telling me about the insurance . . . it means Bolland is—"

"We're going under. If Emmaline-Wattrous even wants the pieces, they will be there for the taking. Our prime dorm space is gone. By the time the lawsuits are settled . . . "

A. J. couldn't bring himself to finish tallying up the body count. Buildings and assets were one thing, the human costs another. The toughest losses to calculate were the people, dedicated professionals who laid it on the line for their students, only to find themselves betrayed, in the end, by leaders they trusted, faculty and administration alike.

"So there's nothing, no way to—"

"Fred Urban saw this coming that night in the snow, watching Clairbourne burn," A. J. forced a grim smile. "*It's over.* Time to break out the shovels."

"Doc apparently must believe you could salvage something. At the very least, it might mean negotiating the merger with Emmaline. He could be counting on you to help them do just that."

A. J. closed his eyes, drew in a long breath before he opened them again. "After today, Joel and Ellison, I don't think I'm up to it, Sam. It's one thing to try to save a place, another to preside over the wake. Our chances are slim to none."

Sam just looked at him, silent, thinking. "This isn't like you," she said slowly. "After all we've been through, just packing it in, giving up."

A. J. shrugged. "I don't know any more who I am or what I

want," he told her. "This place, this business has been my life. I never questioned what I was doing here—well, maybe it's high damn time I did."

"A little late in the game. This place needs you, A. J."

He chuckled softly, ran a thumb along the full curve of her mouth, felt her shiver. "Not a tenth as much as I need you," he said.

"You didn't start this mess, but heaven help Bolland if you don't chose to finish it."

"Ferinelli the Terminator," A. J. winced, his distaste evident. "We have plenty of those types running around here already."

"True, control freaks abound. Unfortunately, not nearly enough of them seem concerned with restoring some sense of integrity to this business. Worst case scenario—my income would feed us both, maybe not filet mignon, but at least tofu," she said. "Think about it."

A. J. laughed, but there was no humor in it. "I am," he said. "I think I could put up with just about anything but a steady diet of veggie burgers."

It proved to be a short, virtually sleepless night for both of them. At first light, A. J. showered, shaved, chose to dress in his traditional teaching garb of jeans and a button-down-collar denim shirt open at the neck. To hell with the Wall Street austerity of a suit. And this was no time to stay away from campus either. Ignoring President Dornbaum's threats, he took up residence at his desk in the basement of the Academic Center trying to maintain the illusion of business-as-usual. He was relieved to find no one had time to change the lock on his faculty office.

The phone was conspicuously silent, suspicious in itself, considering the rumors had to be out there on campus that a coup and counter-coup were in the works. With his door flung wide open, A. J. was well aware of the steady buzz of conversation just out of earshot from passing students, even an occasional faculty colleague.

If someone popped their head in his door, it was an awkward attempt to wish him well. Even the dayshift security guard, Al, who had been charged with policing A. J.'s exit from campus yesterday, put in an appearance. A. J. chose to read it as the guy's attempt, in his own way, to make amends.

Supposedly at 7 AM the full Board met in emergency session. A scant hour-and-a-half later, it went into executive session, holed up in the conference room of a local motel owned by one of their numbers. A deceptive calm prevailed on the quad. Classes changed, students complained about exams, and on the surface of things, the business of higher learning went on. As so many other times in the institution's long and troubled existence, its fate was being decided behind closed doors.

Shuffling the deck chairs—A. J. couldn't seem to shake the image—with the proverbial ship's bow already thrusting heavenward. He made no illusions that in the faculty and staff offices around him, the survivors had begun to jockey for spots in the lifeboats, every man for himself.

Around six in the evening, with still no word, A. J. went home. At seven the phone rang. It was one of Doc Radisson's friends, a Bolland graduate and long-time Board member, requesting A. J.'s presence at the President's office. Slipping this time into his bankers' gray suit and power tie, he complied.

For better or worse, the maneuvering was over. At the door, Sam simply held him close.

"Win, lose or draw," she said, "I love you. What ever you or they decide."

A. J. found the administrative lot deserted except for a handful of cars, any one of which would have decimated his entire salary for a full year. Given that company, it wasn't tough to slip his wisp of a Toyota into a narrow spot relatively close to the door. He'd forgotten his coat and a freezing rain had begun to fall. It was turning the walks and lawn into a treacherous soup of ice, moldering leaves and mud.

At the entrance to the administration building, he impulsively stopped, turned and looked back over the darkened campus behind him. The fortress-like bell tower was bathed in light from the giant spotlights at its base, soaring upward into the fog. Brooding, he thought, beautiful.

His own mood in the past few hours had gone from incredulous, angry beyond belief, to anxious and finally resigned, as he mourned a heritage squandered and a future compromised. For all the misgivings he had shared with Sam, fact was, he still cared about the outcome more than he was prepared to admit. Cared more than any sane man had a right to care, knowing what was to come.

His footsteps were muffled by the thick, though aging, carpet of the hallway outside the administrative offices. Dean Bremer's mahogany outer door was closed but inside the glassed entrance to Dornbaum's suite, an unfamiliar female face presided over the desk guarding the inner sanctum. Her most recent predecessor in the office—Bremer's one-time assistant and the woman who had been willing to perjure herself in Sam's grievance as her ticket to the presidential suite—was gone.

"Dr. Ferinelli, I assume," the secretary-in-residence flashed a shy quirk of a smile. "They'll be pleased to hear you've arrived."

What a difference twenty-four hours can make, A. J. thought as he followed the woman—Francine, she introduced herself in passing—through the door into Dornbaum's private conference room. He still half-expected to see his unsigned resignation letter still lying there on the coffee table, its discreet little penciled X's staring up at him.

Instead, he saw three men in business suits, Doc Radisson in khakis and turtleneck, and two expensively dressed women arrayed in a semi-circle of chairs, looking at him expectantly. All of them, A. J. recognized, were Board members with the exception of one of the women, in her mid-fifties with silver hair and a pale designer suit—clearly a power-hitter in the room. Her face seemed familiar, but A. J. couldn't place it or recall having met her before.

A single chair was free. It was Doc Radisson, A. J. noticed, who nodded in that direction, urging him to join them.

"I'm sure you're wondering why you're here," Doc said.

It didn't require a reply. Something of A. J.'s nervousness must have shown in his face. Doc got right to the point.

"First off," he said, "as your newly appointed interim CEO at Bolland, I want to reassure you immediately that you're a tenured full professor at this institution. I say that, regardless of the unfortunate confusion surrounding the issue of late."

A. J. nodded. "Your clarification is most helpful. Thank you."

His job was safe. And for the moment it seems Doc himself was going to try a hand at the helm.

"Second," Doc continued quickly, "It is our intention to offer you, officially, the position of interim Academic Dean and head of the Bolland merger negotiating team. Effective immediately. That comes with the clear understanding—in writing, that you will retain your tenured status and all of the seniority that goes with it."

"And," Doc continued, "it is important you know this

235

arrangement was approved by a majority of the full Board in emergency session. The people in this room are only here to convey the will of the Board and assure you of their support."

Doc gave him time to breathe—let the import of those decisions set in before continuing. Merger was a foregone conclusion in this game plan.

"You are charged with saving as much of the Bolland faculty and staff as possible," Doc continued. "You are also empowered to negotiate buyouts with faculty and staff as needed. Ultimately, as operations are merged with those of Emmaline, the goal is to preserve as much of the unique character, contributions and heritage of Bolland as humanly possible."

"Of course," he added, "this recognizes also the . . . superior fiscal and related resources our sister college brings to the bargaining table."

A. J. couldn't help noticing Doc had worded his announcement to exclude any need—or logical spot—for a statement of acceptance. For now he was assuming it as a given.

"And the current administrative team?" A. J. said.

Doc's voice hardened. "If you mean President Dornbaum and Dean Bremer, they submitted their resignations to the full Board at noon today. The resignations were accepted."

A quick nod was A. J.'s only visible reaction. It was done.

"In order to expedite the transition," Doc said, "I suggest by tomorrow you move your office from the academic building to the former Dean's office. There you will have full access to the documents you need."

"And the ground rules," A. J. said, "for negotiating staff-related issues?"

Doc didn't mince words. "Strictly programmatic. Legally as of noon today, the Board declared financial exigency and filed for bankruptcy—we're dissolving the institution."

So much for tenure and seniority. By opting for dissolution, the Bolland Board was in a position to circumvent both. They could and most likely would pink slip the entire faculty and staff, allowing Emmaline-Wattrous to rehire strictly as departmental staffing needs dictated. No guarantees and no holds barred.

"Legally?"

"This is fraught, of course," Doc conceded. "Court battles are

236

possible. But we've retained a New York-based law firm with vast experience in this area. They've assured us this approach offers our own negotiating team—and the equivalent from Emmaline-Wattrous—maximum flexibility in integrating staff from the two institutions."

Gutsy, A. J. had to admit. Lentz and his cronies would have tried to hold out for a marriage-of-equals arrangement in order to save the Bolland name. Emmaline-Wattrous would have been forced to honor the Handbook, rehire Bolland's faculty on a seniority basis, regardless of merit or past performance. It was something no sane person would concede. The reformist Board members had engineered a clean sweep.

A. J. shifted in his chair. "I want to commend the Board on its courage," he said, "in making these tough decisions. I can only hope the faculty and staff will cooperate."

"We believe they will," Doc said, "if you're leading them, Professor."

First Sam, now Doc. "I don't expect an answer to the offer tonight," Doc said. "I'll be in my office tomorrow morning."

A. J. smiled, stood, assuming it was his cue to leave. "I'll stop by around nine," he said.

"We still need to wind this up," Doc told him, "all things to which you should be privy. First, however, I would like you to meet my colleague, the President of Emmaline-Wattrous College, Dr. Elizabeth Cordova."

Her hand extended, the woman in the pale cream suit rose to meet him. Stunning, that much he noticed, dark hair and eyes. Her smile was broad, self-assured—genuine.

"Dr. Ferinelli," she said warmly. "It's a great pleasure. I've heard so much about you, look forward to a long and productive working relationship, starting now. We have a tough job ahead of us but one, I believe, that will greatly enhance the quality of education for all of our students."

It was total surrender, the ultimate concession, having her there. Shocked at first by the arrangement, A. J. felt tongue-tied as a schoolboy as he returned her greeting.

Still, by the time he eased back in his chair again, he had begun to accept the woman's presence as reassuring. Openly and without equivocating, Emmaline's CEO was a full party to the ongoing discussions at Bolland The woman's choice of words, her whole demeanor left no doubt Emmaline was coming to the process out of a genuine conviction that student learning comes first and foremost. He couldn't have lived with any less—not, and be a part of it. From a purely selfish perspective, even with merger and all the ax wielding bound to go with it, A. J. also got the message. He was not going to wind up in a bread line.

The rest of the meeting, to which he was now privy, was an odd mix of bunker politics and a guarded inter-institutional love-fest—the latter dictated by the presence of President Cordova in the room. Quickly the Board got down to picking A. J.'s brain about the resources needed to identify and protect the most valuable human assets Bolland was bringing to the merger. No small job, setting the rules. For the most part President Cordova simply listened, nodding occasionally and interrupting only to request clarification as to what Emmaline staff would need to do to make the negotiations as fair and amicable as possible.

Their official proceedings over, the board members shared with A. J. their respective marching orders that would make his job as head of the Bolland negotiating team easier. Feeling like a fifth wheel during all their insider leave-taking, A. J. was about to head for the parking lot himself when eyebrows lifted, Doc signaled him to stay behind for a de-brief.

Exhausted and emotionally drained, he reluctantly agreed, though by now his thoughts had leaped ahead to one goal and one only—to home. Late as it was, by now Sam would be worried sick waiting for him. Alone with his ostensible boss-to-be, A. J. added his congratulations to those expressed by the Board.

"Ferinelli, what can I say," Doc said, clapping him lightly on the shoulder. "Welcome aboard, yet again, hopefully under a lot less ambivalent conditions than your former administrative appointment."

"I appreciate your confidence—"

"But," Doc finished for him, "you need to talk to Sam."

A muscle jerked along the line of A. J.'s jaw. "Yes."

"You're concerned what this could do to her, her new position with Emmaline."

A. J. drew himself erect. "In a word, yes." It wasn't the whole truth.

"I've run into her a couple of times on the Emmaline

238

campus," Doc reminded him. "That woman is tempered steel—a keeper. I, for one, would bet a year's revenue at this place she will tell you loud and clear, if she hasn't already, to go your conscience. And we both know where that would take you."

"I'm not sure I have a right to put her in such a position."

"Her choice, not yours."

"Still, it has to be asked."

"In your shoes, man," Doc's eyebrow arched, "while I was at it, it isn't the only thing I'd ask."

Their laughter echoed in the now deserted presidential suite. A. J. waited while the new CEO closed up shop, clicked off the lights, and by the time they hit the parking lot together, any doubts A. J. had about Doc Radisson's personal loyalty in all this had been silenced. Still, he had never seen Doc in this capacity before, his political game face on.

A. J. had to know. "You realize," he said, "for one ugly moment in Dornbaum's office last night, it occurred to me that you may have suspected for some time maybe even knew this was coming or at least a variation on a theme—my firing, the attempt to pin the insurance fiasco on me."

"And that I sat back and let it happen," Doc chuckled softly, his expression unreadable. "Not my style, Ferinelli. Of course I suspected all along what Dornbaum might do if cornered, yes. And once the insurance issue surfaced, he had his excuse, which partly explains my phone call to warn you the minute I found out . . . moot, unfortunately. By the time we caught up with one another, the man already tried—very publicly—to throw you under the bus."

It was an apology of sorts, one that begged the question. Still, it was something.

"You saved my reputation," A. J. said, purposefully left the issue of his job out of it. "If anything is left of Bolland when this bloodbath is over, it's to your credit, Doc. I truly believe that."

"And I'll expect you in my office at nine, track shoes in hand. The clock is ticking. If we don't hit the ground running, all bets are off," Doc said.

"And President Cordova?"

"I wanted her in the meeting, so everyone—you included—could see she's a straight shooter. Emmaline-Wattrous could be behaving at this point as if they had us by the throat. You

239

heard the woman. They've had their own problems over the years, but know what the bottom line is. Students. She'll keep her people in line. I'm convinced of it."

"I also understand the need for spin from our side," A. J. said. "When push comes to shove, I'm not all that certain how folks on campus here are going to react when the pink slips start flying. And I'd be willing to bet there are going to be one heck of a lot of nervous alums wondering if we all have lost our minds or what's left of them."

Doc winced. "True enough. Which is why I'm counting on you to run the shop on this end so I can get out on the road and do what's gotta be done. While we were making nice and pressing the flesh in my new office, Francine was sitting out there booking red-eye flights like a woman possessed. Bottom line, I suggest you get a good night's sleep, Ferinelli. It may be the last either one of us enjoys in a very long time."

Sleep was the last thing on his mind. Adrenalin on overdrive, A. J. aimed the Toyota in the direction of home. *Sam.* Somehow just the sound of her name was enough, repeating itself over and over in his head, to steady his racing heart. For once the front door key actually worked, first try.

He found her ensconced on the living room sofa with her laptop, engrossed in concocting strategies for beefy guys in armor striding across a craggy heath, up to their ankles in mud and gore. It never ceased to amaze him, though she was hardly a gamer, how adept she was at tactical software.

"Playing Civilization . . . I love it," he chuckled softly. "I come home from the wars to find you spear in hand, doggedly staked out defending home and hearth, fearless, ready to take on the marauding hordes."

"Heads rolling, the skies raining arrows—dead on target, skewering the bad guys. I thought it fit."

She flashed an anxious grin, put the game on hold and invited him to settle in alongside her. His own mood a mystery even to himself, A. J. drew her into a lingering embrace. It became one of those moments of clarity that come just before the storm hits. He knew what he needed to do.

Sam let out her breath in an impatient rush. "Nice," she said, "but it would also be nice if you cut to the chase."

"It's done," he told her, "or just beginning, depending on how you look at it. Doc and the Board have taken over, are dissolving the college as a legal entity. Emmaline has started to pick through the spoils."

Her eyes never left his face. "And *you*."

"Interim Dean. Head of the merger negotiation team."

Sam let out an audible sigh of relief. "Thank heavens."

"I'm not so sure about that but at least Doc's running the show," A. J. said, "considerably less scary than some of the scenarios we were imagining."

"So, you told him, then, you would accept."

"I said I'd think about it. There was someone I felt I needed to consult first."

"Jake, of course, to nail down a contract. After what happened with Dornbaum and Lentz, I don't blame you for—"

"I meant *you*," he corrected her. "I wouldn't even think about taking a job as a janitor on the night shift until I was sure you would be there at the end of the day, through whatever comes. Though under the circumstances, sickness and health, all the rest of the parade of horribles on the traditional list seems way too depressing."

"I don't blame you for being a skeptic," she grimaced. "Last time you asked me what I thought about a change in job description, I was out of town on the first bus. Sorry about that. I am not about to make the same mistake twice."

A. J.'s forehead creased in a puzzled frown. "I guess I wasn't making myself clear . . . am certainly a little rusty at this. Maybe it would have helped to pick up a dozen roses for Dutch courage on the way home, but unfortunately they're a hard commodity to come by in the middle of the night around here. True, I haven't got a ring . . . "

"A ring." Sam's eyes were wide, questioning.

He hesitated, took a deep breath. "What I'm trying to say, in my own apparently clueless fashion, is that I'm asking you to *marry* me."

Silence. Sam flushed, paled, her shock and confusion apparent.

"You *really mean it*," she breathed. It wasn't a question and she didn't give him a chance to react. "I don't . . . can't begin to pretend to know what to say."

"*Yes*, I hope."

241

"Just out of the blue like this," she said slowly.

"*I love you.* And if anyone out there in rumor-monger heaven isn't aware yet we're living together, they won't be for long if I take the job—fraught when we're both working for denominational colleges. And sooner or later, guaranteed, it will become an issue."

Indignation flared in her eyes. "Let them talk!"

"Sam, be reasonable. I can't drag you through that. I won't. Not after everything you went through on the Bolland campus.

She just looked at him, jaw tight, inscrutable. "I appreciate you're only trying to protect me," she said. "Misplaced, but well meant. What we already weathered together since October would have sent most couples to divorce court a long time ago."

"My point exactly. So, marry me."

"I can't imagine the crew you left back there in the Board room lining up to toss the rice either. It isn't much of a stretch to argue my going after the Dean was what brought this whole apocalypse down on Bolland's head in the first place!"

A. J. forced a smile. "It should come as no surprise to you that Doc Radisson, thinks you're the best thing since sliced bread. Though I would agree it's probably not a good idea to invite any of the Bolland faculty . . . "

Sam appeared anything but amused. "You forget, I work for Emmaline now. You're going to have to hang tough, grovel, plunder and pillage to protect your people. I can almost guarantee my colleagues will be terrified Bolland's problems are going to pull our faculty and staff down the drain, too. And meanwhile there I am—"

"Sleeping with the enemy."

"Name it honestly for what it is," Sam bristled, "we'd both be caught in a conflict of interest, or worse—rubbing the relationship in their faces. Forget your credibility, it would be shot to hell."

The tension level in the room was escalating by the minute. This wasn't working out the way he had intended, not by a longshot. At least Sam hadn't rejected him outright. A. J. momentarily shot a glance at the ceiling, closed his eyes, waiting for his pulse to steady.

"Do I detect a prayer for divine intervention?"

"Try a devil of a headache," he muttered.

At something she must have read in his face, Sam softened her tone. "Please understand, how difficult this is," she said. "You have no idea how terrifying—and yes, absolutely *miraculous*—it is for me

242

to even *think* about the M-word without going into cardiac arrest or winding up back in therapy, whichever comes first."

"But . . ."

"Timing is—"

"Exactly the point," his mouth felt stiff. "When *would* a right time be, *if ever,* provided I take this job. Right after I nail Bolland's doors shut or maybe end of the month when the first of the pink slips hit the mail? I doubt even by the time I'm a hundred-and-ten that the survivors will bring themselves to forget, to say nothing of forgive anyone who presided over the bloodletting. If we take such reasoning to its logical conclusion, you and I have just become the latest casualties of the merger, this whole tragic mess—something I am *not* willing to risk. Not now. Not ever."

A. J. broke off. His heart ached worse than his head, when all he wanted to do right now was take her in his arms and make love until nothing mattered any longer but that they were together.

"For the record, I would get down on one knee, start over," he told her, "if I thought it had a snowball's chance of changing the outcome."

"Which brings us right back to where we started," Sam averted her gaze. "We know how we feel about each other. Anniversaries are only dates, times—meaningless."

"Numbers. Your specialty. Next thing you'll be telling me, this isn't personal," he said.

"If it's personal you want, all right, *truth.* Borderline catatonic as I feel right now, I'll say it," Sam exhaled, drew in an audible breath, "you know I love you, more than I ever thought possible, especially if you consider marriage was never Priority One on my to-do list. But if you're talking about sending out announcements in the immediate future, I'm sorry, this conversation is over. Nonnegotiable."

The hell of it was, she had a point. But then so did he.

The silence between them was unbearable. On a desperate sigh, A. J. reached out across the metaphoric divide that had opened on the sofa between them, gently drew her to him and buried his aching brow against the silk of her hair. Her body at first was stiff and unresponsive in his arms but gradually, on a sigh herself, Sam finally gave in and let him hold her.

"I'm sorry, truly sorry if you . . . if I hurt you," her voice shook as she said it. "But I had to tell you the truth."

"I realize that."

They made eye contact. A. J. could read the uncertainty, the genuine regret in her upturned face.

"In my defense," she said, "it's no great secret delicate interpersonal diplomacy tends to send me running for the hills. I think it's fair to say a marriage proposal qualifies."

"But you're still here."

"Go figure, yes," Sam's eyebrow arched. "Although you know me. For one wild second back there, in my head anyway, I was already on the way out the door."

"What changed your mind?"

Sam winced. "I couldn't remember where I left my shoes."

It took a nano-second for her sheepish confessional to register. Wide-eyed, anxious, she was watching him, waiting for a response. When one came—sidesplitting, tears-to-the-eyes laughter—it momentarily shocked the both of them.

"You're finding this funny."

"Sam . . . sweetheart, sometimes laughter is the only thing that makes any sense," A. J. managed to gasp, "Just do me one favor. I would be truly grateful—if asked—you would decline any and all offers to serve on Emmaline's merger negotiating team. I'm really not sure I'm up to going head-to-head with you over a board table."

He freed up a hand so he could brush back a strand of her hair that had strayed across the curve of her cheek. Sam shivered, met his quizzical gaze with a questioning look of her own.

"Freckles," he said. "I had forgotten how much I love the dusting of freckles across the bridge of your nose."

Her frown was back.

"Not to worry," he added quickly, "I won't push the M-word again, I promise you. Not until you tell me you're ready."

Finally, a hint of a smile began to play at the corner of her mouth. "One thing I won't ask you to postpone . . . ever," she said softly. "And at the moment, Ferinelli, you're the only one here with a headache."

After everything that had happened in the last forty-eight hours, he didn't need a second invitation. Words were his business and they had failed him miserably. Right now, it was a whole lot safer just to love her.

Chapter Eighteen

Daylight came. With it came the inevitable.

Bolland College was in its death throes. The face A. J. encountered in his bathroom mirror was haggard and drawn—less the ravages of surviving an administrative assassination attempt, he decided, than the outcome. To compensate for all the stress, the Board simply gave him more—they kicked him upstairs. By now A. J. knew the players only too well and how they operated. He felt like a shellshocked fellow-inmate suddenly put in charge of the asylum, without the benefit of straightjackets.

When he checked in at Doc Radisson's office around nine, he found, to his chagrin, after all the soul-searching with Sam much of the night, his acceptance of the interim deanship was a forgone conclusion as far as his new boss was concerned. Doc was making some last-minute phone calls, packed and ready to head for the airport on his emergency junket to reassure the alumni. After a hearty 'welcome aboard,' A. J.'s new boss invited him to set up camp in Bremer's former office.

A. J. stood for quite a while in the doorway before he could even bring himself to enter, much less take his new boss up on the move. Knowing what Sam had gone through in sight of that ostentatious desk was tough to stomach. He didn't have long to think about it. A phone call from Dean of Students Fred Urban only confirmed what A. J. already suspected. An unofficial "hit list" had already begun circulating in the Bolland camp with the names of faculty who were slated to be axed after the merger. It wasn't identical to A. J.'s intuitive, off-the-record body count at the executive Board meeting last night, but close enough.

Sad, he thought, that all the effort and intelligence going into campus intrigue hadn't been spent on quality teaching instead. The outcome just might have been different.

The morning had only begun. Barely an hour later, history professor George McDowell was storming the secretary's desk in the Dean's office. Over the intercom Francine scrambled to run interference, but in the background A. J. could hear the voice of his one-time mentor—brutal and abusive—demanding an appointment.

"Of course I'll see him, Francine," A. J. said evenly, "send him in."

Make a note, he thought, to apologize to the poor woman. McDowell's diatribe out there was intended for him. He didn't have long to wait to experience the tongue-lashing first hand.

"You two-faced bastard," McDowell's eyes were fierce, his hands coiled into tight fists at his sides. "They must have promised you one hell of a lot to sell out your friends and colleagues, these students . . . this college!"

Stone-faced, A. J. took the verbal assault in silence, felt the words strike as they were intended to do—penetrate, tear open his insides. McDowell was only getting started. He lowered his voice, but not the force of his words.

"You could have had it all. Power, the respect of your peers. But *you* bought survival. Tell me, old friend, was it worth it?"

"George, I understand your . . . appreciate where you're coming from. But we'll never agree on this."

"Agree? You . . . *bastard* . . ."

McDowell's shoulders slumped, suddenly too small for his accustomed tweed jacket and professorial elbow patches, his Oxford colors tie. This was not the same man who had stood outside A. J.'s garage when Sam's harassment case first became public, what seemed now like half a lifetime ago. *That* George McDowell was confident of his knowledge and experience, self-assured and in control. Some time in the last six months, this professor and colleague—a man A. J. deeply respected—had become a brittle shell. Wasted and spent, he was old, not just in years but spirit.

"Add it up," McDowell said, "or get Pomerantz to do it for you. Add up the collective years of professorial experience you're selling down the river here. Whatever you tell yourself, it's on no other basis than whether or not the person sucked up to the administration in this godforsaken place."

To a gentleman of the old school, gutter language came hard. Still, what McDowell felt clearly smacked of such abhorrence, it crossed the line toward obscenity.

"Forget that I've only got a couple of years to retirement," McDowell reminded him savagely. "Forget there are at least a dozen of us in the same friggin' boat. To go down like *this*, after a lifetime of service—"

Let the man vent, A. J. thought, although it was getting harder and harder to listen to this. The tragedy was real enough, one of careers cut short and talent wasted, but all that had nothing to do with supposed loyalty toward a system where employment was considered an entitlement.

"There are worse ways," A. J. said stiffly, "far worse ways to end one's career. And personally, I've been experiencing way too many of them of late."

McDowell's head jerked up. "I fail to see what you—"

"Try working alongside faculty who have forgotten what teaching means," A. J. said, unable to contain his indignation any longer, "or who are using those young intellects out there to achieve personal ends that have nothing, nothing at all, to do with truth or knowledge or the life of the mind. Try playing games with no winners, that only tear and wound and corrupt the soul of a place I loved . . . still love, I tell myself. Even worse, try living with the Clairbourne fire and those kids who died in it. You *do* remember Clairbourne, George?"

"*What . . . about . . . Clairbourne*—"

A. J.'s voice shook with quiet fury. "In my heart and gut, I believe it is not out of the realm of the possible that somebody on this faculty talked an arsonist into setting that fire, George."

McDowell had gone deathly white, recoiled as if physically struck. "How *dare* you suggest one of our own might be—"

"I wasn't *suggesting* anything at all, George," A. J. said, overwhelmed by a sadness so profound, it drained the rage out of him in a heartbeat. "But if there is something you want or you need to tell me . . ."

"Ferinelli, I wouldn't give you the time of day!"

Shaking and visibly disoriented, McDowell was looking straight through him. Hands braced against his desktop, A. J. watched his one-time mentor and friend draw himself up, turn and walk out of the room. The heavy door to the Dean's office swung open, then shut—without so much as a sound—behind him.

There are times so bleak, so terrible they cleave a person's soul and the wounds they leave, or at least the scars that follow, are there forever. For A. J., his wife's death had been such a moment. George McDowell's visit was another.

In one split-second in the Dean's office—a space and role he still really could not conceive of as his—A. J. Ferinelli knew his life had been built on a lie. For as long as he could remember, certainly in the years that propelled him through graduate school and into the ranks of the professorate, he had believed that in knowledge there is integrity, decency, hope. If human beings only become literate and humanized enough, they will not kill or maim, ruthlessly or wantonly destroy. They will not toy with other people's lives for the sake of personal gain or mere exercise of control or ego.

That faith died. It died in the instant he knew—not suspected or feared, but knew—that George McDowell had firsthand knowledge of why the Clairbourne fire had been set and how.

Proof was another matter entirely. But A. J. knew it for truth just the same. Just as he knew he could not live with what this community had become.

There had always been colleagues who decried the fact education was 'becoming a business'. A. J. was not one of them. What tore at his soul was not the pragmatic demand for accountability when it came to books and chalkboards and computer terminals. He couldn't even argue with the need to maintain student-teacher ratios, despite all his maneuvering with the course schedule over the years to keep enrollments in his Con Law class down, if not to a sane at least a manageable level.

What stuck in his craw, ate away at his sense of integrity, was how tawdry and unviable that business was becoming, the futility of affixing blame or finding solutions. *We are truly the last of the dinosaurs,* he thought. *We cling to feudal illusions about our profession even in the face of a mountain of irrelevance that could sweep our species, liberal arts education, out of existence entirely.*

Meanwhile board members like Lentz, long since removed from the mainstream of their own often failed corporate careers, played God with colleges like Bolland as if this were their own private sandbox, their last bastion of control. Faculty forgot their missions in a war to preserve styles of learning out of synch with the needs of the very people they presumed to educate. And caught in the tug-of-war, staff and students fixated on immediate needs that often had little to do with what true and relevant education is all about.

There were no winners in this deadly game. And indeed, a game it had become.

Somehow A. J. got through the day, answered memos, returned phone calls, sat in on a round of negotiations at Emmaline. Another week passed with more of the same, then another. Well past close of business on a Thursday night, A. J. got in his Toyota yet again and drove home. Sam's car was nowhere in sight—her hours were becoming as crazy as his own. If she really was going to be late or had a dinner meeting, she normally checked in.

Missing her, needing to hear her voice, A. J. slung his suitcoat over a chair in the entryway. Like an automaton he allowed himself to be drawn to the blinking rhythm of the light on the answering machine.

"Professor Ellison has been shot."

Ellison, *what*? A. J. replayed the terse message from campus security a second time before the words began to sink in. It was the very last thing in the world he would have expected to hear, no matter how many times he replayed it. He couldn't even pretend to guess how the already traumatized faculty and student body at Bolland would react to the news.

Whatever he felt personally was beside the point. It was up to him, officially, to respond. With Doc Radisson on the road, the campus was de facto in A. J.'s hands. A quick phone call to Security confirmed the barest of details. What he learned was quite enough. In police custody was the husband of one of Professor Ellison's students, a woman the sociologist supposedly had been seeing after hours, and not in the interest of offering professorial advice. Allegedly in a jealous rage, the husband had gunned him down point-blank in his office. Ellison had been life-flighted to the state university medical facility over the mountain.

A. J. wasn't looking forward to the long drive to the medical center in Ontowona, but at least it would be a chance to think, get his head on square, figure out how to handle the situation. Except once behind the wheel of his Toyota, A. J.'s thoughts came rushing at him with the blinding randomness of the oncoming headlights in the spring dusk.

Surreal, beyond irony, all of it. Bremer had been the notorious womanizer. It was inconceivable that Ray Ellison—seemingly above an intimate connection with anyone—would be the one to wind up facing retribution at the hands of an irate spouse with a handgun.

Equally surreal and incomprehensible, graduation was coming hard upon them—Bolland's last. In the steamy calm of his bathtub a few days ago, A. J. had found himself idly scanning the first tentative rosters of graduates, sounding out the names to the hard tile walls and penning in phonetic cues to avoid the most obvious errors.

An ambivalent and powerful thing, *naming*, a spiritual act in even the most primitive of cultures. Behind the calling of the roll of graduates lay not just four years of individual achievement, but centuries of tradition that had little to do with final exams or grading curves or credit loads. Whatever manifestation of the Good Housekeeping seal the graduates found thrust into their outstretched hands—the twelfth-century sheepskin, a rolled and beribboned scroll or an empty diploma case with its ultimate contents dependent upon criteria as mundane as paid parking and library fines—the outcome was identical. Another class was leaving its alma mater for the unknown.

And to seal the centuries-old ritual of passage, A. J. as the Dean would call out the student's name, strong and proud, as it had been given at birth. Syllable by syllable, graduates would hear themselves called to a future no more certain than in their initial violent coming into the world.

Right now, A. J. had naming of his own to do, only of a very different sort. Sam and Professor Julie Schechter. Joel Van Susten and Andy Duncan. Three Malaysian students whose names he could not reliably pronounce and who had not even lived long enough to see their fleeting moment center stage. The list was growing. George McDowell, then the names on the faculty merger hit list. And now Professor of Sociology, Ray Ellison, lying hooked to tubes and sophisticated technology in an aseptic room far removed from the pomp of gowns, hoods and the illusion of freedom—academic and otherwise—that had defined his life.

Graduates all, A. J. thought, of Bolland College. Teacher and pupil alike they had become bound together in life lessons more lethal than any of them had ever envisioned, as shattering as those gunshots echoing along the hallway of a deserted academic building.

This was his world—this, his community of scholars. A. J. had known nothing else for the whole of his adult, professional life. On some level, he realized, he had never known it at all.

The parking lot of the sprawling medical center in Ontowona was bathed in orange neon, amazingly full of vehicles considering the lateness of the hour by the time A. J. arrived. In contrast, the facility's intensive care unit was dark, hushed, a shrine to electronic miracles and human ingenuity. A male technician in hospital greens verified the professor's identity and relationship to the patient, then cautiously gave him permission to pass.

This was a place for family. Ray Ellison, it appears, had none. Deans and colleagues made poor substitutes. Still, in the end it was Bolland the man had listed in his wallet for official purposes as next of kin.

"The patient is conscious—barely," the guardian of the inner sanctum warned. "The anesthetic still hasn't completely worn off."

On the phone, campus security had said something about surgery. "Current prognosis?" A. J. said.

"Critical. The head wound did some damage. It could have been a lot worse There's some memory loss in such cases and most likely speech impairment. But the second bullet, apparently as the victim fell, was just as traumatic."

"Second," A. J. repeated. That fact went beyond his hasty briefing.

"The second shot damaged several vertebrae, lodged near the

spine," the tired-looking male medical staffer in institutional green began, rattling off a combination of numbers and letters that made no sense whatsoever to A. J. under the circumstances. The bottom line was something else entirely. "The present paralysis could be, most likely *is,* permanent. In all likelihood, he'll never walk again."

A muffled alarm had begun sounding on some piece of equipment in another curtained alcove. The scrubs-clad technician scampered to respond, leaving him suddenly alone at his colleague's bedside. As A. J. slid onto the hard institutional chair, Ray Ellison's eyes flickered open—held momentarily, then closed again. Even lost in the maze of tubes and wires, the stark white of the hospital linens, the man's face had lost none of its accustomed sharp-angled intensity. Fierce and uncompromising, that face had intimidated and terrified so many students over the years.

A. J. had seen the sociologist in action in the classroom. Ellison was a pacer as he taught, tight-coiled, ready to pounce on the unsuspecting, the fuzzy thinkers and those for whom the study of sociology, the task of understanding the human community, was only a blip on a transcript en route to a diploma.

Tragic, A. J. found himself thinking, for all of the man's study and erudition, his theoretical knowledge of the perils of collective behavior, it had come to this. But there comes a time to suspend judgment. Though after all that had happened A. J. could not pretend to that particular response, he managed what could be interpreted as compassion.

"They say you're going to make it, Ellison," he said quietly. "We . . . your colleagues will help in any way we can."

He was pronouncing a death sentence all the same. Memory, words, the restless leonine pacing as a lecture flowed out from this man's mind and psyche into a waiting classroom—all that was gone.

Ellison's eyes blinked again, connected. What A. J. read in them made any more words unnecessary. It was a bottomless pool of hate.

The return drive over the mountain seemed endless. Sam had been on her way home when she had picked up the news about

Ellison on the radio herself. Bone tired, she listened without comment, strangely detached, as A. J. unpacked it all. There were days that defied easy summation.

"I wish . . . I'm not sure what I wish," she told him when he finished his grim narrative, "except to come up with something, somehow that might make all this any different for you. Easier."

"You already did. Just listening."

Sam was holding something back. A. J. could feel it.

"One of our Emmaline security guards is moonlighting from the Sheriff's Department," she said finally. "Apparently the late night news is going to break the story that law enforcement found a body in the campus landfill a few days ago. They believe it's Henry Putnam. The suspicion is exposure or alcohol poisoning—an autopsy is winding up, as we speak. Based on the time elapsed, the condition of the body, the guard says it's going to be tough to confirm exactly what happened—"

"Did the guard connect it to . . . say anything about the Clairbourne fire?"

Sam shook her head. Their eye contact communicated for them.

Factor in Joel Van Susten's vicious encounter with Ellison, now this, with McDowell's recent visit to A. J.'s office. Suddenly the historian's behavior made complete and utter sense. Ellison and McDowell knew more about the fire and Putnam than they were willing to admit.

"What are you going to do?" Sam said.

A. J. shrugged. "Go to the police. Tomorrow is certainly soon enough. Ellison is going nowhere. They're likely to question McDowell, if they haven't already. But of course now he'll be waiting for it—won't let his guard down again, especially not with Ellison lying there in that hospital bed," A. J. shrugged.

It was a dead end. Whatever link existed between the two professors and Putnam's lighting that match, in all likelihood, no one would ever know.

Chapter Nineteen

O hallowed halls, our fairest Bolland, we . . .

For A. J. , the assumptions behind the banal tribute to Alma Mater suddenly had taken on a whole new imperative. Bolland college had stood and struggled as an institution for a hundred fifty years. In less than two months their venerable 'spiritual mother' would cease to exist as an independent seat of higher learning. From Day One as A. J. walked to the negotiating table, he had a sense of the clock ticking, compressing time with the surreal inevitability of the Clairbourne dormitory crashing into its foundations the night of the fire. It took incredible force of will to keep the horrific image from surfacing, unbidden, again and again in the black recesses of his memory.

At least Doc Radisson had been right about the ground rules. Elizabeth Cordova, the Emmaline-Wattrous President was not disposed to gloat or arbitrarily slash Bolland's personnel to protect her own—which made the actual merger negotiations far more civilized than they probably deserved to be. A. J. quickly was coming to respect his boss-to-be as advertised, a highly capable administrator who saw in this tragedy an opportunity for her to strengthen both institutions.

The blame-game had ceased to have any relevance. Still, as

the losses began to mount, A. J. began to feel the weight of the collapse coming to rest squarely on his shoulders. These were his friends and colleagues whose lives and livelihoods were in jeopardy. Objectivity was impossible. Every choice, even to save what could be seen as 'one of his own' at Bolland, became a no-win victory. It became a trade-off in which some other name, until now unfamiliar to him, became a life brutally interrupted.

Some compromises were more obvious than others. If the choice came to axing Fred Urban or a newbie first-year Student Dean at Emmaline, there was no choice. Emmaline was going to need every bit of experience it could get to handle the awkward, painful transition ahead.

And one was taken, the other left. That ancient textual account of the End Times kept stirring in A. J.'s head as he weighed the alternatives. He found it grimly appropriate, considering the denominational origins of the two institutions.

Although neither school made an issue of theological litmus tests, A. J.'s own comfort levels with those traditions had undergone radical transformations over the years. A lapsed Episcopalian at the point of his marriage, he periodically had joined Anne, a Methodist, in her observance of the major festivals of the church year. Some of that lingering receptivity to the religious he chalked up to his childhood Italian-American upbringing. Some—though he rarely allowed himself to think in those terms—stemmed from a latent personal openness to the notion of the Sacred.

All that ended abruptly with Anne's death. Since her memorial service, A. J. had excised religion entirely, or at least the practice of it, from his life. It had become a debilitating canker feeding on his grief until he could no longer bear to utter 'God' and his own name in the same sentence.

And yet here he was, one of a handful of colleagues, playing God himself, day after day, with impunity. Not surprising, in his bleakest moments, the dense biblical poetry and language, the powerful stories of cosmic wrath and retribution, mercy and grace, justice and forgiveness came welling out from the recesses of his adolescent past. Among them were half-remembered tales of Lot's bargaining with the Divine, a man desperate in his eloquence to divert the Armageddon threatening to eradicate two communities with which his life was inextricably bound.

Goodness knows, Bolland and Emmaline-Wattrous were facing fire and brimstone of their own. The magnitude of the collective staff and faculty cuts was so great, the two campuses so small and their rumor mills so efficient, the decision was made to handle the surgical strikes in layers across the board, rather than a sector, division or department at a time. That way all were equally safe, equally at risk. A. J. found it to be a leveler of sorts, to keep the process honest. Survivors of a given round temporarily breathed a sigh of relief, but with the clear understanding there were no guarantees that the reprieve was permanent.

The rapid pace of the restructuring was at once a blessing and a curse. Doc kept reminding A. J. of the old Dutch proverb, that kind surgeons leave stinking wounds. There wasn't a lot of time to mourn when the cuts just kept on coming.

There were also no gut-wrenching repeats of George McDowell's reaction when the faculty first heard what A. J. had been hired to do. With its leadership core in disarray, the Bolland faculty was all but mute through the waves of pink slips—almost sadly so, given their accustomed feistiness in the past over far, far less.

As academic officer in charge, A. J. personally delivered the dismissals, his red-rimmed eyes and breaking voice irrefutable testimony to the human costs. In the wake of the fire, even the students could not bring themselves to mount a protest. As the bloodletting progressed, a sizable number of students had begun to try to work the system in order to make sure Bolland's name and colors appeared on their diploma cases, this one last time. Whatever it took.

A. J. knew the grief of losing his family with brutal finality at the hands of a drunk driver. In a sense, he was losing one again. *His campus family, however dysfunctional.* Only this time it was he who was at the wheel, stone cold sober and in control of his faculties. The irony, at times, was unbearable. In those moments of searing introspection, Sam Pomerantz alone stood between him and the abyss.

Graduation was less than a month away. It had to be well past midnight and something in the rise and fall of Sam's breathing as she stirred alongside him in the darkness, told A. J. he wasn't alone with his thoughts.

"You can't sleep . . . I woke you."

Her audible intake of breath was an answer of sorts. "Yes, and No. I was half-awake already."

"Insomnia?"

"Just wondering," she said, "wondering what would Anne have made of all this—watching you tear yourself to pieces trying to save this place, those people out there."

A sliver of moonlight was filtering in from the bedroom window, enough so A. J. could see her watching him intently. Her upturned face was pale, inscrutable. He couldn't allow himself to dwell on the fact the pressure must be getting to her, too. Not and retain any pretext of sanity.

"She put up with a lot—even in those glory days," he said slowly. "My teaching and all the prep time that went with it, the office hours, perpetual on-campus squabbling, endless plotting in George McDowell's basement. Every spare minute I buried myself in my research—as unrepentant an alpha dog as the rest of them."

"Sometimes I think workaholism is an unwritten requirement for tenure. We even organize ourselves into 'disciplines'. Not exactly a call for moderation or a balanced lifestyle."

"Perhaps," he said. "But at what point does that single-mindedness become selfish, even narcissistic? At the very least, I was careless—*care less,* taking for granted the needs and the loyalty of the people who loved me the most. That day Anne drove alone over the mountain to the clinic, she just shot me one of those 'looks' when I told her I wouldn't be coming with her. 'Like boys, squabbling in your playpen over there. Don't you worry, I'm keeping a tab, plan on collecting one of these days.' That was the last thing she ever said to me . . ."

His voice broke off, steadied again. "I swore, no more, never again. Yet here I am, obsessed with finding some deeper meaning in this catastrophe—keeping us both up half the damn night. You would think two decades of research into why communities flounder should have taught me *something*. The dynamics are hardly a mystery. Look for Armageddon when ideologies or political frameworks become more important than people or human growth, when moral rigidity seduces people into believing they can know all the questions, much less answers."

"Tough stuff, watching communities die, utopian or not," Sam told him. "I can't bring myself even to go back to Phrenel Springs—abandoned grain elevators, boarded up store fronts, vacant farm houses with broken windows and shredded curtains stirring in the wind . . . "

"Believe me, when I was ten, Brave New Worlds seemed a heck of a lot more substantial, worthy of emulation than anything I saw in suburbia. Little did my folks know what they were unleashing when they took me on a trip to Pleasant Hill, Kentucky."

"The Shakers, I assume."

"For starters," he chuckled softly. "Grad school was like giving drugs to an addict. Waldensiens, Shakers, Pietists—those incredible back-to-back utopian models in New Harmony, Indiana. Parallels still pop up from time to time. Sixties communes. Jonesboro. All of them seeking truth in isolation—with the culture of Academe no exception. And not many happy endings in any of it. A primal urge . . . like trying to recapture some long lost Eden."

"Still, not all of it for naught, I have got to believe. Monasticism fits the mold and at one time those communities kept civilization alive against some pretty formidable odds."

"You're right, of course," he said. "The secular models certainly had their moments, too . . . devising revolutionary educational systems, breaking down gender stereotypes, creating economic systems that equalized wealth when robber barons were still running amok elsewhere. The Chautauqua movement bringing culture and learning to the wilderness—"

"Glorifying the life of the mind. I remember some lofty words to that effect forged in wrought iron on the very gates to the Bolland campus."

"Something I'd rather forget as I start to break out the padlocks!"

Her breath was warm against his skin. "Well, if it's letting go you're after," she said, her voice husky with longing, "I think I could come up with a couple of suggestions . . . "

"Sam," he said.

"Yes . . . "

"Nothing. I just needed to hear your name."

When he drew her to him, it was with the desperation of a man struggling alone in deep waters. Their love-making quickly took on a fierce intensity that left them both spent, clinging silently to one another in the darkness. On a shuddering sigh, A. J. closed his eyes, felt her breathing steady, then his own.

Sleep came in spite of himself—though precious

forgetfulness, Elysium, was tougher to come by. In the fleeting hours until dawn, he found himself visited by recurring nightmare visions of dormitory roofs imploding, molten fire and ash raining down upon them from a black and angry sky.

Commencement. The week and then the day was hard upon them, a rite-of-passage made all the more ambivalent by the conclusion of the merger negotiations.

Ink had been put to paper. The traditional solemnities would honor not only individual academic milestones completed, but would mark Bolland's last hours as an independent institution of higher learning. The final terms of the negotiations could well have been far worse. Twenty of the Bolland faculty, a mix of tenured veterans and nontenured instructors, plus some fifteen staff had survived the cuts.

A. J. waited until the last possible minute, the night before the Saturday event, to haul out his ceremonial academic garb. Sam stood watching him take the gown and hood out of their protective wardrobe bag, shook her head.

"Leave it to academe to think up an outfit like this," she chuckled softly.

Suspended precariously on a wire hanger from the bathroom door, the flamboyant maroon and black academic robe from his Alma Mater looked so much smaller than life, even a little shabby around the edges, after all the Convocations and Commencements it had witnessed. Sam tugged in vain at the wrinkles on one of the garment's flowing sleeves, trying to smooth out the worst of it.

"The thing is hotter than Hades," A. J. grumbled, "and par for the course, it's going to be in the high eighties out there."

Sam laughed. "What would you expect from a profession that manages to reverse the seasons. The calendar reads September and nature begins its annual deathwatch. Meanwhile out on the quad another class of freshmen shows up to start their educational journey. Spring comes for the graduates amid lofty talk of new life beginning. And what do they do? Deck themselves out in all their finery, caps and gowns and tassels for one last, bittersweet goodbye. To boot, we call all the hoopla 'exercises'—then we all sit there immobilized far too long, wondering when those gosh-awful speeches are ever going to end."

"I don't know about the graduating class," he grimaced, "but I, for one, am going to reek of mothballs."

"Not if I can help it."

Over his protests, she took it upon herself to put a steam iron to work on the gown and hood, had already begun hauling out the board and press cloth. As she took the velvet beret that went with the get-up out of its plastic storage bag, she looked around for somewhere to stash it, gave up and hung it on the door knob. The thing looked vaguely silly taken out of context—the stuff of last-minute cobbled-together Halloween costumes.

"By the way, I hear they've finally assigned you an office," Sam said, visibly impatient for the iron to heat.

Given his mood, the less he thought about what did or didn't await him at Emmaline, the better. In the great personnel shuffle, A. J. was among the few former Bolland faculty who were slated to be transplanted physically to the central Emmaline-Wattrous campus—strange as it was to think in those terms. About a quarter of Emmaline's staff and faculty would then move to vacated offices at Bolland At least initially, such exchanges would be based on clusters of academic majors to encourage better integration of personnel.

"I'm told it's Harter Hall," he told her. Harter was the central administration building, in itself an unsettling prospect.

"Clear across campus." From her own office, she meant.

"Close. Closer anyway than the two of us commuting alone so much of the time these past few months. At least now we can share the drive, carve out more quality time."

"Dodging those gravel trucks heading over the mountain toward the construction site east of Emmaline," Sam grimaced. "I was thinking more along the lines of a genuine weekend alone. No committees, no finals to grade, just you and me and my wildflower book, though the book is optional. I can't even imagine how painful, how awkward the whole transfer of power thing is going to be tomorrow."

"Mercifully, Doc Radisson made it clear at the last cabinet meeting—no formal, public nailing-shut-of-the doors. He already turned over the keys privately, so to speak, to Emmaline's president early in the week. Most of the pink-slipped personnel won't clear their offices until the Thursday after Commencement weekend. All that takes at least some pressure off the moment."

Iron in hand, Sam was zeroing in on a particularly stubborn crease around the black hash marks on one of the flowing sleeves of his doctoral gown. In trying to evade the sensitive velvet fabric, she managed to get her fingers instead. Sam let out a pot-scorcher sequence of oaths that left her flushed, embarrassed.

"Blister," she gasped. "Damn . . . that . . . smarts . . . !"

A. J. quickly sprinted to the kitchen for some ice. Meanwhile she was frantically rummaging in the medicine cabinet for something to put on the burn.

"Enough already," he said, "call the job good, Sam, before you immolate yourself. It's far better than anything I would have come up with."

He hadn't asked her to press the blasted gown in the first place, but she had insisted. Despite her best efforts, the cloud of scalding droplets from the steam vent kept missing their target.

"As good as it's going to get," she muttered.

"More than anything, it would mean a lot . . . I hope you plan on coming to graduation tomorrow," he told her. "The Convocation begins at ten, Commencement at one, though I'll probably head over to campus at the crack of dawn."

Sam clicked off the power switch on the iron. It wasn't as easy to shut down what he read in her face, to watch her worrying, grieving for and with him.

"Sorry, can't, unfortunately," she told him. "Command performance. I've been meaning to tell you I won't be there. Counseling is on stand-by, me included, getting Emmaline's own graduation lists ready for our doings on Sunday."

The cord to the iron had become snarled around the doorknob. With a swift motion, A. J. leaned over and disentangled it.

"No problem—it's probably better this way," he said after a while. "And since you're tied up, I may as well stay on after the ceremonies and clean out my office, or make a start in that direction anyway. With any luck, I should be home when you get back from Emmaline."

He hadn't volunteered and she hadn't asked, except in passing, how Bolland's survivors were handling the upcoming contract deadlines with their soon-to-be new employer. There was some stonewalling, understandable under the circumstances. Anything short of a last-minute concession to the inevitable could be construed as tacky, if not downright callous. But then, desperate times can call forth desperate responses, and to date, all but a handful of the Bolland faculty in question had signed their new faculty agreements.

A. J. was not one of them. If pushed on the subject, he would have been hard pressed to explain the lapse, even to himself. Any way he cut it, this was shaping up to be a long, anything but peaceful night.

By the time he arrived on campus next morning, fortified with even more caffeine than usual, the parking lots were already beginning to fill with vehicles of family and graduates alike. Forecasters were predicting rain on and off most of Saturday. Taking no chances, maintenance had set up the chairs and a dais both on the lawn and in the gym should the event need to be moved indoors. The latter proved an unnecessary precaution.

By mid-morning the campus was sweltering under overcast skies, with temperatures and humidity approaching record highs for May. Wide-brimmed mortarboards and SPF 30 notwithstanding, the upturned faces in the graduate section were sunburned, expectant. Their black armbands were restrained as far as gestures of protest go. Otherwise, the senior class behaved pretty much as any other graduates before them. Laughter and tears abounded. There was amazingly little posturing. The memories the valedictorians chose to share revolved around one another and their personal stories as much as about this place—or their future as alumnae of an institution that had ceased to exist.

The rest of the official speeches were mercifully brief even low-keyed. Faculty had debated behind closed doors, discussions to which A. J. wasn't privy, about the possibility of a boycott. But in the end they turned out in force, grim-faced, their gowns and hoods creating the familiar rainbow of color as they processed across campus from the arches of the academic building to the quad. Reserved faculty seating was up front and dead ahead of the platform on which the dignitaries were sitting. All the while A. J. clutched the formal platform book, intent on the names on the roster of graduates to come, the faces of his colleagues imprinted themselves in his memory, survivors and casualties of the merger alike.

When it was all over, he quickly forsook the platform, struck off briskly across the quad, alone, en route to his office. A familiar face stopped him dead in his tracks. *Joel.* A. J. turned the name over a second time in his head before risking it out loud, half-expecting his former student to vanish like a mirage, a distinct possibility given the waves of heat shimmering on the quad.

"Van Susten—I wouldn't have expected you here"

Their greeting was awkward. Prolonged conversation was going to be a tricky business in the crush of parents and tearful students around them.

"Bolland's last graduation . . . I wouldn't have missed it for the world. So, it's true, then," Joel said, "the two Boards have approved the merger."

"Signed, sealed—delivered. The press releases went out yesterday."

A. J. tugged at the fastener on his Oxford-style academic gown. It took a while, but he finally succeeded in shedding the unwieldy garment in favor of tie and shirt sleeves.

Joel was avoiding his gaze. "You must have been through hell and back," he said.

Anxious, A. J. realized, wondering what spin to put on his former professor's status. *Protective.* Something in that touched A. J. more than any single gesture in that long day fraught with poignant moments.

"Could have been worse," A. J. forced a twist of a smile, "although a colleague or two might dispute that."

He was replaying in his head the rows of faces of the faculty at the graduation ceremony. George McDowell wasn't the only one who had his doubts about what Bolland's interim dean in the end had been willing to negotiate.

"And Sam . . . Ms. Pomerantz?"

"Settling in at Emmaline-Wattrous. She's going great guns expanding their developmental programs."

"Glad to hear it. She was sure in the right place when I needed her," Joel told him. "But then so were you. I hope you tell her I tried to look her up, both of you."

"Of course. She'll appreciate that."

"It's long overdue . . . I didn't want to leave here without telling you. I don't know how I'd have handled any of it, back then, without your help. But then I'm sure you know that," Joel hesitated, finally came straight out with it. "Have you seen him . . . Ellison, since the shooting?"

"Once, briefly," A. J. nodded. "He's out of ICU but not out of the woods or the hospital. He's not allowing visitors. It looks like the man is never going to be able to teach again."

Joel chewed at his lower lip. Whatever he was thinking, he chose not to articulate it.

"You and Ms. Pomerantz were right, by the way," he said instead, "about grad school. I decided to enroll at Carnegie-Mellon. Summer school starts in a month, in the political science department."

Apparently the semester Joel spent in his dad's auto business had worked a major miracle. "So not the Law after all."

"A double degree."

A. J. blinked—about the time it took for Joel's pronouncement to register, Law and Political Science. This was A. J.'s own course of study his former student was describing, *disturbing on any number of levels*. He sensed Joel watching him, intent and unsmiling, anticipating his reaction.

"An interesting choice," A. J. said finally.

"It worked for you."

"I would rest a lot easier if you told me it works for *you*," A. J. said pointedly. "For what it's worth, I, for one, had no notion what I was getting into at the time. I think it's safer to say, you *do*. I assume you'll be shooting for a partnership with some advocacy firm . . . maybe governmental work. Though a dual degree certainly seems a bit like overkill."

Joel grinned, shot off the punchline. "With any luck when I finish, I hope to do a couple of internships, get some hands-on stuff under my belt. By then I thought maybe you might consider me if there's an opening for an adjunct at Emmaline-Wattrous," he said coyly.

A muscle began to twitch along the ridge of A. J.'s jaw. "You're . . . ," he started to say *kidding*, caught himself, "you're serious."

For the life of him he didn't know whether he should drag his former student into his office and verbally knock some sense into him or privately give thanks that in spite of everything, Joel was picking himself up, was dusting himself off and moving on. The hell of it was, the gesture was meant as flattering, most professors' wet dream if it came down to it. Except somewhere in A. J.'s head darker voices threatened to assert their claim on him as well. *So, this is what his life's work had become—to clone yet another generation of potential Ferinelli's, Ellison's and McDowell's.*

Joel was looking at him strangely. "I may be out of line . . . stop me if I'm wrong," he said, "but word on the street has it you will be taking over the chair of the Poli Sci department at Emmaline."

"That seems to be the plan."

A. J. hadn't intended to be so gruff or evasive. Truth was, in the end he hadn't thought about his own survival, much less tried to make it happen. Even raising the issue made him extremely uncomfortable. Late in the merger negotiations, an unknown hand had penned in A. J.'s name under the new roster of full-time faculty at Emmaline-Wattrous. Even tougher to stomach was the asterisk appended, apparently administrative duties went with the package.

At first he was too stunned someone had intervened, had taken the decision out of his hands—too preoccupied with winding up the negotiations to either protest or ask exactly what all of that meant. Then, to A. J.'s dismay, the Emmaline-Wattrous president had approached him personally a week ago about leading the accreditation self-study the college had ahead of it over the next two years, a major challenge given the merger.

"You are . . . I assume you're going to sign on the dotted line," Joel said.

An unfortunate choice of language, given the blank signature line on his contract. "I'm considering it."

There was an uneasy silence. It was finally Joel, not A. J., who intervened.

"What ever comes of it, I just want to say, they're lucky to get you!" Joel flashed a self-deprecating smile. "Classes start in a week. I figured, okay, why wait until Fall . . . take it easy first semester, get my feet wet in summer school. It's been a while since I forced myself to sit down and really study."

"Like riding a bicycle. Just do yourself a favor and memorize all those damn court cases, Van Susten. I seem to recall—"

"That surreal Con Law quiz you sprung on us. Yeah . . . well, a joint degree is sure going to test your bicycle theory of scholarship. I've got the feeling I could be in for a rough ride."

Had he ever been that young? A. J. knew such brutally self-critical moods as well, had felt them himself standing in line at the graduate office to confirm his own course schedule, now so many years ago. He knew on some level if he would have had a son himself, the proverbial apple couldn't have fallen closer to the tree.

"None of that has to be written in stone, Van Susten," A. J. told him bluntly. "A bit of advice worth pondering."

"I realize that . . . you have no idea," Joel said. "My old man was pretty damn worked up on the subject. I finally told him whatever happens, *I could have been a contender* is one epitaph I don't want on my tombstone. All those months I was licking my wounds and selling cars, I kept thinking about the crazy skeleton in your office with the Carpe Diem sign around its neck. If it comes down to it and I can't hack it, you can remind me of this conversation. But I'll guarantee you this, Prof, it wouldn't have been for lack of trying."

Mercifully no response was required. Decked out in dark dress slacks, white shirt and tie, Andy Duncan had spotted them and was headed their way. Grinning from ear to ear, the guy launched into one of those impromptu air guitar scissors leaps, but unfortunately in the process he half tripped over his academic gown still draped Batman-style around his shoulders, narrowly missing a close encounter with the rim of the marble fountain at the base of the carillon.

A. J. fought a smile at the get-up, quite a change after four years watching Andy prowl the campus decked out in surplus military gear. The young man's course work wouldn't be officially completed until August, but then in a rare display of nostalgia, the student actually had owned up to wanting the Bolland seal on his diploma. It was the least A. J. could do to finesse it.

The professor shifted his own robe and other trappings so he could shake the young man's hand. "You did it, Duncan."

"Almost, anyway," Andy managed a sheepish smile. "Nothing stands between me and boot camp at this point but Elizabethan Poetry or the Harlem Renaissance. The English Department and I are still negotiating. Except Joel here still keeps trying to persuade me it would make a lot more sense to forget the Marines, enroll in a crash course in Arabic somewhere, keep the old gray matter intact as long as possible. He may have a point."

"You know if you ever need a reference, Duncan, I'd be happy to fire one off. If anybody could ferret out the bad guys running around in the bull-rushes, my money's on you!"

Duncan flushed. "Thanks, Prof. Really . . . for everything."

If anything, the noise level around them was escalating considerably. A couple of graduates had taken off their shoes, rolled up their pant legs and were squaring off for a water fight in the reflecting pool at the base of the carillon. Time to pull the plug.

"Before we all get too much older," A. J. said, "I ought to get going and let the two of you do the same, hoist a glass or two, for old time's sake." It was as plausible an exit line as any that came to mind.

"You're welcome to join us—"

"Sorry," A. J. forced a smile. "The battle plan is to turn Bolland's Academic Center, including my old faculty digs, into temporary student housing, ASAP. Which leaves me with a car full of empty boxes to load, pack and haul over to—"

"Van Susten and I would make short work of it," Andy Duncan persisted, "just say the word."

A. J. could well imagine how their little blitz of a moving job would turn out. "I appreciate the offer, really," he said, "but I've got it covered. Just celebrate, you two. You've certainly earned it."

Andy frowned, his expression uncertain, before slowly he extended his hand again. "Prof, it's been real!"

Joel took that as his cue to pull his former professor into an awkward bear-hug of a farewell. "Look, if there's a free weekend," he said, "I'll try and get back this summer sometime. I mean, only if you and Ms. Pomerantz—"

"Of course. You're welcome any time."

"You'll write?"

"Email. Wonderful invention, Van Susten."

With a thumbs-up gesture to them both, A. J. slipped off into the crowd. The wall-to-wall leave-taking going on around him made it impossible to look back.

Chapter Twenty

The academic center basement was eerily quiet as A. J. steeled himself to hole up in what had been his faculty office all those years in order to finish his packing. Amazing what cardboard can hold. No less amazing was how memory-laden an accumulation of books, files, and bits and scraps of a career four walls of a faculty office could retain over time.

His professional life history was buried among all that clutter. A manila folder yielded up the yellowing citation from his first teaching award, dated his second year at Bolland. Dust had contributed a patina of time to his doctoral thesis, crammed tight into the back of a fireproof file drawer.

A. J. chuckled, remembering the all-but-the-dissertation paranoia that had once led him—while that bit of scholarly hubris was still in draft form—to keep the latest revisions and box of research notes stashed alongside the bed every night in case of fire in his seedy graduate school apartment. He and his roommate used to kid about it. So had Anne, when A. J. told her about those days.

"You actually slept with the darn thing," she shook her head. "Figures. I always pictured you hunched over some steel-mesh cell in the library, cranking out the pages with quill and ink, with cobwebs dripping from a green eye-shade!"

Anne. In a lower desk drawer he unearthed a small cache of framed photos of her, face glowing, along the glen trail at Morgan Ford Sanctuary. Below it was his favorite, a shot of her sitting on a Fire Island beach, staring out over the ocean. The photo was taken during what they affectionately had called their honeymoon to meet his folks. The homecoming was a full year after their impromptu moment of truth before the Justice of the Peace. Behind her was a hillock of sand crowned by a stand of wild beach plum. A blade of sea grass was tangled in her hair, mute evidence of their love-making.

He instinctively had stashed the photos in the drawer for safe-keeping early on in his relationship with Sam, only now remembered they were there. He made room for the frames in a box with newspaper clippings and several old Bolland yearbooks. In the process, he stopped to take a swipe at the cloudy surface of the glass.

When he next checked his watch, a good two hours had passed. All that remained to sort was a small heap of unopened mail and memos lying on A. J.'s desktop. Suddenly aware how tired he was, he slid into his desk chair, rifled half-heartedly through the 'to do' pile. One last-ditch chance, he thought, to weed out anything urgent and discard or box the rest.

He hadn't remembered even receiving the slim campus mail envelope, no return address—had avoided opening it at the time on the assumption it was from Personnel, chiding him about the contract deadline. No time like the present. A. J. retrieved the single sheet of crisp linen bond and scanned the contents. The memo line leaped out at him: *The H.N. Reuter Prize Honoring Exceptional Scholarship and Teaching.*

A. J. quickly scanned the contents. A week before graduation, the body of the letter informed him, the faculty had voted to give him the prestigious cash award, the last ever—thirty-five thousand dollars, no strings attached. The signature on the notification letter read, George Fulham McDowell, Division Chair, Humanities and Social Sciences.

It was as if an iron vise had tightened around his chest. With a single stroke of the pen, it was all there—recognition from his peers and the funds to pursue high-level scholarly research, the moment of a lifetime, a professional triumph, total and complete. And it was his erstwhile mentor George McDowell who had made that possible.

Beyond irony, A. J. thought, how life gives with one hand and rips the heart out of you with the other. A year ago, grateful, he would have taken McDowell's gesture at face value, the heartfelt expression of respect from a senior faculty member for his long-time protégée and friend. But that was then. In the new normal of the merger, if his former mentor had wanted to express his most profound censure for what A. J. had done at Bolland, he couldn't have found a more pointed or cutting way to do it. *Blood money*, George's signature told him. *Blood money, bought with a ledger of lives interrupted and careers abruptly ended.*

"I thought I'd find you here," a voice said from the office doorway—male, familiar.

Startled, A. J. tossed the letter on the desktop. Just how long had his boss and friend been watching him? "Doc. I thought you would have—"

"Bailed by now. Me, too, actually. I packed up most of my stuff yesterday," Doc said, "was just over at the administration building taking one last look."

A. J. stood, unkinked his back, then shared a collegial hug with his boss and friend. It was the gesture of survivors contemplating the crater-scarred battlefield behind them.

"I shudder to think," Doc said, "what it's going to be like if I ever do this kind of housecleaning over at the practice. It will be horrific enough just shoveling out over there after these past few months on half-time Bolland detail."

"Believe me, avoidance has its merits."

Doc exhaled sharply. "President Cordova tells me that's not all you've been avoiding."

There was no mistaking his reference. *The unsigned Emmaline-Wattrous contract.* A. J. stiffened, managed to keep his expression neutral. "There's been a lot on my plate," he said.

"What does a signature take, two seconds?"

But then that wasn't the issue. And they both knew it.

"When I asked you to take the interim deanship," Doc said slowly, "we discussed how tough this was going to be. If I had seriously thought it would jeopardize your career, I would never—in all conscience—have asked or encouraged you to do the job."

"I know that, Doc."

"So then, Ferinelli, cut to the chase."

270

They both knew what refusing the contract would mean. Given his age and the tightness of the teaching market, for all intents and purposes A. J.'s academic career would be over.

At the bottom of the drawer he had been emptying, A. J. spotted yet another stray Bolland catalog from several years back, lying amid the clutter. Irrelevant now. He casually snagged it, then tossed it into the maw of a huge carton labeled crudely in permanent marker, Dumpster Run. That left just the announcement of the Reuter Prize still lying there on the desktop, waiting for a response. Without a word, A. J. picked up the letter, fingered it thoughtfully. He offered it to Doc who quickly skimmed the contents, smiled.

A. J.'s eyebrow arched. "You knew about this."

"You deserve it, of course."

"Coming from the faculty, exquisite timing," A. J. winced. "Some just might read it as a collective dagger thrust on the way out the door. Fire a boatload of tenured faculty, Ferinelli, and then head off for the Bahamas to celebrate, on us."

An explosive out-rush of breath summed up Doc's spin on things. "Damnit man, you didn't cause what happened here. You did a heroic job of protecting as many of your colleagues as possible. They may not know that or care what the effort cost you, to say nothing about ever acknowledging it, but they owe you a hell of a lot!"

A. J. felt the familiar start of a headache, half-closed his eyes, willing a serenity beyond his grasp. "Thanks . . . thanks for that," he said, "but—"

"But I see you're hell-bent on penance, apparently. Prepared to sacrifice your faculty line, your career or both on the altar of the merger."

"Slipping my name on the list of survivors wasn't my idea in the first place," A. J.'s jaw hardened, knowing full well now that Doc must have been the one to intervene. "It's ridiculous given the bottom line. I've seen the books, if you remember. My full-time salary as a senior professor could easily fund a slot-and-a-half for junior level instructors, one from Emmaline and one from Bolland, better in the long run for everybody."

"I beg to differ, Ferinelli."

"With all due respect, what I do about a contract with Emmaline-Wattrous isn't up for discussion. You hired me to do a job. I did it. Let the chips fall where they may."

Doc's shaggy brows tightened in a frown. "Survival guilt. Whatever you're feeling, man, believe me I've been there. Anger, denial—it's the predictable list. I've lost a patient or two in my day. You never get used to it, you shouldn't."

This was not just about career choices any longer, it could be their friendship on the line. A. J. grasped for the hard edge of the desktop behind him, steadied himself.

"So, tell me, Doc . . . I'm curious what you say that doesn't make you feel like a hypocrite of the worst order. The body is barely cold—family members haven't picked up their cell phones to start calling their lawyers, *yet.* You're feeling responsible as hell, wondering how you screwed up, and some grieving kid just stands there calmly telling you how grateful they are for everything you did."

Doc's eyes narrowed. "There's something you're not telling me here, Ferinelli."

"I've been in this business half my life," A. J. shrugged, "watching my colleagues lifting up the accumulated wisdom of humankind, far too much of the time to the bored, the sleeping and the indifferent. We all do it, hang on the fantasy, dream the dream of that one student out there we could truly reach—the one who picks up the torch. Professional vanity, I suppose. And heaven help me, if you're talking about a disciple ditching the old nets and following the master, Joel Van Susten was mine. On some level, I find myself regretting that fact as profoundly as almost anything that has happened in the past six months."

"Van Susten. He's the student who crossed swords with Ellison and dropped out. You made sure the kid graduated."

A. J. chuckled softly. "Be careful what you wish for. Joel showed up this afternoon on the quad looking for closure, bursting to tell me he had just enrolled in grad school in Political Science and Law, pathetically grateful for every damned platitude I ever doled out in the name of mentoring. And even after all academe did to him, the poor guy is still hell bent on heading down the same godforsaken path I took."

"There are worse legacies, Ferinelli."

"Right now I can't think of many of them. Oh sure, I just stood there nodding and making all the politically correct noises. For the life of me, self-serving to the end, I couldn't bring myself to tell him the truth."

"Enlighten me."

"How manipulative I felt, most of all that he credits me with inspiring his visions of the future. Hells bells, the kid wound up trying to reassure *me*. Even knowing what he knows, he still wants a piece of this business, which is more than I can say for myself right now!"

With an impatient gesture, Doc extended the letter with the offer of the Reuter Prize in his friend's direction. It was almost as if daring him to take it.

"And *your* mentor, the Civil War buff?"

"McDowell," A. J. winced. "You've seen the termination lists, will have to forgive a terrible pun, but I believe the term of choice at moments like this is, the guy's *history*. Basically, I threw him under the bus—early retirement, saved two junior faculty lines in the process, but not before helping steer the arson investigation in his direction. Now there's gratitude for you!"

"At least our erstwhile Dean is still unemployed."

Not for long, A. J. found himself thinking. Men like Dean Wilton Honore Bremer seemed to have an uncanny way of landing on their feet. Re-folding the Reuter letter, A. J. started to toss it into the to-shred box, changed his mind and folding it, tucked it into his shirt pocket.

"Go figure," he grimaced, "regardless of what the motives were in awarding the grant, my first instinct was still to take the money, head off to some archive, write my damn book, get it over with. Then maybe I would finally get up the guts to draw a line under it all. Sell shoes, shovel manure, anything but teach."

"And what does Sam say about all that?" Doc said. "I grant you're entitled to a mid-life crisis, Ferinelli—life beats the crap out of you, so you hide out in a hole somewhere to regroup. My ex-wives will be happy to attest I've had my moments, including one go-round when I kayaked from the St. Lawrence to the Mississippi. But then I didn't have Sam Pomerantz to come home to either."

A. J. flinched. At least Doc could have had the tact to keep his outspoken approval of his choice in women out of the mix.

"This soul crisis of yours," Doc persisted, "does she—"

"Sam senses something is wrong, of course. But I . . . we haven't talked about it, no, not in so many words."

A. J. felt a band tighten around his heart at the thought of telling her. Filling the last of the boxes, he had come across the outline of the seminar Sam had given on learning styles her first semester at Bolland, long before he truly knew her, loved her so much it hurt.

If he took the Reuter and went off somewhere, Sam couldn't just pick up and go with him, that was a given. Nor could he ask it of her. The battle to build her programs and a future for herself at Emmaline-Wattrous lay dead ahead over the next six months to a year. It would take every bit of skill and passion she had to make sure it succeeded. She had come too far, risked too much to just chuck it and follow him.

"So ask for a postponement. The Reuter, as I understand it, is a fairly open-ended research grant. What is your specialty, anyway? If you told me, I'll confess I've forgotten."

"So have I, most of the time these days. I wrote my thesis on governance and systems failures in isolationist societies. Before Anne died, I was beginning to recast it as a monograph, *Governance Models and Systemic Failures in American Utopian Communities*". My God, what was I thinking?"

Doc managed a grim laugh. "Sounds suspiciously like the kind of field work you and I have been doing the last couple of months."

"I found the crazy manuscript in my files. Would you believe, I ended the thing with a quote from H. G. Wells—obsessed with utopias in his own right, if you recall. *Human history becomes more and more a race between education and catastrophe,* the guy said. Factor that one into the events of the past six months."

"And you truly think somehow your abstract what-iffing about Paradise Lost is going to gain you some kind of closure, make some sense out of Bolland?"

"Delusional to the end," A. J. shrugged. "Or maybe it's just tangible proof, I keep telling myself, that something of what matters or mattered to me will live on . . . in spite of or because of everything. Right now I would pretty much settle for either one."

For a split-second, raw anger flashed in Doc's eyes. "Life is *living*, Ferinelli," he said. "Damn tough to pin down in a card catalog. The sad part of all this is, you're a damn good administrator as well as a teacher and the self-study underway at Emmaline needs a strong hand now, not a year from now. Accreditation could be riding on it, given the merger, and Cordova makes no bones about it—she needs you over there. So help me, I can't just stand by and watch you toss all that in the proverbial pail. Not and live with myself."

"Right now the only decision that makes any sense is channel surfing with the remote," A. J. bristled. "If I take a sabbatical in the mood I'm in, I'm afraid I might just start scouring around instead for some public defender's office in need of a paralegal and never come back. Woefully overqualified for looking up case numbers in some law library, I grant you, but then it certainly makes me employable—the price is right."

Silent, the two men just stared at each other. "Before you do anything rash," Doc said evenly, "let me talk to President Cordova. You've got a whole summer ahead of you—take a short leave of absence if you need to. Go to Timbuktu, if it'll get your head on straight. Postpone the grant or cram in enough research over the next couple months to write your damn book, but in the name of all that is holy, man, don't let Bolland take you down with it. There are too many casualties out there already. Your name on the list is one I don't think I'm prepared to live with."

It was silent in the room. But then, there wasn't a heck of a lot more either one of them could say. Awkwardly, Doc took his leave.

A. J. knew the man would make good on his promise. Contract or no contract, Doc would make sure he had a job to come back to, if it came to that. All of which left him with just as many question marks as when he started.

Fortunately the only work on the calendar for the foreseeable future was chain gang stuff, the backbreaking job of loading the small mountain of cartons into his Toyota, one trip at a time. Repeat the drill on the other end and stash the boxed up vestiges of his life at Bolland in the relative safety of his garage. The mindless shuffling back and forth would keep him from dwelling on the obvious. On some level, all of this might be futile.

Sam had every right to expect, even demand, that he take the Emmaline-Wattrous offer. He had asked her to marry him, put that possibility on hold only because she asked it of him. If the tables were turned, he had no idea whether or not she would do the same.

Sweat was soaking through the back of his dress shirt by the time A. J. made his third box-run from campus. He pulled into his driveway in time to catch a woman ringing his front doorbell—certainly not the break he was anticipating. Petite with hair close-cut, a sandy gray, the woman turned at the sound of the Toyota behind her, made eye contact. A. J. cut the engine, jaw tight, took his time throwing on the hand brake and retrieving the keys from the ignition.

Bea McDowell. He hadn't seen the woman since his wife's funeral and the immediate months thereafter. Those anguished encounters were a far cry from Bea's incredible and frequent soirees at which he and Anne had feasted on exotic canapes before settling down to some of the most elegant dinners either one of them had ever experienced. Ever the consummate hostess, Bea McDowell had always been impeccably dressed, charming even the dourest of faculty curmudgeons with her warmth and Southern grace.

The Bea McDowell waiting for him on his front porch certainly was not the one in his memory banks. Dressed in jeans and a faded paint shirt, she had a tentativeness about her—fragility even. Her car keys were still in her hand, as if she had been seriously contemplating changing her mind about the visit. A. J. recognized it now, her oversized steely blue Buick snugged alongside his curb.

Forcing a cautious smile, A. J. crossed the lawn in her direction, waiting for some signal how to greet her. She gave it, a mute and lingering hug. Ultimately, it was he—not she—who chose to end.

"It's good to see you," he told her.

Bea nodded. "I wasn't sure if I'd catch you."

By way of response, A. J. leaned over and unlocked the front door, stood aside to let her pass. Bea hesitated but finally took several tentative steps into the living room. He eased the door shut behind them.

The sound appeared to startle her. "I really can't stay . . . "

But then she made no move to go. Nor did she react, one way or the other, to his offer of coffee. As he pulled himself together enough to retrieve the custom grind from the refrigerator then scare up water and a filter, he caught glimpses of her in the living room still standing where he had left her.

A. J. tried to take in the room from her perspective. The evidence of Sam's touch over the past weeks and months was everywhere. Anne had enjoyed, was amused by Bea's relentless mothering, including her persistent decorating advice, when she first tried to turn the austere bachelor digs into a home on an assistant professor's salary. George and Bea had no children of their own.

"I was worried you might be . . . I saw the open garage, the boxes," Bea said as A. J. reappeared with the coffee. "I . . . we need to talk."

She took the mug of steaming, fragrant brew he offered her, then sought out a stiff-backed chair facing the new couch he and Sam had picked out together. Easing his aching body back on the sofa cushions, A. J. focused on the wall of picture frames behind his visitor, two of them skewed to the rest for all of Sam's efforts over the months.

"We're moving, too, you know," she told him in her subtle drawl, "back to North Carolina. I have family there. We're selling the house, may already have a buyer."

"I heard," he said. "It must be difficult after all these years."

Her voice was barely audible. "He'll miss you," she said.

A. J. forced himself to meet her steady gaze. It was the last assessment of George McDowell's state of mind A. J. would have anticipated. He was thinking about the Reuter letter and the spin he was inclined to put on it, logical enough after the last terrible time he and McDowell had really talked.

"We have no sons," she told him bluntly, her confidence visibly building as she spoke. "I think George always fancied you as some sort of spiritual successor. Your relationship, all of those years together meant, still means a great deal to him."

"I owe George a lot."

Even after all that happened between them, the admission came easier than A. J. once would have thought. For a long moment Bea just looked at him.

"He doesn't know I'm here," she told him. "But it needed to be said, you needed to know."

"Thank you."

She wasn't finished. "And I ought . . . want to thank you, too," she told him, "for helping my husband, tough as it was, especially when he was making his peace with what was going on at Bolland and his role in it, unintentional as it may have been. Last night, he finally told me the truth, how difficult things had become in the past months."

"Bea, you don't have to—"

"Yes," she said firmly. "Yes, I do. It would kill him to tell you but you need to know this. For both your sakes."

Like most faculty spouses, Bea McDowell had heard her share over the years. Impassioned vent sessions were part and parcel of the academic game. Mostly it was a lot of rhetoric and posturing, radical and off-the-wall, fueled by bourbon and frustration. No one took it seriously. Once spoken—in fact—rarely acted upon.

When all that had changed at Bolland, it was hard, if not impossible to pinpoint. But change it had.

"Coffee," A. J. said. "I think we could both use a refill."

He fumbled with the unwieldy pot, left a sizeable pool of liquid around the base of the mugs in the process. When he finally returned to the living room with her mug, Bea sat staring down into its murky depths.

"I guess I should have suspected something," she said finally. "Ray Ellison's visits at the house became more frequent. George seemed more moody and distant. I was in the laundry room one night just outside my husband's study, heard Ray speculating out loud about tactics to make the institution worthless to anyone contemplating a takeover. It was no secret dormitory space was among Bolland's most valuable assets, he said. I never thought about it again. Until the fire."

"And they found the bodies," A. J. said.

Bea was clutching at her mug as if her life depended on it. "Ray Ellison showed up . . . drunk, the night after the fire," she said softly. "It was late—after midnight. I could hear the two of them arguing in George's study. Just words here and there, but enough to know George was in trouble. He said something about conspiracy. Blackmail. Ellison kept shouting George down—finally he left. Yesterday, getting his academic robe of the closet, George broke down, admitted he knew Ellison had gotten the custodian drunk the afternoon of the fire."

"Putnam."

Bea nodded. "After they found those kids' bodies apparently Putnam was out of control—threatened to go to the police, claiming Ellison had put him up to it, that he had been guaranteed the dorm would be empty. Ellison wanted George to go back to campus with him and talk to the man."

"And did he . . . ?"

A shadow of pain darkened the woman's delicate features. "No. I think he suspected Ellison could have played more of a role than he was willing to admit, could be dragging George into it to save his own hide."

"Bea," he said carefully, "does George know if the supposed meeting with Putnam ever took place?"

"Ellison claimed the custodian never showed up. But of course, when they found the body out there at the landfill, it made George wonder." Bea looked down at her hands, visibly distraught.

"George never talked about it to me again," she said. "But since all the speculation about Putnam hit the papers, he was even more distant, shut up in himself."

"For all their suspicions, the police never found any evidence of foul play."

"We aren't talking about legality or the law, A. J.," she told him quietly. "You, of all people, ought to know that. And you *know* George—you were, hopefully still are, his friend. With George, this is about conscience."

It was so still in the room, he could hear the ticking of the antique mantel clock Anne had given him for their fourth wedding anniversary. Always ten minutes slow, it had become a kind of perpetual joke between them—a symbol of whimsy and humanity in an age of digital watches and their illusion of technological perfection. Clocks have hands and faces, or ought to. They work in spite of the imprecision and uncertainty that come with time passing. As much as we want to quantify certain moments, their ultimate meaning, the truth of them is all too often beyond rational knowing.

"And Joel," A. J. persisted. "Did George say anything when Joel Van Susten tracked Ellison down, confronted him, when the kid nearly wound up in jail."

"He . . . if Ellison told George anything, I never heard about

279

it," her voice was sad. "My husband certainly realized how much that young man meant to you. I only know Ellison stopped coming to the house. And now, of course, since Ellison's shooting and with Bremer gone . . . George and the Dean had been at Oxford at the same time, you know."

"I heard that," A. J. nodded.

"You ought to know, too, George found the whole circumstances surrounding the Dean's departure especially painful—what happened to that young mathematics instructor. He still finds it hard to believe how indefensible the man's conduct had become. And then when we heard about Ellison—"

"I went to see Ellison right after the shooting," A. J. said. "From what the doctors say, he'll never teach again."

Bea's eyes hardened and she drew in her breath, let it out in a painful rush. "I consider myself a Christian woman most of the time, don't put a whole lot of stock in Divine retribution" she said, her voice almost inaudible. "But when it comes to Ray Ellison, I'm not so sure. Bringing myself to forgive that man . . . I believe that may just take me a while . . . "

The silence between them was awkward as A. J. watched her struggle to compose herself. If the time had come for true confessions, there was one more loose end. A. J. had to know.

"I saw George," A. J. told her, "after the so-called hit list of faculty started circulating. He came to my office."

"Angry about the firings, he told me, but never at you. Angry at Ellison—at himself, all of them. When there was no insurance, George knew it was all over. It wasn't just saber rattling or a . . . game any longer. Bolland couldn't survive it."

A. J.'s voice fell to a harsh whisper of sound. "I understand that George was angry, but it became ugly, Bea. Ugly and personal. Things were said. I would have expected that from Ellison and some of the others. Not from George."

"Whatever he said at the time," Bea finished. "I think my husband truly feels you only did what you had to do."

"I got his letter about the Reuter Prize," A. J.'s mouth felt stiff.

Bea half-smiled. "He did everything he could to make sure you did, insisted it was his name on the announcement. It was the least he could do. You—if anyone, he said—deserve it."

In so many words, it was exactly what Doc Radisson had told him. A. J. just looked at her, felt the anger drain from him in a painful rush of awareness. It was not his mentor's feet of clay that were at issue any longer, but his own.

As a professor, he had flattered himself that his role was to loom larger than life, not merely to transmit knowledge but to use the power of the word to challenge and mold and shape not just the parameters of truth and the human experience, but alter the lives of others, to create the future. The potential for arrogance in that scenario boggled the imagination. At his peril, he had forgotten that how it is done and why, does more as well—over time it changes and shapes the mentor.

And arrogance it had been to pretend himself capable of discerning the anguish playing itself out in his mentor's life and heart. It was nothing short of arrogance to pass judgment on Joel Van Susten, on the hopes and aspirations of a student he himself had nurtured.

Without a sound, Bea had begun to cry, her eyes still fixed on the empty mug in her hands. "He . . . this has made him old, A. J. The clinic is talking about bypass surgery."

Without thinking, A. J. was kneeling alongside the straight-back chair, carefully easing the mug out of Bea McDowell's shaking hands so he could clutch them tightly in his own. His voice was low.

"As faculty we make our living with words, Bea," he said. "It's easy to forget that once a word spoken becomes fact, it takes on a reality of its own from which we can't easily distance ourselves. I would be grateful when the time is right, if you would tell him . . . tell George how much I truly *regret* that we . . . that it ended this way. Not just for Bolland. For us."

He saw Bea smile. Gently she extracted a hand so she could brush at her tear-streaked face, then she drew herself up, stood. Imperceptibly, her shoulders straightened.

"Yes," she told him. "I will. He loves you, A. J., always did. We both do."

Her hug said the rest. This was most likely the last time he would ever see either of them again.

A. J. stood in the doorway until Bea's car was out of sight.

When he turned to start back into his empty living room, the air felt suddenly stifling, closing in on him. Bracing himself palms spread against the hard edges of the door frame, he waited for his head to clear.

That scarred wood took the weight of everything Bea had told him, all the agony of the last nine months, the losses that came before in his life and those, unnamed, he knew were still to come. Shoulders shaking, frozen there alone with his grief, A. J. Ferinelli did what he had not been able to do—had needed to do—so often since the terrible night of the fire and all that came after. He wept.

Gradually, his desperate outpouring of grief spent itself. The sun had sunk below a thickening cloud bank on the horizon. It was almost dark when A. J. forced himself to retrieve George McDowell's letter about the Reuter Prize from his briefcase. He laid it on the coffee table.

Sam was still at Emmaline. A. J. waited for her on the couch in the living room, drained and only half-conscious of where he was, staring blankly at the empty straight-back chair where Bea had spilled out the secrets of her heart. He felt as alone as a man can be.

Chapter Twenty-One

It was dark when A. J. heard the key in his front door. Disoriented, he heard someone groping in the hall for the switch for the overhead fixture. A harsh light flooded his living room and threw everything into sharp relief.

"You look like death," Sam said.

Even in the mercilessly revealing light, he found himself thinking she had never looked more beautiful. It had been unseasonably hot the last few days and she had taken to wearing these understated tank-top sundresses—like everything else she wore, feminine without flaunting it, conjuring up the familiar ache inside him. Straightforward, no frills, lovely. Like Sam, herself.

She made no move to join him, but instead busied herself clicking on less obtrusive lamps around the room, then eliminating the glare overhead. Slowly, his eyes adjusted. From the safe confines of the sofa, A. J. processed the taut, anxious set of her features.

"Bea McDowell came to see me," he said.

"After graduation . . . with George."

"Here," he corrected her, "a couple of hours ago. Alone."

"I had heard they were moving—assume you weren't

expecting her."

Haltingly he told her all of it. Sam's face turned from pale to flushed, then ashen, a mirror of his own reaction when Bea first told him of Ellison's complicity in the Putnam affair.

"What are she and George going to—?"

"Get out of here," A. J. shrugged. "I force-retired the man. It's a good question what an academic does—*after*. George always jokingly said he would tend his roses, except he and I both knew as he said it, this wasn't just a job for that man, Sam. It was his life."

"Living isn't teaching," anger crackled in her voice, fierce, shocking him out of his detachment, "and life isn't just some abstract linguistic or philosophical exercise on the meaning of it all, the ultimate what-if. If you ask me, you and I have been indulging in that kind of *bullshit* way too much lately. Hell-bent on studying community? Here it is. Right in front of you. Life is about risk and caring, about relationships, flawed and messy and real. It's about George and Bea, it's Joel and those students you care about so much. It's *us*. Or at least I *thought* it was us . . . "

When he didn't respond, he saw her shoulders slump, read the awareness in her eyes. Someone must have talked to her, most likely Doc or President Cordova.

"It's true, then," she said dully, "you didn't sign the contract."

"No."

"You're just walking away. And you never had the simple courtesy to warn me this was coming."

"Sam, it isn't that simple."

He started to tell her about his encounter with Joel at graduation, the letter about the Reuter Prize and its horrific timing, the shattered illusions behind all of it. Doc offered, he said, to buy time so he could sort out his options. Sam was having none of it.

"Nice. Except you and I know what's really going on here. It's your version of closure, the accident all over again. You're going to take the Reuter to get as far away from this place as you can, write your damn book and then never come back, to Emmaline or the job. Or me, for that matter."

A. J.'s mouth felt stiff. "I'm sorry that I haven't been . . . should have told you what—"

"*Sorry?* Trust me, you don't have a monopoly on that," her

laughter ended on a rising note, almost a cry. "This isn't over, only beginning on some level. People around here are grieving, angry, confused and they need you. I need you."

He wished to heaven he could switch loyalties and campuses like a change of socks, with a wave of some wand wipe out how shattering it had been to play God with the lives of his friends and colleagues. If only he could do what his training had conditioned him to do when confronted with an ethical dilemma—to talk it out until it ceased to matter what he thought or felt, trusting somehow a path opened in the process, one he was prepared to take.

"For what it's worth," his mouth felt stiff, "I love you, Sam. Nothing can change that."

She just stared at him. Something already had changed, and they both knew it. Doubled over as if in pain, she had turned her back on him, unable to continue.

That finally got him on his feet. Even as he drew her back against him, hands cradling her bare shoulders, A. J. felt her wordless struggle. At all costs, he realized, she was not going to break down in his presence. "Sam, don't—please don't."

"You just expect me to take this, watch you bury yourself alive again, only this time in some moldy archive, heaven knows how far away, while you track down all those 'perfect', fatally flawed communities of yours. All that while I'm supposed to just put my life on hold after everything we . . . A. J., we talked about your research, just a few weeks ago. And you never said a single, solitary word about any of this. The possibility of the Reuter, the contract deadline, none of it."

In his defense, the Reuter had been unthinkable, totally off his radar at that point. Still, there was nothing he could say to make this right. "You deserve better," he told her, "deserve more than a burned out hulk of a human being. I need to be more than that, to myself and to you."

"Sometimes life is just showing up—not original maybe, but it fits. The gospel according to Sondheim. *We're still here*, both of us, and that's—"

"Not nearly enough," he said, "not for either one of us. If I just sign the faculty contract like this, I'd wind up hating myself. In time, I think you'd come to feel the same way. I couldn't live with that."

Though her eyes were still clouded with tears, the worst of her anger had begun transforming itself to a quiet despair. Going on autopilot, A. J. steered them both to the sofa. They settled in there, Sam nestled tightly against him, close—but with dark unknown waters already beginning to rush in between them.

"Jake always warned me about letting academe and its mystique get to me," he said. "Stick to the law, the guy said, nobody has any illusions about lawyers. We lawyers play to win, charge exorbitant fees, celebrate with Cuban cigars and chalk up another W on the tote board. Cynical real-politik, Jake said, but then nobody makes any bones about any of it either."

Sam's hand was clutching his. It was cold to the touch, trembling.

"You forget, I came here too needing Bolland to be some ivy-covered shrine to truth, beauty and wisdom," she told him. "Even after reality set in and I wound up at Emmaline, even after I vowed to protect myself from ever letting a louse like Dean Bremer hurt me that badly again, I still cannot bring myself to believe a college campus is just another place to punch the clock and earn a nickel, or love is hopeless or unattainable. You may not see it that way or want to hear it, but watching you struggle to challenge the assumptions you had made about your life and your work has kept my sanity these past months—in some perverse way has given me hope."

She shook her head. Her choked burst of laughter ended as quickly as it had begun.

"Like ships passing in the night, the two of us," her voice was low. "You were ready to commit back then when you were still trying to help *me* pick up the pieces. Under duress you agreed to wait until I was ready to talk about us, the future. Well, for what that's worth, I am—ready to talk, little good it does either one of us."

They had switched grounds with a vengeance. A. J. could only guess at what it cost Sam to rise above her loveless childhood and a lifetime of unfortunate choices when it came to men, to concede she needed his presence in her life, long-term.

His voice was tentative, barely audible. "I can't ask you to understand," he said. "You gave us another chance when I took on the problems at Bolland in the first place. I need that same trust now—more than ever."

"You also told me I would never regret it."

Sam, the words went unspoken against her hair, d*earest, dearest Sam.* Something of his anguish must have communicated itself.

Her voice was tired. "Being a wannabe gamer has its moments," she said. "Great therapy—replaying the siege of Carthage. The ancient Romans would have had a simple solution for this whole mess. Just sow the Bolland quad with salt and then plow it under. Tempting—and one thing I certainly *did* learn back home in Dakota was to handle a tractor."

A. J. laughed, but Sam didn't join him. "It's getting late," he said. In more ways than one.

An uncomfortable silence prevailed as they hit the kitchen, put together a makeshift dinner, then headed off for bed. Visibly exhausted, Sam drifted quickly off to sleep. Alone with his thoughts, A. J. lay there wide awake in the darkness alongside her as the minutes crept toward morning. A terrible heaviness had settled in around his heart. Even his wife's death had not left him so totally without faith in his ability to cope.

The obsession with Bolland, centering his life on the rhythm of academic life, had been a demanding mistress with which not even his beloved Anne could compete. If anything, Sam's attempts to understand, even empathize, only widened the gap between them. She would never hurl the truth back at him, but sometime since that morning in the corridor outside his basement office, she had grown beyond him.

Loyal as she was to her work, the students, even to Emmaline-Wattrous, A. J. knew academe was not the love of Sam's life any longer. It was *him* she loved. And heaven help him, she deserved the same in return. He had to find a way to begin again. Trouble was, he had stood at this watershed, had stared profound personal loss in the face once before, knew for him anyway how it had ended.

At first light, A. J. gave up on ever dozing off. Sam was still sound asleep. Gently disentangling himself, he showered and shaved, made coffee. As he passed through the living room, he noticed the Reuter prize announcement was still lying on the coffee table where he had left it. Retrieving it, he headed for the garage.

287

It took a while, but finally he found the last box he had packed at Bolland. On top was the to-do file in which he had stashed, among other things, the unsigned Emmaline-Wattrous contract. A. J. slipped McDowell's letter into the file and closed the box. Out of sight—but very much both still on his mind.

Be careful what you wish for. The phrase kept running through his head. He had never once considered what achieving those youthful goals might cost him. If Bea McDowell were to be believed, his mentor's role in awarding him the Reuter Prize was a powerful vindication, perhaps even George's way of bequeathing a way to live with all that had happened in the last nine months. And yet, if he used the money to leave Emmaline-Wattrous—either to make his peace with or to leave academe for good—it would have become a hollow victory.

Two of the people A. J. cared about most in the world, Sam and Doc Radisson, already had weighed in on the subject. His place was *here*, not off in some musty archive in a quest for the best of all possible worlds.

By the time Sam woke, A. J. had breakfast on the table. She too showered, changed and then joined him. It was as if their heart-to-heart last night had never happened. A. J. sat nursing his coffee while he watched her polish off her French toast, all the while not touching his own.

"I'd ask you about the state of head and heart," she said finally, "but not at the risk of launching World War III."

A. J. winced. "When you fell asleep last night, I had plenty of time to think about it."

"I see."

"You added it up yourself. Anne dies and I bury myself in my teaching. Bolland dies and I'm looking for the exits. Some just might chalk it up as a character flaw or at best a colossal fear of change, of becoming irrelevant, not just in the classroom, but even to myself."

"Nice try, but if you're trying to get rid of me, no deal," Sam managed a wan smile. "Tough stuff to find out your profession and workplace are no better, or worse, than any place else. At least instead of bemoaning the darkness, you did something to try to make things better. Anybody in their right mind who had to make the choices you did the past few months has a perfect right to complain about burnout."

"Believe me, Sam, if this were just a funk, we wouldn't be having this conversation."

Sam squared her shoulders, her voice steady as she said it. "For now, it's my last word on the subject. When all is said and done, I truly believe, this is where you belong. It's who you *are*."

They had arrived at a truce of sorts, to agree to disagree, and leave it at that. The rest of the weekend passed in mindless domesticity. Monday morning Sam went off to work in Emmaline-Wattrous as usual, while A. J. shuttled again between the two campuses tying up loose ends. Gradually it became possible for him to time his schedule so the two could commute together. If Sam sensed he was going through the motions, she obviously was choosing not to confront it.

By now it was late July. The boxes and debris from his office on the Bolland campus languished in the garage. He couldn't function at Emmaline-Wattrous if he kept working out of a briefcase in the cafeteria. Without fanfare one Tuesday morning, A. J. loaded the clutter from the garage into a rental van, then spent the better part of a day moving in to the office space President Cordova had set aside for him.

Sam freed up part of her afternoon to help. She hung drapes and arranged his memorabilia, putting her stamp on the room as if he were about to set up shop there permanently.

It was the first time A. J. had spent an entire day on the Emmaline campus since the merger. He had to admit he had never really looked at it critically before, as a student would, taking a measure of the place. The view of the quad from the bank of nine-over-nine windows in his office was impressive. Well cared for shrubs and a stately arching canopy of maples framed the crisscrossing walkways. Where Bolland was all red brick and Georgian columns, the atmosphere here was monastic fieldstone and weathered slate—a look he had always associated before with barbed wire and maximum security guard towers. Still, on the inside, the Emmaline buildings were cozy, far less institutional than the ambience on the Bolland campus.

Most striking, under President Cordova's administration, a point was made of mixing faculty and administrative, even student work space and offices. His own was on the second floor, tucked away at the end of the hallway, close to the presidential suite. On the same corridor was a spacious meeting room shared by both student government and the college's Board. The Student Life sector was housed on ground level in the campus' only large residence hall complex. The bookstore was in the library, combining books to borrow with books to buy.

The arrangement was unusual, thoughtful he had to admit, a leveler of sorts, holistic. But it was tough, knowing Fred Urban would not be ensconced there. His friend and colleague would be riding out the transition for the foreseeable future as administrator-in-residence on the Bolland campus.

The painting was done. The furniture settled in place. As A. J. and Sam stood back to admire her decorating handiwork in his new campus digs, he read the questions in her upturned face—ones she had been too politic to ask. Would he, in fact, ever put this all to use? With what could have passed for a smile, he leaned over and brushed at a smudge on one of her cheekbones.

"Ya done good," he said. "Worthy of HGTV. It's beautiful."

"Practice makes perfect. I *have* done my share of moving, too, you know."

"I especially like the dark wooden blinds against your psychidelic neon yellow on the walls."

"Hardly neon," she grimaced. "Golden Wheat, the label said. I figured it's harder to be depressed living with latex sunshine around you 24-7. Worse comes to worst, you can spring for dark glasses."

The aged mahogany slat blinds had been gathering dust in a corner of an Emmaline storage closet when Sam liberated them. Their finish matched perfectly with the woodwork and huge built-in floor-to-ceiling bookcases dominating an entire wall in the spacious room. A Guatemalan weaving in primary colors, a gift from a former student that had hung in A. J.'s old office, offset the austerity of a black futon, Sam's replacement for the wretched overstuffed sofa she had refused to let him move. She also insisted on bringing some greenery indoors in the form of several hanging plants and something she called a corn plant that already had designs on the ceiling.

"These will up the oxygen content a little," she said. "A good thing, a healthy shot of O_2 is just what the doctor ordered for clearing your head. I put in a requisition for maintenance to install a grow light."

Still grumbling, with some difficulty A. J. hooked the last of the hanging pots over an antique bracket that was part of the original furnishings in the room. Sam had even remembered to bring a watering can.

"All this flora is going to die of neglect."

"By the time you get back," Sam insisted, "the corn plant will be poking through the roof."

They laughed, suddenly awkward with each other. *When* he got back. A. J. landed a quick kiss on her forehead, wanting to shut out what he saw in her eyes. For all her brave words, Sam was steeling herself to the possibility he would take the Reuter money for his research junket, and beyond the year's hiatus, all bets were off.

Finally she came right out and said it. "Have you thought any more where you might—?"

"I've been doing some looking around," he admitted reluctantly. "The money could easily fund a cross-country swing, hunting down regional Shaker and Pietist archives. Then, too, Jake has been after me for years to think about a pro bono scholar-in-residence position at a legal aid clinic he knows in Harrisburg."

Sam turned, moved toward the huge bank of windows. Although she seemed caught up in the view of the campus below, the set of her shoulders told him otherwise.

"There's really no good time to bring this up," she said, "but I've been thinking, too. Maybe it's time I bring some of my things back to my rental here in Bradenton. A year is a long time and that commute—well, you know. You've been doing it yourself."

A. J. felt his mouth go dry. She was thinking of moving out.

"I agree, the drive can be tough," he said slowly. "Sometimes I catch myself dozing off on the home stretch even when we commute together. I wouldn't want you to make a habit of driving that route alone."

Sam turned his way, flashed a weak smile. "The merger may be a fait accompli, still given the crazies out there, you'll probably have to get a housesitter yourself for this place while you're gone."

"Recent grads or a nontrad. I've done it before."

The thought of someone else sharing that space—*their* space—was unthinkable. But Sam was right, something had to be

291

done. Classes were starting in less than a month.

That night, for the first time, he sensed how hard Sam was trying to protect herself from what she truly believed was the inevitable. They held one another as if any moment of intimacy might prove to be their last. Spent physically and emotionally, A. J. had closed his eyes, only half thought he heard her voice beside him in the darkness.

"We aren't as far apart as you think, you know," she told him, "struggling to live with failure, compromise. The Dean told me today that Emmaline-Wattrous faculty has voted to put expanding the remedial program on hold."

A. J. mentally shook himself alert as her words hit him. It seems he wasn't the only one with secrets. He should have asked, he thought, suspected. Something.

"I had no idea," he said slowly.

"I knew for some time this was coming, but didn't have the heart to tell you. You had quite enough on your plate."

"Damage control."

"Twenty students—maybe more—will be forced out in math and the sciences alone. Those kinds of numbers make less of a ripple on total enrollment, of course, since the merger."

Worse than he would have guessed. "A heck of a way to generate a more viable headcount. You're an amazing teacher, I'd be willing to bet an equally tenacious administrator. Your time will come over there."

"A guy has gotta hope," Sam sighed. "At the moment it's pretty much back-to-the-drawing-boards."

"Elitist stereotypes die hard—I'm hardly in a position to offer you pearls of wisdom. Some colleagues still think poli sci isn't even a science, much less a 'liberal art'. Such hairsplitting, of course, is nothing like the kind of street fighting you're going to be facing.

"The students," she said. "I just keep telling myself to concentrate on the students."

We humbly here sweet Wisdom's light pursue. McDowell had quoted those same lines from the Alma Mater to him years ago, when A. J. came to him, distraught that over half the class had flunked the first exam in his Constitutional Law course.

"The rules are simple, Ferinelli," McDowell said, "it's risky

292

to try to run with a torch. And a liberal education is a marathon not a sprint. You educate one student at a time, as well as you can for as long as you can. It's never enough, but you use the time you've got, knowing you rarely see the outcome. You just trust and do it, hope to goodness they can use something of what you give them."

A. J. shared the story with Sam as they snuggled alongside each other in the dim light from the lamp on the bedside table. "Amazing what sets us off on a course, sticks with us over the years," she sighed. "My advisor freshman year was this little slip of a nun who could barely see over her desktop. Day One she set all of her budding scholars off on a quest to write these gosh-awful personal and professional growth plans. Already up to my eyeballs in structure around there, I dug in my heels, was putting it off as long as possible. Finally the woman called me in and read me the riot act. It seems I was the only hold-out. Bad timing. I had been up studying for an exam most of the night and wasn't in the mood for lectures on the subject, so I pretty much told her what I thought of the whole business."

"I would have loved to see you giving the poor woman attitude," A. J. chuckled softly.

Sam grimaced. "In retrospect, I can't believe I did it or that she let me rant and get the frustration out of my system. 'Is that it?' my advisor said finally. Typical me, I shot from the lip. *Besides, what happens if I don't grow*, I said, all fiery indignation, *What then?* She just looked at me hard for a moment, hit me with this knowing little look. 'You can do that, Pomerantz, of course,' she said quietly. 'But if you don't grow, you *die*.'"

Sam broke off, hesitated, began again. "Why the woman saw my personal enlightenment as her own raison d'etre, I'll never know—still, I'm grateful. No risk, no growth. Trust me, I never forgot it."

"Tough stuff for a freshman."

"At any age. But then we know the alternatives."

A. J. drew a harsh breath. "You're right of course," he said. "If I had to point to a single factor in Bolland's downfall, it would have to be fear of change. The more the academy seems to decry the loss of tradition, claws and fights to entrench itself in the legacy of the past, the less it seems capable of reforming or renewing itself. No big surprises there. A lot of the political models I've wrestled with over the years turned to rigid contracts and social structures in pursuit of their ideals—the beginning of the end."

"Scary times for us *dinosaurs*," she said softly, "your word, if I remember correctly, the very first morning in your office. Prophetic—who knew."

By way of response, on a sigh, A. J. coaxed her back into his arms, her body fitted spoon-fashion against his own, shutting out for the moment everything but the reality of her presence. Even in their twilight world where nothing seemed constant but the overwhelming inevitability of change, he could still see her incredible eyes, her knowing hint of a smile, sense the laughter bubbling up inside her. In spite of, because of everything.

Beyond reason, the kind of chances they were finding themselves challenged to take. As for Sam's dogged faith in him, he had to admit, it just might be the greatest gamble of all.

Chapter Twenty-Two

Early August. Summer semester was all but over. By now Sam was cranking out endless drafts of Learning Center events calendars for Fall while A. J. was meeting almost daily with President Cordova and Emmaline's deans, hammering out last-minute strategies for integrating the two faculties. The sand was sifting downward in the glass. Since A. J.'s heated encounter with Doc Radisson in the basement of the academic center after graduation, there had been nothing but official silence on the subject of the unsigned Emmaline-Wattrous faculty contract. In a word, his future was as murky as ever.

Campus mail usually showed up mid-morning and again mid-afternoon in the Emmaline administrative office building. When late in the day, a student intern hand-delivered an envelope to A. J.'s office with "Board of Directors" as the return address, he assumed his grace-time finally had run out. Either Doc as Co-chair of the Board or President Cordova or both were issuing an ultimatum.

Instead A. J. found a fax of a newspaper clipping, dated earlier that day and forwarded to the Board from the campus Public Relations office. Attached was a sticky note with Doc's distinctive scrawl.

"Thought you'd want to see this ASAP," the note said. "Cordova is on top of it, has been talking with the family."

The source was a small town weekly in North Carolina. *Professor George Fulham McDowell,* the obituary began. At that point, A. J. ceased reading, although the man's list of achievements and honors stretched on for another six column-inches. Family, the article ended, planned to bring the body back to Pennsylvania for interment. Memorials should be made to the Bolland alumni scholarship fund at Emmaline-Wattrous College.

As a reality check, an antidote for the depression that had all but reduced him to existing on autopilot, the fax machine's single sheet of ultra bright copy paper was devastating. What in the hell had he been playing at? A. J. had justified the pervasive malaise about his career path since Bolland's last graduation as a soul crisis, some sort of cosmic struggle to regain control of his life. In fact, never had he felt less in control, of anything than in this moment. Hands shaking, he keyed in the sequence of numbers at the bottom of the email.

"McDowell's," a voice said.

"Bea, it's A. J."

"You know, then."

A. J. scrambled to collect his thoughts. "Bea, I'm so terribly sorry. Doc Radisson passed along a fax of George's obituary a few minutes ago."

"We . . . I was going to call, already have been in contact with the President's office," she said. "I assume some of George's colleagues would like to hold a memorial service in the Bolland Chapel. We're thinking about a week from Wednesday."

"If there's anything I can do—"

"George would have wanted . . . I would be very grateful if you would deliver the eulogy."

Through the iron vise tightening around his temple, A. J. forced himself to say it. "Bea, I'm the one who should be grateful. Of course, I would be honored to do it."

She didn't have to spell it out for him. First and foremost, it was not just a tribute to a man and his life Bea McDowell was asking of him. If that were the case, he wouldn't have still been sitting there perched on the edge of his desk, cell phone in hand, long after Bea had broken the connection. He knew without Bea spelling it out for him, she needed a sense of closure. And only he was in a position to help her achieve that.

Alone in his new office on the Emmaline campus, A. J. had a singular view out the bank of windows at the central quad below. An unexpected perk—nice, he had to admit. Even this late on a summer afternoon, a few incoming students and what had to be their parents were crossing the expanse of well-manicured grass, half-hidden by the canopy of trees arching over the winding brick paths. Before his very eyes, the place was coming alive again, its season of rebirth, as it had for so many generations of eager young scholars finding their places in this alien world into which their studies would thrust them.

Thy loyal children, lift the sacred flame. The expressions on those young faces ranged from bewilderment to barely concealed apprehension at what lay ahead. Even with decades of Fall semesters behind him and the Commencements that came after, A. J. knew exactly how those freshmen down there felt.

A glance at his watch said six. Having fun or not, time flies.

On her way to meet him for the commute home, Sam spotted him standing there at the window, broke stride and stopped on the sidewalk for a moment, waved up at him. They made it a habit of late to take turns driving and today, as it happened, A. J. was the one behind the wheel. Out ahead of them as the Toyota's odometer clocked off the miles, the dark ridge of hills surrounding what once had been the independent campus of Bolland College sprawled like some vast fortress against the fiery sky.

Visibly tired and preoccupied herself, Sam made short shrift of unpacking her day. It took considerably more mileage before A. J. finally brought himself to tell her about his own, starting with the call to Bea and what had triggered it.

"She asked if I would be willing to give the eulogy at the memorial service," he said. "I certainly owe the man that much."

When Sam didn't react one way or the other, A. J. flashed a quizzical glance in her direction. She was looking down, intent on unsnarling the strap of the book bag resting on her lap. It had become caught somehow in the wide band of her shoulder harness.

"That can be no small gift . . . words," she said finally. "Literally and figuratively."

A. J. winced. He didn't have to add for Sam's benefit that those three double-spaced pages promised to be the hardest thing he had ever written. She knew.

"When?" she said.

"A week from Wednesday in the Bolland Chapel. Burial is at Allegheny Hills," he hesitated, "where we took Anne . . . "

They had reached the outskirts of Eugenia, the fork in the road where he and Sam usually made a left turn to avoid the maze of one-way streets downtown. Instead, A. J. veered to the right, took them out into the countryside again, due north by the compass on the dashboard. If Sam wondered where they were going, she didn't ask. In a little over three miles, he spotted their destination, mustered up the will finally to tell her.

"Up ahead on the left, those stone columns. I haven't been back since we . . . I should have done this a long time ago," he said evenly. "On Wednesday, before George's memorial service, is neither the time nor place."

He had threaded the Toyota through the crumbling fieldstone entrance, and at a virtual crawl, began to pick his way through the labyrinth of gravel lanes separating the new from the historic part of the cemetery. The trees were smaller now, the rows of markers lay flat against the earth—all of which made it hard to get his bearings. With the Toyota's engine on idle, A. J. flexed his hands on the steering wheel, staring out the windshield.

Finally something caught his eye and he cut the engine. Without a word, he got out, walked around the front of the car and opened the door for Sam.

"I need to do this," he said looking down at her still sitting there, "have for a long time. For Anne, for myself—and I would like to hope, ultimately for us. I would be grateful . . . it would mean a great deal if you could bring yourself to come with me."

Sam deposited the book bag on the floor of the Toyota and got out, closing the door behind her. A. J. could sense her following several paces behind him as he threaded his way through the rows of markers toward an ivy-draped wall marking the outer boundaries of the cemetery.

From the look of it, the grounds crew had gotten behind in their mowing. The open expanse of grass in this area looked more like a meadow than one of those overly manicured lawns on which so many cemeteries pride themselves. *It fit*, A. J. felt a tightness in his chest thinking about it. His Anne always hated sod-farm front yards, made a point of cultivating the sturdiest dandelions on the entire block.

Something about the landscape triggered long-buried memories. A. J. stopped just short of one of the few remaining mature native oaks straining upward toward the sky, found near its base what was eluding him. The plate at his feet was simple cast bronze, devoid of ornamentation. He hunkered down and began to brush with one hand at the dusting of yellowed grass clippings some long-ago pass with the mower had left behind.

With a will of their own, his outstretched fingers tentatively began to trace the deeply cast shapes of the letters, began again. *Anne.* A. J.'s face worked and he choked back a sound, unintelligble, as he silently read the inscription:

Anne Sorenson Ferinelli

Beloved Wife ❧ Mother of Alexander James

Numbers swam in and out of focus, the measure of a life frozen in time, unchanging and unchangeable. Anne had been thirty-eight.

Abruptly A. J. lowered his head, planted his fists hard against the damp grass steadying himself. "I've been such a damn fool," his voice was muffled, thick with emotion. He wasn't expecting a response.

"Your name . . . those initials, A. J.," a woman's voice said, "Alexander James."

Startled, he half-turned toward the sound. Of course. Sam had been witnessing all this.

"Not exactly," he said slowly. "It started out Alessandro . . . Alesso for short as a kid growing up. In Italian, the James would have been Giacomo. It was my one and only adolescent rebellion, cutting myself loose from all that."

"Alesso. You and your father."

"And grandfather," his voice was low.

Naming. He had been thinking a lot about it since graduation—the powerful expectations and traditions behind it. For himself. For Bolland.

The breeze tugged at a tendril of hair drifting across Sam's forehead as she stood looking down at him. Her expression was unreadable.

"By any other name, you *are* that legacy," she said finally, "just as you were and are for George McDowell, as Joel Van Susten will be for you and as I am becoming—I've got to hope anyway—for that tenacious and compassionate nun-of-an-advisor of mine. Gone now, but the woman never gave up on me. Life without her dogged faith in my future would be unthinkable. Things change, stuff happens, death is just a matter of time. Inevitable. But not everybody lives. *That* choice is *ours* to make . . . and ours alone. Lord help me, whatever you choose, I love you, always will."

She took a deep breath, hit him with the rest. "You've needed space to grieve and I've tried to give it to you—for your family, for Bolland and your colleagues, for childhood dreams, the uncertainty of living. Long as lists go. I understand. But then you've brought me here and that has got to mean something. I have to hope just maybe you're finally ready to start to leveling with me, with yourself."

For one irrational moment, he felt the urge to introduce the two of them—Anne and this beautiful, strong, perceptive woman beside him. Awkwardly A. J. struggled to his feet, stood looking down at the grave marker as if only now truly seeing it for the first time.

"Truth is, the two of you would have liked each other," he heard himself say. "It's been a long time coming, but I think I'm finally capable of truly moving on with—"

"Don't think I expect that you . . . you know I don't do ultimatums."

"If not here and now, then when, Sam? Life belongs to the living and Anne would have been the first to remind me of that. The truth is, fifteen years of research and teaching awards, promotions and accolades absolutely pale compared to waking up every morning alongside the woman you love. Nothing, nothing on this earth is worth more than seeing the sunrise through those eyes and tasting that warm body in the night. I love you, Sam. That hasn't changed. I want to spend my life with you—marriage, the whole nine yards, if you can still trust me enough to risk it. That has got to come first. And I've got to believe after all Anne and I, after all *you and I* have gone through, she would most definitely approve."

Sam was already in his arms, her breathing at first as halting, as painful as his own. But in the calm settling in around them like the lowering night, he began to sense the faint whisper of the wind through the grass, the steadying sound of his own heartbeat. Off against the horizon, pinpoints of light began to glitter amid the shifting teals and purples of the sky. It would be dark soon.

"You must be beat," Sam volunteered after a while, "I can drive if you like."

"Thanks. I'm good." Even as he said it, his eyes blinked closed, shutting out the realities of life and death all around them, the terrible fatigue and stress weighing on his soul. "Really, no problem."

Still, her offer was enough to get him moving, carry them back across the darkening field to the car. At the edge of the gravel drive he hesitated, then opened the driver side door for her after all. With a tentative smile, Sam took the keys from his outstretched hand, waited for him to settle into the passenger seat before she began to guide the Toyota back toward the highway and home.

In the end, there are some watersheds a human being faces alone. For A. J. Ferinelli, drafting George McDowell's eulogy had become one of them. The week passed with precious few words, much less thoughts, committed to paper. If there was a way to draw a line under a relationship, experiences, values and choices that, for better or worse, had shaped how A. J.'s life and that of his mentor came together, it seemed to be eluding him.

The morning of the Memorial Service brought with it a light drizzle that cut short the graveside gathering, but once back on campus, the sun cut through the spotty overcast. Bolland's chapel reared up against the hillside like some picture postcard stereotype straight out of a New England travel magazine. Thick ribbed columns held up the red brick portico and a blindingly white spire stretched skyward. The only concession to more contemporary, less Puritanical aesthetics, were the stained glass windows.

Spaced every ten feet along the chapel walls, the glass panels were executed with exceptional artistry and in rich but muted colors, with the blues and golds of the Bolland seal woven delicately into each of the designs. Portrayed on each window were the trappings of the academic life and the traditional scholarly disciplines. They were all there. The Arts and Sciences, the Humanities, Philosophy, Mathematics, Literature and Languages all came alive through the historic tools of the academic trade—scrolls and books, test tubes and beakers, exotic instruments to calculate the mysteries of the universe.

A. J. had seen those same windows many times before in passing, at Convocations and milestone events in Bolland's recent history, always considered them vaguely trite, despite the obvious skill of the designer. Still, as he escorted Bea McDowell and her family into the familiar space and settled into the front pew on the left himself with the assembled faculty, it was if he were experiencing them for the first time.

There it was, their community of scholars, preserved in glowing shards of glass connected to one another by a network of leaden veins, seemingly strong and indestructible. Yet like any organism, A. J. knew with a certainty now, those precious links were both malleable and fragile. Even in the face of the losses that had brought them here, the result was a magnificent living mosaic in which the whole became so very much more fraught with meaning than just the sum of those many fragmented parts. Worth honoring. Beautiful.

He hadn't shared the draft of his speech, more notes really, and Sam didn't ask. When he found her in the packed chapel, made eye contact, he saw she had chosen to sit not in full academic regalia with her colleagues, but alongside Bea. Both women were in simple dark suits, designed to deflect attention from themselves. The older woman's hand was clutched in hers.

The program was beginning. From the back of the room, A. J. heard the combined Emmaline-Bolland student choir launch into the *Alma Mater,* Bolland's. Doc Radisson had been right about President Cordova. That touch had to be her doing. She and Doc, representing Bolland, also went on to share the opening remarks. Bolland's now emeritus chaplain offered an invocation.

Finally, from behind the inlaid Pennsylvania hardwood lectern with the seal of Bolland College still emblazoned on it, A. J. himself looked out at the sea of faces in their academic robes. At either hand on the cold plaster side walls hung traditional alumni banners, faithful

302

to the geography of the merger. Those for Emmaline were now on the east and Bolland's on the west. His voice was clear and strong:

George McDowell was my mentor. He was my friend. He taught me how to put together a decent syllabus and the course that went with it. He coached me through what it took to create a final exam that wouldn't flunk out the entire student body in the process. I'm still working on it.

A faint ripple of laughter greeted that last statement. "I owe him much more than I can express," A. J. said.

George Fulham McDowell loved academe and loved the academic life. He loved Bolland College. As colleagues we fought, long and hard at times, over what that meant. In the process we sometimes frustrated, even disappointed each other. But through it all we shared a deep love for teaching and scholarship, and above all, a love of knowledge.

Loving knowledge is a complicated business. For some in academe it begins and ends with the life of the mind. George McDowell was not that kind of academic. Ultimately, I believe George McDowell understood that 'loving knowledge' in the traditional sense is not enough. To be 'loving', knowledge must be applied in such a way that the life of the mind and building a healthy, balanced community become one.

A. J. paused, feeling the enormity of the words hit home. They were life changing, and the life that they were altering beyond recognition was, first and foremost, his own. Sad, he thought, that it takes a moment like this—to pull us up short and make us confront who we truly are and what our lives can be.

"As professors we teach not only with words but through our actions," he said.

The 'life of the mind' requires, even sanctifies the ability to stand still and look inward to find the truth.

303

But loving knowledge in a broader sense brings with it the expectation that we act—that we do justice and we treat students, one another and those around us with humility and respect.

A. N. Whitehead summed up the distinction so brilliantly: 'Education with inert ideas,' he said, 'is not only useless, it is above all things harmful.'

Loving knowledge is a radical way to transform our work as professors. It begins with the assumption that 'learning' is not a role reserved solely for the undergraduate and that 'teaching' is not exclusively the realm of the professor. To love knowledge and act upon it are qualities every true academic cultivates first and foremost in one's self and then—and only then—successfully in the students entrusted to them. As long as I knew him, George made it his life's struggle to talk that talk and walk that walk. He will be missed.

We professors have enormous power in student lives, George once said, the potential to build or destroy. It is a power that can easily corrupt if we let it. As we practice our craft, we need to be prepared always to examine and reexamine our 'professorial persona', to question whether we are truly dignifying our collective humanity and glorifying a Truth greater than ourselves. Or has our academic 'gravitas' unwittingly become an excuse to love ourselves rather than either knowledge or our students?

Unbidden, familiar words came flooding back from his own childhood, transformed into the language of his profession. *You might have the eloquence of a humanist, divinely inspired, you might make the ultimate sacrifice for what you believe and if there is no love in the doing of it, it is all for nothing. Love forgives, hopes, endures. It never ends.* He didn't trust himself to repeat them aloud.

In a word, it was his life he was staring down as he gazed out over the hushed chapel. If ever he found himself driven to honor the principle of putting his money where his mouth was, this was the time. When he looked up from his notes, Sam's face swam into focus.

It was riveted on his own, devoid of any expression.

I don't pretend to know any more what it means to be an academician, a scholar or a humanist. But I would like to believe I may be learning at long last to live humanely. I believe even in the darkest moments, George McDowell had hope in the future. His final act as an academic shortly before he died was to have the courage to acknowledge his own limits and yet work to secure that future. Through his family, George asked that any memorials made in his name be channeled into a Bolland Memorial Scholarship fund at Emmaline-Wattrous College. It will go to support undergraduate studies for men or women who are committed to further graduate education and a career in college or university-level teaching.

A. J. folded his notes and momentarily closed his eyes. His free hand tightened on the finely polished decorative rail running along either side of the podium.

"Bea McDowell, President Cordova and distinguished guests," his voice was low, "it is with deepest gratitude and respect for my friend and colleague, George McDowell, that I am donating the monies from this year's H. N. Reuter Prize for Distinguished Scholarship and Teaching as an initial gift toward endowing his scholarship fund. *Vive ut vivas!*"

Live that you may live. He couldn't recall how often he had seen Bolland's official motto emblazoned in brass on the seal at the front of the speaker platform or had picked his way idly through the translation from the Latin while someone else up there on the dais in their academic finery poured out their vision, their ideal of academic life. He had seen perhaps, but only now understood. *Vive ut vivas.*

Silence followed that pronouncement. Gathering his notes and awkwardly slipping them back into the sleeve of his academic gown, A. J. left the podium. It had ceased to matter in that moment what his fellow Bolland faculty thought of what he had chosen to do. He only knew this was the most spontaneous act of his life. Its motivation was lightyears beyond anything as simple as the need to forgive or find forgiveness, to atone or redeem political choices and bitter consequences that had driven a wedge between him and his mentor, that had shattered their campus family forever.

If A. J. had to put a name on what he had done, he was casting his lot with community, imperfect and flawed, anything but utopian. Painfully real. As for his research, the definitive book he once had dreamed of writing with the Reuter funds, this too he knew would come in due time—all the stronger, he had to believe, for the context in which he would now pursue them.

Silently, without fanfare, he found himself naming in his heart the living threads that bound him to this place, the survivors and casualties alike. First and foremost Sam, Joel and George, Bea, Liz and Fred Urban, Andy Duncan and Doc Radisson. His Anne was on that list, even Julie Schechter and those three Malaysian students and their families. The courageous bookkeeper, Priscilla. Angry and tortured Ray Ellison. By any other name, those unspoken sounds and syllables of his were a prayer.

The rest of George McDowell's Memorial Service was lost to him, its passing marked only by the printed agenda unfolding in the program booklet in his hands. For much of the time, A. J. found his gaze drawn upward from the unfolding text to the enormous window cut into the far wall of the chapel, a visual symphony of Bolland's colors—the gold and the blue. The artist had taken the imagery from the opening phrases of the *Alma Mater*, the human spirit soaring in ever widening arcs from darkness toward the light.

Emmaline's chaplain had the final word, pronounced the benediction. Alone amid the cluster of faculty in their academic robes preparing for their traditional recessional out of the chapel, A. J. slipped away with the intention of joining Sam and Bea McDowell. He spotted them standing together in the side aisle, Ruth and Naomi at the crossroads, their dialogue hushed, waiting for him. Sam had her arm around the older woman's shoulders.

Plan was for Bea and her family to join President Cordova and the platform party in the Bolland executive dining room for lunch before they left campus. Pleading exhaustion, A. J. declined. A public luncheon was just one thing more than he could handle right now. Bea could read all of that clearly enough in his face. Drawing him aside, she hugged him one last time in the now all-but-empty chapel.

"Thank you," Bea said softly. "I know George would have

never been more proud of you or of anything he accomplished in this place, than at what you just did at that podium this morning. I wish you and Sam every possible happiness. Be good to each other."

A hint of a smile tugged at the corner of his mouth. He didn't trust himself to speak. Instead his hand closed around Sam's. Taking their time, beyond words, the two of them struck off in the direction of the parking lot.

Bea McDowell's benediction surrounded them like the waves of heat rising from the asphalt. *Be good to each other.*

The air in the Toyota seemed unnaturally still. It felt like the uneasy calm that follows a front's passing, when the sky is still a vitriolic green, reminding the survivors how close the storm had come. A. J. fitted the key into the ignition, hesitated.

Sam had turned in her seatbelt and was looking his way. He half-smiled, puzzled at something in her expression—different, luminous, a subtle radiance that he hadn't remembered seeing in quite that way before. If he hadn't been paying attention, he might have assumed it was just the sunlight filtering in through the tinted glass of the windshield in front of her. As he returned her steady gaze, tears began to glitter along the edge of her lashes.

"It occurred to me in the middle of all that, George McDowell wasn't the only one extremely fortunate about the woman in his life," he said, cleared his throat. "Sam, I can't even begin to—"

Her fingertips, laid against the somber lines of his mouth, silenced the rest. *Vive ut vivas.*

For once in his adult life, Professor A. J. Ferinelli didn't weigh or rethink the alternatives, analyze the wisdom or significance of what he was about to do. There was life out there meant to be lived and only he could live it. He just turned the key in the ignition, slipped the Toyota into gear and drove.

ABOUT THE AUTHOR . . .

As wife of a university President-Emeritus and a long-time campus administrator herself, Mary Agria brings an unique perspective to the at times brutal world of campus politics—insights she passionately and thoughtfully shares in *Community of Scholars*.

Ms. Agria turned to novels after a distinguished career as author of numerous non-fiction works in the field of rural community development and work-force issues. Her regionally best-selling 2006 breakthrough novel, *TIME in a Garden*, continues to enthrall new readers and book clubs from coast-to-coast. *VOX HUMANA: The Human Voice* (2007) and *In Transit* (2008) have won critical acclaim in national magazines. Her novels have made her in demand as a writer-in-residence and speaker on the challenges of finding meaning in one's senior years, community gardening, the dynamics of healthy communities and the writing process. Her column "Winning the Rat Race" ran for twenty years in newspapers around the country and led to a college-level text by the same title. She currently writes a popular column on gardening and spirituality, based on *TIME in a Garden*.

The proud mother of four daughters, Ms. Agria loves to travel the globe with her husband, Dr. John Agria—in retirement, a professional photographer. She weaves, enjoys liturgical music and gardening.

For chapters from her novels, essays, special features, photos and calendars of events, visit on-line at maryagria.com

COMMUNITY OF SCHOLARS
BOOK CLUB QUESTIONS

1. A. J. Ferinelli realizes early-on that Sam and her experiences in higher education simply do not 'compute" for him. How do events test his assumptions about his own background   and about his profession?

2. Discuss how Sam Pomerantz's past makes her vulnerable to a man like Bremer. What finally enables her to confront the pattern? How typical is her situation?

3.   Discuss how A. J.'s relationship with his mentor, George McDowell, changes in the course of the novel. How does Sam's mentor play a role in the growth of her character?

4. How does the political climate on campus contribute to community or the lack of it? Discuss how those same dynamics can impact conditions in any work setting.   How typical is this kind of politicized work environment?

5. With which character in the novel do you most identify and why? Discuss the character's role in the story.

6. How does the relationship between Joel Van Susten, Julie Schechter and Liz Diamond parallel the experiences of A. J. and Sam?   Discuss how the concept of mentoring plays a role in the younger and older characters' growth.

7. Discuss how the secondary characters contribute to the sense of community: Eg., Dean Bremer, the McDowells, Fred Urban, Doc Radisson, Jake Burroughs, Julie Schechter, Ja Ron, Professor Ellison, Priscilla Fowler, Henry Putnam and Andy Duncan.   Which characters functioned most for you as catalysts for change?   With whom could you most identify and why?

8. A. J. finds it difficult to get beyond his guilt over the death of his wife, Anne. How does that begin to change and why?

9. Discuss how unresolved feelings of guilt impede Sam in her struggles to make her peace with her past.   What enables her to begin to change?

10. Bea, Doc and Joel take on important roles in the course of the novel. How does their intervention impact the central characters?

11. Discuss the ending in light of the Herbert poem quoted at the beginning of the novel. How does the ending define what it means to live holistically in community?   What do you think ultimately happens to Sam and A. J.?

12. Discuss how the novel changes or reinforces your perceptions of Higher Education, at its best and at its worst.

For more book club materials, author reflections and sample chapters, visit the author on-line at maryagria.com

Coming from Mary Agria . . .

with illustrations by John Agria

inspired by the best-selling TIME in a Garden

Second Leaves

A story about gardening for children

(and the grownups who love them)

Other novels from Mary Agria...

TIME in a Garden

...the 2006 best-seller that started it all. Set in northern Michigan's resort country, this unforgettable story of Eve Brennerman and Adam Groft and their little crew of senior citizens trying to beautify their struggling rural community, celebrates perennial gardening, family and the enduring power of human love.

"We all do battle with stony ground and unseasonable dry spells over the years," the novel begins. "Though we may not call ourselves gardeners, it is the human experience."

"**A compelling read. Adam and Eve in the garden** . . ." Five-Star judge's review, 2007 *Writer's Digest Self-Published Book Awards*, Literary Fiction.

VOX HUMANA:
The Human Voice

The intriguing worlds of pipe organs and weaving come together in this poignant story of love and forgiveness. When Philadelphia counselor Char Howard is force-retired, she returns home to western Pennsylvania and a community of strangers.

"A five-star book in every way. Characterization was excellent . . . fascinating. I learned so much by reading this book. Special . . .excellent work." Judge's review, *Writer's Digest Self-Published Book Awards*, 2007

"a reflective portrayal of the ascent of goodness, reconciliation and love," AGO Magazine, 2007

IN TRANSIT

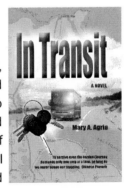

Set in Michigan's Upper Peninsula, *In Transit* is the story of Lib Aventura, a former travel agent, who is widowed only three years after she and her husband sell their East Lansing home and go on the road full-time RVing. Considered "homeless" by her adult children, Lib finds herself thrust into living vicariously with their families until she musters the courage to return to the UP and reclaim her abandoned motorhome. Her journey is only beginning,

"Wisdom, the kind that only a lifetime of experience can give. Like Lib Aventura, may we never grow too old to live." *Dan's Hamptons*, 2008

For sample chapters of her novels, visit maryagria.com